Hassle in the Castle

Juele ran through the gallery. She must get out of the castle at once, but how? She mustn't go by way of her station; they'd be watching that, now. She would have to risk the front entrance.

Terrified of being observed, she felt eyes on her. All the portraits on the walls turned to follow her as she ran. It seemed as though the whole castle was against her. A suit of armor stationed against the wall near the door stepped forward as she dashed toward the exit. It swung its halberd up in an arc, then chopped it down. Fortunately, Juele was quicker than a hollow man. She ducked the sharp blade and kept running into the next chamber.

The entry hall was full of people in elegant clothes mingling and discussing weighty-sounding matters. These officials were no doubt preparing to leave. Perhaps she could sneak out with them. Then she spotted Tanner at the entrance, near the sentries. He must be looking for her.

Juele crouched behind a cluster of statuary. She noticed it looking down at her. To her surprise, it was the griffin and cow from the sculpture garden. The museum must have melded with this part of the castle.

"Is this hide and seek?" the griffin asked.

"Shh!" she hissed. "It's not a game!" Tanner had a dozen guards with sunglasses and whips with him. Juele was terrified. What would they do to her if they caught her?

"What's that?" the griffin asked, his voice getting louder.

"Please be quiet," Juele begged.

The griffin opened its beak to the widest. "She's over here!" it bellowed. . . .

Baen Books by Jody Lynn Nye

Also in this series:
Waking in Dreamland

The Death of Sleep (with Anne McCaffrey)
The Ship Who Won (with Anne McCaffrey)
The Ship Errant
Don't Forget Your Spacesuit, Dear (editor)

Jean Plaquin

School of Light

Jody Lynn Nye

SCHOOL OF LIGHT

A Baen Books Original

Baen Publishing Enterprises
P.O. Box 1403
Riverdale, NY 10471

ISBN: 0-671-57816-2

Cover art by Pat Turner

First printing, June 1999

Distributed by Simon & Schuster
1230 Avenue of the Americas
New York, NY 10020

Typeset by Brilliant Press
Printed in the United States of America

To Aaron,
from his auntie

Book Two of
The Dreamland

Chapter 1

The girls in muddy shorts and T-shirts scrambled madly toward one another as the referee on the sidelines blew a sharp blast on her whistle. From the path beside the field, Juele heard a hollow *poomp*, and a big, round, white ball went sailing high into the blue sky toward the goal at the end of the grassy field. It arced higher and higher, looking as if it might overshoot the goal completely, then began to descend, slowing as it fell. Suddenly it stopped entirely, forty feet in the air.

"Air ball!" one of the girls shrieked. The opposing team started laughing. The defending team looked upset for a moment, then began to laugh, too. The female teacher on the sidelines came forward and planted her hands on her hips to look up at the hovering ball.

"All right, you lot," the teacher called. "Is it really up there, or is someone spinning an illusion?"

The young women all protested at once. "No, Mrs. Cardigan. We wouldn't do that!" But there were a few smiles and nods among the players, saving up the idea for next time.

"Well then, it's stuck," said Mrs. Cardigan. "Would someone please go find the ladder?" A few of the gym-suited girls ran off the field toward a low wooden building behind the second goal.

"Come on." Rutaro nudged Juele. "We have to keep going."

Juele pulled her attention away from the interesting spectacle of students standing on one another's shoulders atop the highest rung of the ladder and lifted her belongings. She followed the stocky young man, her new

1

mentor, along the path that led past the playing field toward the cluster of buildings that was her greatest desire in all the Dreamland: the School of Light.

Glowing with promise, the lofty white buildings beckoned her. Every window had a wink for her. Every turret gleamed with appeal. Every brick and stone promised to whisper inspiration in her ear. Juele was so excited that she was almost vibrating with happiness. She could hardly believe that she was here at last. An aspiring illusion artist such as she would naturally desire to go to the best school in the land, be instructed by the best teachers, and one day achieve great things, but the admission policy of the School board was stringent. You could apply only once in your lifetime. You had to present three references, none of them related to you, and you had to demonstrate marked talent in illusion. No one got in on mere charm.

Not that Juele had any illusions about her physical appearance. In most of the forms the Sleepers imposed upon her, she tended to be on the short side of average, on the average side of beauty, and on the shy side of extroversion. In her travel suit—a blue fitted jacket and skirt that were more comfortable than stylish—she knew she looked ordinary. Her hands were the only remarkable feature she had. They looked *capable*. Long and thin, short and strong, dark-skinned, light-skinned, missing a finger or a fingernail, they still looked as if they could do whatever the mind driving them wished to do. *And*, Juele thought, *they nearly could*. There was plenty of talent locked up in their bones. So much that it surprised her, sometimes.

Her teachers had been full of hope when they sent her off to Mnemosyne. She had been creating illusions, really realistic ones, since she was very young, and her more ordinarily talented teachers had guided her, to the best of their abilities, as far as they could take her. Even though she wasn't quite sixteen, she had long ago passed beyond the abilities of any other artist in the region. Now there was no more that they could show her, yet Juele still had room to stretch her wings. Oh, she loved her teachers, but they didn't understand her or her dreams. She'd heard that only in the School could she find the kind of tutoring she needed to train her talent and become a world-class artist. Even the smallest student who wanted to change the look of the world aspired to come here. The fees the School charged were exorbitant. Her parents had had to mortgage several of their dearest dreams to send her here. She wanted them to be proud of her. As importantly, *she* wanted to be proud of her, too. Oh, please, she begged the Sleepers silently as she approached nearer and nearer to the gleaming pillars of the entrance, don't let this be a Futility Dream, with all my hopes out of reach!

Juele hadn't been idle while waiting to hear whether the School had accepted her. For almost two years she had been seeking new directions in her art. She had no idea whether what she was doing was any good, if it was original or even right to attempt. That was what she had come to find out. She'd packed her bags full of the tools of the trade that she had amassed and stuffed in all the hope she had.

Rutaro, trotting on ahead, seemed to have no notion how much coming here meant to her. But, of course, he must have been here for years already. He seemed so confident. Could he recall that first, precious moment when he stepped through the gate, out of misunderstanding and into promise? It would be hard, but she would succeed—she had to! For confidence, she looked down at her hands, clenching the handles of her suitcase and art box. They exuded capability, and that soothed her nerves. With their help, she could cope.

So, this was the School of Light! Juele thought. She stayed close on Rutaro's heels as he led her under an arch that passed through the base of a tower in the broad face of a building. So far, it lived well up to its reputation. For a moment she put out a hand, hoping that she wouldn't find an invisible barrier. Her hand touched the cool, cream-colored stone. It felt as if it was thrumming with power. Juele stroked it and let her hand drop. Real. It was real, and she wasn't suffering an Isolation Dream that would keep her from getting right into the middle of it all.

Ahead of them lay a square garden gleaming with sunshine. To either side of the corridor, doors opened on bright, airy classrooms full of students. Although they were almost all adults, they wore the look of rapt fascination one normally saw on the faces of children. What were they doing? What were they learning? She wanted to be in there with them. Her curiosity distracted her so much that she forgot to listen to what Rutaro was saying. Hastily, she brought her attention back to him, hoping he thought her inattention was forgivable. Surely he should understand what it was like to come into a new place, particularly this one. Her curiosity was on full alert.

A wave of influence swept through, changing everything in its path as the Sleeper dreaming the province changed his or her celestial mind about how things should be. Juele braced herself for the alteration, savoring it, enjoying it. Influence felt more powerful here than it did in her home town of Wandering, as though the Sleeper had His or Her dream eye fixed on Mnemosyne, and all other places lay in the periphery. A tingle raced down her arms, and she rubbed her fingers over her palms, feeling the electricity of change. In the ever-shifting world of the Dreamland, the creative ones whose minds created the landscape were always experimenting, testing, perfecting. Juele welcomed the changes, though they left her no wiser as to the eventual pattern that the Sleepers had in mind for her. She caught Rutaro looking at her with a curious expression in his eyes. Did he disapprove? She found she'd been made a little taller than she had been and hoped it helped her look more mature.

"We all have a great deal to teach one another, pupil and teacher alike, so you'll find that we're all equal here," he was saying, as they walked out into the full sunshine. The character of the light had altered slightly in the wake of the influence, opening up the skies and making them bluer. "We do talk to one another about problems we have each solved. It is most stimulating to hear what other minds think and aspire to. I look forward to seeing what you have to teach us, too."

"It sounds wonderful," Juele said. "Just what I've always wanted." Rutaro smiled, the corners of his eyes crinkling upward. He was an agreeable-looking but not particularly handsome man, about a head taller than Juele, with intense, brown eyes that seemed to bore into her. He had a small, blunt nose slightly turned up at the tip, but the nostrils curled haughtily in the corners. His hair was a mass of dark curls that fell to his collar, his skin was tawny, and his clothes curiously old-fashioned. She studied them, hoping it didn't look as if she was staring. Under a white artist's smock, which he wore like the robe of royalty, his garments seemed to be about a hundred years out of date. His plum-colored breeches were of velveteen, his shirt of fine white cloth with ruffles at the wrists that fell over the backs of his hands almost to the knuckles. He wore a waistcoat woven in a complicated pattern but subdued colors, as if to say that here was a complex person that one would have to examine closely to understand. She also noticed that he hadn't changed in the alteration, but she didn't dare ask.

"You're wondering about my appearance," Rutaro said, reading her thoughts, with a small, amused smile on his lips. "I am modeling for Peppardine today. He's been working on this period illusion for some time. I have to keep reminding myself of what I looked like, bringing back the same thoughts I had on that day, and mold myself accordingly. I mustn't let the form go, no matter what the Sleepers send. He's counting on me."

"Oh," said Juele, letting out a little breath. So everyone acted as models and teachers—so how did one tell who was a student and who wasn't? How very confusing. She meant to straighten that out at once. She was here to get an education, not just teach what she knew. "Er, who is Peppardine? A teacher?"

Rutaro looked at her as if she had just asked who the Sleepers were. "He is my friend," Rutaro said at last. "A fellow student. And a brilliant artist, as you will find out."

"I'm sorry," Juele said. Rutaro waved away her apology.

"Never mind. This is the Main Quadrangle," he said, holding out his hand to encompass the wide green park surrounded by buildings. Flowers of glorious red and yellow bloomed in artfully arranged beds at the corners of the square. A few trees, venerable and lovely, rose from the perfectly manicured lawn. On a few gray stone benches arranged around the perimeter and in a ring at the center of the garden where four paths intersected, men and women sat or lay. A few were just enjoying the sun. Some of them had sketch pads on their laps. Others had easels or pedestals and were capturing the beauty of the day in small ways. Juele caught sight of a perfect miniature model of the main building forming between the hands of a man with white hair and a creased face. Something in it wasn't quite right, and the man frowned at it from several angles, trying to see what was wrong. Juele knew that kind of concentration. Becoming impatient with his creation, the man waved his arms, exerting his own strength of will, and the building itself changed. Now, model and work matched perfectly. Here, Life imitated Art.

The buildings, like the gardens, were very beautiful. Juele squinted at them in the bright light, wondering if she could tell how they had altered under the influence. Yes, she could. The bricks were longer and thinner, and the lintels of the doors had swan-neck finials on top instead of fan windows. All was still beautiful and in satisfying proportion, with color and texture that was attractive to the eye. The Sleepers certainly favored this place. The last time an influence like that came through her home of Wandering, the whole town square had turned into ramshackle hovels, much to the embarrassment of the town council, who were having a market fair at the time, with a hundred visitors from out of town. Here, it felt as if nothing could be ugly, ever. Then, across the square, Juele noticed a man step out through a section of wall as if it was a door. Behind him she could see a brief glimpse of a corridor and a flight of stairs.

"Oh yes, some of it is illusory, to correct the asymmetry of the real building underneath, and preserve the beauty of the scene," Rutaro said, smiling at her surprise.

"Well, why not?" said Juele, with spirit. "How much of this is natural and how much has been altered by the people here?"

"Well, sometimes the School does it by itself, much in the way a Sleeper maintains the flavor of a province. The place has an overmind of its own. It has a taste for beauty."

"Oh," Juele said. She knew inanimate objects frequently achieved a kind of awareness, even activity. Any foundation in operation for such a number of years might well create its own ambiance. And it *was* an art school. Why, after all, should form interfere with aesthetic enjoyment?

"So what is real, and what's not?" she asked, eager to understand her new surroundings.

"Does it matter?" Rutaro asked, suddenly bored. He started walking again. Juele grasped her bags and hurried along the gravel path after him. Had she made an error on her very first day?

"I suppose not," she said, apologetically. Rutaro waved his fingers, but kept going. The matter was unimportant and was already forgotten.

I like it here, she thought, looking about at the bright colors and happy bustle. All around her, work was going on, questions were being asked, deep conversations were deepening, art was being brought into existence, and all in conscious pursuit of the greatest beauty. Fabulous. She wondered when she might be able to start talking with people, and deepening her own understanding.

For two years, Juele had been working on a style of illusion that she found meaningful. She hoped it would be thought original. All by herself, she had ruthlessly excised from her small images all traces of anyone else's

style that she detected, keeping the techniques that gave
the effect she liked. There hadn't been much left at the
end, leaving her images spare, but what was there was
all hers. She called it "askance reality." It had cynicism,
but appreciation in it and was really best viewed out of
the corner of one's eye. Perhaps her style could use some
more refining before she brought it up in such sophisticated surroundings. She opened her mouth to ask, but
of its own will her jaw dropped agape, leaving her tongue
hanging.

They passed under a narrow stone arch that stretched
like a bridge between two upper-story doors. In the vast
square beyond it was one of the most beautiful fountains that she had ever seen. The tiered, pink marble
basins were shallow, and the rims encrusted with pearls
and jewels rose in shell-like scallops, the water lapping
diamond-bright between them. The foaming jets of spray
leaped up twenty, thirty feet, playing on the air as gracefully as winged dancers. Around it, eight or ten students
were modeling or drawing.

Out of a door to Juele's right, a woman in a long, blue
smock and a preoccupied hurry emerged, walking straight
toward the fountain. Juele lifted a hand to her mouth
and started to call out a warning to her, but the woman
ran slap through the middle of the spray, and came out
without a drop on her smock. *Oh!* Juele thought, letting her hand drop. It was an illusion.

"That fountain is so real!" she said, wonderingly, when
she could find her voice. "But it isn't!"

Rutaro tilted his head and smiled again, that madden-
ing, knowing smile. Bored insouciance seemed to go well
with his costume.

"Oh, you'll learn quickly what's real and what isn't in
the school grounds. Part of your education, really." Rutaro
suddenly didn't want to stand there with everyone looking
at him. He started to walk. Juele stared after him, then
back at the pink fountain, unable to pull herself away.

"It's perfect! Every detail is ideal. Who did it? The
school or a person?"

"Does it matter?"

"No, but . . ." Juele trailed a few paces, still looking over her shoulder, then ran after her guide. "Rutaro, it's amazing. The melding of reality and illusion are seamless."

"Isn't that what you are here to learn how to do?"

"But, I could end up taking classes in an imaginary room!"

"And do you think that won't teach you something?" Rutaro asked, wryly.

Juele laughed, caught off guard. "I guess it would. If something is too perfect, then it isn't real."

"Possibly. Illusion is the manipulation of light, whereas the more gross arts manipulate matter. It's a more subtle control of influence, I feel," Rutaro said, with his arched eyebrows raised, as if daring her to say otherwise. "Naturally, light would be closer to perfection than matter."

Juele looked back at the plumes of water dancing upward, bending outward at the top and flattening out, echoing the shape of the white towers beyond the walls of the square. There was something familiar about the vast battlements and high, blue-roofed turrets. They looked almost perfect, Juele thought, although they were too far away to be inside the school's environs.

"What place is that?" she asked, pointing.

"The Castle of Dreams," Rutaro said with satisfaction. He paused at the edge of the huge quadrangle to admire the effect of water, wood, stone, and shadow.

Juele dropped her voice out of respect for the King, as though he could hear her. "I had no idea how close the school was to the palace."

"It varies," Rutaro said, with a grimace, "depending upon our status of the moment. If we are in vogue, as we are at present, then we are very close to the center, indeed. If we're out of favor, we're on the outskirts of town before you can say 'paint.'"

"Oh," said Juele. "Why are we . . . in vogue?"

"There is an exhibition of the arts being planned at present," Rutaro said, with pride. He preened and fingered his elaborate necktie. "A well-publicized and well-received one, hence our proximity. Her Majesty, the Queen, is the patroness of the arts. Above all the art schools in the Dreamland, she favors us. We are most fortunate." Juele thought the way Rutaro said it that the queen was fortunate to have such a school to appreciate.

"I hope I'll get to meet her," Juele said, then, abashed at her own boldness, added, "or see her."

"Count upon it," Rutaro assured her, blithely. "Her Majesty is in and out of here all the time."

How very exciting! Juele thought. That was something to tell Mum and Dad when she wrote home. Royalty visiting, casually dropping by. In and out all the time. Even if she'd dared, she couldn't have imagined such a thing.

Another wave of influence passed, a mere correction to the one that had gone before. It turned the basins of the fountain blue, and the artists seated around it let out a collective groan. There was much hand waving and erasing of color in the air before they began again to capture the essence of the fountain.

"I've never been in Mnemosyne before," Juele said. "We don't have constant waves of influence running through Wandering like this."

"You'll get used to it," Rutaro said, yawning. He started walking again. Juele hoped she hadn't alienated him with her ignorance. He was the only person who'd spoken to her so far. He was clearly one of the senior students. She tried to guess how old he was and found it impossible to say. He could have been twenty, could have been thirty. She tried to reconcile his young face with his world-weary attitude. Rutaro *exuded* Art. He was at home here, something she felt she had to be, had been craving to be, ever since she had first heard of this school as a youngster.

It was a dream that she was here, almost as if she was a dreamer in the Waking World, experiencing a nightborne fantasy in her mind. How wonderful it would be if only she could fit in here, if only they would accept her. She had never been very good at making friends, although she treasured the ones she had. She suddenly felt small and lonely, and clenched her fingers on the handle of her art box.

"Rutaro?" she asked, timidly. "How long have you been at the School?"

Rutaro shrugged. "It seems like nearly forever." He looked at her with a fond smile. "I think you are just a little older than I was when I came here."

He swirled his hand in a small circle, and beneath his fingers, a scene sprang up, a perfect miniature reality in every detail. Juele gazed at it raptly. She saw three young people—children, really—dressed in their best clothes, huddled together in the corner of a quadrangle that was recognizably the one she stood in today. Rutaro had to be the intense, dark-haired one on the left, with a soft, floppy bow tie under his vivid face. His two friends were a tall, thin boy with dreamy eyes wearing a knee-length coat that only made him look lankier, and a short, belligerent-looking girl with a dark blue dress that fell unbecomingly just below her knees and a big bow tying back her hair. Juele had the sense of the passage of time, and four more young people joined the first three. She couldn't see the newcomers quite as clearly as the three, but there was a rainbow in the sky behind the group, and the fountain in the foreground, different in memory than it was now, tinkled musically. Rutaro's voice was soft.

"It was so good to find others who felt as I did."

"Oh, I know what you mean," Juele said, passionately, gazing up from the image. Rutaro gave her a quizzical look, one eyebrow raised into his theatrically curled hair.

"*Do* you?" he asked. Embarrassed, Juele turned away from his gaze. As she bent closer to look again at the small scene, the illusion faded. "I expect perhaps you do. You'll meet the others in time," Rutaro said, carelessly, flicking his fingers as if to clear them. "Come on. We need to get you settled in. I've things to do before dinner." He beckoned, and Juele trotted after him.

"The philosophy of the School is simple," he said as he walked. "We strive here to learn how to make the best illusions to be found anywhere. In illusion, the skill is to make something look like something else, to disguise the imperfect essentials. To make something invisible is easy. To use actual matter is cheating. The illusion is the art." He ran his hand through a wall that appeared to be white marble inlaid with a pattern of brass flowers. His arm disappeared up to the forearm.

"Oh," Juele said. "But that man, who changed the building to look like his illusion . . ."

"His own style. Not what We think." Juele could hear the capital letter very clearly. But, she thought, who is We?

"We imbue the illusion with importance by using appropriate symbolism," Rutaro continued. "Symbolism is very important. But it is wrong to use symbols that are without meaning. Every object, every color, every shade and nuance adds volumes of understanding, but Nature herself is the most perfect symbol of all."

"I see," Juele said, though she didn't.

"We have students of every age here. Art knows no boundaries," Rutaro said, halting suddenly. "But you *are* one of the youngest students we've ever had. This might be an adjustment for you. You can fit in, can't you?"

Juele steeled herself. "Yes, I can," she said, and with a mental crossing of her fingers, she folded her hands together on a handy beam of sunlight and concentrated. When she opened them, a blue-white unicorn pranced on her palms. It was one of her favorite images, detailed down to the last hair on the goatish tail. The tiny creature lowered its glowing horn to her thumb, and a bright spot of light flashed where it touched.

Rutaro gave her a wry look and began walking again. Juele released the image and let it go back to undifferentiated light, wondering if she had overstepped again. She followed Rutaro out of the lovely square, and into a narrow, dark corridor like the inside of a stable. It smelled not unlike a stable, too, and Juele noticed that the beams holding up the ceiling were rough wood with rusty nails sticking out here and there. People were living in this building. She glanced through an open door and saw the tiniest room, fashioned roughly out of a stall. On the narrow, lumpy bed were piled a few meager belongings. A very impoverished student who couldn't afford anything better must live there, and the administrators fit him in where they could. But as she passed more of the doors, she saw that behind every one was a room as small as the first. All were occupied. This must be the charity dormitory, she thought. Rutaro halted and turned on his heel.

"What residence are you assigned to?" he asked.

"I don't know," Juele said. She found the letter of admission in her pocket and held it out to him. In her hand the piece of paper gleamed bright with high hopes, but when Rutaro held it, it became merely a piece of paper. He stuck out his lower lip while reading.

"Oh," he said. "You're in the Garrets. This is the Stables. This way."

Rutaro turned at the end of the corridor, opened a small door, and guided Juele to a dark staircase that smelled of dust and floor polish. He pointed upward and began to climb. Hoisting her bags, she followed him up the linoleum-covered steps, floor after floor after floor, until her arms were sore and her feet were numb. The stairwell walls had once been painted a cream color. From the edge of the banister to above Juele's head, the paint had been smudged brown-gray by a thousand passing hands, and the plaster was chipped. The stairs spiraled around and up until, when Juele glanced over the banister to the bottom, the lowest levels had vanished in the dark and the sounds in the courtyard had faded to distant murmurs.

At the top a skylight was set into the ceiling. Between festoons of ancient cobwebs, light forced its way through the small, grimy panes of glass. Under the skylight was a grubby, brown varnished door that seemed feet shorter than the ones on the lower levels.

"Here we are," Rutaro said. "Sixteen-D." They passed into a very small reception hall with another sad-looking skylight. In the wall on each side were two small doors with tarnished letters in the center panel at eye level. Rutaro perused the admission letter again and pointed to the fourth door.

"Yours," he said.

The door was smaller and more battered than the one at the top of the stairs. Juele opened it. The room was tiny, and there were *two* beds in it. She didn't even get a room to herself. Juele's heart sank.

"Oh, well," Juele said, bravely. "I'm just happy to be here."

Rutaro didn't seem to hear her. He was good at ignoring things. He stood to the side to usher her in, then turned to go.

"Get yourself settled," he said, over his shoulder, as he made for the stairs. "You can just make your first afternoon class in symbology if you hurry. You'll find Mr. Lightlow quite adequate. I must go to Peppardine before I change too much. See you again at dinner."

"Thank you," Juele called, but he was gone. She heard his boot soles clatter away downward.

She turned to examine her new home. It was a *very* small room. The dingy, yellowing plaster on the walls was cracked, and the only window was high up and very dirty. At the narrow end of the room under a candle sconce stood a single study table and chair. The two beds offered neither privacy nor comfort. They were only a pace apart on the brown-planked floor, and the mattresses were thin enough to pinch between her thumb and forefinger. Juele sniffed. It smelled musty in here, the odor of ages.

She felt miserable enough to cry. Was this the nicest place they could offer her? She had felt so special to be able to come here, one of the chosen few among all aspiring artists in the kingdom, and they had given her a cramped little attic to live in. In a single day she'd gone from being loved and admired in Wandering, the best, a prodigy, a privileged character, to an insignificance in the School's smallest and most wretched accommodation. Was this how things would be here? Should she just take her things and go home? But she couldn't. To learn at the School of Light was her dream. No matter what it took, she would stay.

She must not let physical surroundings break her spirit. Couldn't she fix it up with illusions? Wasn't her skill, after all, what had brought her here in the first place? She looked at the two beds, deciding which one would be more comfortable. The one nearest the door had a teddy bear seated against the flat pillow. The window was in the wall opposite, so what little light they got would fall on that bed. Juele approached it, trying to judge if the morning sun would hit the pillow, or not. She liked to get up with the sunrise. As she made to sit down, the teddy bear blinked its shoe-button eyes at her and growled fiercely, its stitched red mouth opening to show a set of sharp, white fangs. That bed had been claimed by her new roommate, and she'd left her toy behind to hold her place.

"All right, I'll take the other," Juele said. She backed away, hands up, and the teddy relaxed and resumed its backstitched smile.

The other bed was on the shadowy side. Juele sat down on it beside her art box and held the battered case to her for comfort. She felt so lonely. Her friends, her family, and her teachers back in Wandering had been her support group. Could she sustain the promise that she had shown at home without them? Would she make it here? Would she disappoint everybody? Or herself? She had the talent; she knew that. But could she do anything with it that mattered?

She hoped she could make friends. Everyone here seemed so cool, so self-assured, so *busy*. Here she had hoped to find the peer group of which she had always dreamed, the ones who understood her passions, and shared the same kind of talents, so she wouldn't be the only one who knew what she was talking about. She stood up on the bed to look out the little window and saw the figure of Rutaro in his ruffled shirt just disappearing beneath the arch leading to the next quadrangle. He was just amazing. The way he could instantly create a moving illusion on the palm of his hand—so complex it would have taken Juele hours—just filled her with awe. She was fascinated by all the little things in the image she hadn't understood, like the golden circle painted on the ground around the feet of the three children, and the various flowers. All that seemed very *significant*. She wondered if Rutaro would be a friend. If he accepted Juele, she knew she should be able to get along with some of the others. But she didn't want to hang on him. She'd make her own way. It was just going to be a little lonely at first.

She unpacked her few belongings into the chest at the end of her bed. To her surprise, the low box made room for everything she put in it. It was even more of a holdall than the suitcase, which was sometimes a steamer trunk, that she had borrowed from her uncle. She guessed that the box might once have been a whole closet in a nicer house. Someone who didn't want it any more had donated it to the School, where, form following function, it took the shape of a dreary chest in a dreary dormitory. Well, it did its job. That was all she asked of it. The room did its job, too. It would be a place for her to sleep and sometimes, when her roommate didn't need the desk, study. She didn't expect to be spending very much more time in there except for that.

The last garment in her case was a new pink smock, made for her by her mother, whose own artistic bent showed in her talent for sewing. Juele shook out the smock with satisfaction and laid it on the bed to admire the half-length sleeves and the gathers at the shoulders. This was an occasion. She wished her parents and friends could be here to see her put it on for the first time.

But this room was an awful setting for a special moment. Juele stood up and put her hands on her hips. The terrible paint would have to go, for a start. Holding out her hands, she spun a rainbow between them in the air and scrolled it back and forth to see the colors. Maybe a light pink or yellow, just enough to cheer up the room. It was a pity that her talent for the manipulation of dreamstuff didn't extend as far as her talent for illusion. Then, she could change the paint. But Rutaro said using matter was cheating, so she wanted to get out of the habit.

The arc of color bowed up and out between her hands, a trick that had always delighted little children at birthday parties. She brought her hands together to compress the ribbon at the red end of the spectrum. Yes, a nice shell pink. She narrowed her hands around that swatch of color, kept it in her mind, then spread it out as wide and smooth as she could and pinned it in place on the wall over her bed with tacks of thought. Oh, that was much better!

She continued to spread the pink over the walls, pushing the illusion up into the corners with a shove of her palms until the whole dark cube glowed with cheery warmth. Even the sad window seemed to shed more light. Juele felt more optimistic as she changed out of her traveling clothes and laid out a fresh blouse and skirt. Later, she'd design a handsome coverlet and, perhaps, matching curtains. She hoped her roommate liked the same colors as she did. Maybe they could have bedspreads to match. That would be fun.

The personal facilities, as primitive as the room, consisted of large pitcher of water and a big bowl on a stand next to the desk and a covered pail in the corner. She hoped that sometimes the pitcher and bowl changed into a real shower, or—bliss!—even a bathtub. She could form the illusion of a luxurious bath, but it wouldn't affect the underlying reality of a small washbasin, as the pink hid but didn't change the cracked paint underneath. She wasn't that good at manipulating real dreamstuff. That was hard work, and she was not always successful. Still, it would have been nice.

Over the bowl, a small mirror hung on the wall. Juele looked at herself as she dried her face.

"You're here," she said, and smiled at her reflection, which returned a happy grin. It was still hard to believe that she stood in the midst of the actual, verifiable School of Light. The School, and no illusion.

Juele was surprised by the sudden sound of a bell striking three. Like everything else here, the tolling was beautiful, but its form enhanced its function. The lovely round tone was tempered with urgency. Rutaro had mentioned symbology class. She fumbled for the admission letter and read down it for her schedule. There it was: Symbology, 3:00, Prism Building, room 306. Oh, no!

Juele grabbed for her clothes. She hastily buttoned up her blouse—which obstinately grew a dozen extra buttons just to make her fingers fumble—then flung her smock on over it. She grabbed up her art box, started to do up the top two buttons of the smock, and nearly dropped the box. Chiding herself for carelessness, she hurtled out of her room and down the stairs, which were old and slick as grease. She was late! And on her first day, too.

She didn't notice as, behind her, the pink light started to peel at the edges and slide off the wall even before the door closed.

Chapter 2

But where was the Prism Building? In the courtyard outside the Stables, Juele looked around her. The building nearest the entrance to the Garrets had no name plate, and almost as soon as she began to look at it, the structure became a featureless cube of plain, white marble. No help there. She pored over her admission letter, hoping she had overlooked a map. Nothing. But the line of print in the letter noting the time of her symbology class was now in bold-faced type with three exclamation points at the end. She stopped a young man who was passing by.

"Is this the Prism Building?" she asked, pointing at the high, white square.

"No," he said, and went up the stairs. A section of wall opened up for him. He was swallowed up by the darkness within, and the door closed behind him. Juele ran up to look for a handle, but the door wouldn't open for her. Not the right building, but she hadn't asked which *was* the right one. She was off to a very bad start. Better ask someone else, quickly. Time was running away from her.

She spotted a woman teacher in a fluttering green smock cutting across the lawn of the quad.

"Excuse me," Juele began politely, trotting alongside her. "Where can I find the Prism Building?"

"On its foundation," the woman said, giving her a very brief glance. She frowned. "Or, it was this morning. Tch tch. I really couldn't say. So sorry." She began to take longer strides and soon outdistanced Juele. The green smock disappeared under one of the brick archways.

Juele slowed down to a walk, discouraged. She knew about Unanswerable Question Dreams, but she'd never heard of Questionable Nonanswers. She must find someone to ask who made sense. She looked about, but the garden, which had been full of people when Rutaro had walked there with her, was empty. She was alone in it, holding her art box to herself. This was not an ordinary Frustration Dream. This was calculated.

"The place is testing me," she said, through gritted teeth, glaring around at the stone buildings. The windows looked like eyes, watching her curiously. "I do belong here, I do! It isn't fair to expect me to find a place I've never seen without instructions or directions. There ought to be a map here. *Close* to here. If I don't see one soon, I'll have to create one out of real dreamstuff, and make *reality* match." She looked around her, wondering if the School would react to her threat or call her bluff. She could hardly manipulate her own form, let alone reality around her or that of anyone else. Her talent lay in illusion, but she hoped that the overmind of the School didn't know that.

"Hi," said a dark-haired young man, coming up beside her. "You look lost. What are you trying to find?"

"The Prism Building," Juele said, thankfully. She showed him her letter. "Do you see? Room 306, three o'clock. I'm already late."

"Oh, that's easy," he said, with a smile that showed even, white teeth like fence posts. "I'll show you. Please follow me."

The young man crossed the quadrangle into the far corner and negotiated the twisting, winding passageways beyond with confidence. Juele ran beside him, clutching her art box and fretting over each second that passed. What an awful way to start her first day! The young man said nothing more. He must have noticed her preoccupied expression. How kind people were, she thought.

A huge herd of sheep, crying shrilly to one another, emerged from one of the archways and spread out onto the path in front of them, which immediately changed from packed gravel to rutted mud. Juele cringed, picturing the nuisance eating up more of her time. She was late enough as it was. Effortlessly, the young man took her hand and threaded between the sheep, fording the stream of gray, woolly backs almost as quickly as if there was nothing there. He even managed to avoid the sucking mud that pulled the shoes off other people caught in the midst of the flock. Juele was grateful for his expertise and tried to say so. Her voice was swallowed up by the stuttering wails of the sheep. In no time, they had passed the shepherd, an elderly man wearing a smock and carrying a crook. He touched his hand to his hat as they went by. Juele forced herself to smile at him, though she was very annoyed. It wasn't his fault he was a nuisance. The sheep turned aside into a low, stone doorway, and the path dried up into a lane of close-set bricks. Juele trotted after her guide.

Two more turns through the labyrinth of archways, and the young man stopped at the foot of a flight of shallow, stone steps. At the top was a building made of pale gold stone that gleamed warmly in the sun. When a man in a flowing blue smock pulled open the door, rays of light shot off in every direction, striking rainbows off the walls and ground.

"Here we are," the young man said, cheerfully. "The Prism Building."

At last! "Thank the Sleepers," Juele said, with relief. "You've been so very kind." She ran up the steps and reached for the door handle. "Thank you," she said, turning back to smile at her guide.

But the young man had vanished. Where he had been standing was a glass-covered map on a pole painted white. Juele blinked. She didn't know whether her guide had been real or the School had created him to help her. There wasn't time to wonder about it. She was late for class.

The stairs in every flight seemed endlessly high as Juele ran up to the third floor. She looked down the expanse of polished brown tile at the facing rows of huge wooden doors. All the doors in the corridor were closed. Juele approached the first one with trepidation. The number plate said 306. She opened the door and stepped in. A woman in a rust-colored smock and three dozen students looked up from their books at her.

"May I help you?" the teacher said.

"I'm here for symbology class," Juele said.

"You want room 306," the woman said, pointing across the hallway.

"I thought this was 306," Juele said.

"No, this is 300," said the teacher. She smiled, but it was a dismissal. Embarrassed, Juele backed out and closed the door. She looked up at the number plate. It did say 300. She must have read it wrong. Hastily, she scurried across the hall. There, on the room opposite, was the number 306. Hurriedly, she flung the door open. Students sat in desks in five rows of five. Only one desk in the room was empty. Fortunately, it was nearest the exit. She slid into it. The thin, intense, dark-haired man in dark red at the head of the room looked at her quizzically.

"And who are you?"

"Juele," she said. "I'm in your class."

He went to his lectern and turned over a page in the tremendous, ancient-looking leather-bound ledger that lay there. "No, I don't have a Juele listed. Could you be in the wrong period?"

"No, sir," she said, worriedly. The other twenty-four students were now looking at her. "My schedule said three o'clock in room 306. Symbology."

"But this is room 304," the man said, shaking his head. "And you're late!"

"I saw 306 on the door," Juele said, feeling ridiculous.

"Did you?" the teacher asked. "You'd better hurry along."

How could she have made such a stupid mistake? Mortified, Juele picked up her box and fled out into the hallway. It had changed in the last few moments. Instead of a well-lit, wide passage, it had narrowed into a labyrinth. Juele ran from door to door in search of the correct room number. At a distance they all looked as if they said 306, but when she got closer, the numbers changed. 616. 803. 1412. As she passed them, the doors swung open. She kept peering back over her shoulder.

At the extreme end of the narrow corridor, she saw one last door. To get to it, she had to pass through an expanse of floor that was lit from all sides as if by spotlights. As she stepped into the light, disembodied voices shouted at her.

"She's the one!"

"Look! There she goes!"

There was nowhere she could hide, no handy shadow she could dart into. Doggedly, Juele held her head up and ignored them, but felt her cheeks burn with shame. The door retreated from her, and the lighted area expanded as she walked, trying to pretend she couldn't hear the catcalls. At last, the Shaming Voices faded, and the door stayed where it was.

She approached with trepidation and looked at the number plate. It *had* to be room 306. Clutching her art box to her ribs, she tried to approach the room quietly, so as to draw the least possible attention to herself. Behind the door, she could hear a voice droning on, but she was unable to understand what it was saying. But her footsteps on the floor sounded louder and louder, and the bronze knob turned in her hand with a banshee-like screech as the door swung open. Everyone in the room turned to look at her. Juele gulped, feeling her heart pounding, and forced herself to step inside. The door boomed shut behind her.

". . . the development of a coherent theme. You will establish a clear central image, and adorn it appropriately. . . ."

At the front of the room, a tall, austere-looking man with a beaky face, domed head, and deep-set, glowing eyes stopped talking and stared at her. Mr. Lightlow raised an interrogative eyebrow, which climbed halfway up his forehead like a hairy spider scaling a wall. His lip lifted, showing horsy front teeth.

"Yes? How may I help you?" he asked.

Juele remembered the letter in her hand and rushed to hand it to him. He took the paper in his knobby fingers. As she passed it to him, the glowing white page turned to a crumpled, stained, and much-folded scrap. He gave her a stern look over the top of his glasses and sucked in his lower lip under his considerable overbite to read. As he scanned the few lines, his mouth pursed disapprovingly.

Juele waited nervously, her heart pounding in her chest. The teacher was about the same age as her father, with the same gift for silent disapproval. The whole room seemed to be disappointed in her. On a shelf that ran all the way around the room were lines of potted plants. All their leaves drooped sadly, as if they hadn't been watered recently and might not survive much longer. A canary in a cage near the big desk at the front of the room chirped faintly for water. The clock on the wall ticked loudly in the silence, then stopped still. If there had been a spotlight over Juele's head, it could not have been more significant. Rutaro had warned her about the weight given to symbolism at the School. The air around her felt heavy with meaning. Everything told her that she was late. Much too late.

"Class begins at three, you are aware?" the teacher asked, breaking the silence, his eyebrow still plastered high on his forehead.

"Yes, sir."

"Ahem. Then you will not let this happen again."

"No, sir," Juele said, her voice shrinking as she wished she could. "I won't." Mr. Lightlow's eyebrow lowered. He waved his hand dismissively at her. Juele sidled back to an empty seat among the others and sat down. With a foot, she shoved her art box under her seat. Scraping along the floor, it squawked and brayed like a stubborn jackass, sticking out recalcitrant corners like feet to hinder her. Wait *until I get you back to my room*, she thought hotly, giving it a last kick. The other pupils tittered. The boy next to her cleared his throat, grinning down at his desktop, not looking at her. Juele sat with her chin bowed to her chest, abject, wishing herself invisible. The teacher cleared his throat, and continued his lecture where he had left off.

". . . And that's the way I want it. The way it should be. Appropriate, as I said. No more, no less. Now, class," Mr. Lightlow said, abruptly finishing his previously side-lined train of thought. Evidently considering Juele punished enough, he opened a hand in her direction. "I'd like you to welcome our newest pupil. This is Jurrie Caffyne, she's from Wondering."

Juele spoke up, her voice a tentative squeak. "Um, sir, my name's Juele, and my town is Wandering."

"Well, you'd better catch it before it trips and hurts itself!" some wit hooted from the back of the room. Juele felt her cheeks burn with embarrassment.

The professor looked around, his eyes very sharp through the heavy lenses balanced on his nose, and focused upon the offender. The murmurs abated. "That's enough, now. Treat her with the same respect you'd like to have shown you. We have great faith in her. The testers said she showed a good deal of promise. We're counting on her to fulfill it, as we count on each of you."

By the expressions of pain and boredom on their faces, Juele assumed the others heard this speech frequently, probably with the arrival of every new pupil. She looked around hopefully at them, smiling. Many of the students gave her their noses in the air, some so loftily they were no longer attached to their faces, but she got a few friendly responses. That big, rangy girl in the back of the room looked nice, and so did the tawny-skinned boy beside her with curly eyelashes to match his curly black hair. Both of them had on smocks that were slightly worn-looking, sort of fashionably shabby. Was her gown too new? Juele was afraid it branded her a hopeless tyro. Subtly, she laid an illusion of wear on her garment, bleaching the dye out just a bit, showing a loose thread on a seam or two. There. She fit in better with her classmates. She glanced around hopefully to see if anyone noticed her making alterations.

Mr. Lightlow paid no attention to the byplay, and continued with his instructions. "Will everyone please open to section two, on page 43?"

Section two? Juele felt a surge of panic. Wasn't this the first class of the term? Had the semester begun early? She had no book. There hadn't been time for Rutaro to show her where to buy books. What had been in section one? She felt as if she was all at sea. The floor under her chair began to undulate, bobbing her about like a cork. Her stomach heaved a warning. The others giggled.

A heavy volume landed with a thump on the desk in front of her and opened itself to a page. Surprised, Juele glanced up. Mr. Lightlow, his eyebrow back where it belonged, hovered over her. He gave her a patient, kindly look and turned back to the class. Already the horsiness of his face was softening into something more human and approachable. Juele seized the book like a life preserver, and the room stopped rocking.

"Your assignment for this period: design a simple illusion, making use of one or two—no more, this is not a rummage sale—ornaments to indicate that you understood my lecture. Yesterday's lecture," he said to Juele. "I don't expect mind reading. You may review briefly." Juele seized the book and bent her head over the page. The title of the section was "Enhancing the Depth of Understanding." She began to read. The text wasn't too obscure, but what really helped her to comprehend the lesson were the illustrations. A hand-colored woodcut on the next page showed a girl in a white bridal dress. Above her head was a wreath held by two doves, and at her feet was a pool. Juele could see small stones and a fish in the water, so the water was glass clear. The gown itself was very plain, though the classic design lost nothing for lacking adornment. *Purity*, Juele thought, fascinated. *I see*. The picture's not really about the girl, it's about what she stands for. So, what you're looking at may not be what the illusion's *of*. Juele felt a twinge as her mind stretched wide enough to encompass a deep concept like that. It seemed so simple, but so—so complex. She wondered if she was understanding it properly. Juele suffered a pang of doubt. Could this class be too advanced for her? Was her precious admission letter a passport to trouble and humiliation?

"Atmosphere, color, shape, everything must be appropriate to the symbol in question," the teacher said. Juele glanced up. He was pacing back and forth at the front of the room, as if by his energy and enthusiasm alone he could make his students absorb the concepts.

Some of them picked them up right away. Thought balloons rose over the their heads as they bent over their desks. Trained as they were to be visual thinkers, the students' very thoughts were visible. Juele spotted what had to be more advanced pupils. The images over their heads were of the illusion that was taking shape between their hands on the workspaces before them. The pictures within the puffy bubbles changed rapidly, as the students tried to decide what image to concentrate on. Juele wondered if that happened to her when she was thinking. No one had ever mentioned it.

One by one, the desks—form following their function as work tables for students to learn upon—became pedestals and easels. The pupils reached for their own art boxes and began to draw colors out between their hands. Juele looked hastily away, not wanting to be accused of copying from her neighbors. Mr. Lightlow continued pacing, nodding encouragingly as each student's thought balloon became a light bulb.

"If you don't comprehend an image, then ask. If you still cannot get anything to take root in your mind, choose another concept. Better to work on something you don't like quite as much than to make yourself ridiculous utilizing that which your audience knows more about than you. It's so easy—we deal in abstracts every day. All you need to do is make one concept visible."

Juele felt his energy licking out from his mind like

fire and starting to catch on in hers. Why, she could design an image like that, all symbols. It'd be easy. She'd draw . . . the Dreamland! Her desk, sensing her change in mind, tilted upward, growing a shelf just below eye level wide enough for a small illusion, say just a little bigger than her hands. She snatched up the ray of light that fell on the desktop and began to pick it apart for colors.

This would be easy, to show one thing representing another. She hoped her efforts would satisfy the teacher. *Let's see who else can figure out what I'm doing*, she thought, mischievously. *He'll get it right away. I hope he won't say I'm being too ambitious.*

Now, how could she best depict her homeland? Juele fiddled with a cool strand of blue light while she thought. The central part of her image would be a portrait of King Byron, ruler of the Dreamland. The king represented his realm, didn't he, so he ought to be a suitable symbol. Juele had never seen her sovereign in person, but his face was on every piece of currency in the kingdom. She slipped a handful of coins out of her pocket and squinted down at the bronze disks. All she had were small ones, only worth a pencil each, and the image was minute. Juele fingered them, choosing the one with the clearest-struck head. If only she'd been richer, she could have used a big coin, say a chicken, as a model. Or if she had better control of influence, she could make the coins larger, or change all the small ones into a bigger coin of their total value. With the talent she had, Juele could make an illusion of a bigger coin, but the likeness would still be only as good as her skill, and that was why she needed it as a model in the *first* place. Juele looked about her and thought of asking one of her neighbors for the loan of a coin, but quickly decided against interrupting anyone. To show any more vulnerability was to make herself the butt of jokes for the rest of her career here. No matter. She'd do the best she could with what she had.

There wasn't enough light on her desk, so she rooted around in her art box for more, as well as for her palette and some preseparated colors. As a base for her piece, Juele fluffed up an imaginary pillow of cloud in pearly gray light shot through with threads of rainbows. She set her king-figure's feet on it and made him face her as though she was looking down on the Dreamland from a height in the south. He was holding his arms out as if he was walking. King Byron had to look handsome, strong, and noble. Her mother, who had seen him once when he made a royal progress through Wandering before Juele was born, had always said that His Majesty was the very epitome of nobility. Her parents had deep respect for the monarchy and the Sleepers themselves. Juele imbued the image with appropriate reverence for her king and country.

Everything in the Dreamland seemed to come in sevens, to correspond with the number of Sleepers. Juele drew King Byron wearing seven garments, one for each of the seven Provinces; and a silver necktie to represent the great river Lullay. No, a scarf. A long scarf, with seven tassels, for each major tributary. And a belt made out of sharp stones, also in seven sections, for the ring of mountains that surrounded the land. Each of the garments had to be beautiful, and they had to fit together, but be distinctly different in style.

Let's see, she thought playfully, the right boot for Swenyo, and the left for Wocabaht, and . . . and the hat for Celestia. After all, the king's head was really in it. Juele grinned at her little joke. A symbol within a symbol that was really a symbol within a symbol. This was fun.

She made the garments fit the character of the provinces. The boot ought to be soft, but waterproof, because Swenyo contained the Sea of Dreams, one of the most interesting features on the map. She didn't know a lot about Oneiros, but it was hot there, so instead of a glove, she made a gauntlet for the king's left hand. It didn't look particularly regal, so she studded the straps with gold studs and applied some mystic looking runes. By the same token, the trousers representing the warm climate in Somnus ought to be short pants, but she didn't think that would be proper or dignified. Maybe she'd make the pants of silk. She used up quite a lot of light getting the sheen just right, but the result looked good, and very comfortable. The coat for Rem was easy. Rem was reputed to be full of fantastic creatures that existed nowhere else in the great Collective Unconscious. She could decorate that part to her heart's content.

Now that the other students around her were at work on their own assignments they paid no attention to Juele. Freed from stinging remarks and odd glances, she could concentrate on what she was doing. She was aware of Mr. Lightlow passing among them, humming wordless approval under his breath.

"Mmm-hm. Mmm? Mmm-hm."

Juele started to hum to herself in counterpoint as she formed the coat on the figure's torso. She embroidered the tunic front and back with vivid depictions of unicorns, dinosaurs, dragons, basilisks, elves, and camelopards. Juele wove little bits of color into the gauntlet of the glove that represented northwestern Elysia. The Wocabaht boot would be rakish and dashing, as she'd heard the denizens of the second province to be. She ought to put it on reversed, or inside out, to denote the backward character of the province. Well, the minds of the Wocabahters weren't backward, but their seasons were. When it was summer everywhere else in the Dreamland, it was winter there, and vice versa. She tried turning the shoe around to face back-to-front and heard a little laughing trill. Derision from one of her classmates?

No, the sound had come from the canary. Juele looked up at the cage hanging near the teacher's desk.

Though no one had approached it, the yellow bird sang brightly, gargling and splashing the water in its silver bowl. Its distress had all been an illusion, Juele thought, catching the teacher's eye upon her. So the canary was an indicator of the teacher's mood. That would be useful to know in future. She bent to work on her assignment.

The figure of the king was prettily bedecked, but stiff and lifeless. *Concentrate*, she chided herself. What were the other aspects one associated with the king? He was not only handsome, but charming. Using a very small tool, Juele tried to mold the face into a more regal, but attractive aspect than the portrait on the coin. She worried that she was spending too much time on the details and not enough on the symbols. The scarf was important. It had to be just the right color of blue-silver, and it had to start on his right shoulder, go one and a half times around his neck, and trail off down his back. And the belt mustn't have a buckle. She had automatically put one in. The ring of the Mystery Mountains was unbroken, and she knew it. Clicking her tongue, she erased the clasp and joined the two front sections of rough rock together. She wondered if the image looked enough like the king. Well, she'd know if it was still handsome and noble-looking when it changed in the next wave of influence. If it kept its attributes, that would mean that the image echoed the real king, who was only just beyond the wall in the Castle of Dreams. Juele felt a pleasurable shiver. She'd heard stories of the royal family all her life, and it was a thrill to be so near them. She hoped she'd get to see them once in a while. Or, even, just once.

Juele shook her head in wonder. Only a day ago, she'd been a nobody in a small town. Now she was an accepted student in the finest school in the land, right there in Mnemosyne, not five minutes walk from the Castle of Dreams and the king and queen.

"I'd like to make an announcement, class," Mr. Lightlow said, circling about the last easel and coming to light on the front edge of his desk. "About Her Majesty, the Queen."

Juele felt as if the teacher had been listening to her very thoughts. She started, accidentally jostling her illusion and spoiling the edge of the cloud pedestal. Irritated at her own clumsiness, she fluffed out the gray mass and plumped it up again. She put her hands in her lap and focused all her attention on Mr. Lightlow. He smiled at her.

"As you may know, Her Royal Majesty, Queen Harmonia, takes a very personal interest in this School, and we are very proud of her patronage. Our School has already been engaged by the Crown to provide a number of new illusions to decorate the palace and other public spaces around Mnemosyne, to be unveiled at the beginning of our public gallery show. Some of these are already under way. Her Majesty has announced that she will be visiting the school next week, in advance of the gallery opening. Please be on your best behavior. Her Majesty has let it be known that she wants a portrait of herself made, with an eye toward having it displayed at the gallery, and thereafter hung in the queen's private hall in the Castle of Dreams. On the day of her visit, she will choose one of our students to receive the commission as the artist."

The class chattered excitedly among themselves. Juele breathed a sigh of delight. Her mother had never seen the queen. Juele imagined Her Majesty to be tall and regal and beautiful, and possessed of every ideal characteristic. If the queen came into the classroom, perhaps Juele could manage a small image of her to enclose in her promised weekly letter home to her parents. But Her Majesty wanted a portrait of herself. Wouldn't it be fabulous if she selected Juele as her artist? Juele heard laughter behind her and looked up above her head. There, in *her* thought balloon, was exactly that image, of Juele painting an image of a gorgeous, motherly woman in ermine and pearls. She blushed and waved an embarrassed hand to dispel it.

"As if you have a chance," the redheaded girl next to her hissed spitefully.

"Huh," grunted the heavyset girl in the back of the room. "As if any of us does." In embarrassment, other thought balloons around the room vanished. They'd had the same fantasy as Juele. "Most likely it'll be one of Them."

"Them?" Juele whispered. "Who's Them?"

"You don't know who They are?" the black-haired girl

on her right asked, wide-eyed with scorn. "Where did you come from, the moon?" Suddenly, Juele felt her chin seized by the grip of influence and forced to turn to face toward the head of the room, where Mr. Lightlow held their eyes.

"I have finished with my announcement. You may continue with your work. Thank you." The invisible finger and thumb let go, and Juele's chin dropped.

Juele's neighbor, also freed from mandatory attention, gave her a disgusted look through her eyelashes and bent over the colorful construction on her easel. Juele couldn't tell what the image was supposed to represent, and she shook her head regretfully. It was difficult to come from the very top of her class at home to the very bottom here. She'd have to climb up all over again. It meant a lot of hard work. Juele wasn't afraid of that, but she feared being unable to make friends among those who ought to be her peers. Was her neighbor a very advanced illusionist? What were the senior students like? The red-headed girl tossed her hair in an unconsciously impatient gesture, and Juele copied it.

She turned back to her easel, and poked at the image of the Dreamland king until she was satisfied that if she fiddled with it any more she would ruin it. She heard humming behind her, then a shadow fell across her desk. Juele looked up as Mr. Lightlow crouched down beside her chair.

"Uh, sir," she said. "I . . . I'm sorry, I guess I missed the first class session. I didn't know. I was told that term didn't begin until today."

"Terms are always ongoing at the School," the teacher said, as offhandedly as Rutaro might have done. "For you, term did begin today. Someone else's may end tomorrow, or never. Barriers are largely an illusion, whether of time or matter. You missed nothing after you came in, did you?"

"I . . . I hope not," she said.

"Let's see what you've absorbed, then." He fluttered his fingers at her to make way. Juele ceded the seat to him at the easel, and he sat down to have a closer look.

"Not bad for a first try, Juele," the teacher said, in a low voice, but not so low that the other kids near her couldn't hear. A few of them were stretching their ears out to listen. "Your portrayal has a very suitable level of realism. It's purely associative, of course. I'm curious: why did you use only one adornment? You could have featured two."

"One!" Juele exclaimed, almost indignantly. *Look at all the detail*, she nearly said, but stopped short of letting the words out of her mouth.

"Yes, one," Mr. Lightlow said. He took up a small beam of light and stripped away all but the red to use as a pointer. He tapped it against the base of Juele's work. "Your only associative symbol is the cloud pedestal."

"What about the scarf-river and the mountain-belt?" Juele was rather proud of those. She had forgotten the pedestal. She'd come to think of it as simply the base on which her light sculpture rested. Of course, it stood for the intangible character of the Dreamland.

"Those are only characteristic features, like the garments," Mr. Lightlow said, tilting his head. "Plain as the nose on your face. That's a feature, not an attribute. You couldn't consider your nose indicative of your character, now could you? Unless you're a nosy little meddler, and then it should stick out where it'd be *obvious*, eh? Surely you can see the difference." He tapped her nose with his forefinger for emphasis. Juele gave the teacher a hard look. None of her teachers at home would have criticized her so harshly. He dropped his hand and drummed a fingertip on her easel. "On the other hand, the pedestal displays a specific attribute of the Dreamland: its ethereality. I assume that's what you mean to depict."

"Yes." She had been right; he hadn't missed her meaning at all. Her sense of outrage faded quickly, and she became eager to explain. "I read in school that the king's title is 'His Ephemeral Majesty.' I thought it would fit."

"That's quite right, and it does. Well, you did quite nicely for a first attempt, really," the teacher said, picking up her sculpture on the flat of his hand and turning it this way and that. "Nice representation. Yes. The garments are a much better way to express the changeable nature of the provinces than representing them as parts of the body, since the Seven always exist, but they change as the Sleepers dreaming them change, as you or I would change our clothes. Yes, I like it."

"Thank you, sir."

Juele felt very pleased. Her teachers at home might have treated her with more respect, but this man's approval meant something because, for once, she didn't know more than he did. He was just in his critiques, and she could live with that. She relaxed.

"So, will it pass, sir?" she asked.

"Yes, it should," he said, handing the image back. "Keep going. Let's see how it looks when it's finished." Juele held her hands apart just far enough not to squeeze the work flat. An illusion might have no substance at all, but if one didn't believe in its character, it didn't exist properly. Mr. Lightlow nodded down at the little construct, then met Juele's eyes. "But you need to study the terms we use, so you know the difference between an attribute and an ornament, for example."

"Yes, sir," Juele said.

"Idiot!" hissed the girl to her left. Juele pretended not to hear, spreading a skin-colored mask over her face to hide the angry blush she knew was rising. How was she supposed to know the meaning of terms before she had ever heard them? "Oh, look, you got the face wrong."

"What?" Juele asked, looking at her sculpture with alarm. "What did I get wrong?"

"He should look more stupid, dear," she said, with a feline grin.

"Don't you think it takes a talent to run a kingdom?" Juele asked.

"No, dear, it's easy," the girl said, languidly. "Everyone does what you tell them."

"If everyone did what I wanted, the Dreamland would be a far more beautiful place," the black-haired girl said.

"If you please! I applaud initiative, but I would prefer you draw within the set lines, you know," Mr. Lightlow said. Juele chuckled, but the students nearby groaned. Another time-worn joke. "In time, you'll learn how to make a thing that represents an abstract concept. Without editorialization!"

Juele looked up at him. "I'm looking forward to it, sir."

The teacher looked at her face and smiled slowly, having evidently decided that she meant it. He raised his eyebrow at her, and, humming under his breath, passed on to the next student.

"Sucking up won't help you pass," the blond boy behind her hissed under his breath. Juele looked around, and the young man made an ugly face. Mr. Lightlow's humming turned to a sudden interrogative "Hmm—mm?" The boy gave her a cool, triumphant glance.

"Shut up, Cal," the heavyset girl in the back grunted at him, and glanced under her eyebrows at Juele. "Never mind."

"It's impossible to please everyone," Juele said, with a friendly grin for her defender. Both girls looked at Cal, who curled his nostril. His assignment was so fuzzy that Juele couldn't guess what it was. It dawned on her that Mr. Lightlow might have had the same trouble.

"And just what is that supposed to be?" the girl asked, peering forward over Cal's shoulder.

"Something you're completely unfamiliar with, Gretred," Cal said, haughtily. "Logic." But he leaned forward and stuck his elbows out around the sculpture, and his arms became a miniature embattled wall hiding it from her gaze. A couple of the other students within hearing snickered, and Juele grinned with them. Cal glared up at Juele, who turned around and went back to her own work. Someone, probably Cal, had painted a mustache on her king. She erased it, shaking her head, and continued pottering over details. A twitch to the sleeve here, a tug on the hem there . . .

The familiar sensation of passing influence welled up around her while she was fixing the color in the mountain belt. Warily, Juele held onto her desk and looked around, wondering what kind of changes the Sleepers were sending.

The wave came through from the front of the classroom. The canary's chirp deepened to a rough squawk as the bird became a multicolored parrot on a perch. Mr. Lightlow's very ordinary smock turned rainbow colors, his skin darkened, and he grew a pillbox-shaped hat on his head. The flow of energy was invisible, but as inexorable as the tide. Juele was used to the calm changes visited upon her small town. Here at the center of the kingdom, everything was more intense.

The invisible swell surged over her, raising the front of her easel several inches. The floor bulged itself up to a new level several inches higher than before. Juele grabbed for the desk, fearing the passing wave would buck her out of her seat. The desk's smooth-sanded surface roughened to hewn planks. Juele's hands, clinging to the edge, lengthened and deepened in color to a rich brown. The back of her easel levered up, followed by the forelegs, then the back legs of her stool, threatening to tip her off. Juele felt a thrill of fear. The students to either side of her stopped what they were doing and held on to their seats.

The table undulated energetically. Juele feared for the safety of her sculpture. When the swaying stopped, she examined her small work cautiously. Miraculously, it had remained intact. Though the garments had changed color and style, the king had stayed very kingly. Juele was pleased. So she had crafted a reasonably true image. On closer scrutiny, she discovered that a few details had changed in ways she didn't like. The tunic seemed too long. She pursed her lips and tilted her head to and fro to give herself different angles of perspective. Well, maybe it wasn't too long, but the collar and shoulders would have to be padded. Juele played with the image, winding and unwinding strands of light to see how it would look both ways.

❖   ❖   ❖

The clock on the wall chimed five times. Juele looked up at it in amazement. The time had ticked by twice as fast as usual while she'd been absorbed in her work. Another wave of influence must have come through, too, for the teacher's pet had returned to being a canary, and the students were all different colors and heights from when she'd last paid attention. Thoughtfully, she poked one more time at the cloud pedestal, then clenched her hands together. She was finished. She must do nothing else. Not bad for a first attempt, she thought definitely, admiring its symmetry and color with a critical eye. If she touched it again, she'd ruin it.

She opened her art box and carefully placed the image inside. The others around her began to gather up their things, stowing away their works in containers and pockets, between the pages of books, and under their hats. Their pieces were lovely and amazingly complex. Juele found it difficult to tell whether most of them were finished or unfinished. She looked down at her work, suddenly despairing of being able to design anything as brilliant as they had. But she vowed she would try. Perseverance had brought her here, and it would keep her here, no matter what. The warm feeling of happiness in just being at the school came back to her, and she shivered inwardly, enjoying it.

Packing away was finished, but no one moved. The class watched until Mr. Lightlow, again at the front of the room, nodded his head, then the noisy scramble for the door began. Juele stood up and shouldered her art box.

"Read chapter three for next time," the instructor called over the din. Juele picked up the big book and stowed it in the capacious pocket of her smock, where it folded down obligingly into the thickness of a pamphlet. Juele was grateful; that probably meant the book was to be a true help, not a hindrance. She hoped she would be able to absorb what it had to teach her.

As she filed out after the others, Mr. Lightlow closed one protuberant eye in a sly wink.

Chapter 3

Juele was jostled from all sides as the other doors in the hallway opened, adding their throngs of students to the crush already in progress. Ahead of her were a few of the girls from her class. They'd seemed interesting, if not immediately friendly. She wormed her way politely as she could through the crowd, trying to keep an eye on the copper-bright head of the girl who had sat on her left. Juele ducked under the limb of a tree creeping from one side of the hall to the other and found herself directly behind the redhead.

"Remember me?" Juele said, clearing her throat tentatively. The small sound was lost in the echoing racket. The redhead must not have heard Juele. She addressed a remark to the small, thin girl on her right.

"What do *you* think about the exhibition, Bella?"

"Pathetic!" The other smoothed her long hair. It was so dramatically black that Juele suspected enhancement, be it dye, influence, or illusion. The shining tresses weren't styled, but looked stylish all the same. Juele did her best to catch up beside the two girls, hoping to join in the conversation. The art box beating a painful tattoo on her hip, she opened up her stride. No matter how quickly she walked, they kept at least a pace ahead of her, without any apparent effort. "An attention-getting device. The real sign of insecurity, dear Daline." The black-haired girl waved her hand, a graceful gesture denoting complete scorn.

Juele increased her pace to a run, just barely keeping up behind the others, who, though they were only ambling, were covering ground at a remarkable rate.

"Are you showing anything in the exhibition?" she asked the two ahead of her. They turned their heads about an eighth of the way around, almost acknowledging her, but stopped well short of eye contact. Juele addressed the redhaired girl directly. "I liked the illusion you made in class. You meant it to be Aspiration, didn't you?"

"Yes," Daline said. "Simplistic exercises," she sneered, turning to her friend. "One wonders why we're kept back doing busywork when we're capable of so much."

"Hmmph," the other agreed.

"How long have you been here?" Juele asked. Other young men and women came out of lecture rooms she passed, glided ahead of her, and struck up conversations with each other, forming a solid row of shoulders in front of Juele that spread from side to side of the corridor. "Er, excuse me." Juele ducked under elbows and between books and boxes, but never could break into the front row. Everyone seemed so much taller than she was. All she could see now were the smocks of the people clustered around her. She caught tantalizing bits of gossip from the students sailing ahead.

"Did you hear what They're doing?" "Yes, it sounded like nothing at all, but when *They* . . ." "Well, my dear, the silly old woman asked me what it all meant, and *I* told *her* . . ." "Sad, sad, sad, but what do you expect from townies?" Juele jumped up and down as she ran, trying to see the speakers. Suddenly, the whole mass came to a halt at the top of the stairs. The crowd seemed to thin slightly so Juele could see ahead of her. Poised beautifully with her hand on the banister was the black-haired girl.

"Oh—" she said, as if surprised at the huge following she had amassed. "Dinner at five thirty, all?" Her eyes brushed Juele's briefly. They didn't linger, but they didn't shut her out, either.

"Yes, of course." Juele shouted out her joyful assent with the rest. "I'll be there." No one paid attention to her, but she didn't mind. Any small step forward was welcome.

❖   ❖   ❖

Juele trudged up the long stairs toward the Garrets, her heart lighter. If she'd had the breath, she would have been whistling. Symbolism was going to be *fun*. She was going to like Mr. Lightlow. He didn't let her off easy, but he showed appreciation for what she did do right. She'd take care to read her schedule in more detail. She never wanted to be late like that again. It was just too embarrassing.

The tower clock outside chimed five and a half times. Juele peered out one of the grimy windows in the stairwell. Almost time for dinner. What she wanted right now was to lie flat on her bed and rest for a moment before changing. A little privacy would do her a world of good.

When she opened the door at the top of the stairs, she pulled the long strap off her shoulder and started to swing her art box into the tiny room, then pulled up short. A girl was standing in the way. Juele yanked her arm back to avoid hitting her, and felt it wrench halfway out of its socket from the box's weight. She staggered backward, pulling herself up only in time not to fall down the stairs. Just to be awkward, the box had grown far beyond its normal size and transmuted into solid steel. Juele smiled shyly as she hauled the recalcitrant container screeching into the room by its strap, mentally promising it a thump on the lid later.

"Hi," she said to the stranger. "I'm Juele."

The young woman smiled back, just as shyly. "My name is Mayrona." Taller than Juele and very slightly built, with a worry line in the middle of her forehead, Mayrona was dressed in a pale blue smock whose color and cut really didn't suit her well. Though her other features were small, her eyes were large and dark, with a look that suggested she might start like a deer if Juele moved too quickly. She might have been about twenty. "I . . ."

"I . . ." Juele began at the same moment, and they both laughed. "You first."

Mayrona sighed. "I was really hoping for a room of my own."

"Me, too," Juele admitted, as Mayrona backed up a pace to let her step inside. The room seemed even smaller than it had in the afternoon. They had to edge around one another so Juele could get to her bed. "I guess they're short on decent quarters—oops, no offense," she said, quickly, turning on her heel toward her roommate.

Mayrona had a pleasant, but worried little smile on her face. "None taken."

Juele was relieved. They were getting off to a good start. Then she looked around. Her pretty colors were gone! The décor had returned to dowdy paint and faded curtains. Juele felt huffy. Maybe the other girl liked living in squalor, but Juele was accustomed to something better. She beat down the furious words before they escaped from her mouth. She was resolved to try and make the best of it. The two of them had to live together, for however long it took the School to solve its obvious housing shortage.

"I . . . guess you didn't like the changes I made this afternoon," Juele said, very casually, though she wondered if steam was coming out of her ears from the pressure of her thoughts. "I'm so *very* sorry. I guess you have your own ideas. I should have waited to ask."

"Did you try?" Mayrona looked genuinely surprised. She threw up her hands. "Oh, it doesn't help. Anything you do disappears in a minute. I've been attempting to put nice curtains in that window for a month. I drew the nicest illusion you ever saw—white cambric with pulled-thread embroidery, and a shiny brass rod—and the left panel vanished before I had even finished the right half."

Juele, who had managed to decorate the entire room in next to no time, did a quick mental summing up of her roommate's abilities, for all the other girl was several years older. She shook her head sympathetically. "Is it against the rules?" she asked gently, ashamed of having been sharp.

"No," Mayrona said, with a sigh. She plumped down on her thin cot and picked up her teddy bear. It snuggled into her arms. She put her cheek down on its head. "Not officially. The administration doesn't care at all. As far as they're concerned, you could use influence to bring in a swimming pool, so long as it's an *aesthetic* swimming pool."

"Influence is not my strong suit," Juele admitted, opening her footlocker to put away the art box and take out her dinner dress. She peered at the folded heaps of underthings in the chest. Hadn't she left the dress on the top? She stacked the underwear on the bed, followed by her good cloak, which had been on the bottom of the chest—she was sure of it—and almost everything she owned before she discovered her nice dress on the bottom. No, not quite at the very bottom, Juele had to admit, when she lifted it out. Underneath it was one lonely pair of socks. Patiently, Juele repacked everything into the chest. It had the same pawky sense of humor as her art box. She slipped off her day smock, blouse, and skirt, and folded them neatly away.

"Nor mine," Mayrona said. "It's the School. Itself. It wants us to live like this, so we'll appreciate beauty when we see it. It's hard to fight it."

"We'll beat it," Juele said, with determination, pulling her good dress on over her head and reaching around to fasten the buttons. "Are you coming to dinner?"

"Thank you, but I can't. I have a late study period for shadow at six. Extra credit for tomorrow's class."

"I'm taking shadow tomorrow, too," Juele said, pleased. "We could study together."

"Oh, I would like that," Mayrona said, with an eager smile. Juele felt a tingle of pleasure—she was making her first friend. "What hour?"

Juele reached for the paper that was never far away from her hand, and read the list. "It's my noon class."

"Really?" Mayrona's eyebrows went up, and her big eyes widened. "You're an advanced student, aren't you?"

"No, this is my first day," Juele said, torn between pride and dismay.

"You must be. Shadows are so short at high noon.

That's the hour they teach the real refinements. It's much easier to work with shadows when they're longer, at other times of day. At least," Mayrona said, with humorous self-deprecation, "that's what they tell me. My class is first hour. Just after sunrise. Life study is my real favorite."

"We can still study together," Juele said, hopefully. She was determined not to lose her chance at making a friend.

"I'd like that," Mayrona said. She had a sweet, wistful smile. "Are you dining with anyone?"

"Some of the people I met in symbology," Juele said.

Mayrona made a face. It reflected Juele's own doubts about her fellow students, but if she wasn't willing to put herself out to make friends, she'd never succeed.

"Have fun," Mayrona said. With a sigh, she sat down in the shabby chair on her side of the room and opened a book with pages displaying various shades of darkness.

"Thanks," Juele said. "See you later."

Advanced shadow? Juele wondered, as she headed down the stairs toward the dinner hall. All right, then, how *did* she measure up with the other students? She'd never seen her assessment, that sort of thing being absolutely confidential. But the administration had chosen her classes for her. They must believe that she could handle the toughest of a tough course. She hoped so. After symbology that afternoon, she was feeling very humble.

A homey clattering and good smells came from a set of double doors opposite the entrance to the dining hall, which proved to be in the end of a side wall in the long room. As she passed inside, the smock over her shoulders turned into a more elegant open robe. Its fronts hung straight down as if weighted, and a tiny pattern of silk embroidery decorated its hems and sleeve ends. The hall clearly had an enforced dress code. Everyone else's costume was similarly transformed, although with varying ornamentation. Juele guessed that the people with elaborate designs were professors, or senior students at the very least. Passing along the aisle toward the far end, in gowns as majestic as royal robes, must be the chancellor and the other officials of the school. She could see near her only a couple of gowns as humble as her own.

The dining hall was an ancient, huge, dark room. She had an impression of a lofty ceiling, but the weak, yellow light couldn't seem to reach all the way up to the rafters. Around the walls hung paintings in ornately carved frames. All of the images were too dark for Juele to distinguish. She could see tiny bronze plaques underneath each one and wondered why the names had been written too small for anyone at floor level to read. Perhaps when she ascended to loftier status, such things would become accessible to her.

Juele surveyed the dark wooden tables and unpadded wooden benches that had been polished smooth by generations of smock-clad bottoms. At the remote end of the room, there was a dais. The single table upon it was surrounded by chairs with high, carved backs and colorful cushions. The lighting was also different for those in the most favored places. Globes of brilliant, diamond-white light hovered at the center and either end of the high table. The rest of the School would dine under gloomy, yellow glows like dying suns. Juele just knew it would make the food look awful.

She found a seat in the middle of a bench facing the dais between two groups of students who had come in together and were engaged in enthusiastic conversations. The group on her left was discussing sports; the group on her right, politics. The sports group, a hearty bunch, paid no more attention to her than they did to the uniformed servers putting down food in front of them. An energetic young man with broad shoulders and a toothy grin, erected an illusionary field right in the middle of the table to demonstrate his success of the day. The end zone was on top of Juele's plate. As she took forkfuls of strong-smelling fish mousse from around the goal, the young man, suddenly reduced to the size of her hand, evaded hundreds of monstrous opponents and at the very last moment dove for a tiny ball. Juele watched raptly, forgetting to eat, as he launched the ball through the goalposts. Thousands of invisible fans cheered. The next moment, he was beside her again, and his companions were slapping him on the back and laughing.

"Congratulations!" Juele said, offering the young man a smile when he glanced her way. "That was terrific!"

"Thanks," he said, grinning, and turned away to listen to a girl at the end of the table. Juele swallowed her next question, and, with a shrug, went back to her dinner.

The food appeared to vary depending upon whom it was served to. Juele watched plates of the same fish mousse she was eating turn into shrimp cocktails or lobster salad as they were put down before certain well-dressed students. They must be on a more expensive meal plan, she realized, taking another bite. Hers was modest, but positively lavish compared with a few of the others, who were dining on eel and carp.

During the soup course, she leaned over to listen to the group on her other side. A most earnest young man set his open hands so they were parallel to one another and kept leaning toward them as if he was concentrating all his energy and essence in the space between his palms. The others stared intently into that space, but Juele couldn't see anything there that made sense. Many nebulous forms floated around, and every time the murky colors or shapes changed, his listeners *ahh*ed or *ooh*ed in a significant way.

"It's a conspiracy, you understand," he was saying. "Misdirection, malfeasance, categorical misrepresentation of a highly advanced degree that the public does not even suspect!"

"So how do you know about it?" Juele asked, curious.

The young man glanced warily at her over his shoulder and met her eyes for one brief, significant moment. "The sealed chamber . . . has leaks." The space between his hands showed a pinpoint of light in a murky field. Juele thought she saw the shadow of a man slip through.

"This sounds very exciting," she said, intrigued.

"Exciting! The safety of the free world is at stake!" said a serious young woman wearing round, black-rimmed glasses. She regarded Juele with a suspicious glare. Juele was taken aback. She was only asking questions, yet they treated her as if she was not only a stranger, but dangerous. The others huddled closer together, muttering darkly among themselves, "Trilateral, Marxist, Greenpeace, right-wingers, worldwide financial markets, brink of civil war." Juele, understanding none of the jargon, let her mind wander.

The door opened, and Juele looked up, hoping Mayrona might be arriving at last. Instead, the late-comers were teachers, prompting the students to rise in waves as they passed. Following the others' example, Juele sprang out of her seat. Mr. Lightlow passed, wearing a gown the color of intelligence with some kind of symbols on the sleeve. She smiled up at him, but he did not look her way. Behind him was a woman who appeared not to be wearing a robe at all. It wasn't that she was naked. Her clothes were invisible. Between her neck and her knees, there was nothing at all. Juele could see the wall quite clearly through her. She was delighted with the complexity of the moving illusion and wondered when she could take the woman's class.

Two instructors came in together wearing charcoal gray robes over their evening clothes. Juele guessed they must be shadow teachers. Behind them were three colleagues in bright peach, sky blue, and warm, buttercup yellow. Juele was curious what the various shades and symbols stood for. She started to ask her neighbors on the left about them, but found the political group had been replaced by another bunch of senior students, talking with animation, but in very low voices. She cleared her throat politely.

"Excuse me?" she began, shyly. They didn't appear to see her. "Hello? Can I ask you something?"

None of them acknowledged her. It was as if she was invisible, or not properly existing. She checked to make sure she *was* there, then waved a hand before the eyes of one young man. He kept talking without interruption. She wondered if she should draw attention to herself in some way, like creating a spotlight that shone down on her.

"May I ask . . ." she began again. One of the young women tossed back her long hair with one hand. Juele recognized the gesture. She had changed to dishwater blond, but Juele recognized her as Daline, the red-haired girl from symbology class. The brunette at the end of the table had had black hair earlier. Juele remembered that she was called Bella.

"Are you going to make a fool of yourself again?" Bella asked, with a superior smirk in her green eyes. She nudged the others. "Here's the child I was telling you about. Made an idiot of herself in front of Lightlow." She laughed contemptuously. Her companions exchanged sly looks.

"I didn't . . . !" Juele began. Defending herself was futile. Nothing she said could change their minds or their fatuous expressions. These people are jerks, she thought. She was rescued by the server, who reached down on her left to remove her plate and replaced it from the right with the main course. Juele smiled up at the uniformed woman, then immediately buried her attention in her food, pretending she had an appetite. Mayrona was the only nice person on this whole campus. Juele hoped that she wouldn't find she was more advanced than Mayrona in every subject. Her roommate would probably stop being so friendly if Juele constantly outshone her, but . . . but she would if she had to. Juele refused to be less competent than she knew herself to be. She shot a sideways glance at her classmates, now making comments about someone at the next table, and sighed. It could be a long, lonely term. She huddled over her plate. Illusions, usually unflattering portraits of other people, spun unhappily on the table amid their creators.

Juele caught a flash of gleaming white from far across

the room. She looked up at the dais. Rutaro sat facing
her at the high table. He was giving a vigorous expla-
nation of something to a group of his dinner companions. So different from the languid gent who had shown
her around the school. He was dressed in a fine suit of
soft, dark gray, more modern than the one he had been
wearing earlier, but he retained the floppy cravat. His
features had altered to a slightly more patrician cast, as
befitted his current situation. He wore a robe on his
shoulders, but his was pure white, as were those of six
others seated at the high table with him. *Those must be
the friends he spoke of,* Juele thought, and studied them
thoughtfully.

On Rutaro's left was a handsome, thin man with
floppy, light brown hair. On his right was the one to
whom Rutaro was giving his closest attention, a dark, truculent woman with a bow in her hair. The others had
their backs to Juele. She could only see their faces when
they turned to speak to one another. She saw a small-
boned woman whose gracefully waving hands looked
exquisite even from this distance. Beside her was a fiery,
redhead woman who was taller than any but the handsome man and had an innate elegance that made Bella
look like a ragbag. Helping the woman to sauce from a
china dish was a quiet, thin man with short, blond hair.
The last was a boy who appeared to be about Juele's
age—fifteen years. Rutaro finished making his point, to
the doubtful expression of his companion, and glanced
up for a moment. Juele waved energetically, hoping he
could see her.

"Who are you waving at?" Cal asked.

"Rutaro."

"You know one of Them?" Daline asked, astonished.
The other members of the clique stopped talking for a
moment to stare.

"Well, sort of," Juele said, surprised by the look of
respect on their faces. "Rutaro showed me around the
campus this morning. I think he's supposed to be my
student adviser."

Eyebrows all around the table raised high. Juele wondered what Rutaro and his friends meant to the School. If they were dining on the dais with the professors and the chancellor, they must hold a place of honor, but to shock the fashionable set, they had to be something really special.

"Well," Daline said, in a slightly thawed tone, "Maybe there's something redeemable in you after all." She looked at Juele out of the corner of her eye.

"Well, thanks," Juele said, indignantly. The others seemed amused. Juele held her tongue as she realized she was on the verge of snapping at them. These people will be your classmates for years to come, she told herself. You want them as friends, not enemies. Humbly, she looked down into her plate. Her half-eaten meal was swept away to the left, and a dish containing a narrow slip of pie replaced it. She took a bite. The sweetness of it hurt her teeth and gummed up her mouth.

"Hurry, or we'll be the last ones in at the coffeehouse," Bella told her group. "They always stare at latecomers." Juele looked up hopefully and met her eyes.

"Can I come, too?" she asked.

"We can't do a thing if you followed us," the girl said, grudgingly. "You might as well."

Juele felt an upwelling of happiness inside her. The last few bites of pie tasted like ambrosia.

Her companions had very peculiar manners, Juele thought, as she walked with them across campus, but she admired their style. Tagging along at the back of the group, she attempted to walk with the same airy swing as Bella, but her adolescent hips refused to coordinate with her knees. If she couldn't ape their gait, she could at least wear the same world-weary expression. Her lips folded together at the corners and pressed outward whenever she wasn't talking, and she let a genteelly scornful crease fall between her eyebrows. Already she felt superior to the way she had been earlier. And these people weren't so rude to her if she said nice things about them. Bella, in particular, liked to hear how clever she was. Fortunately for Juele, she had thought the older girl's work was clever and offered honest praise of it that made Bella purr. The green eyes slitted, and the points of her ears sharpened just a little bit.

The moment they left the dining hall, their robes reverted to smocks. Juele made hers look more like those of the clique's. She could not yet put her finger on what quality it was that made slightly beaten up garments seem so elegant, but whatever it was, she wanted it. They *belonged* more than she did. As they mounted the stairs to a building in the residence area, Juele tried the hip swing again. Her second attempt was better. Maybe all she needed was practice. In time, if she became similar enough, they should like her.

"What is this place?" Juele asked.

"The coffeehouse, dear," Bella said, in her most bored tone. In spite of her voice, she seemed anything but detached. Her eyes sparkled as she looked around her.

Juele didn't really see what was so wonderful about her surroundings. They had entered a hallway with a dimly lit, high, painted ceiling, but that was the last detail Juele could distinguish clearly. She had to pull in her elbows to keep from being crushed in the crowd. The smoky air was thick and tasted like the dregs of a cup of coffee: bitter, oily, dark, and tired. She kept her eye on Daline's fair hair as the girl pushed her way into the very heart of the mob.

Juele looked around her. Except for her classmates, she recognized no one. Faces swam up indistinctly out of the gloom and disappeared again. They seemed disembodied because nearly everyone in the room was wearing black under their smocks. For a moment, she lost track of Daline. Fighting her panic, she tried to cut through the miasma with a thread of influence, but it was at once swallowed up like a minnow in a pond full of pike. Something about the atmosphere in here was predatory and dangerous. Juele felt a little afraid of it as she edged further on into the room. It was very hot, and she felt her palms and forehead growing damp.

"Drink?" A rail-thin man with dark, bristling jaws and long, greasy hair underneath a black beret edged sideways toward her between two pale women in black. His eyes were half closed, as if his eyelids were too heavy to keep all the way open. He had a small, cylindrical glass half filled with amber liquid in each hand, and he extended one to her. A heady scent wafted toward her from the glass, teasing her nostrils.

"No, thanks," Juele said, looking at the liquid with alarm. Would he insist that she took it? To these people, liquor might be some kind of treat or entertainment and behave as such, possibly to become caviar or television in the next wave of influence, but to her it represented a frightening adult thing. If she accepted it, it might become a tax demand or something else that she felt unready to handle.

"Oh," the man said, flatly. "You're temperate. How dreary." He slipped away into the smoke. Juele thought that she must have flunked a test of some kind.

"There you are," Bella said, appearing suddenly by her side. She thrust a tall glass into Juele's hand. "Here. This is innocent enough for a tot like you. You've got to try and act like you fit in."

Juele accepted it with a look of gratitude for the older girl. She pushed aside the tiny paper umbrella and sniffed the bright orange liquid in the glass. It smelled like fruit juice. Harmless enough. She took a gulp and found the liquid very sweet, almost syrupy, and gently warm in her belly.

"Thank you," she said. Bella eyed her with bored impatience.

"Try not to be so small town," the girl said, and disappeared back into the mass.

Juele clutched the glass. Among the intense, black-clad people gathered here, she had never felt so unprepared. What was she supposed to do here?

"Three dimensions are so limiting," said a man's voice

that rose abruptly over the hubbub. Curious, Juele made toward it, keeping the glass close to her so it wouldn't spill.

"Abandoning dimensions is to draw more attention to the bounds of your work, rather than to the work itself," said a woman's voice. Juele edged her way closer to listen. The speaker, dressed in black like the others in her circle, but wearing a deep-gold smock on her shoulders, put the thick white mug she was holding into one hand and drew a nebulous figure on the air. Juele peered closely, trying to see what it was. The woman turned her head to stare at Juele, and Juele withdrew hastily. She took a sip from her orange drink.

"I can't be bothered by worrying about the limits of other people's perceptions," said the man. He was short and stocky, definitely taking up three dimensions himself. He grasped for the woman's illusion and drew it out in several directions at once. Parts of the misty whiteness disappeared. Some wisps would reappear in other places at different intervals, and others changed shape and color where they were. Juele wondered how he had done that. Surreptitiously, she drew a wisp of white smoke out of the noisome fog that surrounded them, then tried to detach pieces of the being of the illusion while making it still the same illusion. It was surprisingly difficult, made even more so by the fact she could only use one hand.

Silence fell. She looked up. The man and woman were staring at her. With a guilty start Juele let the mist evaporate. She backed away, and the circle closed. Juele turned away and went to wander the room.

Everyone there talked in hushed, intent voices, in small groups wreathed by the smoke that seemed to rise out of the very floor. Juele dipped in and out of various conversations. Some of the chatter was interesting, but much of it was obscure or over her head, in some cases literally, the talkers bobbing up near the painted ceiling. Many of the others were huddled in twos and threes around low tables lit by a single dim candle in a dark orange shade. Juele only glimpsed the faces, thrown into deep, sinister shadows by the dancing flame. Occasionally someone pushed by her, a man or woman in stark black, carrying a tray of glasses or coffee cups.

Now that she was over her initial nervousness, she was grateful to Bella and Daline for letting her come. In her fantasies about the School of Light, she had pictured this kind of gathering, where people talked about Art and Higher Concepts, and discussed Beautiful Thoughts. She sipped her drink and listened for a while, then moved on through the fog to the next group. People drew small illusions in the air that danced on the fumes and faded away as they talked. Waves of influence, both Sleeper-induced and driven by those present, changed the floor plan and people's appearance, yet always left the atmosphere obscured so that Juele couldn't see anyone but the people who were immediately around her. It was so dark that she slipped between two couples and walked straight into a wall without seeing it.

Her head rang. She fumbled for the glass, hoping she hadn't spilled it. Someone grabbed her arm and turned her around. Juele cried out in surprise.

"Shh! Don't make a fool of us," Bella hissed, leaning close to her as the crowd pressed about them again. Her dress had turned black, and her dark eye makeup stood out stark on her pale face. Daline and the others were behind her.

"I'm not!" Juele exclaimed, louder than she had intended. Everyone else abandoned their illusions and conversations to look at them. Her head felt rubbery. Was it the air, the drink, or the overwhelming pressure of influence in the room? She saw a ledge and put the glass down. Whatever was in it was affecting her head. "I'm sorry. It was an accident."

"Be quiet," Bella said, furiously throwing up a wall of illusionary smoke around them that stifled her voice. "People will notice you. The *wrong* way."

"Ah, there you are!"

The curtain of smoke parted, and Rutaro appeared.

Her companions hastened to make way for him, standing back as far as they could with awe on their faces. His white smock had lost none of the glamour it had had in the dining hall. It glistened like a pearl in the gloom. Juele studied the embroidery on the sleeves and hem. It changed constantly from one set of complex patterns to another, or was it just her muzzy-headedness that made her think so? The dinner suit under the smock was flawless, and Juele let out a little sigh of satisfaction for something that looked so right. Rutaro smiled at the small sound. His large, dark eyes were sharp, even in the half-light. The others regarded him with awe, but he only spoke to Juele.

"I hope you are getting along well," he said, with a charming little half-bow. Juele's classmates behind her nodded their heads violently up and down, willing her to say yes. She wanted to please them.

"Yes," she said, obligingly. Her classmates relaxed.

"Good," he said. "I was telling my friend Mara about you." He put out a hand behind him, and the woman with the bow in her hair who had been sitting near him at dinner squeezed in. She had on the same kind of white smock he did, over an old-fashioned yellow dress that came down to her knees and was somewhat too tight, as if she'd outgrown it, but kept wearing it anyhow. "I was telling her about the artists sketching the fountain this afternoon, and how impressed you seemed by it. You remember."

He held up a hand, and in it was a perfect little image of a fountain with blue, scalloped bowls and an upright pipe like an open lily. Juele studied it, and wrinkled her brows.

"That's not exactly the way it was," Juele said, eagerly. The others gasped, but Rutaro paid no attention. She put out both hands and willed the image of the fountain as she remembered it into being on her open palms. There was so little light in here that she had to concentrate hard, but color pooled on her hands, and she molded it. The top of the fountain had looked more like an elaborate candlestick, with scrolled details spiraling all the way around it to the base. She thought she got it just right, and nodded, looking up at Rutaro for approval.

"I think it was like this." She looked at Mara over the tossing plumes of water. "It really was beautiful. It looked so real, and then a woman walked right through it!" She did her best to reproduce the teacher in green passing through the carved pool.

"Not a fluke," Mara said to Rutaro. "All right."

"I told you, dear," he said, closing his palm on his own illusion. The fountain folded up and vanished. Mara nodded curtly and sidled through a group clad all in black, who made themselves thinner to open the way for her.

Rutaro smiled paternally at Juele. "Come to us tomorrow. There are some more people I'd like you to meet."

"I'd love to," Juele said. "Where do I . . . ?" He ignored her question, as usual, and strode off. What a man for a dramatic exit. Juele looked after him to see where he was going, but the crowd closed behind him. He hadn't forgotten her. She was glad. The other people in the Salon turned away and went back to their whispered conversations. The excitement was over. Juele started to let the little illusion on her hands fade, but Daline grabbed her wrist.

"Not so fast. I want to see," she said. She stared at the fountain and looked puzzled. "What's so wonderful about that?" she asked Bella, who also leaned in close to see for herself.

"Who knows, with Them," Bella said, with a wary look over her shoulder to see if anyone else was listening. "I mean, it's representational, and all. Hardly cutting edge."

"Is that really bad?" Juele asked, worriedly. "He seemed to like it."

Bella and Daline looked at one another. "I *suppose* not," Daline said, exasperated. "If *he* liked it."

"She did, too," Bella pointed out, with an eye on Juele. "You could tell."

"What you see isn't necessarily what *is*, darling. You know that."

"Would I dare to second-guess one of Them? Do I look stupid?"

"I suppose not," Daline said. She nibbled on a scarlet-varnished fingernail and considered Juele thoughtfully.

Juele glanced in the direction Rutaro had disappeared. "Where am I supposed to go to meet them?"

"We'll show you," Bella said. "That's easy. Anyone can find the Ivory Tower, but not just *anyone* can get in. But seeing that he specifically asked you . . ."

"Thank you," Juele said, ignoring the young woman's insulting tone. "That's very nice of you."

Bella shrugged, as if ashamed to be caught doing anything nice, but her attitude was marginally less distant than it had been. "We're going into town tomorrow morning."

"Into Mnemosyne? Can I come with you?" Juele asked at once.

"If you're there at the gate when we're going," Bella said.

Chapter 4

Juele tiptoed up the long staircase, clutching the banister for support. She was very tired and feeling unsteady. To her amazement, the clock on the tower in the Quad showed the time to be well after midnight. She ought to have been in bed ages ago.

Bella and the others had scarcely noticed her thanks and farewells as she left the Salon. They were deep into an esoteric conversation that sounded more interesting the farther away she got. It drew her back, but her conscience convinced her to go by reminding her that she had classes the next day, and besides, wonder of wonders, she'd been asked on a shopping trip. Still, it had been hard to make her feet cross the threshold into the fresh air. Some day, Juele vowed, she would be in the midst of everything going on and not get a bit tired.

A wave of alteration had come through just as she started across the moonlit campus. Her head and her feet had gone very small at either end of an unusually attenuated body. Her neck was a long, thin pipestem, her waist not much thicker. Her legs were spindly and fragile, at least twice as long as usual. Juele teetered along, praying she would not fall over and break herself. Every time she looked at the ground, it had dropped farther away. The altitude made her giddy.

The innocent-tasting drink Bella had given her must have had some kind of intoxicant in it, after she had carefully refused an obvious liquor. She'd never really consumed intoxicants before. What with the lateness of the hour, a lungful of atmosphere from the Salon, and the drink in her head she was finding navigating on her

58

pins very difficult. She teetered this way and that on the steep stairs.

How silly she must look. A giggle made its way up from her middle and tried to escape out of her mouth. Juele refused to let it, fearing that she would wake up everyone in the Garrets. The giggle tried to get out of her any way it could. Juele held her ears and her nose and crossed her legs to head it off each time. It finally retired back to her middle to sulk. Juele crawled up the last flight of stairs and prepared to creep into her room, until she saw a sliver of light under the door.

"Mayrona?" she asked, in a very low voice.

"I'm awake," Mayrona said. Juele stood up. She had to duck her head to miss the lintel as she tottered into the small chamber. The older girl was sitting up in bed with a book on her knees. A faint, orange-yellow glow hung over her head. She closed the book and reached down to slide it under the bed. There was no space for bedside tables in the room.

"It's very late."

"I'm sorry," Juele said, folding her long legs onto her cot. "Bella and Daline took me to the Salon. Everyone was having the deepest conversations. Do you ever go there?"

"Why, yes, now and again, when I need my consciousness stretched," Mayrona said, with a little smile. "It's not always a pleasant or a comfortable place."

"But it's intense," Juele said, passionately. She kicked her shoes off and felt in her footlocker for her nightclothes. "I've never been anywhere like it. There was one man doing something really interesting with time and space. I didn't understand exactly what he was doing, but it was different from anything I've ever seen. I mean," Juele said, self-deprecatingly, "I haven't seen that much, but I feel like I was in another world. May?"

"Yes?"

"Is it bad to create representational illusions?"

"No, not at all. Most illusion is representational. Why?"

Juele ducked her head to undo her shoes, avoiding Mayrona's curious eyes. "Well, I made an image that looked like something I saw earlier, and the others sneered at it."

"Who did?"

Juele looked up, and Mayrona smiled at her.

"Well, Bella and Daline and a boy they called Cal."

"Bella Luna isn't bad, really. And Daline Catnap is just jealous of other people's talent. Cal's Cal. Pay no attention."

"Oh, no! They're really good. I saw their work in class."

"Take my word for it," Mayrona said, settling her pillow down flat. "They don't like it when other people shine brighter than they do. If yours was good, they'd rather fill their mouths with cement than say so."

"And they called them Them," Juele said, thoughtfully, pulling on her nightdress and climbing into bed. She wondered if Rutaro's interest in her was genuine, or if he would be like the clique, and wondered how to put her question into words to ask Mayrona. "What's so special about Them? I can see that everyone respects Them, but why? You know, he was really nice to me, but he ignored everyone else." She reached for the reading light over her bed. It was a candle, so she had to snuff out the wick with two fingers. She snuggled down under the comforter and pulled it up to her chin. "I think he made the fountain wrong on purpose."

"Well, that's very interesting," Mayrona said quickly. Juele looked at her, wondering if she was being sarcastic. "I've got an early class. Good night." She extinguished her own nightlight, grasped the edge of her coverlet, and turned over. The quilt encased her like a cocoon. Juele looked at the featureless expanse of cloth in dismay. Even the teddy bear had turned its back on her. So much for her hopes of late night chats and sharing of confidences. The School was proving to be nothing at all the way she had thought it would be. Everything pointed to one long Frustration Dream. Feeling suddenly cold, she pulled her own blanket closer.

"Good night, then," she said to the moonlit lump.

✧   ✧   ✧

Roan Faireven shifted from foot to foot as Micah, Historian Prime, droned toward a conclusion. His declamation had begun approximately two shifts of influence ago, while the sun was still above the horizon, and the small, old man was now well wound up in the endless and knotted threads of his narrative. Roan's father, Thomasen, a senior Historian, deliberately grew a long beard and mustache to hide the monumental yawn he could no longer suppress. Roan's friend Bergold, another Historian of importance, carefully slid his mouth around to the back of his head so it could gape without offending the king. The shorter man glanced up at Roan with a playful gleam in his eyes. They looked odd in a face without a mouth. Roan wished he was capable of changing himself. He simply had to stifle his boredom and try to force his own yawn out his ears instead of letting it escape between his lips. Not that Micah would have noticed if the ground itself had opened up a chasm at his feet.

"You would find it fascinating, Your Majesty," Micah said, his voice rising and falling at last in the inflection of someone who was about to stop speaking at last. "Dare I say—" he stretched a finger and thumb to the sky to pluck down inspiration "—you might find it *enjoyable*."

Silence fell in the audience room. A few sighs of relief stirred the air. Surreptitiously, several of the ministers present brushed away the remains of scattered thoughts that had fallen onto their chests or around their feet while they'd been listening. Roan swallowed his yawn, and his eyes watered. Beyond Micah, in the smallest of the three thrones on the low dais at the head of the chamber, the Princess Leonora undid the swag of opaque blue silk hanging across the lower half of her face and sent him a sweet smile. Her eyes, currently the same blue as the silk, twinkled at him. Roan returned the smile warmly, loving her with all his heart. Leonora did not usually go veiled, but in such intimate quarters, it would have been too obvious if she'd gaped right in the face of one of her father's most trusted ministers. The volume of her costume disguised furtive movement, if Roan dared to suggest even in his own mind that such an august lady might twitch or fidget when trapped in place by the demands of courtesy. Her small feet in their blue silk slippers remained motionless on their pedestal as though made of china.

This was the smallest and most intimate of the king's audience chambers, used for what His Majesty called "informal chats." Here King Byron spent a good deal of his private time. Though everything was made of the finest materials, the decor was modest compared with the opulence of the public rooms of the castle. At present, the walls were painted a soft bluish white and hung with watercolors and the occasional framed memento. Tables, candlesticks, vases, desks, and cabinets were of classic lines without a hint of gold leaf or gem incrustation. Even the thrones were simple carved wood with embroidered cushions. Every piece of furniture or ornament was a personal favorite of the king. Anyone who was summoned here to this innermost sphere was either a close and trusted friend or in very deep trouble. In this case, Roan suspected that His Majesty was kindly saving the rest of the court from what he and those others present had just endured. The king sat with his legs crossed, elbow on armrest, and chin on palm, listening. He was an excellent listener.

"Enjoyment is not the point," snapped Synton, Minister of Continuity. The stout man moderated his tone as he bowed to the king. Three senior Continuitors standing behind him bowed low, too. "Observation of a rare phenomenon is a matter for history, Your Majesty. It's quite serious. Such an event as a Cult Movie Evocation gives us a special insight into the Waking World. We so seldom have a mass coordination of so many sleeping minds all focused upon the same event."

"Though in this case," said Carodil, the Minister of Science, a narrow-faced woman with teak-colored skin, "the event surrounds a fiction! A story! It should not be incorporated into the Akashic Records as if it was fact!"

"But the concurrence of millions of minds on a single subject is the event of importance," Micah said, urgently. "Creative thinkers, many of them. Not of the level or the power of the Sleepers, but, nevertheless, vivid!"

At the mention of the Sleepers, eyes all over the room slewed toward Roan. He was known to resemble one of the Seven Sleepers who dreamed the Dreamland in their Hall underneath the Mystery Mountains beyond the source of the Lullay River. Ever since they had returned, Roan had been unable to shake his traveling companions' belief that he was in some way a manifestation of the First Sleeper, the one who dreamed the province of Celestia. All right, that grand being had looked a lot like Roan, but that didn't mean a direct connection. All the attention was embarrassing.

He was still having difficulty reconciling his new status. A few of the companions who had been with him in pursuit of the scientist Brom and his nefarious Alarm Clock were making the matter worse, ascribing a kind of divinity to him by identifying him as a Sleeper made flesh. Some critics said he'd suborned or brainwashed them. He hadn't. What he and his companions had seen, they'd seen. There *was* a Sleeper who looked like Roan. His companions had meant well, but it hurt his credibility. Roan had heard rumors that he was a god now. Once the stories had gotten out, some hysterical people in Mnemosyne had asked him to perform miracles for them, which of course he could not do. He could never be certain if they believed it seriously, or if they were trying to make a fool of him.

Of those present, only Bergold and the princess had been with him on the perilous journey that had taken him to the Hall where he had seen his avatar. The others believed or disbelieved the tale, depending on their faith in the credibility of their colleagues, and on how much they approved or disapproved of Roan. To many of the Historians and as many of the Continuitors, the unchanging Roan was a freak, an aberration against normality. Ordinary Dreamlanders changed several times a day.

Those who controlled a good deal of influence could alter themselves whenever they chose. Roan commanded a considerable amount of influence, but nothing he did made the slightest difference to his appearance. He didn't mind his immutability. It was rather an advantage in his job as the King's Investigator, since no form of influence could change him. His identity was never in question, making him the perfect messenger for vital communications from the king.

The critics in the royal court who disliked Roan and thought he was a freak were now convinced more than before that he was unnatural. His father Thomasen was tarred with the same brush, or limned with the same holy light as the father of an avatar—or did he have anything to do with Roan's conception at all? (Roan's mother insisted that he had, of course. She had clucked at the idea that Roan was anything but a normal baby, whatever they'd seen in that silly cave.) Most of the Historians and the Continuitors, particularly Synton, treated him more than ever as a peculiar untouchable.

"Your Majesty, I have mentioned it before," said Synton, with the air of one tearing open an old wound. "If . . . this being is the perfect image created by a Sleeper, he should change, and that is that. It is the way of the Dreamland, of which his avatar is one of the Seven Pillars. Why does he not follow his own rules?" Roan opened his mouth to protest, then shut it again. How could he defend himself? Bergold, bless his kindly soul, stepped in at once.

"Stability is a trait we prize in the Sleepers. Roan represents a kind of stability, one we have not previously known. Every Sleeper is different, is that not correct?"

"Well, yes," said Synton reluctantly. "But things that stagnate are symbolically dying."

"He looks healthy," Bergold said cheerfully. "I tell you, I was there. The world did not fall in. Roan defended us, prevented an evil plot from disrupting the Sleepers' dreams of us all and destroying the Dreamland." There were shudders all around. "Drop the subject, eh, friends?"

Bergold suggested kindly. "Roan is not inimical to anything. He is beneficial."

Roan felt uncomfortable being discussed like a laboratory specimen. The hugely magnified eyes of the Continuitors and Historians focused upon him looked like bloodshot basketballs, and there was no escape from them. He fidgeted.

"So much slips through to us from the Waking World, enlarging our understanding," Bergold added quickly, drawing attention away from his friend. "We can discount the events and items that are clearly part of the work of fiction, but who doesn't enjoy a good story, eh? For myself, I'm looking forward to seeing snippets of the movie itself. I hope it's an Action Blockbuster."

"I am fond of those myself," Thomasen said. "In preference to Horror Spectaculars or Epic Romances."

"Well, I shall be going," said Romney, the Royal Geographer. "Chances are that the event will change the landscape around it, and I mean to see how. It's a valuable exercise in minds over matter, if you will forgive the epigram."

"I understand the points made by all of you," King Byron said, sitting back in his easy chair. "It is a matter of importance, and indeed, I might enjoy it, but I shall contemplate it from here in Mnemosyne. I have seen at least one in the past, as I am certain you recall." The ministers nodded. Roan knew they were as familiar with the king's past activities as they were with the celestial phenomena. "I do not need to see it myself. I delegate both of you," he nodded in turn to Micah and Synton, "to make arrangements for others to enjoy it in my name. How about you, my dear?" he asked the queen. "Will you go and observe this phenomenon that has so exercised our experts?"

"Of course not, my love." Queen Harmonia smiled at her husband and bestowed a gracious, if long-suffering, look at the courtiers. She was a beautiful woman. Her daughter did not much resemble her physically since she began to change at her own pace and style, but Leonora had inherited her grace. "Out in the wilderness?"

"Bolster is hardly a wilderness, mother," Princess Leonora said, very patiently. "It's a big town. What if it is an Epic Romance? You do enjoy those. Think how nice it would be to see it firsthand."

Queen Harmonia fluttered her hands delicately, and the rose-colored silk fell back from her slender, pale wrists. "But with all those strange germs? I don't think so, darling. Besides, I am to open the new gallery at the School of Light."

"Hasn't that happened yet?" King Byron asked. "Your artists are everywhere in this castle. One can't set foot out of a door without tripping over one of them, my dear."

"Those artists are the ones working on the commission for the castle environs, my love," the queen said, with a gentle smile. "They're very excited about being asked. They are so eager to please."

"They're a trifle precious, if Your Majesty will forgive me," said Synton. "Don't know they're being dreamed, some of them."

"And, if Your Majesty will permit me to say, they are a little intrusive," Carodil said, leaning forward on her tall walking stick. She usually appeared to be in her forties, but today she was somewhat older, with graying hair and deep lines around her mouth and eyes. "One would almost accuse them of listening at keyholes, eavesdropping on policy and so on."

"If they offer you any good advice," Micah said to her with a snort, "take it!"

"I have great expectations of them," the queen said, imperturbably, ignoring the disagreements between her ministers. "It will take all my time to prepare for the gallery opening. I should hate to be tired out from traveling, when they are expecting so much of me. With regrets, honored friends, I shall not go."

Roan and the others bowed to her decision, though privately Roan thought that a pair of talking, animate scissors that could cut the ribbon and make a few remarks would fulfill all the function the queen would serve at the gala. From his experience, the people at the school were impervious to any celebrity except their own. Royalty was almost redundant. And yet, the staff and students of the school showed Her Majesty infinite courtesy at all times. They were proud of their royal patron, as indeed he himself was, but they felt that they merited the acclaim, whereas Roan never felt entirely worthy of the kind attention lavished upon him by not only the queen, but the king, and especially Princess Leonora, who had agreed to marry him. The last thought made him glow inwardly with happiness. Fortunately for the princess's modesty, he never manifested his emotions bodily. There was some benefit to being a freak among Dreamlanders, who were ever-changing, according to mood, influence, and the will of the seven Sleepers. Roan never changed. His tall, dark, good looks had always been with him. Well, at least he possessed a superior control over influence, no matter what the others whispered behind his back. He had his sanity, and in the Dreamland, that meant something.

"Will you go, then, Your Highness?" Micah asked, turning to the princess.

"I would love to, Historian Prime," Leonora said. "Providing Master Roan will escort me."

She gave Roan a tender smile, and everyone looked at him. He felt his cheeks burn, but he was pleased. A warm, comfortable thrill glowed in the vicinity of his heart. The flowers in the vase on the table near his elbow turned from prosaic chrysanthemums to jasmine and orange blossoms. The air filled with their sweet perfume. No one laughed. Roan was grateful. *He* might not ever change, but his influence was more than sufficient to alter his surroundings, if unconsciously at times. The truth was that he couldn't wait to marry Leonora.

His connection to the Sleepers didn't impress the king as much as his heroic action in stopping the threat to the Dreamland. Roan was proud to be a patriot, but he couldn't have done anything else. Luckily, the king was not angry with Roan for having taken the princess

Leonora on his escapade with him. He hadn't, for one thing: Leonora had followed him at considerable risk to her own safety on behalf of their homeland. True, Roan could have tried to send her home, but she had helped to stop the renegade scientists. Roan did not think he could have accomplished that end without her. She had proved brave and resourceful, and it made him love her more than ever.

They had returned to a heroes' welcome in Mnemosyne. The king deigned at last to grant Roan's dearest wish, to marry the princess. However, His Majesty, a most protective father, didn't specify a date. Leonora continued to ask every day when her father would allow her to set one. Roan did not mind. He *would* marry her one day, and that was all that mattered.

"Your Majesty," Roan said, "I would be honored to escort Her Highness, but if virtually the whole of the court is going to Bolster, who will be here to assist if there is a crisis? Perhaps I should not go."

"If it is known the entire court is in Bolster," the king said, "then people will undoubtedly bring their crises to the ministers there."

"With the utmost regret," Roan said, with a rueful look at the princess, "I should stay and assist you by keeping an eye on things."

Byron gave him a fatherly smile. "Go, young man. It will be all right."

The aged Historian Prime manifested a pair of scissors and clipped himself free of the mass of threads of his original narrative, then kicked them aside. He brushed down his plum-colored robes. "Well, Your Majesties, I wish I could persuade you to change your mind. Everyone else is going. Crowds will be there from all over the Dreamland."

"Good!" King Byron said cheerfully, clapping his big hands together. "If everyone is going, then I shall have a vacation from the endless streams of courtiers and supplicants. I shall enjoy myself here."

The chief continuitor pursed his lips. "I probably

should not go, either," Synton said, importantly. "My function is not to be influenced by new events, but rather to prevent aberrations from normal trends. Although many of my ministry will go—the opportunity is rare, but as His Majesty said, not unprecedented."

"Suit yourself," Micah said, with a look at his colleague that showed what he thought of non-independent thinkers and favor seekers, although Roan thought he was probably relieved. Now the Historian Prime would be the sole ranking minister in charge of the observation, and he would not have to worry about the security of the royal family in the midst of unstructured dreams. They would all remain safely behind here in Mnemosyne, the responsibility of the royal guards, under the command of the worthy Captain Spar. Nor would Micah have to concern himself with his nearest rival looking over his shoulder. Anticipation of such freedom made him expansive. He leaned back and rested his palms on his thin chest. He grew feathers and wattles like a pleased rooster ready to crow with inward delight. "We will bring you back an accurate and most detailed account."

"Hmmph!" Synton grunted, looking like a disgruntled crow. "That will be new." Micah's comb stood up, and the pinfeathers on his neck bushed out.

"Thought you didn't approve of anything new," Thomasen said, playfully, slapping his senior on the back. Micah, now a true bantam cockerel, started to circle his rival. Synton stretched out his ebony-plumed neck, looking for an opening to peck.

"Gentlemen, gentlemen," the king said, with a warm and fatherly smile. "We all serve the Sleepers best in our own way."

The king's blithe statement was meant to soothe the ruffled feathers of his ministers. Instead, it caused every eye, human and avian, to turn Roan's way, making him feel very uncomfortable.

Chapter 5

Breakfast, after the dull misery of her dormitory room, was homey and comforting. Juele waited in line behind half a dozen other sleepy students. She slid a tray along a wooden track, peering over it at the glass hatches to see what she would like to eat. None of the food on offer was terribly inspiring, merely fuel for the day, but it was all familiar. Grain flakes in bowls, eggs cooked any which way, and tea and toast seemed to be the items most common to the few who were there for an early meal, although there was room for variation in the hot food section. Depending upon who was reaching for what, a plate containing an ordinary cooked breakfast of bacon and sausage and fried sliced tomatoes might become chunks of fish in white sauce with chopped onions with rye bread. Or kedgeree, rice porridge, and pickled vegetables. Or cold pizza, its congealed white cheese faintly greasy on the hot plate. Juele made a face and picked up the nearest dish, and was relieved to see the exotic foods on it give way to a fruit-covered waffle and a couple of sausage patties. The food smelled good. She was hungry, and not feeling adventurous. The Salon had been an exhausting experience, but so exciting. She hoped she would be able to go there again soon.

She was on her own. Mayrona had gotten up and gone out to her shadow class before Juele had awakened. Juele regretted not having a chance to ask Mayrona's forgiveness for keeping her up past midnight when she had a dawn class. In future Juele promised herself she wouldn't come in so late, for either of their sakes. She was weary, too. Only the prospect of her trip into town and her new classes put spring in her step.

The great dining room wasn't so overwhelmingly glum in daylight. The windows, set high into the wall above the oil paintings, threw rays on the darkly varnished paneling, picking out a ruddy tinge in the wood, and gave a gleam to the gold frames. The serving ladies, wearing shapeless black uniform dresses under white aprons, all looked like someone's mother. The last one, who handed her her pot of tea, gestured kindly toward the tables.

"Sit where you'd like, dear," she said.

Juele glanced around. At the ten tables, there were only eight people, one to a table, and all strangers. But breakfast, being a casual meal, might be the ideal time to strike up an acquaintance. She smiled tentatively at the first person to meet her eyes, a man in his thirties with a bushy beard and a tweed suit. Hastily, he looked down at his food. *All right*, Juele thought, *not him*. Palpable tension built and mounted as Juele walked through the hall. The people she passed quickly turned their attention to their breakfasts. She felt almost physically repelled away from some of the benches. No one else would meet her eyes. Too shy to intrude deliberately on any of the preoccupied diners, Juele chose one of the two empty tables and put her tray down on it. Once she made her decision, the room seemed to relax again.

The next person who came from the serving line, a plump woman with a long tail of black hair, took the last empty table. The room filled again with tension, like an unpleasant aroma. Juele watched with interest as the following person, a slightly balding man with a long nose, had to sit down at a table already occupied. He maneuvered carefully so he was not directly beside another human being (or otherwise—the girl at the farthest table from the door, under the dais, was eating like a bird, standing on the edge of her plate on tiny clawed feet and pecking away at bacon and toast). Subsequent diners arranged themselves in a kind of table chess, sitting as far from one another as possible until propinquity was absolutely unavoidable. Only after there were more than three people on a bench did anyone begin to speak to anyone else, and only in a gentle murmur quieter than the sound of footsteps on the stone floor. Two more people had joined her table, both intent on their own thoughts and meals. They weren't close enough for easy conversation. She would have to shout, and she didn't feel comfortable breaking the silence.

She started to pick up a piece of toast, and the tray vanished from the table top. Juele looked up, wondering where it had gone. Suddenly, the room shifted position. Juele let out a squawk of surprise. Her tray was in its place before her. The room hadn't moved, but she had. A fourth diner, an older woman with very dark eyes, had joined them, and the three already present at the table had automatically been rearranged to accommodate her. The room itself was moving people, Juele thought indignantly. *Well, what if I'd like to sit with someone?*

The arrangement left her across from a man with a brown beard and heavy eyebrows. She gave him a shy grin. With a look of surprise, he picked his napkin off his lap, wiped his mustache, and tossed the napkin onto his plate. He got up and stalked out. Juele looked after him, shocked. She hadn't meant to offend anyone. Was it forbidden to take any notice of one's fellow breakfasters? She spread her napkin on her lap and began to eat.

"New here, aren't ye?" a thin voice asked in plummy tones. Juele looked at her companions. None of them glanced up from their meals. The voice didn't sound as if it was coming from beside her. Juele cast around for the speaker. She heard a thin whistle overhead. "Up here, child."

Puzzled, Juele looked up, and met the eyes of one of the dark-varnished paintings on the upper walls across from her. "That's right, gel. How d'ye do?" The portrait depicted an elderly gentleman with a round face. His thinning white hair was pulled back into a queue and tied with a ribbon. His prominent blue eyes and apple cheeks bulged with good humor, and the painted grin was amiable. Apart from the meticulous representation of a ruffled jabot at his throat, his costume had been only roughly sketched by the artist. Juele got the impression of a dark, fine fabric suit, but little detail. "Eh? Hard of hearin', are ye?"

"No, not at all," Juele said. "I'm doing fine, thank you. How do you do?"

"Well enough, well enough," said the portrait. "Devil it is that children don't eat decently these days. What's that flat thing there?"

"A waffle," Juele explained. "It's made of flour and eggs and, er, ironed."

"Ironed! Hah! Looks like they didn't get all the lumps out."

"No, sir," Juele said.

"You ought to have meat! Go up and tell those drab-feathered harpies to give you a good slice from a haunch of venison, child!"

"Let the girl dine in peace!" snapped a voice from a darkly varnished canvas. Juele could see little of the face except for the glint of the image's eyes and a line showing the curve of an ample jaw. "Too early in the morning for heavy food *or* talk. Imposing your palaver on her, indeed!"

"Oh, you don't mind a bit of fatherly concern, do ye?" the first painting asked. "All well meant, truly, all well meant."

"I . . . suppose not," Juele said, eating a bite of sausage, wondering whether she'd be better off with the attentions of a friendly bully or a considerate curmudgeon. The first painting let out a triumphant crow, so she swallowed hastily and added, "Sometimes, that is." The second painting emitted an amused snort.

"Might we make your acquaintance, gel, if it's not too much trouble?"

"I'm Juele Caffyne," she said. "I've just arrived at the School."

"Gladiolus Mignonette," said the cheerful face. "First

Chancellor of the School of Light. Proud to meet you."

"Darius Somnolent," said the gloomy face. "Second Warden. A pleasure."

"I'm very happy to know you, gentlemen," Juele said. She glanced up at the clock that hung on the wall above the door. The time was fast approaching nine. She ate the last bite of waffle and put her fork down. "I'm sorry, but I have to go. It was nice to speak with you."

"Never fear, never fear, you'll see us again," said Chancellor Mignonette. "We never go far. Ha ha ha!" Warden Somnolent turned his shaded face away even farther from view with a rumble of disgust.

Juele stood and picked up her tray. Where did one put dirty things, she wondered? She heard a gasp of surprise and saw a sea of faces turned her way. Everyone was looking at her. She heard mutters and whispers of "new, doesn't know." Confused, she sat down. A young man with a defiant expression got up from his place, and keeping his gaze focused on Juele, walked away, leaving his plate and cup behind on the table. Another diner left, abandoning her dishes where they lay. But the dinner ladies walked toward the tables clucking and shaking their heads. Juele thought for a moment. Her natural impulse was to tidy up, but that seemed to go against tradition. Yet the way she had been raised, cleaning up was the considerate and expected thing to do. She sat frozen as her upbringing fought with peer pressure. Well, she must not be forced out of doing what was right.

She rose, hands on the tray, but the stares were so onerous they felt as if they were pressing against her. Juele felt the force of opinion as strong as influence around her limbs. She slid the tray along the surface of the table. The hiss it made was as loud as a waterfall in the silence of the hall. At the last moment, she lost her nerve and walked away without the tray. She couldn't do it. One person, the newest and youngest student at the School, could not force herself to be openly different, not on her very first morning.

On her way out of the hall, she passed the dinner ladies. They looked disappointed, but unsurprised.

The pressure abated once she was outside in the sunshine. She stood for a moment, just breathing, wondering why she felt so guilty about trying to do things the way her mother and father had taught her. Rutaro was right: the School had its own opinions of how things should go, and they didn't coincide with the way things were outside the walls. She didn't like that very much. It was rude to leave messes for other people to clean up. Was she meant to defy convention? There was a lesson in this, but she didn't know just at the moment what it was.

The clock began to chime nine. Juele started, not wanting to be late for her date with Bella and the others. She made for the gatehouse, almost dancing with anticipation.

Last night, the others had caught her off guard with their mode of dress. As Juele was getting ready before breakfast, the shabbiness of her small room gave her an idea. She'd be in full style when she joined the clique. None of her clothes were of the correct chic black, nor did they have the insouciance of anything worn by Bella's set, but she had a dark green blouse and skirt that she had put on under her smock.

Now, with the greatest of concentration, the same she'd devote to a class assignment, Juele constructed a dense overlay illusion of dark black shadows on the skirt and billowing blouse, even touching her lips with the same hue, the way she'd seen Daline made up the night before. She laid a curse of shabbiness on the smock, making the sleeves appear as if they'd been sanded almost bare, and graying the fresh, light pink cloth to the miserable tint of a hundred washings. If she'd dared to do that to her real garments, her mother would skin her alive, no illusion!

Juele stopped before a shaded window to admire her reflection. The effect was all that she could hope for.

The smock was threadbare, like a rag out of the cleaning basket, and the underneaths looked smoky and mysterious. Around the black lipstick, her skin was bleached almost colorless. Brilliant, she thought. She added an illusion of a more sculpted jaw and a slight hollowness around the eye sockets that made her look five years older. Now she would look like one of them.

Feeling a little naughty and not at all like herself, Juele sauntered toward the gate, past artists catching the early morning light on their easels and small knots of people in smocks chatting. She patted a few of the hundreds of bicycles milling here and there throughout the campus. Never in all her life had she seen so many. There were bicycles leaning against walls, hitched to posts and stands, espaliered against walls, halfway up staircases and trees, and simply wandering freely. Nobody seemed to own any particular steed; if one needed a ride, one reached for the nearest set of wheels, and off they'd go!

She didn't see the clique right away, until she was almost at the door of the quadrangle—and if Daline hadn't tossed her head in that very characteristic way, she would not have recognized them. Bella, blond today, wafted her hands expressively, describing a minor illusion on the air. They were clustered on the path not far from the entrance to the school grounds at the far end of the playing field, chattering in loud voices. None of them were wearing black! Not one! The girls were all clad in very smart dresses of muted earth tones, and their smocks, worn unbuttoned over these outfits, had a soft luster as if they'd been woven from cashmere or camel's hair. The boys had their hair slicked back. Their shirts and robes were dyed in rich colors, but their trousers were the same neutral color as the girls' smocks.

Juele slid to a slow walk, hoping they hadn't seen her. But of course, they had. As one, the whole group turned toward her and began to laugh. There was no escape from their scorn. Laughter bubbled up out of the pavement, echoed out of the nooks and crannies, of the vaulted ceiling of the gatehouse, came down from the very skies. Other people on the grounds turned to look at what was so funny. Juele's face burned with shame. She felt like ducking behind the wall to hide, but forced herself to keep walking forward. As she passed under the cool shadow of the gatehouse, she started to undo her work. If she was quick, she could don a mass illusion to make the dark clothes look like velour so the black would seem deliberately chic. A glance down told her that she'd failed. She didn't have the knack to give the outfit that tailored fit without the help of a mirror. She was mortified. This was a Humiliation Dream of the lowest level, above only stark nudity. Even then, she wouldn't have had a choice of what she was wearing; this time she'd done it to herself. Tears stung Juele's eyes, and she stumbled to a halt. She should turn back and go to her room. She could study her symbolism textbook until her noon class.

As if sensing her withdrawal, Bella waved and called out to her.

"Oh, darling, we're not laughing *at* you, we're laughing *with* you. Come on." But the girl's tone still had that derisive note in it. Juele started to back away.

"No, I'd better stay here and study," she called to them. "I just came to tell you . . ."

"Come *on*," Bella said, impatiently, stamping her foot. "We're going in a moment. It just won't be the same without you. Come on."

Juele was barely mollified, but she felt the force of invisible hands on her back pushing her forward. Very reluctantly, she crossed the playing field to join the group. It was the longest walk she had ever taken in her life. Bella came up in the last ten feet and clasped her firmly by the upper arm, steering her toward the others.

"Good!" she said. "Juele, meet Soma, Sondra, Erbatu, Colm, Tanner, and you already know Daline and Cal."

"A pleasure," Juele said, smiling hopefully at them. She expected them to snub her the way they had the day before, but to her surprise, they clustered around her.

"Darling, how do you do? How *do* you make your hair do that?" Sondra asked. She ran a hand down the length of Juele's hair, though never quite touching it. Puzzled, Juele put her hand up to her scalp. Unless it had changed since she'd looked in the glass a hundred yards ago, her hair was stick-straight and medium brown.

"Do what?"

"*So* nice to meet you," Erbatu said, grasping Juele's hand in an iron clasp. Her hands were very large, and the nails were perfect ovals. She was dressed in the statutory taupes and tans, which went well with the deep tone of her skin. Her curly hair was combed fiercely back and secured at the nape of her neck with a tortoiseshell comb. She had a bright, multicolored scarf around her neck. Juele peered down at her own hands for reassurance. They looked equal to any task. So was she, she reminded herself. She was here by invitation.

The others introduced themselves, with elaborate gestures and eye-rolling. Juele viewed Colm with fascination. His coloring was entirely without black, like a pastel painting. His hair today was somewhere between blond and red, his eyes a surprisingly pale blue, and the skin of his rounded face and pudgy hands was light with a dusting of freckles. It was only the sharp pupils of his eyes that reminded Juele he wasn't as soft as he looked. None of them were.

Once the introductions were over, the group settled back to the conversations they'd been having before she arrived.

"Darling Daline, your ensemble is so beautiful today, dear," Soma said. She held up a hand as if searching for a word. "So . . . original."

"Oh, Soma, thank you so much," Daline said, the gray of a knife's edge showing in her eyes between her mascaraed lashes. "I must say your look today is . . . classic. Did you find that dress in your grandmother's attic?"

The air between them became dangerous and sharp to the touch. Their very breaths clashed noisily like swords sharpening. Juele decided she'd better keep well back out of the way. The others listening looked amused by the scathing byplay and were not at all concerned. Juele was a little puzzled as to the source of the disagreement between the two girls. To her eye, they were dressed almost exactly alike.

She'd never known anyone at home like the clique. They sent out such mixed signals, she couldn't guess what to expect. Today, instead of being haughty and aloof, they were almost overwhelmingly nice, but Juele felt that the change in manner was only an outward one. They paid one another extravagant compliments, but the kind words were always spoken with a sneer, as if the speaker would rather die than be in the same condition as the person to whom she was speaking. They accepted comments with a casual toss of the head and a quick laugh, appearing to be carefree, no matter what had been said to them. It inhibited Juele, who would have offered them wholehearted friendliness, if only she wasn't afraid of having it thrown back, ever so sweetly, in her face. Juele saw images of knives in the back, stumbling blocks ahead on the pavement, and small, looming clouds that threatened to hang over their heads, but the group seemed to avoid them all.

"Let's go, my dears," Bella said, with a glance at a tiny gold watch on her wrist. "I've got things to do later." She sauntered toward the gate, mincing along in her dainty shoes. The others fell in line behind her. Not wanting to have any more attention paid to her outfit, Juele kept well to the rear of the crowd and sought to remedy the situation.

Nothing in the Dreamland remained the same for long. She ought to have guessed that the clique would change what they considered in vogue. They were creative thinkers, like herself. They wouldn't stay fixed on the same idea forever. The only one of the group wearing dark colors, she felt rather like the missing tooth in an otherwise perfect smile. Quickly, she let go of the overlay of black, letting the green of her costume show through.

The threadbare illusion on her smock was harder to dispel. She'd worked hard on it, and it was fixed in her mind. The smock held on to its ragged appearance despite her efforts. Look new, she pleaded with it. You *are* new. My mother finished sewing you only two days ago.

The group turned out of the gate into a small residential avenue lined with white-painted cottages and young trees. Juele eagerly drank in all that she could see. Within the confines of the school, all the buildings were very grand and had an air of ponderous authority. She rather expected Mnemosyne itself to be similar. It *was* the capital of the Dreamland. But instead she passed by houses and buildings not too different from those in Wandering. What made them seem different was the aura of importance she sensed. Whereas her village was an ordinary place, this was the capital city of the whole world.

The paved sidewalks were full of little children playing, romping about with jump ropes and balls and tricycles. On the front porches, mothers rocked babies and chatted with their neighbors as the men walked out of their front doors, kissed their wives, and donned their hats before walking out of their garden gates. Juele felt a little homesick watching all those happy families. A part of her wished she could be the same as they were. She gathered up a fold of the cloth in her hand and squeezed it, seeking something of home in the cloth. She felt it squeeze her hand back with familiar maternal warmth. Her mother must have left a little influence in the garment for love. Juele smiled, remembering that she should be happy to be where she was. She had the best wishes of all the people at home behind her. In no time she'd get over feeling lonely and out of place. She looked down at herself and realized she'd let her whole illusion slip, age makeup and all. Her pink smock glowed like a petal in the spring sunshine. She undid the two buttons at the top so it swung open like the others' and looked every bit as nice. When she looked up, Soma was staring at her.

"My goodness, how changeable of you," the older girl said.

And then the superior, derisive, snickering laugh. Hurt, Juele started to retort, but she clamped her mouth shut on the angry words. *Everybody* changed in the Dreamland. It was *normal*. Soma watched her with a half smile on her face, waiting. Juele suddenly saw the trap looming, a big, metal, sharp-jawed thing with a cage behind it hovering just above her. Soma was trying to draw her into one of their mannered exchanges. Juele knew that if she fell for the bait, she'd never escape from the endless round of insults. She didn't understand the rules, and she didn't feel capable of improvising a clever retort. Carefully, keeping angry words from fighting their way out over her tongue, she smiled at Soma.

"Thank you," she said, and immediately slowed her walking pace, so the other girl overshot her. Soma, startled that her victim had refused to play the game, sped up further to catch up with Erbatu. The trap itself vanished. Left alone, Juele concentrated on her surroundings.

The group turned out of the avenue onto another tree-lined road filled with pedestrians and slow-moving traffic. Juele looked back to note the name of the street from which they had just come. Just as she caught sight of the sign, lettered in gold on a black slate high up on a ridged gold pole, a horse-drawn carriage rolled into the way, blocking her view. When the carriage drew off, the street looked the same, but the sign was nowhere in sight. There wasn't another on any of the other corners. She realized that she had better pay close attention to the way home and hoped the streets wouldn't rearrange themselves while she was gone. She couldn't be late for her afternoon classes.

"I can't stay out past twelve," Juele said, raising her voice over the traffic so the others could hear her. Only Cal and Bella glanced back at the sound of her voice. "I've got shadow and color today."

"Then you'd better watch the clock, hadn't you, darling?" said Erbatu, fluttering her hand casually as she

walked. The others gave a disinterested sniff or a chuckle.
Juele drew back. She'd have to rely upon herself. These
people would love it if she humiliated herself again, and
they wouldn't do a thing to help. Subtly, over the course
of several blocks, Juele changed the shade of her own
overdress from light pink to a rose taupe so she matched
more closely with the day's fashion. Bella, whom Juele
had already picked out as being the nicest of the crowd,
gave her an approving nod.

Juele caught more than one person staring at them,
and many a couple drew together and murmured something to one another as they watched the group of students go by. A man driving a landau coach past them
looked openly envious. Juele edged closer to the others.

"Why do they keep looking at us like that?" she asked.

"It's the smocks. Everyone knows we're from the
School," Cal said, with a superior sneer at a milkman
driving a wagon filled with cans and cows. The stocky
driver looked as vacant as his bovine passengers. "Peas-
ants. We're as far above them as the Sleepers."

Not from where Juele stood. Some of the curious
onlookers had to be royalty, or at least very wealthy, from
the abundance of gold jewelry and fine clothes they wore.
She pointed this out to Cal, who shook his head. "Mere
things. They have material wealth, but they'd die to have
the talent we possess. They can never get where we are."

A broad, green parkland opened up to one side of the
street, and the students crossed over to walk along it.
Juele admired the handsome elms and beeches, green
with new leaves, and stared in appreciation at the majestic oaks with their strong branches stuck straight out as
if defying gravity. Not far from the walk, there was a lamb
perched on a bench, its white, woolly head bobbing as
if it was dozing. At the sound of their footsteps, it startled
awake. It noticed Juele, blinked, and then baaed loudly.
Suddenly, a lion leaped out from behind a bush and ran
toward them. Juele gasped.

"Look out," she cried, preparing to run for her life.
The others turned. The lion reached the lamb, which

clambered down off its bench. Then the two animals lay down together side by side in a most artistic fashion, with the lion's sandy, tufted tail wound protectively about the lamb's small flanks.

"Oh, how wonderful," Juele breathed. Her hands itched for her art box, wishing she had something with her to record the image.

"Hackneyed," sniffed Daline, giving it no more than a momentary glance. "Trite. Ignore them."

"Ignore them?" Juele asked, dumbfounded.

"Happens all the time," Daline said, rolling her eyes toward the sky. "It's the smock, darling."

An orange tabby cat, on its way along the gravel path that paralleled the sidewalk, leaped to chase a yellow butterfly in the sun. Juele cocked her head at it with interest. The bright colors hovering over the green grass presented another very artistic prospect. The others hurried her on, not letting her stop to look. The cat seemed to shrug. He ceased his leaping about and nonchalantly resumed his walk as if nothing had interrupted him. Across the broad lawn of the park, a shepherd and a goose girl clung to one another, looking deep into one another's eyes. Around their knees peered a representative from each flock.

Juele stopped short. This scene was too wonderful to pass by. She could at least make a sketch of it and put it in her pocket to work on later. Such a romantic couple. And how cute they looked, with the sheep and the goose looking suspiciously at the other around their guardians' legs. Juele couldn't resist another moment. She could just do an outline and fill it in when she got back. She reached out for a strand of sunshine and was pulling it to bits when a shadow cut off her source of light. The filaments of light unraveled and faded.

"We don't have time for that, child," Sondra said, flipping her hand casually, as if she'd just been brushing away a fly. "There are better things to do."

"It won't take a moment," Juele said, wistfully. As if they could hear her, the goose girl tilted her head back just a little to gaze into the eyes of her lover, who smiled a warm, protective smile. Juele's heart ached for them. The others took her by the shoulders and walked her away.

"Pay no attention to them at all," said Bella, turning Juele's head forward with strong fingers as an eagle flew to the top of a flagpole and posed with its wings out. "Such exhibitionism. Everybody wants to be a model. If you make an image of one of them, the others will never let you alone. We'd be here for years!"

More animals came into view, flinging themselves into all manner of picturesque attitudes when they saw the students in smocks. Juele sighed, seeing one artistic opportunity after another fleeting as the others kept her moving along, pulling and pushing her.

Chapter 6

Beyond the park, the city changed from avenues and parkways to busy streets. Juele stared around her in wonder, ignoring the amused expressions of her companions. Pedestrians hurried along the sidewalks, shooting glances out of the corners of their eyes at the students, who sauntered at an easy pace, giving her lots of time to rubberneck. Traffic on the roadways was heavy. The vehicles were mostly animal-drawn or human-powered, like carriages and rickshaws, but they were interspersed with motor cars and singular conveyances of every description. Between two red sports cars with balding men at the wheels stood a black goat with a woman in green on its back. Behind her was a stone vehicle with animal skins for the roof. Its driver's bare feet stuck out below the frame. Three rows ahead Juele saw a man in silk clothes and a felt cap sitting bolt upright on a flying carpet. Behind him on the carpet, a very thin man in a double-breasted suit and eyeglasses was laughing loudly at his own jokes.

At the corners, the vehicles bunched together in impatient files, nose to tail like performing animals in the circus. At predetermined intervals, they zoomed ahead, spreading out along the length of a city block, until they bunched up again at the next corner, where cross traffic hurtled past. Juele soon learned to associate the stop and go with the antics of the signal devices. On the nearest corner, a small girl spun around on her heel. When her back was to the cars, they drove forward as fast as they could. When she faced them, they had to stop. At the next intersection, traffic was controlled by walls that rose out of the pavement and dropped to allow passage. The signals never seemed to change fast enough for the drivers, who honked and shook their fists and made winding signs with their hands. Juele's companions pulled her across an intersection while a red and green whirligig in the center showed a red panel to her side of the street. An alarming screech erupted behind her, and she jumped up on the curb to avoid being run over by a man on a huge, square vehicle that left a streak of smooth ice behind it. She never saw any traffic like this in Wandering. But this was Mnemosyne, and everything was much more intense.

The very buildings gleamed with self-importance. When she had arrived the day before, she had seen very little of Mnemosyne between the train station and the School. She'd been so focused on finding signs of the School, she had had no interest in anything else. Now her eyes and ears were wide open, and she was absorbing as much of Mnemosyne as she possibly could. The guidebook that her grandmother had given her as a going-away present said that a million people lived here. She couldn't conceive of so many people at once, but here they all seemed to be, hurrying places, changing, interacting—a mosaic of busyness.

The others lacked appreciation for the novelty. Probably most of them came from Mnemosyne in the first place. That would account for their sophistication and detachment. The students walked with an air of superiority, which seemed to be borne out in the manner people made way for them wherever they went. It was nice to be deferred to. Juele swaggered along behind her comrades as they walked in the sunlit streets, enjoying the view and the awe of the crowd. She paid just enough attention to their path so she wouldn't get lost going back.

The architecture impressed her hugely. It had changed entirely overnight from the gleaming white city she vaguely recalled seeing out of the train window, to a more bustling town of golden stone. The glass in the windows was cut and beveled to pick up every sun gleam and throw it back in a hundred directions. The stone of the walls and buildings was also cut with an artisan's hand. The multiple styles standing side by side ought to have clashed, but they didn't. Shops with ornate carvings on their walls stood beside offices of classic architecture through whose handsome wooden doors stepped men and women wearing business suits, or togas, or stovepipe trousers and crinoline skirts. It all seemed to fit together into a picture that Juele would have titled "City." Its form was its function.

Between one block and the next, Juele sensed a wave of influence passing over them. The buildings on the street became just slightly more ornate. Bronze ornaments, green with the patina of age, blossomed on the doors. Doorways grew classic-looking porticoes, and the wrought iron gates in between doorsteps twisted into more elegant patterns. The clothes of passersby altered slightly to match as well. So had the garments of the students. The others remained in their guise as fashionable young ladies and gentlemen, though now the boys wore blazers and straw boaters, and the girls were in form-fitting dresses with big shoulders, the smocks open swing coats that fell to the knees. Juele felt a breeze blow past her knees, and looked down. To her horror her clothes had become a pinafore with a white apron over it and shoes with bows. The changes drew chuckles from her companions, and the invisible audience laughed loudly at her. She was embarrassed, and annoyed with the Sleepers. Her clothes were little-girly, were they? She threw on an overlay that looked exactly like Bella's elegant outfit, not caring if it was too old for her, and stalked after her companions.

Now the whole of Mnemosyne seemed determined to show her she was too young. The buildings along the roads rose up in their foundations until the shop doors and windows all seemed to be above her eye level. Stairs were too high. She had to stand on tiptoe to see into the windows. Alabaster statues that flanked and guarded the steps leading to the entrances wore sour expressions like hall monitors. They gave her haughty glances as she

went by them. Juele stared at them, very impressed. If
this was just the shopping area, what must the center
of government be like?

Everything changed slightly as the group went along,
shifting to accommodate the crowds. The sidewalks widened or narrowed, according to the influence exerted
either by the pedestrians or the shops themselves. One
massive store occupied an entire city block. Pillars rose
from the pavement to its grand roof where flags flew in
the breeze. A street with few shops on it changed so that
it looked trendy and the shops were exclusive boutiques,
isolated stores enhancing the glamour, however imagined,
of their emptiness by making it seem as though exclu-
sivity was their purpose. On the side streets, small shops
opened out from the sidewalk, more inviting and friendly.
She felt far more comfortable in the little places oper-
ated by one or two employees. Still, she followed her hosts
through the posh stores, giggling when the others made
comments about the displays or the clothing that "townies"
were wearing, or Sleepers protect them, the tourists. The
students' smocks set them apart in an important way from
the townsfolk, sort of above and separate, as if they were
walking within a great glass bubble that nothing outside
could penetrate. Juele started to enjoy the stares and
admiration. She was, after all, part of the elite. If they
were admiring the clique, they were admiring *her*.

Juele turned her nose up with her companions' at the
sight of a woman, badly dressed and ill-prepared, running along after a smartly turned out man in a suit. She
must have been after him for a job, because he kept
dandling a slip of green paper just out of her reach. Juele
felt sorry for her, as she clearly needed it. Juele was
grateful that such a thing wouldn't happen to her. Illusions were always in demand. She had talent, and she
would learn to use it even better than she already knew
how.

Following close behind in Bella's footsteps, Juele
managed to jump up the marble steps before they grew
taller than her legs could manage. The group sauntered

into a dimly lit boutique. The walls were painted a chic, in-between pinkish-grayish-brownish color that Juele couldn't find a name for. Very little merchandise was on display, a sure sign that this was an exclusive emporium. Juele studied the one dress, two sweaters, two necklaces, and one pair of shoes arrayed on pedestals about the shop as if they were fine art. She rather liked the dress, although the price tag shocked her. Two hundred chickens, for a simple linen frock! The shoes cost even more. Juele was almost afraid to look at the necklaces, even when they stretched and twisted attractively in their display case like a pair of cats in the sun.

"What junk," Daline said under her breath to her friends. The group stopped looking at once, and swept out. Only Juele smiled at the proprietress.

Daline repeated her comment in store after store, haughtily dismissing everything on offer. But Juele saw no junk. To her, it all glittered and glowed. She hoped she'd never forget the moment of awe she felt at seeing so many beautiful and well designed things. She wished she could be as casual as her companions were over the wonders of the capital city. Instead, she felt she was one of the rubes gawking in the shop windows of whom the clique made fun.

The very most exclusive stores had dark glass windows, difficult to see through, making one think there was something to be sought after behind them. One of them had obscured its windows so much that Juele could see herself reflected as if in a mirror. She shaded her eyes, trying to see in. Bella stalked right by it, taking Juele by the arm as she passed.

"Too uninteresting, dear. What are they hiding?"

"Hiding? Oh." Juele hadn't thought of it that way. She and Bella walked off a few paces. As if in desperation that its audience was going away, the window cleared. A single dress was on display, a gaudy orange tea gown with fluff around the hems and wrists. This time, Juele felt as if she could snub the shop herself. What a ridiculous rag!

The others were also experts at debunking the mystery of some very elegant-seeming goods. Tanner in particular was top-notch at spotting the sorts of illusion used to enhance their appearance.

"Do you see that bag hanging on the hook?" he asked Juele, peering out of the corner of his eye toward it. Juele tried to look at it without turning her head.

"Yes," she whispered.

"Looks like leather, eh?"

"Yes."

"Old shoelaces, I assure you. Someone just combined the stuff. Shoelaces'll hold things in, tie 'em up, hold 'em together, like a bag's supposed to do. They got an illusionist to put a fancy overlay on it so you can't tell it was never leather before."

And once he'd explained it, it was easy to see what he was talking about. If something hadn't been handcrafted from pure, new dreamstuff into the very best design, Tanner seemed to know. She began to tell the truth from illusions, where badly done enhancements were made, especially the join between the material used and the overlay. In another scantily furnished boutique, Juele picked up a sweater, and her hand automatically went to the place where the illusion making it look like angora was the weakest.

Bella gave her a knowing nod. "There, you see? It should be in a seconds bin, not costing *real* money."

"Young ladies," said the shop owner, a statuesque woman with pince-nez glasses, drawing herself up furiously until she looked like the eagle on top of the flagpole, "this is a first-class establishment."

"Yes, with economy-class goods," Bella said, in a bored voice calculated to infuriate, and just loud enough that the customers across the shop looked up at the sound. The owner pointed at the door.

"Get out of here at once."

"I am a customer," Bella said, surprised.

"Not here, you are not, you impertinent minx," the woman said. Just for a moment, Bella's elegant outfit slipped a bit, and Juele spotted the broadcloth smock under the cashmere. "How dare you say things like that in my shop! Go away. Now! Before I summon the police."

"We were leaving anyway," Cal said, taking Bella's arm. Bella shook him off and stalked out with her head high.

"Don't come back," the woman's voice hissed as she shut the door behind them. Bella was angry because the woman had used influence to nudge her out physically.

"How dare she insult me like that, her and her tatty goods?" Bella grew toweringly tall with rage, and she looked positively formidable. Her nails grew out into talons, and her brows drew down in the middle and shot off into black points at the outer tips. Batlike wings grew out of her back, right through the smock. Juele was alarmed at her transformation. The others, indignant about their friend's treatment, had grown and changed, too, but not nearly as tall or as furious looking.

A large beetle with red eyes appeared by Juele's ear. Alarmed, she shooed it away. Buzzing loudly, it flew over her head and landed on Erbatu's shoulder. The girl's hand sprang to the place where it had landed, then her eyes turned the same color as the beetle's.

"This place needs renovating," Erbatu said. Her red eyes glowed. "It's ugly. There should be more beauty here." The bug flew from one student to another, biting each one in turn.

"A little something for contrast," said Colm, his light eyes blank expanses of brilliant blue-white light that shaded at once to crimson.

"Yes," Sondra hissed. "We'll improve this pathetically designed city. If they don't appreciate us now, they will in a moment."

"Wait, it was only one person being rude," Juele said, trailing along in alarm.

"A microcosm of the whole mundane city," Cal said, lisping a little around the fangs that grew out of his mouth. "She said it, but they're all thinking it!"

"*That* should go, for a start," said Daline, pointing at a stop sign. "It interrupts the flow of the natural energies here." She held up her hands, forming light, and suddenly, the stop sign was gone, concealed in a illusion of transparency. Cars and carriages, and especially bicycles, suddenly went into confusion at the intersection, as their guidance was removed. Horns blared, horses screamed, and Juele cringed as she heard the sound of metal hitting metal. Two bicycles, front fenders locked together, limped to the curb as their riders began to unfold card cases and exchange documents. Juele was alarmed at so many people trying to get through the same small space at once. But as this was the Dreamland, and the townsfolk adapted very quickly. One man got out of his car and ran into the middle of the street. He held his hands straight out from the shoulders, and everybody stopped dead, including, involuntarily, the students. The man beckoned to one lane of traffic, holding the other at bay with his free hand. His clothes slowly altered to a traffic cop's uniform as he directed first one lane of traffic, then another, safely through the intersection. Pedestrian traffic resumed, too, and streams of people flowed toward the students, broke around them like waves around a rock.

"Form follows function," one of the boys said, automatically. The older girls grimaced at him.

"But why?" Erbatu asked, petulantly. "Form should be attractive, whether or not it suits the specific function. Look at this!"

The nearest lamppost shimmered as she wove an image around it. Juele watched, fascinated. Erbatu was a most advanced student. Though light still came out of it, the lamp became a huge pink bunny rabbit.

"Stop that!" A woman coming out of a store rushed up to confront them. Her round eyes were all but popping out of her pale face in shock. "You evil children! How dare you pervert the Sleepers' will? That's not a proper source of light!"

"So what?" Erbatu asked, insouciantly, examining her pointed fingernails.

"You change that back at once!" the woman insisted.

"No," Daline said. "Tch, tch, how pedestrian you

townies all are." The students behind her folded their arms.

The woman threw up her hands. She looked around, then hurried away. She called back over her shoulder as she went. "You are evil! Perverted!"

But we're not! Juele wanted to say to her. *Nothing's been changed, really. Even the stop sign is still there.* "It's just an illusion," she called after the woman. "It'll wear off soon."

"Pathetic," Tanner sneered. "You have to explain it to them." The others grinned slyly and walked on. Juele followed, feeling troubled. Bella and Daline were walking at the head of the line. Juele ran up to them. Their red eyes regarded her.

"Shouldn't we tell that woman it will be all right?" Juele asked, cocking a thumb back over her shoulder.

"Who?" Bella asked, though clearly she didn't care. "There's no one here."

"That woman. She thinks you used *influence* on that sign!"

"Why should you care what a townie thinks?" Tanner asked, with a sneer. "Or are you . . . just auditing? You're not really a student?"

Juele cringed. "I'm a *student*," she said, very boldly, bracing herself for the attack.

"Well, then?" Tanner said in a very mild voice, raising an eyebrow. "Do you always reveal what's behind an illusion?"

"Um, no," Juele said, after a moment's thought. She felt as if she was getting out of her depth with them again, but Tanner gave her a brilliant smile.

"Of course you wouldn't," he said. "Of course not." Erbatu jostled his arm and winked. Juele relaxed, just a little.

She trotted along with them, hating herself for being so fearful. She cringed every time one of the clique looked at her, wondering if she would have to withstand a fresh assault of their insults and arrogance. They were clever. There was an art in the way they were playing with her. They never hurt her so much that she felt as if she ought to turn back and return to the school on her own. They knew she wanted to belong, and it made her vulnerable to all their teasing. Juele summoned up all her meager resources of influence, not to change her outward appearance, but to thicken her skin against verbal barbs. They're harmless, she told herself. Just words. But she knew it wasn't true. Like influence, words could destroy. To belong, she had to do what they did.

Seeing her resolve waver, the red-eyed beetle landed on her shoulder and buzzed in her ear.

Chapter 7

Once the mischief bug had bitten them, the clique couldn't seem to resist playing practical jokes on innocent passersby. Juele went along with them at first, but she became worried the longer the mood went on.

"Look!" Cal said, pointing to an old lady walking a huge brown and gray dog just ahead of them. The old woman stopped to look into a shop window full of lamps, and the dog sat down next to her feet. Cal grinned, looking feral. "Perfect." He spun together a ball of light between his palms and flicked it over the dog just as he walked past. The others huddled in a shop doorway, looking around the edge to watch. The dog was swallowed up in an envelope of illusion that shrank its image to that of a small ginger cat. The dog, not knowing it was a cat, stretched up a hind leg to scratch its ear.

"She's going to be so surprised," Sondra said, a feline grin on her own face. "Wait, look!"

Ahead of them, a couple of smaller dogs wandered along the pavement. They spotted the cat and galloped toward it, teeth bared and growling.

"Oh, this is better than I thought." Cal clutched his ribs, giggling. Juele stared as the strays attacked the "cat." To their surprise, instead of running or puffing up into a hissing fluffball, it grabbed one of them by the scruff and shook it, tossing it into the gutter. With a look of bewilderment, the stray ran away. The clique howled with laughter. The other dog barked fiercely, circling. The defender tracked it, eyeing its movements. The strange dog leaped, and the two of them clutched each other, rolling up and down the sidewalk, snarling. The "cat" sprang loose, grabbed its opponent, and with a mighty twist of its frail-looking little neck, slung the other dog two storefronts away. The loser scrambled up and fled, yelping. Cal laughed so hard he went boneless like a slug and started to slide down the wall.

The old woman ceased her window shopping and turned a pleasant face toward them. Cal hastily pulled back his illusion and favored her with an innocent smile. She turned to pat her dog, who had resumed his seat behind her as if nothing had happened.

Flushed with this success, the group spotted another dog lying on the pavement beside a post outside a shop across the street. The fluffy terrier had been tied up with a leash by its master or mistress, who must be in the store.

"My turn, my turn," Daline cried, her wings rattling with glee. She whipped up a ball of light between her hands. This one flew out and surrounded the dog, but instead of changing, the dog vanished!

Juele stared at the empty place. What had Daline done? Had she destroyed it? Then she listened. She could hear the dog panting. It was there, but invisible. Not that Juele had never seen people walking invisible dogs, but this was different. The leash lay slack as if it was abandoned. The group clustered together on the pavement, waiting.

Within a few minutes, a man with fluffy hair similar to the terrier's came out of the shop door. He saw the empty leash and started looking about. Soma and Sondra jumped up and down and patted Daline on the arms with glee. Juele giggled at first, but became concerned as the man grew more frantic.

"Shep! Shep! Here, boy!" His face turned into that of a small boy's, and his lip quivered as if he might cry. The leash stood up and whined. Juele's companions were slapping each other on the back and guffawing.

"All right, I saw that," said a booming voice behind them, clapping a hand on the nearest winged shoulder.

"You all put that back like it was. Give the man back his dog." Juele spun on her heel to see a huge, broad man in a blue uniform with shiny buttons down the front. He was big enough to block out the sun. His face was shadowed by a tall, dark helmet.

"A copper," Cal said, alarmed. He bolted off the curb into traffic, which whined and veered to avoid him. Daline and Bella opened their batlike wings and flew upward. The others started away in several directions. Not knowing why she was doing it, Juele found herself running away, too.

She didn't know where she was going. Her feet slapped down on the pavement to the rhythm of her thoughts. *I'm sorry sorry sorry....*

A long, blue streak came from behind, circled around to her left side and arrowed in front of her. Unable to tell what it was, Juele skidded to a halt as it arced back around her right side. She turned on her heel to see. At the very end of the blue streak was a gloved white hand. It was an arm! The arm contracted on Juele, drawing her back the way she had come at a rapid pace until she bumped into the others, who had been herded into a little knot by some unseen power. The long arm of the lawman reeled in like a rope being coiled up until it was the same length as the other, the hand of which was holding a small notebook. The empty hand reached into his breast pocket for a pencil.

"All right, that's enough," the policeman said, as he wrote on a page. "Interfering with private property. Interfering with *public* property. Resisting arrest."

"We're not under arrest, are we?" Colm asked, his pale cheeks bleached alabaster white.

"Not if you put things back the way you found them," the policeman said. "I shall have to report you to the chancellor at your school." He tilted his helmet up so Juele could see his face. His features were large, not unfriendly, but, at the moment, very serious. "Your audacity is going to land you in hard trouble one day."

"Our *audacity*," Bella said, "is how our creativity comes

to be expressed. We're artists, above mundane considerations like the law. Like you."

"Watch your lip, miss," the officer said. "Now, restore things to the way they was."

"Oh, how dreary," Erbatu said, tilting her head back to look at the lawman, who was unmoved by her reaction. "How *pedestrian*." The rest of the clique still attempted to look bored, but Juele felt the strong bond around them and pushed at it. They were powerless to get away.

The policeman noticed her gesture. "You aren't going anywhere until you undo your damage. You illusionists, you like your games, but you can't do much compared with really influential people."

"You don't *know* the power of illusions," Daline snarled at the policeman, flexing her claws. "You have no idea how much more powerful illusion is than reality."

Juele thought Daline was talking just to make herself feel less helpless. Not only had the officer prevented them from getting away, he was able to keep them from doing anything but what he instructed. They were only artists. They could influence people's emotions and thoughts, not their bodies or their surroundings. Art had little practical application in the real world. As real as the Dreamland was, she amended.

Acting as though they were condescending to do the policeman an immense favor, the clique undid all the pranks they had perpetrated. The officer trailed along behind them, keeping track of their actions in his notebook. The man with fluffy hair was overjoyed to see his dog again, and the little animal jumped up into his arms. They became surrounded by a rosy glow. Juele shot a look at her companions to see if any of them was creating it, and decided that it was the man's own Dreamer's idea of bliss and contentment.

"Now, that there light post," the policeman said, checking off the last deed in his notebook. A look of mischief passed among the clique. Tanner pointed up the street.

"Over there!" he cried. At the end of the block, a plume of fire licked up out of the pavement toward the skies. The policeman put his whistle in his mouth and ran toward the blaze, hooting in alarm. The clique laughed as the influence holding them drained away.

"How easy it is to fool the poor idiots in the civil service," Tanner said, shaking his head scornfully. "Come on, before he figures out it's a sham."

"But what about the streetlight?" Juele asked.

"It'll change back to normal by itself in a while," Erbatu said, with an elegant flourish. "It'll be good for the townies to experience our talent in the meantime."

"Are we going home?" Juele asked.

"Certainly not," Bella said, springing to life again. "I haven't finished my shopping yet."

The interruption by the policeman had actually been good for breaking Bella's fit of temper. Her fury had abated. Her wings shrank away, leaving her looking fairly ordinary in her camel-colored smock and smart clothes. They'd passed through another wave of influence somewhere: her hair was black instead of blond, and cut just below the jawline in a smooth line. The other furies slowly resumed their reality as art students, each of them new versions of their former selves. Juele peered sideways into a shop window. The red light had faded entirely from her eyes. She was glad.

Juele lost count of all the twists and turns that Bella took. They emerged into a broad square with a small garden and a fountain in the center. Juele jumped as she looked up. Looming over them were the turrets of the Castle of Dreams. They must be very close to it. The walls were of brilliant white again today, but a different shape. The building was still huge.

"It's so beautiful," Juele said, gazing at the sunlit windows. "Is it true that the castle is always a thousand paces by a thousand?"

"Mere facts," Daline said, impatiently, picking up baskets from a shopfront barrow, then putting them down again. "Shopping is much more interesting than politics." With a look of regret at the gleaming tower, Juele followed the group into a small a small cul-de-sac lined with shops. Most of the store facades were adorned with cutout trim under the eaves and multiple colors of paint, as if they were wearing too much makeup.

"It's . . . quaint, isn't it," Juele said, with what she hoped was the right amount of tolerant amusement.

"*We* like it, dearie," Soma said, the glint of her eyes warning Juele from making any more comments. It was hard to tell what they liked and what they didn't. Let strangers beware of mixing up the two! Juele said nothing more.

"Here it is, darlings," Bella said, slowing to a stop before a wooden door that stood open. Juele peered inside the dim shop. It was very small. She could see small spots of bright color and light and the silhouette of a face that turned toward her. "Wait for me. I won't be a tick."

As soon as she was gone, the others separated into twos and threes to talk, leaving Juele by herself to study the street. If she'd had to pick a word for it, she'd choose "cute." The gingerbread cottage in the heart of the loop was a bakery. Its wicker displays were tilted forward, full of pretty cakes and cookies that tempted the eye. The flower shop next door tried to outdo its rival's appeal with colors so bright they overlapped into the next spectrum. The scents of both shops vied for her attention, shoving one another out of the way under her nose. Juele smelled first flowers, then sweets, then flowers again, until it blended into a fragrant muddle. But it was the shop just opposite her that caught her eye. It gathered all the sunshine in the short block in its bright windows. The glass was cut to reflect the morning light off in a thousand different directions. One bit in a corner particularly attracted her attention. A narrow prism gleamed diamond bright, casting a thin rainbow down off the window and onto the pavement.

Curious, Juele went over to look at it. She picked up

the dainty strand, which relaxed and lengthened in her hands like soft putty so that it maintained contact with the glass and the ground. Such an interesting bit of light. It would be very pretty as the accent in one of her askance reality illusions. She twisted the rainbow around so that the length crossed over itself and pinched the resulting loop loose. It glowed brightly in her palms with a brilliance like nothing she had ever seen before. She started to put it in the pocket of her smock when a huge hand reached down and grabbed her wrist.

"Well, well, well, wot's all this, then?" Juele looked up in horror. A huge policeman in a blue uniform with a tall black helmet stood over her. He had just appeared out of nowhere. Were the police following them now, just because of the incident with the stop sign? He frowned down at Juele, the big black mustache under his nose drooping disapprovingly. "You can't just take something because you sees it sitting about, my girl!"

"But it doesn't belong to anyone," Juele said, alarmed. She gestured at the rainbow, now flowing like a waterfall against the wall of the shop. "It was just here in the window."

"You can't remove something from a shop window," the policeman said, blowing out his mustache to either side like a party favor. "That's stealing! You 'and that over and don't do it again, and all will be well."

"I'm sorry," Juele said, chastened. In trouble twice with the police, and she'd been in the city such a short time! She dropped the gleaming hank of light into his white-gloved palm.

"Run along, then, run along," the policeman said, not unkindly, waving a black club slung from a thong on his wrist. He walked off, whistling.

She slunk back to where the others were waiting. Fortunately, Bella had come out of the store and they were all clustered about her, so nobody had witnessed Juele's humiliation. Juele made her way back into the group to see what they were all exclaiming over. Bella displayed an ornate paper fan.

"Where did you say it was from?" Sondra asked.

"Oneiros," Bella said, flicking the fan open with a quick jerk of her wrist. "Isn't it pretty?" As she moved it, different images emerged on the thin surface.

"Very pretty," Juele said. She watched a donkey cart carry a woman and a boy in plain clothes with big hats to protect them from the sun across a picturesque, sunbaked landscape. "How do they make an illusion like that?"

Bella snapped it shut. "It's not an illusion, child. Illusions are created. This is real. It's a sight someone saw. It's a scenic view, captured on specially treated paper. A record. An archive. They make thousands of these in vacation beauty spots."

"Totally representational," Daline said, with a sly look at her friend. Bella raised an eyebrow and gave her friend a catlike smile.

"But if they captured the view, what's left there?" Juele asked, trying to grasp the idea of a bit of captive reality.

"Not much," said Cal, with a shrug. "That's why the landscape's so bare. The more people who visit a beautiful location and take in the sights, the less that's left. That's why I never tell anyone where I've been. Don't reveal your sources, that's what I say."

"No one would dare poach one of your sources, dearie," Erbatu said, batting her eyelashes at him. "They wouldn't want to." Cal twisted his lip at her.

"But, even bare, it continues to be beautiful," Bella said. "Its function doesn't really change. I require inspiration from reality for my illusions, and I prefer beauty. I like it."

"Oh, we like it too," the others chorused, including Daline, who had only been teasing her friend. A clique was a clique, and they stood together.

"Me, too," Juele agreed, but she spoke too late. Her admiration fell into a pit of silence and hit bottom almost audibly. Cal snickered. No one jumped to her defense or tried to ease her embarrassment. She wasn't yet a part of the group. One day, she thought. If she was more careful, more observant, and had more experience, they'd accept her fully.

"One more stop, darlings," Bella said, putting the fan away in her bag. "I want to see how Davney is getting along." She turned to Juele with a casual air. "You haven't visited the castle, yet, have you. Come along."

Chapter 8

"It's not that impressive," Tanner protested, but his words rang hollow as Bella steered them up a steep road along which ran a stone wall twice the height of a man. Juele touched it as she walked, and felt a tingle of power race along her nerve endings from her fingertips. Of all the important buildings in Mnemosyne, here was the most important. She was nearly out of breath with excitement when they got to the top of the slope, where the featureless wall gave way to pillars with a high arch between them. Spread out like the wings of a book were twin gates of fancifully wrought iron. Guards stood to either side. They were clad in uniforms that made them look extra brave: red tunics buttoned up high under the chin, black trousers with a gold-and-red stripe up the outer seam, and shiny black boots. They clasped silver-tipped lances that rested on the ground at their side. Their metal-and-leather caps were shiny as glass, and they stared straight ahead from under the dark visors, daring all foes to try to pass. Juele felt a thrill as she walked between them to behold the Castle of Dreams.

Juele caught her breath. Before her, the great keep rose many stories into the air. The walls were of stone as white as salt with glittering diamond windows sparkling at intervals. The top edge of the building was cut in heavy square battlements. At each corner were mighty towers broader at the base than the top, as if they had melted slightly under their own weight. Pennants at the peak of each tower house flew proudly in the wind. The castle had an air of having been in the same spot forever, ponderous but not unapproachable. *I will protect you*, the keep said. It was secure and serene in its own strength.

Between her and the keep, however, the castle grounds were lively. The main entrance of the castle, double doors of mahogany twenty feet high, stood wide open. People were coming and going freely through a courtyard busy with carriages and cars. Dozens of small buildings had been built against the inner side of the curtain wall, and in every one Juele saw the tools of a different trade: weavers at their looms, tanners cutting strips of leather, telephone repair men bent over their receivers, a blacksmith hammering red-hot metal, and in one shed hung with mystic-looking draperies a woman in a turban leaning avidly over a glowing crystal ball. Men with wide-brimmed hats, bandannas tied around their necks, and blue jeans walked up and down exercising bicycles, horses, and other steeds. A skittish tricycle broke free of its handler and started racing toward the path, scattering people as it went. A bicycle let out an alarmed squeak and rolled hastily after it. The pair was pursued by a couple of the ostlers, waving ropes.

Juele heard strains of music and peered around her for the source. It would seem the king was fond of all styles. She watched musicians in full tuxedos wheeling odd-shaped instruments in and out of the main entrance, a string quartet sawing away in a knot garden beside a fountain, a harpist on a lawn at the side in front of a pair of French doors, and a T-shirted man with long hair striking the strings of an electric guitar under the curve of a balcony. The harpist, a small blond lady in a long dress, swept her arms back and back, brushing the strings, tossing off arpeggios in handfuls and sending showers of song everywhere. Heaps of discarded notes lay around her, still sweetly singing. Juele was delighted.

"There's so much going on here," she said. "Such . . . such variation."

"Oh, well, you'd expect it, wouldn't you," Erbatu said, raising her eyes to the sky and shaking her head. Though she pretended to be bored like the others, Juele was

thrilled. She stared as intently as any tourist would at
a party of men in felt pillbox hats decorated with long
pheasant feathers, colored hose, and short, gorgeously
embroidered tunics with long furred sleeves that nearly
brushed the ground. The shoes were of red leather, narrow, twice as long as their feet and curled over at the
tips into ram's horns. A few of them had codpieces to
match. She and the others peered out of the corners of
their eyes and giggled.

"Renaissance," Sondra said, tossing an airy gesture
toward them. They were walking with a short, thin man
in a black broad-brimmed hat and long coat with a four-
in-hand tie looped under his bearded chin. "La Belle
Epoque." Behind them was a man in a translucent tunic
with starched pleats. "Seventeenth dynasty."

Pedestals and easels had been set up about the hand-
somely kept grounds with works of art very much in
progress. Most of the places were unoccupied at present.
Juele stared at a sculpture consisting almost entirely of
mannequin arms and wondered what it meant. She was
delighted by a pile of soap bubbles crowning a big ball
of water perched on a marble plinth. Their slight pink
sheen glistened with rainbows in the sun. The blow-wand
and bottle on the grass nearby suggested that the artist
had been called away hastily.

"There he is," Bella said, distracting Juele with a tap
on the arm. Purposefully, Bella led the others down into
a corner of the garden that sloped into the corner of the
curtain wall opposite the front gate. There, beyond a
narrow clock tower, a high brick wall about four meters
wide curved partway around one of the pedestals. A
crowd had gathered on the other side, and were hop-
ping up, trying to see over it. A young man in a mustard-
yellow smock stood behind his easel on the other side,
scooping handfuls of matter from one part of the mass
on his table and slapping them onto other parts. He
stroked his chin with his fingers, then picked up a long,
sharp tool with a fork on the end.

"Davney!" Bella called, when they drew closer. The

young man turned around. He palmed back long, light-brown hair and grinned at them. He had a long, thin chin and very square, white teeth.

"Bella, come and see," he called back, waving the chisel. Bella minced daintily down the slope, careful not to catch the heel of her high-buttoned shoes in the grass. Juele trotted after her, followed by the rest of the group.

"Juele, this is Davney Farfetch," Bella said, holding out her hand to the young man. "Davney, Juele started yesterday. *They've* taken an interest in her."

Davney raised an eyebrow, and Juele caught a glint in his eye. "How do you do?" he said.

Juele started to reply, but Erbatu clutched Davney's arm and turned him toward his work. Juele closed her mouth on her greeting, and kept the protest she felt from coming out. "Darling, it's going marvelously. It was twice as big yesterday."

"I'm beginning to get it distilled down to the essence," Davney said, crossing his arms and tapping his chin with the end of the chisel. "I'd like to get it reduced to a mere concept, but that's not what they want. Or so they keep telling me." Juele studied the mass on the table. It was an untidy, multicolored heap of matter that began to shift shape as she looked at it, but not into any configuration that she recognized.

"It's not illusion," she said.

"No," Davney said, watching her curiously. "No, the customer asked for nebulosity, and the customer is right when the bread is right." He jingled a few coins in the pocket of his smock. "And the bread is very right, indeed. Of course I'd rather be working in illusion, not getting my hands dirty."

"Who is the customer?"

"Why, the Crown," Davney said, raising his eyebrows into his hairline. Juele watched with interest as they settled back in place one at a time. "Public sculpture, for edification of the masses."

Daline looked at Juele as if pitying her for asking a

stupid question. "Don't humor the child, Davney. She should have been paying attention."

"Well, it could be an endowment," Davney said, with a grin and a shrug. "Or I could be a nuisance."

"You *are* a nuisance," Bella said fondly. The artist went back to work as he chatted with them. He gave the matter on his table a slap, and it straightened up, quivering, and assumed a shiny, translucent texture like marble. Juele realized the shape was meant to be a kind of a bird. It had a long neck and a sharp beak. Its tail stood up in a huge fan, and the eyes at the end of the blue-green feathers winked at her. As she watched Davney manipulate the nebulosity, the peacock seemed to shift to catch the best light. It was really very pretty, though she wasn't sure she dared say so, remembering Daline's sneer about representational art.

"Do you like working in the castle?" Juele asked, when Davney paused to contemplate his work.

"I'm pestered half to death with people coming by all day to look at my work. Don't put me in it, they say," Davney said, painting a quick illusion over himself of a double-chinned man in black. "I don't know art, but I know what I like," he sneered, in the guise of a rail-thin woman with a long face. He dropped the illusion and grimaced at his friends with his own face. "*I'll* say they don't know art," he said bitterly, slapping a double handful down on the back of his sculpture, where it spread out into scale-shaped feathers. "Oh, they say they like it, but they *don't* understand. That's why I put the wall there."

"It's an illusion?" Juele asked. The crowd of people was still there. She could hear their voices and occasionally see the top of someone's head as they leaped up and down.

"Of course, child," Soma said, with her superior smirk.

"I had to," Davney said, giving her an apologetic grin. Juele decided she liked him. "I wasn't getting anything done. *They* think the peacock represents a peacock." He looked amused at that. His friendliness was for other art students only. Juele was glad she could be included in his regard. Though she was curious, she didn't intend to ask *what* the peacock represented and look like a fool again in front of the clique, but he was so kind, she felt bold enough to ask the next question that popped into her head.

"*Why* a peacock?"

"Why, it's the perfect symbol of self-deception," Davney said, with a grin. "Even if the peacock looks around, it can never see the truth, only the gaudy illusion. It shows the futility of the physical world, how all appearance is merely a surface illusion, and one has to strive to maintain the illusion, whether of beauty, strength, control . . . or dignity." He beckoned her around to the back of the pedestal and showed her the ridiculous fluffy underfeathers beneath the magnificent tail. "As you can see, I *am* putting all of them in it." Juele laughed.

"Have you had any time to work on your piece for the exhibition?" Sondra asked.

"No, not yet," Davney said, with a shrug. "I'd work on them both at once, but I don't want commercial taint in my own exhibit. I've got the thing roughed out in my room. Nothing to it," he assured them, slapping another handful of nebulosity onto the base of his design. He raked at it deeply with the hand tool and the matter spread out to became peacock toes. "I have plenty of time. I'll just finish it when I'm through with this. Shouldn't be more than another few days on configuration."

"Have a look at this, Dav," Tanner said. He pulled his hand out of his pocket and stretched out a hank of light. It was brilliant with rainbow glints. "Just something I picked up in town. Pretty, isn't it?"

"Very," Davney said, admiringly. Juele looked at it. She recognized the crystalline reflection and bit her lip angrily. That was the bit of light she had been playing with outside the sweet shop. He had stolen that, after the policeman had told her it was wrong to take it. Then, Tanner looked up at her under his lashes while he was talking to Davney. At *her*? Did he want her to say something

nice about his find? No! Juele realized, with dawning
shock. *Tanner* had made the illusion of the policeman
to drive her away. She stepped up to him, her anger
making her tall enough to look him right in the eye.

"You tricked me," she said.

"Who, me?" Tanner asked, dangling the little rainbow
from one hand to another. He didn't like having his prank
exposed, but he was enjoying his audience. Juele was not.
Daline and Cal looked amused and the others seemed
bored. "But you believed it! What are you going to do
about it?" He held out the strands, sharp and beautiful
as when she'd first seen them. That diamond bright light
attracted her, and she nearly reached for it, but didn't,
knowing he'd snatch it away if she put her hand out.
Instead, she closed her hands into fists.

"I'm not going to let you get away with it again, that's
what." Juele felt very bold, and wondered whether she
ought to say more, when Bella came up and touched her
on the shoulder.

"It's just before noon. If you want to get to shadow
on time, foolish child, you'd better run."

Juele looked up at the clock. A quarter to. She turned
to Bella. "Thank you," she said. "Thanks for letting me
come along today. I had a good time, and I learned a
lot."

Bella was startled, but looked pleased. Daline wore
a blank look for a moment, then pursed her lips ironically.

"Gracious, you must be easily amused," she said.

"Well, thank you anyway," Juele said, doggedly. She
walked away, her back pricked for the sound of derisive
laughter behind her. It didn't come, but she kept feeling as if it might. When she was out of sight of the group,
she started running. She was still fifteen and a newcomer.
This wasn't her world yet.

"Heavens above, girl, not so dense! You'll obscure the
detail. Now, mix in some white light."

Juele sat at a bench up to the elbows in yellow illusion. It was as thick as mustard, and she couldn't see

her hands through the mass. She was mixing it with her fingers, trying to feel the difference between this color and any other. She couldn't. It felt like light, insubstantial and faintly warm.

Unlike Mr. Lightlow, Mr. Cachet tried to impress his information upon them by pure volume. If a student didn't understand him, he increased the size of his voice until she did. His barrel chest was good for resonance, and he made full use of it. The very rafters shook when he shouted.

Trying not to lose the brilliance of the color, Juele shook it off her right hand and reached into the bar of blinding white light shining down on the far edge of the table for a handful. The moment she drew it into the yellow mass it lightened, but the tone changed. With a groan of impatience, Juele concentrated on changing it back again. Mr. Cachet boomed an order at some-one nearby, and she jumped, scattering light everywhere. She gathered it back up and kept mixing. The white light thinned down the mixture enough that her hands appeared in the midst, the plump fingers she had at this moment stirring and flipping the insubstantial color as though they were not quite attached to her, but not enough to make the hue completely translucent. There, she thought, pleased. Yellow!

"Very good!" Mr. Cachet shouted close to her ear. "All right, you can put that away! Stand up! We're going to work on ensemble coloration. Did everyone bring the pastels we made last week?"

Gretred, who was also in this class, nodded and held up a neatly bundled mass of pink. Juele worried that she would be held responsible for not having pastels, since she hadn't been at the previous class session, but quite a few of the eight students looked guilty and shook their heads. With a growl, Mr. Cachet threw open the big cabinet at the front of the studio and started tossing hanks of color at each of them. Juele put up her hands and caught a cluster of blue that ranged from sky blue to deepest midnight. She felt a tingle in her palms as she handled it and realized that blue *felt* slightly different than yellow. She digested this information with pleasure as Mr. Cachet ordered them to stand in a circle.

"The benefit of ensemble work is not only to show how your vision works in connection with other artists, but to strengthen the parts of your own work that are unique to you," he said. "You learn to complement one another."

"But . . ." began a young man with a goatee who was standing near Juele.

"But, what?" Cachet asked, rounding on him.

"We can't combine illusions, can we? It's like influence," the young man stammered. "You can only use your own." Juele nodded. That's what she had always believed.

"Of course you bloody can! This isn't combination, but collaboration," Cachet boomed. "Know the difference! Were you asleep last week, Sangweiler?"

"I . . . I think so," the young man admitted, sheepishly.

"Hmph. I hope that you gleaned as much from your dreams as the rest of your classmates did from *my lecture*. Do I make myself clear, eh?" He peered around at all of them. "Right. I'll set the design."

With one hand, he began to draw on the air. He made great sweeping motions, leaving behind black outlines of a house, with a rolling field and a pond in the foreground, and a broad sky with fluffy clouds in the background.

"Just a little prosaic, eh?" Cachet chortled, to the groans of his students. "You can play with nonrepresentational art when you can respectably produce representational. You need to know how to draw a plain image. Do you understand why?" Juele nodded hastily along with the others, but he pointed at her. "All right, Juele! Tell us why!"

"Uh," she said. She knew so well instinctively, but could she put it into words? "So someone looking at art knows what they're getting feelings about?"

"A little incoherent, but fundamentally correct! It's the *bones* of the illusion—the bones! If you don't know what's at the basis of your images, if you can't inform your fancies with your knowledge of the plain, how the night-mare do you expect anyone else to comprehend a higher chord? Eh? You need a grounding in the classics. So, give your best efforts to this very ordinary image, if you please."

Awkwardly at first, but gradually with more gusto, the students drew out sheets of color and placed them where Mr. Cachet directed. The boy with green began by out-lining the foundations of the house and barn and circling the pond in bright emerald. At the teacher's order, he left a thin wash across the pond's basin and a trace in the ivy around the farmhouse door. Next, the girl with black thinned it to pale gray, with which she painted the barn and silo, and swept a light haze in the lower sky. The effect was quite interesting. Juele could see gaps between the gray and green where not enough light had been used to fill in. Gretred stepped forward to paint the house in pink. She dotted the grass with flowers. Juele was next. She spread blue across the sky, filling in as best she could over the buildings, but not over-running the outlines of clouds waiting for Sangweiler, the student with the goatee, who held the white light.

"Now, the pond," Cachet said, pointing. "I want to see some good layering here. Gives luminescence."

It was meant to reflect the sky. Juele filled in the irregular outline very carefully, even drawing her finger through to show where the edge of the cloud would be. Maybe the student with gray could limn the shape and make it look more real.

"No, more blue!" Cachet shouted. "That's *light* blue, girl. I want darker."

Juele's hands shook as she tried to change the shade. As the blue deepened, the area it covered seemed to contract. She had to stretch out the edges to fit again, and it lapped over onto the green of the grass. She was nervous, having the teacher shouting at her while she was trying to concentrate. Making clowns, unicorns, and balloons for toddlers' birthday parties was easy compared with this!

"No, darker! Darker! Good night, girl, you'll never amount to anything if you can't follow a simple instruction like that. What a pathetic effort. I'm sorry to be in the same room with it. Are you sure you ought to be here, and not at some provincial center of learning for the colorblind?"

Shamed, Juele spread out a fresh sheaf of blue. She was so embarrassed that it was an effort to raise the color to its place. It was a dark blue this time, dark, dismal, sad, sorry blue to suit her state of mind.

"Not so dark, girl," Mr. Cachet said in a much gentler voice, thoughtfully studying it as she tacked it into place. Juele hastened to lighten the pond slightly. "That's more like it. Now, do you see what you're capable of doing? You can imbue even the most ordinary thing with your emotions. Even if it took shock treatment. Good job."

Juele brightened at his praise, and the pond glowed with her mood.

"No!" he shouted. "Think of what you're doing! Separate your work from your personality. Project less of yourself into your art." Juele corrected the image, to Mr. Cachet's approving nod. She stepped back, thankful to be finished, as Sangweiler stepped forward with his hands full of white light.

"But, isn't art a personal expression?" Gretred asked, as they watched the student install highlights and clouds.

"Yes, but you can explore many ways of being. Any Dreamlander changes, but through illusion you can appear to change without actually doing so, or appear in ways different from the manner in which you have really changed. There's your art, and your personal expression to boot. Next time," he shouted, as a siren sounded the end of class and Juele gathered up her box, "I want you to bring in two-toned light. And I don't want to see a roomful of sky-blue-pink, do you hear me?"

Chapter 9

"Hurry, Juele," Daline said. "Turn at the next passage." Her cheeks, fashionably plump as befitted a girl of a century past, were flushed with excitement as she pulled Juele through the twists and turns of the buildings around the oldest quadrangle in the School. The other girls patted their thick rolls of hair back into place on top of their heads. Juele felt her own hair being bounced out of place as she was pulled along, and her shins being bound in the long, tight skirt of her dress, as she dodged to avoid the ubiquitous bicycles, but she was very happy.

Shadow class had been fun. Most of it was concepts she'd already learned or explored on her own, and she could work on refinements of her technique. Color class had been a real eye-opener. Her dorm room, when she went up to change for dinner, had captured a little of the day's light and was less dingy than the day before. And in the hall, over the meal, the clique had actually addressed a comment or two in her direction. Not at her, for a change, but to her. True, they were inviting her to make remarks about people they chose to smear, but they were *including* her.

Juele had listened, happy to be even marginally a part of the group. She couldn't quite bring herself to say anything insulting, but membership in the clique was fluid. Some people, like the nice Gretred, would never be members, but others were In or Out, depending upon the whim of the group. Juele was marginally In, and she wanted to stay there. Each time a reply was expected of her, she had aped an innocuous comment, facial expressions and all, that she had heard Sondra say that morning. "Well, you would *expect* that of her, *wouldn't* you?" she said. They seemed to be more than satisfied with it. The truth was that they were excited about Rutaro's invitation and had all but forgotten she was attached to it.

"I wish Mayrona was coming with us," Juele said, as they hustled her along, but their ears appeared to vanish, avoiding her words. The clique just wouldn't hear of associating with someone outside their number. At dinner after the soup course May had come over to their table to say hello. Juele was glad to see her, but the others hadn't seemed to notice that she existed. Only the flicker of Bella's eye assured Juele that May was neither illusionary or invisible. She was just Not There to the group. She was Out. Mayrona appeared to expect nothing better. She had turned away with a friendly smile for Juele. When the meal had come to an end, Juele had also spotted Gretred by her stooping posture, and started over to say hello, but Bella and the others pulled Juele along like a caboose toward the door. She waved helplessly at her friend over the tossing waves of humanity behind her. Her feet had hardly touched the floor as she was carried out of the dining hall and into the twilight. Momentous things were happening, and she was happy to be a part of them. She could bring her other friends into them later.

"Just through here," Bella said, with a firm hold on Juele's other arm, drawing her into a very narrow covered lane lined with bicycles. "There, dear. Isn't it ideal?"

The lane opened up into a square garden. At its center was a tall, round, white tower as lovely as any in the Castle of Dreams itself. Its walls were smooth, with a silken sheen in the blue evening light that made the tower glow like the moon. Juele wondered if it was really made of ivory. Not likely, she decided. Most probably it was made of metaphor, like everything else here. Around it were beds of finely crushed stone with perfect flowers growing in them, ivy climbing up the walls in a dark green curtain. At the top was a single window, lighted from within. She could see movement behind the yellow square, but was unable to tell what or who it was. She knew that she wanted with all her heart to see what was up there. Looking up at it Juele felt conscious of the momentousness of the occasion.

Plenty of people felt the lure of the unattainable Ivory Tower. Attracted by the purity of its shape, students and dons alike coming from the small passage or out of the buildings in the square attempted to go inside. They started for the three steps, started to put their hands on the wrought bronze handrails, and were repulsed by an invisible force. They were not even aware that they had failed to go in as they turned away. Some of them walked as though they were climbing invisible stairs.

Juele approached toward the steps and put out a hand for the banister, expecting all the while to be thrust back, but the moment she touched the smooth bronze, she felt that it was all right to continue. The sensation was not quite welcoming, but far better than merely tolerating her. Juele glanced back at her companions for comfort. Bella, Daline, and Cal, who had stayed very near, crowded up behind her, following quickly in her footsteps to avoid being shut out by whatever force prevented entry to everyone else. They were afraid of being excluded, an unusual demonstration of vulnerability for them.

There were no rooms on the ground floor. The entry contained only an ascending spiral staircase that hugged the cylindrical wall on one side, but had no visible means of support on the outer edge. Juele mounted the steps, feeling uneasy. The steps were not unlike the flights in the Garrets, but were in perfect repair. The walls were freshly painted, and an almost new-smelling strip of Oriental carpet going up the risers was deep and soft under her feet. She didn't know why she should be so nervous; she was here by invitation. Her companions looked just as uncomfortable as she felt. They couldn't be as bored as they liked here. It was a far more exclusive venue than they were used to.

They climbed up and up until Juele could not guess how many stories they had passed. It felt longer than the sixteen flights to her dormitory, yet she never passed another doorway. Suddenly, she was at the top. Through the open door, she heard the sounds of soft music and low conversation, and felt a welcoming warmth. She stepped into a cosy room full of people chatting in small groups. The chamber seemed small, but so many people were gathered here that she had to revise her estimate of its size. The moment she passed over the threshold, her clothes changed. Juele was glad that her one dinner dress was of a classic cut, because it was able to be transformed by the prevailing mood in the room into yet another classic design. The hem surged upward, revealing her knees. The long sleeves vanished entirely, leaving wide shoulder straps framing a modest scooped neckline, and the cloth turned from peach silk to black georgette. The style was mature for her, but no one seemed to disapprove. She looked quickly down at her feet, which were now shod in low, black silk pumps. Whatever caused the influence did not intend for her to totter along on spike heels. Juele was thankful.

As to who or what had caused the alteration, she did not know. It felt a bit like a wave of Sleeper-induced influence; not quite as powerful, but every erg as focused. Juele would have liked to take a moment to identify the difference, but that seemed less important now than taking in her surroundings.

The room had a smoky atmosphere like the coffeehouse, although she saw no apparent source of smoke. The fume seemed to be deliberate obscurement, not a physical manifestation. Around her were faces that she had seen throughout the campus, including, in the corner, one of the sheep. A lamppost was involved in an intimate conversation with two people who kept looking furtively about them. Juele felt very nervous. All the people kept glancing toward the middle of the room, so as not to miss anything that was happening there. When something struck them as funny they threw their heads back in ripples of mannered laughter, but always checked to make sure their merriment was approved by whoever or whatever lay unseen on their other side.

Juele smiled at a couple of young men in dowdy smocks worn open over jeans and stained T-shirts. The least well-dressed and most ordinary-looking people stood nearest the walls. They stopped talking to stare, and moved to make way for her. Beyond them was a man and woman in huge-shouldered clothing of deep brown and maroon. The woman was made up with slashes of dark color on her eyes, mouth, and cheekbones. It was very deliberately shocking, but not so wild as the girl in the short, tassel-covered dress who blinked at Juele through false eyelashes as long as her hand. She broke into a vibrating dance that made all the fringe blur. Juele blinked back at the young woman, gave her a polite smile, and kept going. The costuming, for costumes they were, and the general appearance of the visitors became more flamboyant and less modern the farther into the crowd she went. Juele felt her own clothes changing in response to the general mode of each layer. She still couldn't see what was in the center of the room. She moved forward through the spheres, conscious that people were looking at her. Somewhere in the third or fourth ring, she lost track of Bella and her companions. They had blended into the crowd, which parted so she could come forward toward the light in the center.

It was Them. All seven of the people in white smocks who had been at the Chancellor's table at dinner sat in comfortable chairs in a circle before the hearth. The logs burning in the fireplace produced bright yellow firelight without a single smut of soot. An elegantly curved, wooden dresser covered with a lace cloth stood against the side of the round chimney that rose up to the ceiling. On it was a china tea service and several bottles. Hanging in the exact center of the room was a bright crystal lamp with seven branches, shedding beams of light on the individuals in the circle.

Juele looked at them curiously, pleased to be able to

get a close look at Rutaro's friends at last. They seemed ordinary people, perhaps more perfectly groomed and polished than most people at the School, but the perfection wasn't an outward veneer. It came from within, as if all the world was arranged for their pleasure. The seven were dressed in fashions of an antiquated cut, though quite as ancient as the clothes Rutaro had been wearing when he'd escorted her from the gate.

At their elbows stood small tables for the stemmed glasses or coffee cups they held. One of the young men had a long, thin clay pipe between his long, thin fingers. The teenaged boy brandished a sketch pad and a pencil, and as he tossed off a quick drawing, the image would hop from the page to hover in the air, adding to the fume, as did some of the obscure ideas issuing from their mouths. All of Them were intent on their conversation, as if no one else was in the room. Juele started forward, then hesitated when she felt an invisible barrier. The movement attracted the seven's attention. All of Them looked at her. She took a pace backward.

Rutaro leaped up and came toward her with his arms outstretched, and the barrier melted away. His hair was still curly, although his skin was fair with ruddy lips and cheeks. He looked like a mature cherub, except that his eyes were deep with ancient wisdom. "Ah!" he exclaimed, taking both her hands. His fingers felt cool and very strong. "You're here."

"I wasn't sure if I . . ." Juele began, glancing over her shoulder for her companions. The crowd had closed around them, blocking Bella and the others out.

"And who among us is at first, eh?" Rutaro said, drawing her farther into the circle. He looked her up and down with approval. Juele's clothes had altered when she'd entered the innermost circle to a cool, ankle-length dress of violet lawn with sprigs of lace down the front and on the tight-fitting sleeves. She felt a little smug, as if she had done something very clever by having only one good dress. "Welcome to our little fortress of Idealism. Everyone, this is Juele. Juele, you have already

met Mara." The truculent woman gave her a curt nod.
"Helena." The elegant woman who'd had red hair at
dinner had equally glorious upswept blond hair now. A
large dog sat at her feet. She stroked its head as she
smiled at Juele. "Von"—the young man with the pipe.
"Callia and Soteran"—the small-boned woman and the
teenaged boy, whose face seemed centuries old or newborn, depending upon the angle one looked at him. "And
this," Rutaro said as if giving her a special present, "is
Peppardine."

A pair of wide, dreamy eyes met hers. They were a
deep blue like a cloudless sky, with thick, long lashes that
would have been a fantastic dream for almost any woman.
Peppardine's mouth was wide, too, and it curled up at
the corners into a charming smile that creased his thin
face pleasantly at the corners of his thin nose. He chose
to let his wavy, light brown hair fall over his collar and
hide all but the lobes of his ears. Peppardine rose to his
feet and took her hand in both of his. He was very tall.
Juele felt a tingle race through her at the touch of his
long fingers, felt herself drawn deeply into his eyes. Her
lips parted involuntarily.

"I am very pleased to meet you," Peppardine said,
nodding his head gravely. "Rutaro has been full of enthusiasm about you."

"Mmph!" snorted Mara, who turned her head to stare
at the fire, breaking the spell of Peppardine's voice. Juele
flinched, hoping she didn't object to her being there.
Mara always seemed so angry. Juele's eyes flicked back
to Peppardine, who gave her a sweet, slightly sad smile.
He was very attractive, and it wasn't just his looks. Juele
felt something warm to melting point inside her. He was
special. No wonder Rutaro referred to him with such
respect.

A cold, hard arc was pressed into her hand. Her fingers automatically closed around it and identified it as
a glass.

"Please," Von said, waving the pipe in the direction
of an empty armchair with tapestry cushions. Juele was

certain it hadn't been there a moment ago. "Make yourself comfortable."

Juele sat down in the chair and found herself teetering on the very edge of the seat. It had moved! She stood up and started to lower her bottom to the cushion again, but it shifted as soon as she was close to it. The others had gone on with their conversation. Only Rutaro and Peppardine were watching her. She felt her face grow hot. This was a test of some kind. Scrutiny made her movements seem more awkward. With her free hand, she clutched the chairback and tried to maneuver it under her. It bucked like a colt, shying away from her. Any moment now it would dump her on the floor, and that derisive laughter that had been haunting her since she had come to the school would flood the room, disgracing her in front of her mentor and his friends. She didn't want to appear a fool. Hardly anyone appeared to be accepted by the Idealists. Only a few of the people in the room stood within the invisible circle that surrounded Them, and no one else was sitting down. If she lost this chance, she might never get another one. The others ignored her discomfiture, carrying on with their conversation.

"No, Von, dear, you're wrong," Callia said, shaking her head. Her very long red hair flicked to and fro at the ends. "The truth of illusion is in its accuracy. It must portray ideally what it represents. If not, then you aren't making illusions; you're cartooning."

"But your symbols and ornaments don't appear with these images naturally," Von said, drawing an image in the air that Juele didn't dare take the time to look at. "When will you see someone in a supermarket holding a lit candelabrum?"

"That's composition, not invention," Soteran said.

"This is the Dreamland," Helena pointed out, with a warm laugh in her rippling voice. The large dog at her feet became a huge purple-gray slug, but she continued to pet it. "Don't say such things can't exist together."

"But are they *right* together? Are they beautiful?"

Rutaro asked, passionately, flinging out his arms. "The trouble with naturally occurring dreams is that they seem so thrown together."

"Do you question the minds of the Waking World?" Peppardine asked in his gentle voice.

"Not at all! I blame the structure of the Dreamland for not making better order out of the marvelous images it is given!"

"I prefer the felicity of natural composition," Peppardine said. Rutaro turned red with indignation and blew up to several times his own size. "Now, don't do that, my friend. Compare for yourself. Here is a scene of the utmost natural character." The image of a grassy sward filled half the floor between their chairs. On it was the miniature figure of a maiden walking. She was dressed in white with a picture hat on her long red hair. Her flowing yellow dress was blown against her back and right leg, outlining her right hip. Overhead were the familiar images of the sun, a cheery bronze countenance wreathed with a corona of flame, and the wind, a lead-colored face with its cheeks puffed out and mouth open. A pair of birds flew overhead. "Here is a properly artistic and managed scene." It looked almost precisely the same, but the girl's skirt was now blowing straight in front of her in the direction she was walking. The faintest air of flute music twittered in the background. The birds were now seen to be bluebirds, flying ahead of the girl in the same direction she walked. They were shadowed perfectly against the clouds. Rutaro said nothing. In a moment, he deflated and managed a sheepish grin.

"Well, it is more artistic that way."

"That's only because you like redheads," Helena said, with a knowing smile.

"And prefigurative symbolism," Soteran said. "Tedious, but necessary."

"That's *exactly* what I mean," Rutaro said, pointing at the boy. "Direction, that's what's needed in dreams. Too much randomness is confusing."

Listening all the while, Juele tried to force the chair

underneath her. No matter how she tried, she couldn't get the seat all the way underneath her. It would only give her a few inches to perch on, never quite enough to be comfortable. She couldn't continue to fight with it, fearing the onset of derisive laughter, but the longer it took her, the more of the fascinating discussion she missed. She hardly understood a thing they were talking about, but that didn't matter to her.

She saw unmistakable signs of envy among the bystanders that someone so young and so new had been invited to sit down with the great ones. Little did they know what a precarious perch that was, not only physically but intellectually.

Juele would not be beaten by a mere piece of furniture. With all the skill she possessed, she put together an illusion that extended the chair forward, matching color and texture. Her tailbone might be the only thing on the cushion, but it looked as though she was resting on it the full length of her thighs. Rutaro's eyes crinkled at the corners with amusement, and Peppardine gave her an approving nod. Juele glowed inside. She felt as though she had passed.

While the conversation shifted to a lively discussion of the shades of pink that most accurately represented sunset, she sipped the contents of the glass in her hand. The grayish liquid made her gag. It tasted salty and very sour, like olive brine. Although it was free of intoxicants she didn't like it, but she understood that it would not be polite to refuse it. Very reluctantly, she took another sip, suppressing the urge to shudder. Helena glanced at her, and Juele felt the shape in her hand change. She looked down and found that she was holding a piece of paper with A+ on it circled in red. Another glass, a big soda frappe full of foaming pink and blobs of ice cream, appeared on a small table at her elbow. Juele suppressed a squeak as the chair snuggled forward under her bottom, giving her a more secure seat. She'd passed another test. The rule seemed to be that they approved of her if she accepted whatever they gave her, in the same way she that would accept whatever the Sleepers' influence might send. How odd that there were seven artists, too. The fact must be significant.

"What do you think of First Impressionism, Juele?" Von asked, sitting back with his white clay pipe held lightly between his fingers. Bubbles rose airily from its bowl. "Does it deserve to last, or should it be superseded?" Juele paused, as all of the seven turned to look at her.

"I . . . don't know," she stammered, her heart pounding. She'd never heard of it.

"It's a trifle uninteresting as a subject," Peppardine said, gently putting an end to the tension. Juele was grateful to him.

Helena tilted her head. "Juele, Rutaro said you are very good at reproductions."

"Um, that's very kind of him," Juele said, wondering if it was a dig for showing him up at the coffeehouse the night before, but her friend just gave her a languid little smile. He was watching the proceedings, not interfering, but not helping her, either.

"Not at all," Mara said firmly. "He doesn't give compliments lightly."

"Oh." Juele felt her cheeks flush hot.

"Would you just do a little thing for me?" the elegant woman asked. "Any little thing you like."

"I . . . of course. What should I do?"

Von took the pipe stem out of his mouth. "You're in Lightlow's symbolism class, aren't you?" Juele nodded, feeling a moment's panic. They didn't want to see her homework assignment, did they? "Can you make us an image of him?"

"It's just a little thing," Helena said, with a friendly smile over the rim of her cup. "I'd consider it a personal favor. A mere nothing, you understand. Just an minor request. A bagatelle."

"Of course I will," Juele said. She held out her hands and, as always, was comforted by their strong, capable shape. Soteran leaped up and pulled a small table in front of her to use as an easel.

A couple of the Idealists nodded between themselves, and Juele wondered if it was anything significant. Obviously these people were the movers and shakers of the school. To judge even by Rutaro's offhand illusion when he'd been showing her around, and the images the others casually drew in the opaque air of the salon, they were the best of the best. She had fallen in amongst the elite. She wasn't at all sure she could go on belonging to them, but wouldn't it be nice? It would be so nice if she could.

Out of the blob of light, Juele carved the best likeness she could of Mr. Lightlow, the way he'd looked at the harrowing beginning of her first class. She'd never forget that moment. With a thumbnail, she smoothed a strand of light into the bald dome of his head, then carved out the deep eye sockets under the shelflike brow ridges. His hair was a peculiar shade that she struggled with for a moment, until she realized she could borrow the color of Peppardine's hair and add a touch of red. The horsy teeth and jaw looked almost exaggerated though they were no more than the literal truth. Her memory wasn't lying, to judge by the grins on Rutaro's and Soteran's faces. Feeling very daring, she took the last bits of light, and made an image of the canary in its cage, and hung it up by the teacher's head. She folded her hands in her lap, afraid to do any more lest she ruin it.

"Bravo!" Rutaro said, applauding.

"*Very* nice," Helena said, tilting her head, swanlike, for a better look.

"Are you enjoying symbology?" Peppardine asked.

"Oh, yes," Juele exclaimed. "It is a lot of fun, but it is so new."

"Anything worth learning may well be difficult," Helena said, kindly, with a wave of her hand. Juele envied her the effortless grace she possessed. "We've also heard reports of your work in shadow and color, but have you ever worked on sound?"

"A bit," Juele said. "But I'm sure anything I've done is minor compared with you. Er, here at the School."

She looked around to include the bystanders and found they were now obscured by a silent wall of white. Von gave her a charming smile.

"So we won't be interrupted," he said. But it was a temporary exile for the people beyond. The press of influence among the crowd was to make its presence felt, and the seven really did seem to enjoy an audience. Very shortly the veil thinned, making those beyond look as though they were embedded in milky glass. No one outside the innermost circle could approach, but they were there and listening.

The milky whiteness around the inner circle changed, and now the rows of onlookers resembled a huge oil painting swimming out of a deep-colored background.

The room changed in appearance from time to time, growing chandeliers from the ceiling or gas sconces along the walls; carpet, tile or polished wood on the floor. Curio cabinets, plants on pedestals, and a long case clock made brief appearances. Paintings, works of art, and folded greeting cards popped up on the mantelpiece and were gone within instants. An alabaster statue of a man with ungainly hands and a head too large for the body appeared and disappeared in between topics. People, too, came and went. Juele looked at Helena's slug-dog. It was now a handsome man who sat cross-legged beside her on the floor, staring up at her with adoring brown eyes. Helena glanced down at him now and again, with an indulgent smile.

"My protégé, Borus," she told Juele. The others favored her with indulgent snickers. She patted the man on the head. "He's good looking, don't you think?"

"I . . ." Juele stammered, reluctant to say something about a person right in front of her. "Um, artistically, he's very, er, winsome?"

Rutaro chuckled. "Really an apt word for him, Juele." No one looked at the poor man on the floor, who continued to gaze at his patroness. Juele realized that in spite of Helena's purported championship no one took him seriously.

"Oh, dear," Helena said, looking into her coffee cup. "It's empty."

The man leaped up and took it from her and shot to the sideboard to refill it. "He's a dear," Helena told Juele in a low voice. "Such talent, too. I have great hopes for him."

Juele just smiled. She didn't know what to say.

Borus presented the cup to Helena with a deep bow. She took it, and gave him a pat on the arm for thanks. He regarded her with awed gratitude and sank to his knees beside her. She paid no more attention to him than she would have a court jester or a television situation comedy. It figured that he sometimes became a dog.

The seven's conversation ranged widely among artistic subjects and matters of philosophy. Juele sat agog with fascination, hoping she could learn something from them, but they spoke all at once and changed topics frequently. Their ideas buzzed about their heads like flies, zooming outward among their listeners. Juele was eager to absorb as many of the little gems as she could, but a lot of them were beyond her grasp, both intellectually and literally. Her first attempt to capture one was embarrassing. Callia emitted a marvelous notion on proportion. It flew away from the small-boned woman, heading up and to the left. Juele jumped up to follow it, hands at the ready, and almost collided with an avid woman on the periphery who dived in and made an expert grab, then popped the ball of light in her mouth. Juele sat down, frustrated, wondering if she'd ever remember the concise way Callia had explained nonconverging lines. When the next idea came within her reach, she leaped up and gulped it down like a frog and found she'd internalized an opinion on supplementary color from Soteran.

Each of the tempting morsels of theory, anecdote, opinion, and gossip were snatched out of the air on the wing by the tongues of onlookers, making the lucky recipients shine just a little with borrowed glory. Most were devoured by the people in the nearest rings, leaving none for the outermost, who had to rely upon what they heard from the ones who had absorbed the wisdom directly.

"May I ask something?" Juele said, and felt like clapping her hand over her mouth when they all looked at her at once.

"Go right ahead," Rutaro said. "We're all friends here, aren't we?"

The others nodded, but Juele's mouth was dry. "I . . . um, is there a reason—I mean, can you tell me why you're dressed this way? In this old-fashioned style? The last wave changed everyone else, so you must be holding on to this shape. I mean," she said, feeling herself blushing fiercely, "you can say if it's none of my business."

"It's very observant of you," Peppardine said, in his grave way.

"We really haven't said all we intend to say about the era that has passed," Von said, picking up one leathershod foot and hooking it over the arm of his chair. Juele could see that the shoe was buttoned up the side. The shoe itself had been sewn by hand. She used her newfound skill at detecting fakery that she'd learned that morning with Bella, but if their dress was illusion, it had been done in a way so detailed and so well-grounded that she couldn't tell at all. "People are so in a hurry to run away from their past. Looking forward should not prevent one from looking back."

She thought that was very interesting, and the respect she had automatically assumed because everyone else seemed to respect them filled in in earnest. They were more clever than anyone else. They did have a better grasp of art theory and practice than anyone else she had ever met. She understood better now why Bella and the others were so in awe of them. Juele felt herself falling into a kind of worship. So long as they allowed her to stay by them and learn, she'd be happy. She only hoped some of their wisdom would rub off on her.

"I often feel it is more comfortable to stay with what came before," Peppardine admitted to her, almost shyly. "The present can be abrasive, and the creative moment is a delicate thing that requires being sheltered to prosper." Juele was flattered that They would trust her, the newest and most inexperienced person there, to understand Them.

"You can't write poetry in a crowd," Mara added in a low growl.

Poetry? Juele looked at her in surprise. She'd never have thought of the brusque Mara in the same breath as poetry. These people were as complex as onions, and they had deliberately peeled away one layer of skin for her to see beneath. Juele was put off by Mara's gruff manner. Now she wondered what else it hid. Mara was an adult but she dressed like a schoolgirl, complete with white stockings and black shoes with a strap across the instep. Perhaps Mara hadn't said all she meant to say about childhood yet. Her curiosity must have shown on her face, because Mara turned away scowling, drawing a veil of darkness between them.

"I'm so sorry," Juele said to the black wall. "I don't mean to offend . . ." Helena clicked her tongue.

"Here, of all places, you must know that the surface image can hide a very different interior," she said.

"Yet, form must follow function," Von said, facetiously.

"Oh, stop," Callia said. "You sound like someone in town. An egg does not look like a chicken."

"To what extent is the egg the chicken?" Soteran asked, looking very old and wise. "The shell is the protective layer, the curtain. One must penetrate the shell to get to the truth."

"Come back again, when we're arguing image, Juele," Peppardine said. She looked at him, feeling as if she could drown happily in his eyes.

"*I'll* make sure she comes back when there's anything interesting to hear," Rutaro said, sharply. Juele jumped, the spell broken. She wondered if she had offended him again. He had such a touchy temper. Clearly, he had claimed her as his protégé, but she didn't really know what the relationship should mean. Rutaro had a powerful personality, but it was Peppardine who attracted her. He had such dreamy eyes. She wondered what it was they saw when they gazed off into the distance. He could return from his reveries with a profound statement that showed he'd been listening to the conversation all along. Juele suspected that though Rutaro obviously liked, treasured, and admired his old friend, he was perhaps just a little jealous of his genius and charm. Rutaro would also undoubtedly scoff if she suggested such a thing. The others of the group were just as interesting in their own way, but the heart of the group was the original triumvirate—Rutaro, Mara, and Peppardine.

"The egg should suggest its origins," Rutaro said. "That is why the School has preserved the original grounds upon which it was built. Very nicely, too. I remember what it looked like before there were any buildings here."

"But I thought . . ." Juele began.

"Did you? What did it feel like?" Soteran asked.

"Well, like a thought, like anyone has," Juele said, timidly.

"Our thoughts are not like those anyone else has," Peppardine said, his blue eyes showing a flash of passion for a lightning-quick moment. Juele quailed.

"*What* did you think?" Callia asked, avidly.

"I thought the school had been here a long time."

"Things are not always as they appear in the Dreamland," Mara informed her severely. That was true. Juele bit her tongue on her next question. "The Sleepers themselves can last for centuries, and so can the direct echoes of their personalities." She nodded her head significantly at the others in her circle.

Juele was wide-eyed with wonder. She had recently heard that an exploration party had discovered the Hall of Sleepers in the faraway Mystery Mountains. More intriguing yet, the rumors also said someone in Mnemosyne had been proved to be an avatar of one of the great Seven, a live copy of one of the greatest of the Creative Intelligences. Juele thought it was possible that it might be Peppardine. He looked like an avatar, if anyone did.

He seemed to be on another plane of existence, as he toyed with tiny illusions more perfect than reality. She peeked shyly at him and wondered why she felt hot and cool all at the same time. Feeling her gaze, he started to glance her way. She hastily turned her head to look at something else and found herself meeting Rutaro's dark eyes.

Rutaro gave her a very sharp scowl. He tilted his head back, drained his drink in a gulp, and nodded significantly at his empty glass. Juele looked at Helena's protégé, who had re-formed as a rangy hound dog asleep at her feet, and wondered if that was how she ought to behave. After all, she was here only because of Rutaro's interest in her. Stifling a sigh, she rose and put out her hand to take his glass.

"No, thank you, my dear," he said, shaking his head with a half-grin at Borus. Grateful, Juele sat down. Thank the Sleepers. Rutaro didn't mean her to be his lackey. Helena's apprentice was in his personal Humiliation Dream, and it was nothing to do with her.

Rutaro went over to the sideboard, which had become a large vending machine. He put a coin into the slot and pushed an oversized button. A stemmed glass clunked down into the dispensing area and filled with wine, accompanied by a hissing sound.

"Are you looking forward to the great event?" Rutaro asked Juele.

"Oh, yes," Juele said. "I can't wait to tell my mother I've seen the queen! That is, if I do get to see her. But I'm so excited that she is coming to visit."

"Not *that*," Rutaro said, waving the thought away with disdain. "We have visitors all the time. The *exhibition*, my dear. The very best—well, second best—of the School's efforts will be shown publicly. It is a great undertaking. I fear that the townsfolk will not quite appreciate what is occurring in their midst, but it is our duty to educate them. It is to be an important undertaking, worthy of everyone's respect and attention."

"Will you all be entering your work?" Juele asked

eagerly, looking around at the seven. "Oh, I hope you are. I would love to see that. It would be . . . spectacular."

The Idealists turned to look fully at her. There were horrified gasps throughout the room. Juele realized she'd been presumptuous, daring to tell Them what they should do. "I'm very sorry," she said, feeling herself nudged just a little farther off the recalcitrant chair.

"No, not at all," Von assured her. "It has been a long time since we showed our stuff. It doesn't pay to get rusty."

Soteran yawned. "We haven't decided. That's why he said the exhibition would be full of 'second bests.'"

"*I* might," Rutaro said, sitting back casually and toying with his glass. Juele saw the next-door ring of people lean closer to hear every word. So did she. "If I did, it would be something big, perhaps, that will knock their eyes out."

"Oh, yes," Von said, with a piglike snort. "You haven't done anything in forever, Rutaro." Rutaro frowned.

"I am secure in my accomplishments. I don't need to display everything like an undergraduate," he said, his brows drawn down like thunderclouds over the bridge of his nose. Tiny bolts of blue-white lightning zigzagged from them. Von ignored the pyrotechnics.

"Well, you've been all talk for years," he said.

"You *have* kept away from producing for a while, Rutaro," Peppardine said, interrupting Von. "I know you're capable of better work than anyone who has signed up to display. Perhaps it would be educational to the School and the public if you would show the perfection of the art to which you have ascended."

Rutaro was clearly stung that even Peppardine had taken the part of his tormentor. He drew himself up, seeming more like a grand statue than a man, and raised his forefinger. "Very well, I shall. I will display. My work will be more magnificent, larger and more complex than anyone else's. I will enter the exhibition!"

Everyone gasped, including those from outside the magic circle. One of Them had spoken. Juele bounced in her seat with excitement. Even her soda bubbled over, splashing joyous pink foam on the table. Something wonderful was about to happen. She wished with all her heart to be part of it.

"Yes," Rutaro said, turning to her almost as if it was part of her fantasy. He leaned over her, hands on the arms of her chair. He was larger than life, his voice booming like a divine pronouncement, and she could hear dramatic music rise up around them. "And, of course, *you* will help me."

"Yes! I'll do anything I can," Juele said, breathlessly, staring up into his face, now wreathed with lightning.

"Good! I am pleased with you. You'll be working quite closely with me."

Rutaro stood up, shrinking back to man-size, and began to pace around the inner circle. Images began to spring from his brow, and Juele tried to guess from them what he was thinking of. She saw flying flags, blocks of quarried stone, a rainbow, and a glorious golden sunrise. Tremendous excitement spread throughout the crowd, but Juele was the most elated of them all. The honor of it all, to be asked to participate in the work of one of the greatest artists at the school. She could learn so much from him, and surely a little of the reflected glory would illuminate the career of a beginner so favored by a master. It would be marvelous!

A voice intruded itself on her thoughts. ". . . don't you think so, Juele?"

Juele was shocked into awareness. Peppardine had been speaking to her. She turned to him, absolutely appalled at herself. From the look on his face, so was Peppardine. He must not be used to being ignored.

"I'm sorry," she said, contritely. "What did you say?"

His face grew long with disappointment, and his brows drew down. The glorious music became sad and died away. He turned away from her without repeating his question. She was devastated, feeling as though a piece of her heart had been torn away. Rutaro looked oddly pleased. Juele opened her mouth to apologize again, but

Peppardine glanced back before she spoke. He smiled. Juele sighed with relief. He was not irredeemably angry with her. She promised herself she would never again be inattentive to him. She wanted so much for him to like her. In the meantime, she couldn't contain the joy of the occasion. A project! A project! She twined her feet together for joy under her long skirt.

"We will have to speak together again soon," Peppardine said, graciously.

"When?" Juele asked eagerly.

"You'll know," Helena said.

"Yes," said Rutaro, whirling and dropping into his seat. "But now you have to go."

"Now?" she asked, disappointed.

"Yes, now. It's time." The table at her elbow and the untouched soda glass on it vanished. Juele sprang up as she started to feel the chair under her begin to recede backwards again. The gentlemen all rose, and Helena offered Juele her hand.

"It's been fun, darling," she said. Juele took the narrow fingers, which slipped away almost at once. The others had stopped talking. All of Them stared at her expectantly. She backed toward the door, feeling the barrier spring up between her and Them when she had moved ten paces. The farther away she got, the more fascinating They became. She couldn't believe They were sending her home so soon, but she had no choice. She was going.

The crowd that had filled the room had thinned to a last few hopeful souls. Juele kept looking back at the Idealists, hoping for a reprieve, but They waited, silent and watching. Trying not to be hurt by the abrupt dismissal Juele gave Them a last smile.

"Good night," she said, and closed the door behind her.

The moment the door snapped shut, raucous sounds like those of a wild party issued through it from the room beyond. Juele heard music, the sound of clinking glasses, laughter, and many more voices than she thought could come from the size of the group she had just left. Juele opened the door and stepped back into the room.

Nothing was happening there at all. No one was in the room now but the Idealists sitting around the fire.

"What do you want?" Mara demanded, lowering her thick brows at Juele.

"Nothing," Juele said, gulping. "I . . . I think I forgot something."

"Aren't you sure if you forgot?" Rutaro asked brusquely.

"How can you be sure if you forgot?" Soteran asked, challenging his friend. "Isn't uncertainty the nature of forgetfulness?"

"It is the assumption of knowledge which makes us aware of the depth of ignorance," Peppardine said. Juele sank immediately out of her depth. The floor opened and swallowed her, dragging her down out of sight. She panicked, clawing at the walls. A Falling Dream might kill her. Not so soon, when she'd only just come to the School, her heart's desire! But, no, she wasn't hurt. The unseen force dropped her lightly onto the floor at the foot of the spiral staircase. Above her, the party noise was louder than before.

Juele picked herself up. Another lesson learned, she thought, as she tiptoed out into the night, although she wasn't really sure what the lesson had been about.

Chapter 10

Juele wandered into the dining hall the next morning for breakfast in a daze. The cloud wreathing her head elevated her until her feet floated just slightly above the floor, so that she was tripping on the tips of loose floorboards and thresholds. She stumbled through the queue, collecting her meal from the smiling dinner ladies, without really noticing what was being put on her tray. She couldn't stop thinking of the night before. The Salon had had real sophistication, even more lofty than the coffeehouse the previous day. And the best thing was, the Idealists had been kind to her.

Juele felt in an odd way as if she belonged more with Them than with anyone else she'd met. They were everything she'd always hoped she would become: intelligent, cultured, commanding, wise, and yet friendly. But the truth was They were even more remote and difficult to reach than the coffeehouse crowd. She hoped that Rutaro meant it when he said she would be allowed to come back to the Ivory Tower when interesting things were happening. Even to be able to listen to Them would satisfy her. She wanted to talk about her good fortune with someone.

She glanced around at the nearly empty hall, trying to decide where to sit. At breakfast the day before, Sangweiler, the bearded student from her color class, had sat at table 5. He had seemed friendly, and she wanted to get to know him. She put her tray down on table 5 facing the door, careful to keep toward the end so as not to crowd him.

Sangweiler came out of the queue and nodded sleepily

137

to her. He must have had a restless night. Even his beard
looked tired out. It sagged like a handful of Spanish moss.
On his tray he had a very small plate of food and a very
large pot of coffee. Well, she wouldn't challenge him with
difficult topics at breakfast; she only wanted to chat. With
a friendly grin she gestured at the bench opposite, but
he shook his head with a weary smile and walked to an
empty table. *Oh, well*, Juele thought.

In the meanwhile, Gretred, the big-boned girl from
Wocabaht, came in, carefully balancing books and her
breakfast on a pair of scales that teetered alarmingly as
she walked. She, too, sought out a vacant place, but Juele
thought it was probably because she hadn't noticed her.
Gretred opened a book and began to read while she
spread toast with black goo. Juele picked up her tray and
came over to join her. As soon as she put her meal down,
Gretred vanished. Juele looked around, puzzled. Gretred
reappeared at the nearest empty table. She gave Juele
a shy, apologetic glance and put her nose back in the
book.

But people did eat their meals together, Juele thought
indignantly, stirring sugar into her tea, trying to fight the
feelings of loneliness that roiled in her belly. It must be
possible to have breakfast companions. At the farthest
table, a trio of students were talking about sports, to
judge by the images floating over their heads. How had
they done it?

Juele looked up at the sound of cheerful conversation in the line. A handful of students clustered about
a don in a neat yellow smock came away from the
counter together and made way for a close table. When
they sat down, they displaced the man who had already
been there eating, but they managed to stay together.
So that was the answer, Juele thought, relieved. You had
to come in with someone. She'd find out where Gretred's
room was and meet her for breakfast the next day. If
they were together from the beginning, the room couldn't
split them up.

She didn't really mind being alone today, although it

would have been nice to have someone to share her experiences with. She daydreamed about the Seven through her meal, not at all troubled by the number of times the dining hall picked her and her breakfast up and moved them to another spot. She had really enjoyed meeting Them. They were so at ease with themselves and their talents. She wanted to be like Them. They understood Art, and deep thought, and beauty. There was something fascinating and dangerous about Them.

The night had also given her an insight into the other students. Bella and the others seemed to be confident, but in a strange situation they could be as awkward and out of place as she was. Juele felt better knowing that, even if it didn't change the way they behaved toward her. When Daline came in with a couple of strange students Juele offered her a smile. Daline rolled her eyes toward the ceiling and whispered something to her companions. They giggled. Juele tried not to be hurt.

"Hail, young woman! I say, hello! Hey! I've been hailin' you for an hour!"

Juele looked up at the paintings on the wall. "Good morning, Chancellor Mignonette." She looked for his neighbor, Warden Somnolent, but the canvas beside the red-faced portrait was entirely black. "What has happened to him?"

"Oh, old Sommie? Out of countenance today, out of countenance," the past Chancellor said, nodding until the curls of his wig shed a few flakes of paint. "He's refusin' to show himself, gel. Says he's not appreciated. No waffles today, eh?"

Juele looked down at her empty plate and realized she had no idea what she'd eaten. "Not now, anyhow."

"Haw-haw! Now, when I was a man, I used to have a hearty breakfast. Started with haunch of venison and a tankard of ale. Then I'd go on to half a wheel of cheese and a loaf of bread and *another* tankard of ale . . ." Still listening vaguely, Juele picked up her tea cup for a sip. She wondered what They had for breakfast, and where They ate it. Did They live in the Ivory Tower, or was that only for salons? She could imagine Peppardine in lofty surroundings like that, although Rutaro and Mara would surely prefer accommodations a little more earthy in nature. The cloud surrounded her head again.

"I'd better go to class," she said to the portrait of Gladiolus Mignonette through her haze, and rose, still thinking about Rutaro and his friends. Behind her, the former chancellor was still talking about food. Absent-mindedly, Juele picked up her tray and headed for the hatch.

Suddenly, whispers broke out. Juele sank to earth and stopped in her tracks. What was she doing?

She was clearing up after herself, that's what, she thought, firmly. With an air of defiance, she kept going, pretending she couldn't hear the outrage. At the hatch, she handed over her tray to the surprised dinner ladies. Juele heard more whispers behind her, but now she heard the word "Idealists." The reflected glory of her new acquaintances, if nothing else, stopped them hissing at her. Maybe, with Their backing, she could set a trend. Head held high, Juele marched out of the hall.

Juele was glad to know that Mayrona would be in her section of life study on the top floor of the Madder Building. Most of the others were strangers, although she spotted Erbatu, Colm, and Daline in a cluster near the windows at the back. On that day, the clique was dressed in an eclectic style, as if a basket of multicolored clothes had been thrown into a centrifuge, and each person took whatever was in front of him or her when the whirligig stopped. Juele sighed down at her tidy clothes and pale pink smock, and wondered if she'd ever be able to keep up with the In Crowd. She squared her shoulders and walked in.

Everybody in the room was much older than she was. Juele heard the words "baby" and "child" whispered. All right, so she did look very young indeed that day, with a half-grown tooth in the front of her mouth. She never felt the burden of her youth so heavy as when people called attention to it. With the quantity of influence around her, she almost felt as if she was back in diapers. Juele nodded and smiled at the clique, and they favored her with bored half-smiles. Several of the students were tittering behind their hands at her. Mayrona gestured urgently, and Juele glanced down. She *was* wearing diapers. Some wit had slung an illusion on her. It was meant to be an insult, but Juele found she wasn't upset. She added the illusions of a pink frilly bonnet tied under her chin and a rubber pacifier stuck in her mouth, and went to sit down on the stool beside her roommate. The laughter turned warmer, and Juele felt pleased. It was amazing how much she felt protected by the signs of favor the Idealists had shown her. By the time the green-smocked teacher started her lecture, Juele was able to let the images drop. She was glad to see that her unknown tormentor had let go of his joke, too.

Their model was a live oak in a heavy terra cotta pot. The little tree was *very* lively. It waved its sturdy branches and rustled its leaves, craning this way and that to get the best light coming in from the many windows in the walls and ceiling, forcing the students attempting to model it to erase part of their illusions and start over. Once in a while it tried to hoist its roots out of its pot and wander the studio. The teacher stood by to guide it back to its place so it wouldn't suffer from thirst. There was no water under the tiles to feed it.

In this field of art Mayrona shone. Even in its roughest form, her image captured the curiosity of the young oak. She also caught the jerky character of its movements. Life study was intended to teach artists to animate illusions and make them realistic. Juele had always enjoyed her experiences with it, and considered herself reasonably good, but she picked up a few new tricks watching her roommate. Mayrona's hands moved delicately, drawing out strands of light, building depth without overloading the moving image. Juele had no trouble understanding why this shy girl who had trouble in other subjects was here at the school for art prodigies. The

other students' examples were like cartoons beside hers.
Even Juele's own piece looked flat and dead.

When class broke up, the teacher left to escort the
young tree back to the garden. Juele walked out with
her roommate.

"How did you manage to get all the leaves to move
in different directions at once?" Juele asked. "When I
did that, the ambient light fell wrong."

"I twisted highlight strands into the leaves themselves,"
May admitted, with a shy grin that showed how pleased
she was to be asked about her technique.

"Can you show me?"

May nodded. "Let's nab one of the open studios."

Half the huge rooms on the ground floor of the
Madder Building had been set aside for students to work
on class assignments. At least that meant the administration knew how cramped and dark the dormitories
were. Subtle illusions like painting light on the edges of
leaves would have been impossible in their room. This
way the students were forced out to work in more suitable places.

Mayrona dropped her art box with a thump on a broad
table and pulled up a squeaky stool that looked like it
was constructed from a bundle of twigs woven together
with raffia. Juele tested one and decided the mood of
the Sleepers or the School was rustic simplicity, not
comfort. She elected to stand. May rummaged in her box
and pulled out several small moving illusions. Shyly, she
placed them on the table in front of Juele. A sinuous,
green dragon wound itself in figure eights, shooting a
tiny tongue of golden flame out of its little, dagger-
toothed mouth. A windup dog staggered back and forth,
changing direction whenever it bumped into something.
The last was the figure of a man with golden eyes. He
sat on the table with his arms wrapped around his knees,
staring adoringly at Mayrona.

"These are wonderful. How do you make them look
so alive?" Juele asked, delightedly examining each in turn.

May pulled the man toward her and stretched out the pupil of the left eye so Juele could see.

"There, in the heart of it?" she said, pointing at a glow at the heart of the fovea. "You put sparks in the eyes or along the parts of the image that demonstrate the most life. You already use reflected light to make the eyes three-dimensional, but it's a further spark inside that shows the wit and intelligence of the person, or the vitality of the animal or plant, that reflects the life."

"But how do you do that with a tree?" Juele asked. For answer, Mayrona brought out the moving image of the live oak and began to unwind the strands to show her how it was constructed.

"Tell me all about yesterday night," Mayrona said. "I've never been there. I want to hear everything." Juele described her visit to the Ivory Tower, spicing up her narrative with little images she drew using the bright sunshine that fell on the table. The depictions of the Seven didn't satisfy her. She sighed for Peppardine's easy talent for lifelike sketches, or Rutaro's flamboyance, but the images were good enough to help tell a story. May laughed at Juele's depiction of the pearls of wisdom and shook her head over Helena's apprentice. She tapped a finger down next to the doggy figure at the woman's knee.

"I knew Borus before he fell in with Them. He'd have been better off without a mentor, really."

Alarmed, Juele set down the waving tree. "Did something bad happen to him?"

"Oh, I don't think so," Mayrona said. "But he likes to give up control. He thinks it frees him from responsibility. If he'd been left alone he'd have had to explore his art. Maybe he would have been mediocre—who knows? Now he just does what They tell him. That's what *They* like."

"I don't," Juele said, firmly. "I don't care to have anyone tell me what to do. It's as if there's a School of Light way of doing things, and the way everyone else in the world does things. I feel like I'm in my own

Isolation Dream when I hold on to my independence. I wish there was another way to get along. I like the sense of community here, even in the special groups, but I see people doing things that aren't, well, right. I *want* to belong. Oh, can't I still be me, and be part of the group? I'd like it if others thought more the way I do. Then they'd welcome cooperative independence. And consideration." Juele thought of the fuss over trays in the dining hall, and the way the clique had run wild in town. "I don't like people making a mess just because they can."

"Stop it," said Mayrona. "You'll just make yourself unpopular. You don't like to be dominated, and they don't like it. Coexist. Do what you want, and let them do what they want."

"But they want me to be like them," Juele protested. "They won't like me otherwise."

"But you're not," Mayrona pointed out, with perfect logic. "So long as *you* know who you are, it won't matter what other people do. Sanity equals influence, remember."

Juele thought about that. "Oh."

"Don't let a few days' worth of Them go to your head. They can't protect you from everything. You have to learn to get along on your own. There'll be plenty of obstacles for someone with your talent. People will already have a chip on their shoulders about that."

"But you don't," Juele said.

"I don't care whether you outstrip me," Mayrona said, sincerely. Juele couldn't see a trace of rancor or falseness in her eyes. "You already have. I'll never reach your pinnacle, and I will never worry about trying."

"But that's quitting!" Juele exclaimed. Mayrona shook her head.

"No. I'll reach *my* peak, and be content. You never will be. Never. But I'll have peace of mind."

Juele was confused. Why would anyone stop short of achieving perfection? Still, she found she had more respect for her roommate than before. Mayrona was much more mature than Juele wanted to be. If the price of striving and honest accomplishment was unpopularity, then—then, so be it. By the time she got to the end of her thought, she wasn't quite so resolute as she thought she was.

"I noticed that the click-monsters were being a good deal more friendly toward you today," Mayrona said, with a smile. "You're In with the Idealists, something Daline and Company have never been able to manage in all their years here. Everyone knows it. Word spreads fast around here."

Abashed, Juele looked down at her hands. They were winding an armature of gray light on which she could hang the luminous shadowing for her revised model of the tree.

"I noticed it hasn't made any difference if I say anything dumb, but they're holding back on teasing me quite as much."

May laughed. "Nothing could!"

"It's not going to be any easier to make friends with them," Juele said, looking up into the other girl's eyes. "It's hard being the newest student, and then suddenly being some kind of wonder because They have taken an interest in me. I'd rather the others liked me as me. I'd rather they liked me at all."

"Pedestals are just as much a barrier as fences," Mayrona said. "The ones who will be true friends won't be affected by status. Things change too quickly around here."

Juele said shyly, "I hope you'll be one of them."

Mayrona smiled. "I am. By the way, tell all the gossip! I hear one of Them wants to do a graduate project for the exhibition! That's news!"

"Yes, Rutaro said he might," Juele said. "But why? Surely They graduated long ago."

"No, they never did," Mayrona said. "They've been here for years, maybe centuries, and they've just . . . never left."

"Centuries!"

"Um-hm. Why leave? I mean, they have all they want here. This is the ideal environment for an artist. Rutaro is such a talent. I mean, all of them are extraordinary, but he thinks *big*. Once, just for fun, he made the rain come down in different colors. Then there was the time the campus was full of chickens walking backwards. Everyone thought it was the Sleepers, but it was all an illusion, all for the sake of Art!"

"Rutaro?" Juele asked.

"Right!" Mayrona said, excitedly. "If he's going to do his graduate project after all this time, it ought to be spectacular. And you're going to be included in it. Wish I was."

"I'll ask him if you can help," Juele offered.

"Oh, you don't have to do that," Mayrona protested.

"No, truly! He's going to need more people than me. A lot more," Juele said, remembering the zealous light in Rutaro's eyes when he started to talk about his plan.

"I'd really like that," Mayrona said, her own eyes shining. She bent over her model and started to fiddle with a minute detail in the face. Juele remembered how shy she was. She smiled, glad to have a chance to pay back her roommate's kindness. The two of them worked side by side in companionable silence.

The open studios were not only used for doing homework, but were available for outside projects and personal art as well. Soon they were joined by another student, Manolo.

He regarded them haughtily from very black eyes under long, dark eyelashes. His smock was dark-colored, too, worn over tight-fitting clothes. He placed a blank canvas on his easel just under chin level. Juele watched with interest as he stood before it with his head back and his eyes closed. With an expression of agony, he wrenched open his shirt and took hold of his thin belly with both hands. To her horror, he ripped himself open, tearing entrails endlessly out of himself, and let them spill onto the canvas. Juele cringed as Mayrona led her behind him to see what he had produced. She almost

felt she couldn't look over his shoulder, picturing blood
and body parts, yet the images taking shape, were sen-
sitive, emotional portraits, washed in muted colors that
called attention to the faces in the midst of the faded
surroundings. The people Manolo created were filled with
pain, yes, yet they were sympathetic to one another and
full of plaintive love. Juele looked at the heartfelt adora-
tion in the eyes of the wrinkled old woman for the
impoverished, ill-dressed young couple crouching before
her, and the love they had for one another. How sad it
was, and how beautiful. Juele felt as if her own guts had
been ripped open, felt nerves touched that had never
been touched before. To her surprise, she touched her
cheeks and felt tears. She glanced at Mayrona, who
nodded, her own eyes wet. Manolo was *good*.

Zeira and Corey came in together after Manolo had
rebuttoned his shirt and packed up his finished illusion,
avoiding glancing at the two girls at the table. Tall, hefty
Corey, who took an easel in the far corner, painted word
pictures. He stayed far away from the other artists so
as not to disturb them with the gentle boom of his deep,
melodious voice. Juele heard a low murmur, ". . . the sky
a delicate blue shading to white at the top, flowers of
jewel colors strewn about the grass like confetti. The lake,
a dull mirror to the sky, ripples in thin lines as ducks
glide on its surface. Sheep, white curds on a green sea,
float lightly. Their cries sound sharply over the soft
susurrus of the wind . . ." The image took place before
him, shimmering gently into being.

Juele, inspired by Corey's words, scooted her stool
a little closer to him, earning a surprised smile. She
closed her eyes, thinking of the way the little tree she
was sculpting swayed its branches. In her mind, the tree
was reaching for those beams of sunlight in between
clouds, tasting the water in the heart of the earth. When
she opened her eyes, she saw clearly what she had to
do to make her illusion better. Now she understood her
subject. Juele had never thought of poetry as an art
form. It was beautiful. There must be a verbal way of

expressing every little detail in their illusions. Rutaro and Mr. Cachet were right: they did learn from one another. Happily, she wound shades of gray and white light together. The little tree came together better than she could have hoped, and wiggled its branches in a lively fashion. As soon as she let go of it, it ran around the tabletop, trying to find a way down. It was a true image. Juele was pleased.

"You really are good," Mayrona said, after watching her for a while. Her expression turned apprehensive, and an embossed metal and leather shield sprang into being in her hands. She peered over its steel rim at Juele, prepared to duck down at any moment. "Do you need any outside work? Put a little extra bread in your pockets?"

"Oh, yes," Juele said, puzzled at her friend's defensive posture. "Of course, I'd love to be able to earn some money. There were all those lovely things in Mnemosyne I couldn't afford. Clothes. Reference works. *Books*. Strands of good color cost plenty, too. I mean, I will get by. I've got full board, but I can't splurge on anything. Why did you think I'd get mad?"

"Well, I had to ask," May said, gratefully letting the shield drop. It vanished before it hit the floor. "Many of the students here, and the teachers, too, think that 'commercial' is a dirty word."

"Oh, no," Juele said, relieved. "I used to hire out to put on illusions at birthday parties and special events at home all the time. I like doing things like that."

"Good," Mayrona said, with a smile. "I'll let Festy know you're interested. He coordinates all the requests that come to the school for illusion art. Most of them are one-time jobs, but a few are permanent positions. Part-time, of course."

"That would be great," Juele said, with delight. This was something she knew she could do, and do well.

A bearded, wild man in torn clothes came screaming into the room, waving his arms over his head. "Get out! Everybody out!"

Mayrona glanced at him. "There's the bell. I'd better go."

Juele chased down her wandering tree and put it away in her art box. "Would you like to go down to dinner together?"

"I wish I could. I've got to beg off," Mayrona said, with a fearful look. "I've got a makeup class in chiaroscuro. I need the twilight. I'm so sorry. Maybe tomorrow? I hope we can still study shadow together. I'd like your input."

Chapter 11

Juele changed and went in to sit in the dining hall, arriving just in time for the service of the soup.

She slid into a place at the table nearest the door, squeezing onto the end of the bench beside a cadre of sports-minded students talking about boating. As soon as she sat down, the punters vanished and were replaced by the clique.

"We've been waiting for you, darling," Bella said.

"Oh, I'm glad," Juele said, with a smile. "Hi."

"Tell, tell!" Colm said, taking the spoon out of her hand before she could dip it in the bowl of thick, light-green soup that was set down before her. He ignored her protests. "Nourishment isn't as important as good gossip. You've been avoiding us all day!"

"No, I haven't," Juele protested, trying to take her spoon back. Colm passed it to Daline, who wound it into the fringe of her multicolored shawl.

"We want to hear the whole story, all about Rutaro's project. Everything. Every single detail." Daline gave Juele a sly look. "We ought to be offended that you abandoned us up there in the Ivory Tower. So the least you can do is tell us everything."

"Couldn't you hear?" Juele asked, innocently. "How far back in the crowd were you when he made his announcement?" She noticed Sondra eyeing her dress and sighing. "What's wrong?" She looked down at herself.

The classic frock had taken on the general characteristics of the hall when she had come in, becoming a quiet, dark color under her smock, but the clique was bucking the trend, as usual. They were wearing loud, cheerful colors and crazy patterns. The men had on long-sleeved jackets with straight collars that buttoned up their necks like a tube, and the women's skirts were short enough to expose most of their thighs. Bella's and Daline's long hair fell straight down over their shoulders to the middle of their backs. Sondra's tight blouse bared her midriff, and Erbatu's loose peasant dirndl was almost as long as her skirt. Juele felt like a crow in the middle of a flock of peacocks.

"You're just not one of us yet," Sondra said sadly. Juele didn't know whether the other girl really cared or not, but now the group was studying her dress. Cal had a broad grin on his silly face. He peered at her over tiny, wire-framed glasses. Her soup had vanished, leaving the next course in its place. She bent to eat her fruit salad, but knew the others were still staring at her. Intimidated, she spangled the burgundy dress with a modest daisy print.

"C'mon, bigger!" Colm urged her. At their encouraging nods, Juele exaggerated the flowers until the petals were fat and nearly touching the next daisy. The others must have been exerting influence on her attire too, because it began to change in shape. In contrast to Daline's miniskirt, her dress lengthened until it nearly covered her lace-up boots. Juele sighed. Her footwear had been shoes when she had come in. "All right, that's the way we like it!"

"Now the story," Bella said. She took the spoon away from Daline and gave it back to Juele.

Snatching bites in between illusions, Juele told the story all over again, complete with the finger-pointings and grand gestures that Rutaro had used. "It'll be big," she finished.

"How big?" Bella asked, her mascaraed eyes opened wide.

"I don't know," Juele said. "How big do They usually do things?"

Bella and Daline lifted their eyebrows at one another significantly.

"*Big*," said Bella. "Big equals prestigious. And he said you're to be included."

"That's right," Juele said, remembering the grand fanfare of music that had accompanied Rutaro's pronouncement. "He promised."

"If he wants her, it must be something primitive," Erbatu said, dismissively. "Something in a naive style, then. Otherwise he'd want assistants with more experience."

"It might be," Bella said thoughtfully. "We'll hear more through the grapevine, I presume." She looked almost kindly upon Juele. "And we'll let you know, of course."

"Thank you," Juele said. It would seem they had forgiven her for accidentally finding herself among the School's high echelons. After all, who knew if it would happen again, or how often? She hoped it was soon. Juele squinted toward the chancellor's table. The grand group in white was having a lively discussion, but no one was scanning the room for her. "Will you be going over to the coffeehouse later?" she asked her companions casually.

"Where else?" Daline asked, raising her brows. She tilted her head toward the others. "I suppose we can't do anything if she follows us, can we? There, *or* to that exhibition of curiosities in the museum tomorrow afternoon. It might be amusing to hear what quaint things she has to say about those."

"Not *too* quaint," Erbatu warned, looking at Juele out of the corner of her lashes.

"Of course not," Juele said hastily, promising herself to say only things that she would think out carefully in advance. She didn't care how she had to hold her tongue. They were including her, and that was what she wanted. Course followed course, but Juele hardly knew what she was eating. A sweet taste on her tongue suggested that dessert had been served. When she put down her spoon, everybody stood up, heralding the departure of the dons from the head table. Juele prepared to follow the clique back to the smoky warren for some more stimulating discussion. She vowed this time to accept nothing to drink that looked suspicious.

As they gathered themselves to go, the white-clad form of Rutaro appeared in the midst of the crowd. He was thin and ascetic-looking today, interestingly pale of complexion, but his eyes were dark and intense.

"Oh, hello," Sondra said, coyly fingering her peace-sign necklace. Rutaro nodded politely. He glanced at all of them. His gaze came to rest on Juele's shapeless granny gown with an expression of pain. Juele winced. She knew he liked elegant lines. She thought about changing it, but found the eyes of the clique on her, too. It was impossible to please everyone at once. Juele felt like leaving the dress between them and running away stark naked. Better a Public Nudity Dream than being squeezed between two strong and opposing wills. Rutaro looked deeply into her eyes. Their darkness engulfed her like coffee swallowing a spoon.

"Come along," he said. "We're going back to IT. You may come, too."

"It?" Juele asked, helplessly.

"IT. The Ivory Tower. Come with us," he said, holding out a hand to her.

"Now?" she asked, pulling her gaze from his to glance at the others.

"Now, or never," Rutaro said.

"But what about my friends?" she asked.

Rutaro favored the clique with a pleasant, blank countenance. "What about them?"

They weren't being invited. They gave Juele a black look that they kept shielded from Rutaro. The floor felt shaky under Juele. She looked down. She stood on a tightrope, and the floor had sunk a hundred feet below her. The gulf between the wire and the sides was too far for her to jump. She had to choose. Rutaro's hand started to move away. Juele saw precious opportunity disappearing, but she hesitated a moment before grabbing it and springing forward to safety at his end. His fingers clasped hers tightly.

"I'm sorry," she said to the clique. She could feel her words bounce off their ears. They turned their backs, forming a neon-colored wall, and the gap at her feet widened even more.

"Come along," Rutaro said. He pulled Juele by the hand, and her feet left the floor as she was swept away in his wake.

Juele glanced back at the clique. She'd try to make it up to them somehow later. The flowers came off her dress and scattered in the air behind her like confetti.

Though the School had sustained several changes of influence during the day, the inside of the Ivory Tower had changed little from her last visit. The cream-colored walls were lit warmly by the firelight, and Juele was welcomed to a chair next to Rutaro's that gave her enough seat to sit on, although she spent little time in it. This evening was not dedicated strictly to conversation. Several of Them had small projects they were engaged upon, molding light on small tables like towers or daubing it into empty frames attached to easels. Juele was invited to take a table and work on a piece of her own.

The crowd surrounding Them was as dense as ever, but this time Juele had more company in the charmed circle. Tynne, a woman who seemed to be about thirty, with light brown hair, a turned-up nose, blue eyes, and fair, freckled skin, stood over an easel close to Soteran. Possessed that evening of similar coloring, he could have been her son, except for his serious mien and her open, happy countenance. Soteran, though he seemed about Juele's age, was always solemn. Though his body remained young, his face was often very, very old, making Juele believe Mayrona had been right about how long the group had been together. Manolo, whom Juele had met earlier, sat and watched Callia with his intent stare. He acknowledged Juele's arrival with a friendly expression that transformed his thin mask of a face from Tragedy to Comedy. Borus was present, too, picking apart details on a half-finished sculpture under the direction of Helena, who lounged in a chair that floated several feet off the floor so she could see what he was doing without sitting up. Her languid pose hid an incisive mind.

Von's pipe was not a pipe at all, but a toy to occupy his ever-moving hands. Juele saw it become a yo-yo, a loop of string for cat's cradle, even needles and yarn for knitting. His laziness was a pose. When he chose, he could work with deep concentration on illusions of great internal complexity. Juele envied an inventive mind that didn't see an end to a design, although his current image, a pine forest, looked crowded to her.

She wasn't alone in her thinking. Peppardine and Rutaro, neither of whom were working on anything themselves but were moving among the rest, offering help and comments where they were needed, looked over the current piece in progress, the image of a forest.

"Von, that's so dense it looks like a single, spiky tree," Rutaro said, moving around the easel. Von made no effort to get out of his way, standing his ground firmly as his busy fingers rolled more and more tree boles.

"It wouldn't do the piece a disservice if you opened out a little," Peppardine said pleasantly, standing on the other side. "Leave a little thinking room in your image for your audience."

"I'll do my audience's thinking for them, *thank* you very much," Von said, crisply.

"That's only right and proper," Mara said, from across the firelit circle where she was putting together a still life with cat, "but can you at least finish a thought?"

"What's it meant to be?" Juele asked, studying the piece.

"Why should he name one of his time-wasters when he never finishes one?" Mara snapped, waving a dismissive hand at Von's easel. "You wait. You come back the next time, and this won't be here. It never is. He'll be working on something else. He has more projects under way than any of us, all of them in various stages of incompleteness."

"That's a statement in itself," Callia said, laughing so her sharp white teeth showed.

"It's finished, Von," Mara said, impatiently from across the circle. She was working on the image of a pregnant woman standing on a train platform looking down the tracks with her gloved hand to her lips. She had told Juele it was to be called "Anticipation."

"Not quite yet," Von said, tweaking a minute branch in a treetop half a shade darker. Or was it lighter?

"It's done! Why do you keep fiddling with those details?"

"Being is becoming," Von replied, peevishly.

"But it *isn't* becoming," Callia said. "Not particularly becoming at all. Have the dignity to let your work stand as it is."

"But I know so much more now!" Von protested.

"Than yesterday?" Soteran asked.

"I can improve on what I didn't know then!"

"How can we see your progress if you don't leave us any examples?" Helena asked gently. Helena liked people, with the same intensity that Mara disliked them. Mara's devotion was to her art, her two earliest companions, and after them, the four others of the inner circle. Beyond that, she was brusque, rude, harshly critical, and sullen. But she was honest. If one did something well, Mara never held back from saying so. For that quality, Juele found she liked her. Callia reminded Juele most of the clique. She could make sharp observations that weren't always tactful, and her smile looked hungry. Rutaro was more tactful, but egotistical to a fault. He was intense in his likes and his dislikes. His favorite subject for illusions was women.

"They're such symbols of life, man's gate to immortality," he said.

"Is that what your project will be about?" Juele asked, trying to fit this concept in her brain with the others and becoming overwhelmed.

"Oh, no, that will be bigger," Rutaro assured her, blithely. "Much bigger. Anticipation and preparation is as important as execution. I haven't finished making my plans yet, but when I do, *you* will be the first to know." Juele felt a thrill of pleasure.

"Huh!" Von exclaimed, deflatingly. "And tell *us*, but wait until we're sitting down."

"Don't deride Rutaro until you've finished something yourself," Peppardine warned him.

"Oh, I'll finish this by morning," Von said, turning hastily back to his pedestal. He muttered to himself. "At least I *start* things." Peppardine caught Juele's eye and smiled. He was teasing his friend, and letting her in on the joke.

Juele returned it with her heart on her eyelashes. She was falling half in love with Peppardine, no matter how many times she told herself she shouldn't.

"But you've done nothing yourself," Helena said, looking at Juele's easel. Juele started to make an excuse, but Helena held up a hand before she could speak. "Don't be shy, dear. Let yourself create. I find the evening atmosphere more conducive to art than the starkness of afternoon, don't you? You couldn't ask for a more private, protected place in which to work. Borus, darling, you missed a spot." She pointed at the red urn he was modeling. There was a large gap in one side where the band of posed figures in black he had drawn as a frieze seemed to dance into space. The crowd beyond the circle laughed. Borus's cheeks reddened, and Juele felt sorry for him. She had no wish to expose herself to their ridicule, but Rutaro caught her by the chin.

"Come, dear, let's see your own creation," he said. He picked up the table she'd chosen and moved it closer to the fireplace. He positioned her before it so the workspace was blocked from view by her body or the chimney. "I've been waiting to see this 'askance reality' you've been telling me about." He folded his arms and turned his back on the pedestal, giving her privacy in which to work. "I promise I won't say a thing unless I like it." He smiled at her and looked out across the circle. "Oh, come on, Von, that's enough trees!"

Juele was so grateful for his understanding she wanted to kiss him. She gathered up some of the warm firelight and started to pick it apart. Copying the image of the fountain at Helena's request, or even making a cartoon of Mr. Lightlow didn't make her feel as shy as exposing her own little ideas.

The firelight separated into a lot of yellow and white, with a few narrow tongues of red and blue. Askance reality depended upon being able to catch the eye with distinct images that were easily discerned. Over the last two years she'd gotten good at putting in small details as well as large, even though most people never saw them, since the piece could only be seen out of the corner of one's eye. Her favorite subject was flowers, but that seemed too ordinary to show to Them. Instead, she modeled a light-colored tabby cat with a red tongue and blue eyes. The whiskers were so much fun to do, stretching wires of light out between her fingers like taffy, that she didn't want to stop. She made them very long with a delicate droop. Juele was deeply happy. This was what she had always wanted, to be with other people who made art and talked about art, without any interruption from the outside world.

As Helena had promised, the talk ran to other subjects than art. It ran from philosophy, through gastronomy, and arrived curiously at politics. Juele might have guessed that the Idealists' prevailing view was rather different than those of the monarchy and its ministers.

"Blind chance does not make good dreams," Rutaro argued. "The Sleepers have a right to expect elegant solutions to the problems that they place in our hands, and we let them down. If we ran the world, for example, it would be different."

"More artistically correct, is that what you mean?" Peppardine asked.

"Exactly. Wouldn't that be better? Dreams are handled

in such a crude and haphazard fashion. If I was in charge, problems would be resolved in more artistic ways."

"If you ran the world," Peppardine said, with a half-smile.

Rutaro smiled back with that air of confidence Juele admired. He glanced back over his shoulder at her and gave an approving nod and a thumb's up for her tabby cat. "Yes. If I ran the world."

Chapter 12

Saturday morning was Juele's first opportunity to explore the school on her own. She had no classes, but hadn't yet found any activities beyond homework to occupy her spare time. After taking the time to write a letter to her parents all about her exciting first days, she decided to visit the gallery where the exhibition was going to be mounted.

The gallery was part of the quadrangle nearest the main entrance. The sturdy, serene-looking building had its own garden—a pavilion of turning gravel paths and fragrant, clipped green hedges filled with sculptures. Juele walked the maze, admiring some figures and gawking at others. The area wasn't large, so many pieces occupied the same space in turn at different times. If she wanted to go back and look at a statue she admired, she had to remember how many times she'd passed its location. The section behind a modest screen of larches featured images of large stone ladies with no clothes on, or large stone gentlemen whose stone togas were slipping off, or a host of fantastic beasts frozen in bizarre and uncomfortable poses. Mythical creatures were a hobby of Juele's. She'd become interested in them while studying about the Collective Unconscious in primary school. Some of the beasts represented here were so strange she didn't have any idea what they were. Nor were there any labels or plaques to help her guess. A few of the pieces had been mutilated, either by time or art haters. Some had facial expressions to match their poses, and others were stoically stonefaced. With plenty of leisure time to stroll, she went back to the ones she liked.

She remembered how her first art teacher had taught her to study a piece. "Does it speak to you?" Miss Fanfare had said. "What does it say?"

Many of these pieces had quite a lot to say. " 'Ee, what are you staring at?" asked a voice behind her while she was looking at a sinuous beast, rampant, with a flattened, weather-beaten face balanced on an alabaster stand carved with curlicues. She glanced back into the blank eyes of a griffin with its wings spread, engaged in the act of carrying off a miniature cow. Every feather had been lovingly carved, and the fur of its lion half and the cow had been represented by clever furrowing of the streaked white marble. It stood on a bronze pedestal atop a granite plinth.

"Good morning," Juele said. "Can you tell me what that is?" She pointed.

"Triton," the griffin said, promptly. Only its beak moved when it spoke, but it had a very expressive face. "Not very good, is it? Still, it dates back six thousand years, so they were afraid to leave it out of the collection. He doesn't say much. Whereas I come from the finest classical period. I was carved from sketches of an actual sighting in north Rem. Notice the energy in the lift of my wings, the anguish of my prey."

"Doesn't really hurt," the cow said, diffidently, dangling bonelessly from the griffin's talons.

"*The anguish*," the griffin said, firmly, "shows the helplessness of the people from whom I stole their livelihood. Good, aren't I? You should see me when I'm a dragon stealing the maiden. Be sure and come back to talk with me when they make you write your paper on classic sculpture. It's required in your third year."

"I will," Juele promised. "Thanks."

Juele consulted the directory on a stone plinth inside the entry hall. Only a few rooms of the gallery building were devoted as yet to the upcoming exhibition. The map was very coy about revealing the chambers where the exhibition was to be held. As it wasn't open yet, it probably didn't want to attract too much attention to the unfinished rooms. Since Juele was a student, she thought that reticence shouldn't apply to her, but the map had other intentions. Every time she ran her finger down the list, the print shifted so her hand was resting on a different section, away from the exhibition rooms. The gallery offered her art from every period in history, from Primitives to Technological Visions, just not the upcoming show.

Juele chose to view the classic art that dated back three to five hundred years. The School was reputed to have a huge and valuable collection of both illusion and physical specimens of art in all the styles she knew of, and more she had only found mentioned in texts. The map, as if relieved that she wasn't going to press the issue, showed her a simple diagram of how to reach the viewing rooms she wanted. A yellow line drew itself along the floor toward the first of the corridors leading there. Juele followed it.

She browsed idly through the linked chambers, studying the themes and presentations of the images framed on the walls. There were pieces from the schools of Light Coming from Behind the Subject, In Front of the Subject, the Left of, the Right of, Beneath, and Above the Subject, and very occasionally, Light Coming from the Vicinity of the Viewer So You Could See the Whole Subject Clearly. It seemed to Juele that in ages past, there must just have been less light around than now so that artists couldn't illuminate their paintings properly. She also viewed preserved images of the Indistinct But Brilliantly Colored period, the Indistinct Faces But Defined Detail period, the Dull Color But Gorgeous Detail period, and the Deformed Perspective periods, both Early, where everybody's head was too big for their body, and Late, which showed what were meant to be women, cats, and guitars in blue, or red and black, but so peculiarly made that Juele had to depend on the labels to tell her what they were. Strong feelings emanated from some, clearly masterworks. Some were just clever, making you admire the artist, but not the piece.

Solemn guides on duty at each door changed into more detailed versions of the directory if she asked them questions. Through a door at the end of the cats and guitars room, she came out into a vast paneled chamber with marble floors. All along the walls were rows and rows of refrigerators. Brightly colored art was hung on the door of each with magnets, tape, or clips. Juele stopped to consider the image of a house made of a box with a wedge on top. The artist, she felt, had a definite idea about the meaning of home, and she wondered what it would look like in, say, neo-Cubist, when reality shifted through the School.

This was the first part of the school in which she had seen members of the public. She fought her way through a crowd of short, dark-haired tourists with cameras to a display of signs. The one that seemed to be attracting the most attention said "THIS WAY TO THE EGRESS." The tourists dutifully took pictures of that, and of more displayed art that said "EXIT," "STOP," "DO NOT ENTER," and "INTERDIT."

"I like what they have to say," a pretentiously dressed woman in a trailing red gown, with pearls around her neck, and a cigarette in a long holder said to her friend as Juele ducked between them. "And they say there are no limits in art."

Juele skipped the rest of the exhibits, which consisted mostly of people in tableaux. In one, a woman with very short hair and red lipstick, holding a cigarette with an ineffable air of chic, was leaning over a round, wrought iron table toward a man with an insouciant expression on his face. On the surface between them were glasses of red wine and white pottery plates bearing cheeses and a few chunks of white, crusty bread. She had to be in the right mood to study French Impressionists.

The next room looked empty, but quite a few visitors were shuffling slowly around with thoughtful frowns, in exactly the same way they were in the other galleries. Juele took a couple of paces and gagged. She smelled rotten fish. She craned her head around, looking for the source of the stench, but couldn't see it. How could anyone ignore garbage until it reached a state of putre-faction like that?

A couple of serious men in suits and gray smocks stopped almost next to her. She shifted hastily, hoping they wouldn't think she was the one who smelled like that. The taller, wispier man inhaled deeply, then coughed.

"Awful, isn't it?" Juele asked, politely. Perhaps the garbage was under the floor. It looked solid, but that didn't mean a thing in an establishment full of illusions.

"Marquart's 'Waterfront on a Hot Day,'" said the shorter man. His mouth was a straight horizontal line between floppy jowls. "A masterwork."

"A joke," said the other. "You can't tell me he's ever been on a wharf. The fish smell is artificial. I distinctly detect the aroma of compost. It should be seaweed."

The stink was a work of art? Juele looked at the two men, searching for signs that they were putting her on, but they continued to discuss nuances of the gagging odor in the most serious way. Still talking, they sauntered around the white-walled room, stopping now and again to inhale deeply through their noses. She put a hand out over the area where the vile smell was most concentrated. There was no tactile or visual component to "Waterfront on a Hot Day." It was entirely concocted of smells. As casually as she could, she caught up with the two art critics, and tagged along, listening. They certainly knew their odors.

Juele remained a pace or two behind, but always within earshot, finding something to appreciate in this unfamiliar art form. Her favorite piece was a still life of a bowl of fruit. She smelled each kind of fruit distinctly and had a clear picture in her mind's eye how much of each there was. The artist had almost certainly filled the bowl more than halfway with purple grapes, for the musty sweetness was the predominant odor, but she sensed a mellow banana or two, a sharp pineapple, and a sweet peach. She could even smell the terra cotta of the bowl, mingled with the hot odor of sunshine on clay.

"But of course," said the shorter and stouter of her guides with a stern look at his friend, "it's entirely representational."

"I don't agree," said the tall, thin one. "Observe the nuances, the connotation rather than simple denotation suggesting early summer instead of autumn . . ."

Juele would have enjoyed listening to the rest of the argument, but through the next exit she spotted a couple of figures she recognized. As usual, Peppardine was tall and thin, while Rutaro was shorter and stockier. Curiously, they seemed almost like a visual echo of the two critics in the Hall of Odors. She was surprised to see Peppardine out of the Ivory Tower. His companions roved about the campus frequently, but she had not seen him abroad before.

Unlike the tourists, they looked as though they belonged here, among the exhibits. They moved with a commanding grace, almost as though they floated through reality without it quite touching them. They would stop and regard a display, and nod or frown at one another eloquently, as if they could communicate without speaking. Juele didn't know if it was a special talent they had, or just a product of their long friendship. Their clothes had changed, as if outside of the salon the Victorian influence waned, and their dress became slightly more modern. Looking up from a piece on a plinth in the middle of the floor, Rutaro caught sight of her. He smiled, and Peppardine looked up. They waved her over.

"Good morning, my dear," Rutaro said. "Here to commune with the spirits of the great?"

"The great?" Juele asked, looking with ill-concealed distaste at the exhibit they were standing in front of. Hanging in space were thousands of blobs of dull color—yellow, blue-gray, and grayish brown. It did not impress her. She started to move on to the next piece. Peppardine caught her by the arm and turned her back.

"Look at it," he said softly. "Give it a chance."

Juele gave him a questioning look, but obeyed. As she stared at the blobs, they seemed to draw her in.

Suddenly, the colors became a haze. Within the cloud she saw shapes. People. Buildings. A river reflecting the building, the man standing beside it, and the clouds overhead. In fact, the landscape was so beautiful and realistic, she couldn't understand how she had missed seeing it in the first place.

"It's wonderful," she breathed. "I've never seen anything like that. What is it?"

"We call it a Turner," Peppardine said, "because it turns into a coherent illusion as you watch. Good, isn't it? Hundreds of years old, and it never ceases to astonish me."

Juele stood and gazed at the image with fascination. It wasn't made of whole components, but rather of the shadows in between, imposed upon the color of ground, foreground and background. She was concentrating on the transition between the primary hues when the others started to move away, drawing her along with them.

"Come along," said Peppardine, smiling down at her. "There's more to see." She was conscious of the warmth of his hand on her arm and chided herself. He was so much older than she was that she felt silly allowing herself to be attracted to him, but she couldn't help it. Not only was he handsome and kind, but he represented everything she strove for in her career. He and his friends occupied the highest echelon of respect in an enclave of all artists. What a dream of a place this was! Every mind in the Waking World must concentrate its creative bent right here. And Peppardine was so gentle, unlike his fiery friend. Juele liked and respected Rutaro, too, but he didn't excite this . . . visceral sensation inside her.

They made their way around the room that Juele had been so eager to leave before. She thought she was a good observer, but again and again the two artists were able to point out characteristics of technique that she wouldn't have seen otherwise.

"I feel stupid missing that," Juele said, as Rutaro showed her the underpainting of white that added so much light to a sunwashed image of pottery on a doorstep.

"I wouldn't have noticed in a hundred years." The two men exchanged another of their speaking glances.

"That is why we are here," Peppardine said, solemnly, leading her to the next exhibit with his hand through the crook of her arm. "To learn from the masters. At least these don't rap our knuckles. Well, not often." Juele laughed. Rutaro trailed behind them, glowering. He was jealous that his distinguished friend seemed to be taking over his apprentice. Juele wanted to reassure him that he hadn't been supplanted, that she still treasured him as her mentor, that she was just enjoying Peppardine's company, but it wouldn't have been polite to say anything of the kind. And besides, Rutaro was keeping up a shield between them that repelled confidences even if she'd had an opportunity to whisper. Peppardine, however, wasn't unaware of his friend's reaction.

"We all teach," he reminded Rutaro. "I'm sure Juele holds you in no less esteem for me pouring pedantry into her ear."

"Yes, yes," Rutaro said, impatiently. A dark cloud formed over his head and followed him as they continued their tour of the gallery. His intense eyes glared out of the shadow. Juele tried to pay more attention, but Peppardine was so interesting, she could hardly ignore him.

"Good illusion," he was saying, as they passed image after image, "is indistinguishable from reality by the naked or untrained eye. Bad illusion is when the light or shadows couldn't be coming from the direction they are, or the poses are awkward beyond what muscle or bone would allow. A lack of harmony is bad. The School prefers truthful, detailed representations of reality. So do We," Peppardine said, and Juele knew he meant the Idealists. "Really good illusion cannot be told even by a trained eye."

"Then how do you tell if it's an illusion or reality?" Juele asked.

"Oh, there are ways," Peppardine said. "You'll learn them all, over time."

The next room was full of the sharp edges of Cubist art, showing all the sides of an object at once in a distorted image. Juele was studying a canvas with a large blue and yellow polyhedron interacting with two smaller polyhedrons. A wave of influence rolled through, changing all the art in the room to Impressionist images. Now that it was represented in soft, hazy colors, Juele discovered that the piece she was looking at was of a little girl with long golden hair and a blue dress, dangling a ball of string for a kitten, which looked as soft as a cotton puff. Juele had changed, too. Her plain blue pants and white blouse softened in color under her pink smock and grew fuzzy around the edges. She'd become just a little bit plumper, her wrists delicate and rounded, and her skin took on a lovely freshness that delighted her. Juele reached for the strands of color she had taken to carrying in her smock pocket. She picked out peach, blue-green, and white lights, and tried to capture the nuance to study later. Peppardine chuckled.

"It won't help, you know," he said. "Anything you take down now will alter the very next time you do." Peppardine and Rutaro looked softer-featured, too. The floppy tie that Peppardine favored lost all its body and rolled down his shirtfront into the form of a silk scarf. He tapped his temple. "You have to keep your observations here. That way you won't lose them."

Juele thought about that as she started forward over the threshold into the next gallery.

She was snatched back just in time as four automobiles sped past the door, roaring like tornadoes. Two more, one jockeying to get in front of the other, hurtled back the other way. Rutaro held onto her shoulder as he peered around the corner.

"Badly hung," he said, angrily. "I told that fool Wimster it was much too close to the entrance."

"I could have been run over!" Juele said, trembling. One might suffer for one's own art, but to be killed for someone else's was ridiculous.

"Is that 'Traffic'?" Peppardine enquired as they made

their way gingerly into the room, hugging the near wall.
Juele stayed close to her protectors as cars appeared
out of nowhere in the gallery and raced toward one
another at top speeds along a yellow line on the floor.
The vehicles vanished before they struck the far wall.
More took their place almost at once, racing back again.
He looked disdainful. "Noisy. Smelly. Unnatural and
unrealistic."

Unrealistic? Juele thought. It looked exactly like the
snarls on the streets of Mnemosyne, just blocks outside
the School grounds. There were even occasional drive-
bys in her small hometown. Peppardine really did not
get out often.

"Wimster claims it's a vision of the future," Rutaro
shrugged. "Like 'Cigar' last year. He is hopeless. You can
see that he has a filthy view of the world."

Seeking escape from the racket in the exhibition hall,
they went out into the corridor, making for a grand-
looking doorway. Affixed to a pillar on the other side,
Juele recognized the cloud and crown symbol of the royal
house. Two guardsmen in long green coats and fur hats
saluted them as they walked through. She looked up and
down the long room. Beautiful and valuable-looking
paintings and statues were ranged along the walls to
either side of them.

"We're in the castle!" she said. "But, it's blocks away
from here."

"It's a joint exhibition," Rutaro explained. "It only
makes sense to have them adjoining. And it saves a great
deal of walking. Our dear patroness will enter through
here, after she cuts the ribbon opening the show."

Juele tiptoed along beside her mentor, feeling as if
she was treading on sacred ground. She half expected
the floor to tilt up and send her tumbling back into the
School, but she followed the other two trustingly. They
seemed as comfortable walking the corridors of the royal
palace as they did the passages of the school. Juele
wished she had their confidence.

Among the displays of classical art and portraiture in the long gallery were pieces of less certain technique, obviously student work that would be part of the exhibition. Rutaro and Peppardine stopped now and again to study one, commenting to one another silently. Juele trailed behind them. It was too bad she couldn't read their private language, but she felt the honor of having two of Them all to herself. If Daline and Colm could see her now!

The corridor opened out into an enclosed garden filled with fragrant blue and purple flowers. Juele heard the trickle of water and peered around her guides. A fountain hung upside down in the middle of the square. It had no visible means of support, but the sprays splashed down, then rose up again into the inverted tiled basin.

"Ah!" Rutaro said. "Tynne's work, I see. Very nice, indeed."

Juele raised an eyebrow. "What's so special about this? It's just an upside-down fountain."

"Rain falls down," Peppardine said. "No one thinks that is important at all. But if a fountain plays down, that's Art. It is a difference in perspective."

"I shall have to compliment her," Rutaro said, nodding appreciatively. "It's all I could ask for."

Juele listened to this byplay feeling more confused by the moment.

"That's Art," she repeated, dubiously, trying to understand. The other two nodded as if she had said something profound.

"Yes," said Rutaro, with satisfaction.

The three of them wound their way around the corridors and found themselves back in the long gallery. Peppardine looked up suddenly at a window that appeared in the ceiling and smiled at the others.

"I had better go back," he said. He bowed to Juele. "Thank you for a most enjoyable afternoon." He gave Rutaro a pat on the shoulder and sauntered back toward the exit that led to the School.

"He never does stay out for long," Rutaro said, with a quick glance after his friend. "I think he only comes out to check that all is going well. And, so it is."

"Rutaro," Juele asked suddenly, "have you really been here since the school was founded?"

"You don't know?" he asked, and suddenly the air around them was full of darkening clouds and thunderbolts. The comfortable square of buildings dissolved. They were on the jagged peak of a high, lonely mountain, without a living thing for miles. The sky darkened, and thunder rumbled, shaking the ground underneath them. Rutaro looked fifty feet tall, and his white robe sucked all the light for miles around into it. Juele trembled. She'd made a huge error, and she had no idea how to correct it.

"No," she said, at last. Her voice squeaked.

"Oh," Rutaro said, in a normal voice. He tilted his head, and the sunlight reappeared. He shrank back to a normal size. "My dear, I *am* the School, I and my friends. We founded it years ago. We've been here forever." He waved his arms, and Juele felt a sense of eternity. She didn't know how she knew that's what it was, but her heart and mind seemed to stretch off in every direction at once. Her boundaries returned to her, and she gazed at Rutaro with a heart full of admiration. He was everything she'd ever wanted to be.

The jutting brow of land settled back into the corridor of the castle gallery, the ceiling sealed up, and the uniformed guards saluted them again as they left.

"I have been thinking of the piece you were doing the other night," Rutaro said, looking upwards, but glancing at Juele out of the corner of his eye to gauge her response. "It wasn't . . . bad. But I would like to see you work on catching the eye more quickly. The key to your art form is immediate capture of attention, conveying the entirety of meaning in the first glance. The whole success of the piece depends upon it. I want you to make a simple, small piece with that precept in mind. Can you do that?"

"I think so," Juele said eagerly, trying to imagine an easily visualized subject that lent itself to quick symbolic interpretation.

"Very good," Rutaro said. "You haven't anything else you need to do today, do you?"

"No," Juele said, meekly. She had been meaning to try and find Bella and the others, but if Rutaro wanted her to do something, she supposed mending fences with them could wait. She narrowed her eyes, thinking.

"Bring it tonight, when you come to visit us, and we'll look it over. All right?"

"Yes, of course," Juele said with delight, and found she was talking to an empty room. She spun on her heel, trying to see where he had gone. A low chuckle faded away into the distance. Quicker than thought, he'd spun a moving illusion around himself and disappeared from view before she had noticed. Juele shook her head in admiration.

The piece Rutaro wanted her to do could take her all afternoon. Part of her knew he had given her the assignment to show his authority over her, after Peppardine had pulled her away. Well, who was she to question one of Them? She was being asked back again to the Ivory Tower, and that was beyond price. The advice and guidance she was getting was worth years of instruction. What was a few hours' work compared with that?

The buildings and the quadrangles in the School moved around and changed their shape several times a day, but Juele could always find her way back to the Ivory Tower in the evenings. Some of the time Bella and the clique were allowed to come with her, but they accepted the invitation less and less frequently as days went by. They weren't part of the inner circle, nor could Juele bring them into it, no matter how often she asked Rutaro. She could tell that irked them. They weren't allowed beyond that invisible barrier. Just her. Juele deliberately spent as much time as she could away from the Ivory Tower with the clique, trying to appease their feelings. She even let them insult her, letting the abuse roll off her as much as she could. It still hurt, but if they were able to vent their anger she could still hang around with them.

Juele fell into a cycle of activity. She spent her days in class, her afternoons in study, and her evenings either in the coffeehouse with the clique or in the Ivory Tower, listening to the Idealists expound on every topic under the sun. She felt ignorant as a newborn next to Them and worried that the novelty of having her around would wear off, but on the days she was invited, the shining tower admitted her. So many others were bounced, walking as purposefully away from the tower as they had approached it. She felt fortunate every day that that did not happen to her. Even the long staircase seemed to grow shorter, so she was among Them in the cream-colored room before she knew it. One day she'd be there before she started the climb. Though she rarely understood everything that went on in the salon, she felt honored to be there.

Later, when she was back in her gloomy dormitory, she told Mayrona everything that had happened that evening. Juele lay on her back with her hands behind her head. She ought to be seeing the dingy paint on the ceiling, but instead, it was a moving picture of the evening's events. Sometimes her vision was so vivid Mayrona could share it, too. She was starting to become a visual thinker, like most of the other students.

"And it's amazing, how They keep up the appearance of a hundred years ago, when everything has changed so much since then," Juele said one night, expounding on her favorite subject. "The School's continuity is amazing, too. I mean, the dining hall always looks like a big room with benches. In my school cafeteria, sometimes it would fill completely with water like a swimming pool, and they'd serve the food on rubber life rings. Sometimes it would be an outdoor cookout, complete with mosquitoes. I don't know; I think the sleepers who dream our village must spend a lot of time outside. At least, I guess so."

"That's very interesting, really," Mayrona said quickly. "Well, good night." She sat up and flicked off the lights.

"May, I'm not ready to go to sleep," Juele started to protest, but her roommate wrapped herself in her blankets, paying no attention. She began to breathe softly.

Juele gazed at her in dismay. *What did I say?* Juele thought. *What am I doing wrong?* Mayrona always seemed so friendly during the day, and always snubbed her flat at bedtime. Every night she turned off the light while Juele was still talking. Mayrona puzzled her, as everybody at the School puzzled her. The eyes of the teddy bear on Mayrona's pillow sent two flat glints of moonlight her way as Juele settled back on her pillow and closed her eyes.

Chapter 13

On Wednesday Juele appeared in room 306 at precisely three o'clock, and Mr. Lightlow smiled at her. His canary, its feathers golden, sang a little song for her as she found her place behind Gretred. Almost everything at the School was a delight to Juele, but symbolism was her favorite class, and this was a special day. The queen was expected at any moment.

Instead of its usual industrial dowdiness, the classroom looked newly built. Everything in it bore an air of beauty suitable for the dreams of the Sleepers themselves. The floor, which had sometimes been battered linoleum and sometimes packed earth, was covered in a carpet of thick brown and beige velvet. The very desks were varnished and gilded. The School itself had put on a special face for its patroness. Juele had noticed as she had run across the campus that the gardens were tidied until they looked like enamel paintings, and the clock tower was tied with a big gold bow.

"Has anyone seen her yet?" Juele whispered to Cal, who was dressed all in somber black silk under his smock.

"I did," he said, smothering a yawn with one hand. His skin was pulled tight under his cheekbones, and he had purple smudges like bruises around his eyes. Juele thought he might be ill, until she glanced at Bella and Daline, also pale in black. "Arrived in a floating coach drawn by jeweled dragonflies. Same old thing as always."

"Oh," Juele said. She settled into her seat. Same old thing? How casual he could be about a royal visit. But then, he and his friends seemed ready for the occasion in their elegant black. She suddenly felt underdressed, and thought about edging the red and blue check print of her dress toward the darker scale of the spectrum, so that it might be black, too, before the queen arrived. It was worth a try.

"Oh, stop it," Daline said, noticing the color of her dress deepening and guessing what she was up to. "It's *too* late. You're behind the crowd, *as usual*." The others snickered at her. Quashed, Juele felt herself growing smaller until her feet no longer touched the ground from her seat. Any time she started to feel a sense of belonging rising in her, it could be smashed flat by the clique.

"All right, all right," Mr. Lightlow said, producing a megaphone from the air to shout over the gossiping class. "You will work by yourselves today. Your assignment is to craft an emotion. Symbols to enhance understanding should not swamp the image! Do I make myself clear?"

There were groans from the class, but everyone nodded.

"All right. At it, please." He swung the megaphone, which became a pointer, and began to patrol the room, offering criticism and encouragement here and there. Juele stared at her easel, thinking of the Emotional Impressionist images she'd experienced over the weekend in the museum. What emotion should she portray? Joy would be the easiest, but she didn't feel very joyful just now, after being snubbed so publicly. Mayrona's words came back to her, that she couldn't please everyone, and she knew what a difficult balance she had to maintain with all the people here. She was also nervous about having the queen watching her working. What emotion did she feel confident enough to show to the royal lady? She thought of Mayrona's teddy bear and wished she had such a comfort object nearby. At that moment, a hug from something entirely supportive and nonjudgmental would feel so good.

Her favorite comfort object had been left behind at home with her parents to avoid its getting lost at school. Depending upon the kind of reassurance she needed, it could be a fat tabby cat, or a cushiony brown teddy bear not unlike Mayrona's, but most of the time it was a cotton rag doll with an embroidered face. Juele could see it in her mind, in every detail, the way it had been the last time she'd seen it: limp, faded, and entirely lovable. With it, she could portray the image of "contentment." Responding to her air of readiness, Juele's easel tilted until it was flat.

The colors were easy. She just needed familiar tones. All she had to do was borrow reflections from everything she was wearing except the smock, which was too new to have memories in it. Red for the hair and blue for the doll's dress and eyes came from her despised, unfashionable skirt. Juele drew on her feelings of love for her battered treasure, and the image began to take shape.

"Everyone rise, please!"

Juele was jerked out of her creative trance by Mr. Lightlow's voice. She looked up toward the front of the room and hopped down off the high seat. She couldn't stop staring. The queen had arrived.

Juele had never seen anyone so beautiful. Her Majesty, Queen Harmonia, looked motherly and kind, but at the same time, she was a vision of celestial glory. Under a crown of filigree gold set with sapphires, her black hair was coiled and shining. Her skin was silky and translucent in its perfection. And her eyes—eyes were never that blue. Juele wondered if any of the queen's beauty could possibly be illusion, then chided herself for such an uncharitable thought. Hastily, she forced her mind to think of something else, lest the notion make its way into her thought balloons. With envy and wonder, Juele took in the details of the queen's traveling gown, deep blue velvet to match her eyes, and embroidered with gold and silver.

Behind the queen was an entourage of six. At the fore were two guardsmen in matching livery carrying steel-tipped lances, followed by a pinched-faced maidservant in bonnet and apron, a couple of ladies-in-waiting, and a man in somber black carrying a little satchel. Juele recognized the sort of bag and the metal device hanging about his neck, and realized he must be the royal physician. In the coffeehouse and up in the Ivory Tower Juele had heard conflicting rumors that the queen had chronic ailments or that she was a notorious hypochondriac. She hated to believe anything uncomplimentary about such a perfect person. Perhaps the doctor was just for show. Juele hated to think the queen required him any more than she needed the guards.

The teacher clapped his hands. "Back to work, all of you! Her Majesty does not want to disturb you. She only wishes to observe."

"As if we couldn't see her," muttered Gretred. *As if we weren't aware of her every movement*, Juele thought, trying to keep from peeking at the beautiful vision walking around the room on a red carpet that unrolled itself before her feet. The Sleepers had certainly favored Her Majesty with their very best efforts. She was graceful, and she had a delightful little laugh.

Everyone whispered among themselves or sent surreptitious little pictures to one another's desks about their impressions of the visitor, but they were also aware of the importance of how their assigned images would look. Juele spotted Cal trying to enhance his red-and-black illusion of "anger" with a little extra influence to cover the holes in his design.

"Concentrate," Mr. Lightlow boomed, his stick tapping down on Cal's table. "If you have any extra to give, why don't you use it on your regular assignments?" Cal went scarlet with embarrassment and fury. At once, the blank parts of his illusion filled in, but the whole thing had gone lopsided, instead of being erect with righteous anger. Fuming, he rubbed the whole thing into a pool of color and started over.

The others tittered and bent over their own work to keep the teacher from criticizing it in front of the queen. It was hard to concentrate when one was so aware of the royal presence. But a week in the Ivory Tower in the midst of the crowd around the Idealists was training

Juele to ignore distractions. Firmly she put her mind back
on her work, trying to shut out the fact that the queen
was only a dozen feet from her.

Biting her lip, Juele frowned at the image on her easel.
The shape was coming along nicely but the face wasn't
forming to her satisfaction. No matter how much she
tried to make the doll's mouth turn up, it turned down.
She picked out the stitches over and over again, but the
little red arc kept tipping over. *Oh, come along*, Juele
thought impatiently. *You can't miss me that much.* But
it wasn't the doll's sorrow that was coming through her
hands. It was her own.

"And what are you doing here?" the queen's voice
asked over her shoulder. "Oh, look, the poor thing is
frowning. What is this meant to represent?"

There wasn't time to redo it. Juele looked up. Her
teacher was standing behind the queen, with a strange
expression on his face. Juele wondered hastily whether
she ought to scrub it all out or lie. She sighed.

"Homesickness," she admitted.

"My goodness, that's lovely, my dear. Look at the depth
of feeling, and on such a tiny face," the queen said. "You
artists are so skilled at representing emotions you are
not experiencing. Or, I hope not, my dear." She gave
Juele a smile brilliant with understanding and put a kindly
hand on her shoulder. Juele remembered that she had
a daughter. "Very nice." The hand patted softly, then
lifted away. The queen moved on to Gretred's easel, and
the teacher trailed behind her. "Ah, very nice." Was it
Juele's imagination that Her Majesty sounded less enthusiastic about her friend's work? No, certainly not. When
Mr. Lightlow drew level with Juele, he held his fist out
with his thumb up. A gold star appeared on Juele's desk.

Juele sat staring at nothing, feeling a little kernel of
warmth in the pit of her stomach. The *queen* understood
the feelings of a schoolgirl from a small town. Her
Majesty was wholehearted with her compassion, not using
it as the bait for a trap, like the clique, or making her
a specimen to be studied, like the Idealists. She saw Juele

as an individual, not just one of millions of subjects. Juele felt better already. Now she had faced the fact that she was homesick. The fact that someone else cared made it immeasurably easier to deal with it. She finished up her illusion and saw to her amazement that the doll's mouth had turned upward. Now, it looked contented.

Chapter 14

"Turn a little more this way, dear," Rutaro said, peering at Juele past his upraised thumb. Obediently, Juele swiveled on her heel, trying not to drop the basket of acorns she had balanced on her hip. "That's it. Now, think immature, tender, young thoughts. You are the symbol of everlasting life. Renewal. Springtime personified. Perfect. Now, hold it as long as you can."

The sunshine played on Juele's face and bare arms. She was wearing a pale green, gauze tunic bound with a tie that crossed between her small breasts and tied around her waist, and left her shoulders bare. The light skirt was barely long enough for modesty, and she worried about playful passing breezes lifting it. On her head was a crown of rosebuds that went well with that day's pink-and-white complexion, and her hair, strawberry blond, fell down her back almost to her knees. Rutaro, dark-skinned as a woodland god, kept rearranging the mass of hair so it flowed loosely, draping along her body, but not concealing anything. She thought she looked very pretty that day. From the life-sized sculpture rising on Rutaro's stand, he was exaggerating even that natural beauty to a higher degree than she'd ever look on her very best day.

"Very nice, darling," Callia said, studying Juele critically from her prone position in a wooden lounging chair. "But don't you want her eyes rounder?"

"No, I do not," Rutaro said, with his teeth clenched. "They are fine the way they are." He transferred the glare to Juele. "And don't you change them, either."

"No, I won't," Juele said, shaking her head vigorously.

A few of the acorns hopped out of the basket and landed next to her feet. A white kitten, one of the many animals that posed on the school grounds, pounced out of the shadows and played with them. Rutaro's eyebrows flew up, and he grabbed another glob of shapeless matter and began to knead it into the shape of the cat. Working with nebulosity, he had explained, was a hobby of his. He didn't need it to make durable illusions, but he liked the feel of it. He was as skilled with it as he was with pure light.

"What is all this stuff for?" Juele asked, feeling the kitten roll over on her foot. Behind her, hovering cherubs held up a swag of ivy, and a table at her elbow held a glass of May wine.

"Prefigurative symbolism," Rutaro replied, with a few birdlike glances between her and his sculpture. "It's important to inform the viewer of the eventual outcome of the image they are viewing. For example, I have you looking off into the west, which may denote that you will be going either that direction, or toward maturity. You are young, so I have adorned you with symbols foretelling your future as a generative force, whether that be children of your brain or your body. The kitten is a serendipitous addition, but is only a symbol of your energy as a young animal. I mean that in the nicest possible sense."

"Oh. Thank you, I think." This was more complex and profound a notion than anything she was learning in symbology class. Juele listened with all her ears, trying to commit his words to memory.

"Such foreshadowing is most important in static art," Rutaro continued, turning out a series of rosebuds with practiced hands, "but you'll find it has its place in moving images as well. Most satisfying, to have the alpha and omega of meaning all in one place. Try it yourself."

"I will."

Juele had been flattered to be asked to join the Seven for a day out. For Them, that meant going as far as the courtyard near the tower. The garden had grown to nearly meadow-size overnight, leaving plenty of room for each of Them to pursue their own activities. Von and Helena were off to one side of the green field playing badminton over a net strung on skyhooks. He, in white pants and a flannel blazer, and she, in a long flowered dress with a lace collar, were in elegant contrast to everyone else on campus, who today were clad in blue jeans and T-shirts. Soteran, in a collarless white shirt, acted as referee. Helena's protégé, a dog once again, ran up and down the sidelines, retrieving errant birdies. Mara, wearing a sailor dress too small for her and a bow in her hair, sat nearby on the grass sketching them. A couple of lucky students sat with her, quietly working in their own notebooks.

The group was not alone. Lining the perimeter of the field were hundreds of onlookers, two to three deep in places. Juele saw her classmates, some of the younger instructors, and a host of people, animals, and things Juele didn't recognize. All stared hungrily at the activity going on in their midst. The uninvited crept closer from time to time, but they were always driven back to the edge like shadows by the brilliant sunshine of the Seven. Not a few harsh glances were thrown her way. Juele was embarrassed to be the center of envy by so many. Rutaro, and Helena, when she noticed, told her to ignore them and just pay attention to enjoying the beauty of the day.

"Yes, true promise of things yet to come," Rutaro said, almost muttering to himself, rolling a ball of nebulosity between his fingers. "Appropriate, you know. You do have the talent to make a name for yourself. You could even aspire to join our number one day," he added. Juele quivered with pleasure, but her delight was short lived. "Or perhaps not. I don't know."

"Promise is not completion," Peppardine said. He lay on his back with his hat shading his eyes from the sun behind him. At first Juele thought he wasn't doing anything, until a cloud passed overhead, dropping a shadow on her shoulder.

"Please, will you move that," Rutaro said, standing back from his work for a moment. "It's in my light."

"Sorry, old sock," Peppardine said. The shadow vanished.

Juele looked upward. The clouds floating above the school had been shaped into nebulous figures of classical gods. She of Love and Beauty lounged on a celestial couch near the horizon. The Warlike One stood guard beside her. The outstretched arm of the Thunderbolt Thrower had drifted directly between the field and the sun, but the figure was moving back again toward the group. Juele was amazed.

"Was that illusion, or influence?" she asked.

"Illusion, of course," Peppardine said, sternly. The hatbrim moved, and he sat up, looking stern. His eyes today were a pale green, good for glaring. "I never use anything but illusion."

"I'm sorry," Juele said, with a gulp. "I just wanted to know."

Peppardine never seemed to remain upset for long. He gave her another one of his heartbreaking smiles and settled back again on the grass. Juele sighed. She desperately wanted his approval. He went from cold to warm and around to indifferent so easily she truly didn't know if he liked her or not. Sometimes she wondered if she had imagined the smiles. On the walls of the Ivory Tower were several images of each of the Seven, including Peppardine, but none of his portraits showed him smiling.

"Von twits *me* about not producing more," Rutaro said, conversationally, tapping his easel with a fingernail to make Juele turn around and face him again. Carefully, she rotated back, steadying her basket, which was now full of peeping baby chicks. "But my dear friend here could sell his time a dozen ways from next week and still not satisfy all his patrons."

There came a snort of laughter from underneath the hat. They must be very good friends. Sometimes Rutaro seemed jealous of Peppardine's extraordinary talent, but the rest of the time he bragged about it as if he'd invented it himself. The Seven were full of contradictions. She tried not to be impatient with herself for failing to understand Them. They'd had years, maybe even centuries, to form relationships too complex to be learned in only a week.

Rutaro let his hands drop. "There, that's done," he said. "You can move now." Juele was grateful for the release. Her flesh had started to turn to stone from holding the pose so long. She set the basket down and rubbed her arms with marble fingers until the skin softened to life again. Rutaro set the idealized image of Juele aside.

"That's too pretty to be me," Juele said, waiting as her costume metamorphosed back into everyday clothing. Because she was close to Them, and in their sphere of influence, she found herself in a pale green, knee-length dress. The golden-red hair stayed long, so she pulled the tresses around and plaited them.

"Not at all," Rutaro said. "You inspire me, dear Juele, with your youth and energy. But if you prefer a more prosaic image . . ." He caught a falling beam of sunlight and, molding it between his long hands, created a simulacrum of Juele in her dress. "I think you are very pretty indeed. Isn't she, Peppardine?"

"Oh, yes," the figure on the grass said, without moving his hat.

"And graceful as a gazelle," Rutaro went on, suddenly playful. He took the image by the hand and spun it around. It went skipping about the field, throwing blossoms out of a basket hanging from its wrist. Juele was torn between flattery and embarrassment. The watching crowd stared and *ooh*ed.

"Oops," Rutaro said suddenly. He clapped his hands together, and the image vanished in mid-skip. Juele looked around to see why. The chancellor of the School had come out of a building and was walking through the greatly extended courtyard toward them. His red-banded, gray smock flapped in the breeze behind him, making him look like a parrot with ruffled feathers. He wore a flat black cap that shaded his eyes from the sun.

"Good afternoon, chancellor." Rutaro said respectfully. Peppardine sprang to his feet and took off his hat.

"Good afternoon, sir," he said. "Sir," Juele added, timidly.

"Afternoon, lads, lass," the chancellor said. He was a stout, old man with a long nose and a long chin that formed the letter "C" in profile. "Staying out of trouble, are ye?"

"Yes, sir," the two men responded in unison. Juele waited until the chancellor had disappeared over the crest of the rolling field, then turned puzzled eyes to Rutaro.

"You look surprised," he said. "One must always recognize authority when one meets it."

"I thought you were the founders of the School," Juele said. "Why would you have to show deference like that?"

"For all our influence, we must still have structure and organization. The administration of the School gives us that. We respond well to structure, like a painting does to a frame. There is great beauty in well-exercised authority. By the way," Rutaro said, upending the container he'd been working from to show that it was empty, "I'm out of nebulosity. Would you run upstairs and get some more for me out of the cabinet?"

"Of course," Juele said. She set out at a run for the shining building, about a quarter mile away. The rolling grass added a little spring to her pace. She still wasn't one of them, but she was among them. That made her feel happy.

Nebulosity was notoriously changeable in its shape. Juele had to coax a mass of ball bearings into a box, where it promptly turned into a stuffed octopus that overspread the container in every direction. Impatiently, she wrestled it down the spiral staircase and outside.

She blinked up at the glare of orange light that met her as she emerged. Two identical, handsome, dark-haired men in tuxedos stepped forward. One of them took the box out of her hands, and the other hooked his arm through hers. He had a microphone in his hand, and a spotlight illuminated him from high above their heads.

When he talked, it was not to her, but to the shadowed crowd behind the forest of equipment and the camera pointing her way. She couldn't see the Idealists anywhere. He aimed two rows of dazzling white teeth at her.

"This way, young lady, and get ready for the chance of a lifetime!"

Juele stumbled on the steps of a dais and was helped to stand behind a small fuchsia desk beside two other students. Dozens of men and women in workclothes swarmed around her, plastering makeup on her face, straightening her dress, and pinning a huge name card in the shape of an artist's palette to her collar.

"Now!" said the man with the microphone, pointing to the girl at the far end. Juele squinted and recognized Soma. "Tell me . . . the correct term . . . for a polite nuisance."

For once the young woman had lost her aplomb. She was jumping up and down in ecstasy. "Oh, I know, I know! It's a Fortunate Circumstance!" she shouted.

A huge buzzer went off somewhere, and the audience groaned. The master of ceremonies tilted his head in mock sympathy and shot his arm into the air.

"I'm sorry, but there *is* no such thing as a polite nuisance! Thank you for playing!"

A beautiful, blond woman in a blue, sequined dress took Soma's arm and pulled her off the stage. Juele lost sight of her. The man moved on to the male student beside her. "Manolo," he said in a low, intense voice, and the young man trembled. "Give me . . . in order . . . the correct sequence of the color wheel."

"Red, orange, yellow, green, blue, indigo, violet," Manolo recited. The buzzer went off, and Manolo looked shocked. So was Juele. That's how she had always known it.

"Too bad! That's the sequence of the rainbow! The color wheel is a circle and *has* no correct starting point! Juele!" the master of ceremonies said, coming to loom over her as another young woman led Manolo away. He put an arm around her shoulders and huddled almost cheek to cheek with her. The spotlight beamed in her eyes, dazzling them. "Juele, it's all on you now. What . . . was the name . . . of the First Sleeper?"

Juele looked at him in despair, and moistened her lips when he shoved the microphone in front of her. "I . . . I don't know."

"That is absolutely correct! You *don't* know! No one does!" The crowd began to cheer, and perky organ music started playing. More lights swung, illuminating a blue and yellow box, the size of a small house, and an orange curtain. "And now, the time has come," the MC whispered confidentially into his microphone. "Choose your prize. Will it be the box? Or the curtain?"

The crowd began to chant, some for the box and some for the curtain. Juele was bewildered by the noise and couldn't make up her mind what to do. She'd never fallen into the midst of a Game Show Dream before. "Curtain!" shrieked a high female voice she thought was Bella's. "Curtain!" boomed a voice that sounded like Peppardine's. Her throat went dry.

"The curtain," Juele said, quaking with excitement. More music played, and the curtain swept open to reveal the gleaming white towers of the Castle of Dreams. The MC stepped into the widening stage and pointed.

"You have won . . . a commission for the portrait of Queen Harmonia of the Dreamland! Come down, Juele, and claim your prize!" Dazed, Juele barely held herself up as the two women in sequined dresses pulled her down onto the stage. She had won the commission? She, the least experienced student in the school? But it must be true. The master of ceremonies, never stopping to take a breath, told his cheering audience all about it, then handed her a square envelope with a gold seal, a key, and a small velvet bag that jingled. "Here you are, Juele, and remember us all when you're at the top of your profession. This is the first step on the staircase to the stars! Congratulations!" He shook hands with her. There was more mad applause, and the spotlights went crazy, wagging their brilliant beams all over the sky. Juele held up her hands to shield her eyes from the glare of it all.

When she lowered her arms, the meadow was empty and silent except for the *pok* of a badminton racquet hitting a birdie. An elderly telegraph delivery man was wobbling away down the gravel path on his bicycle. Juele was still holding an envelope, a key, and a velvet bag.

Juele watched him ride off, then tore open the envelope. Inside was a square white card beautifully calligraphed in gold: "Please come tomorrow morning at half past ten," and it was signed over a gold crown and cloud with a single name, "Harmonia." It was true. She had really won the commission.

"Rutaro!" Juele shrieked.

Rutaro abandoned his easel and came running. The rest of the Idealists followed, curious about the uproar, and with them the entire crowd of spectators. The whole meadow seemed to contract about Juele until it was the same size it normally would be, but with ten times the people all peering over one another's shoulders. The crowd pushed apart to form an aisle to permit the Idealists to come through without touching them. The mass spread out to make a ring, giving Juele a little breathing space. She was so overwhelmed she couldn't speak. Shaking, she held the card out to her mentor, who read it with raised eyebrows.

"Very nice, my dear, very nice," Rutaro said. He passed it to Peppardine, who smiled at her through his eyelashes and gave it to Helena.

"But what should I do?" Juele wailed.

"What you do best," Rutaro said, blandly, retrieving the embossed card from Von and handing it back to Juele, who clutched it. "Keep on as you have. The queen knows you're not a master illusionist yet. But she sees something in your work that she liked. Concentrate on that."

Juele was not comforted. What was it the queen liked? And what if she couldn't do it again?

Chapter 15

"Hello? Is anyone here?"

Juele's voice echoed up into the rafters of the vast stone chamber, where it was lost in the gloom near the ceiling, forty or fifty feet over her head. She stood just inside the threshold of the entry hall, clutching her art box under her arm. There had been sentries outside, but once inside the castle, she couldn't see a single living soul. The walls and floor were plain, smooth, gray stone, like the sides of a cube. She would not have guessed the castle could be this empty when she'd visited the grounds with the others. Even now the gardens were heaving with people: artisans, tourists, courtiers, and her fellow artists. Juele felt a small twinge of despair. She'd said good morning to all of them, but no one would meet her eyes. Juele was afraid she no longer existed to any of them. She was Out, and it was all because of the queen's letter. The clique could tolerate her becoming intimate with the Idealists, or possibly winning the commission, but accomplishing both piled insult on top of outrage. She was so excited about coming to the palace and seeing the queen, but no one would celebrate with her except Mayrona, who had once again abruptly cut off her congratulations the night before to go to sleep. Mayrona was nice, but her behavior was so strange, not friendly at all. Juele was getting her education and opportunities, but at the expense of companionship. It wasn't at all that she wanted to go home. Perhaps if she could be a different person here, she would be happier.

The worst part was that down deep she felt like a fraud. She didn't deserve any of the good luck that had come her way. She was the least experienced person at the School. What would the queen do when she found out Juele wasn't really an artist yet? Throw her in the dungeon?

"Hello?" she called again, her throat strangled with nerves.

Suddenly, she heard a low rumbling that grew louder and louder as if something heavy was lumbering toward her. A pair of double doors at the rear of the chamber was flung open, and a wide, weighty roll of yellow carpet, as tall as she was, thundered through, unrolling as it went. It bounded toward her. Her heart pounding, Juele jumped out of the way before it flattened her. She watched, wide-eyed as the carpet finished unwinding. Standing on the last six feet was a willowy man in a white wig and a gorgeous, blue silk uniform laden on the shoulders, sleeves, and buttonholes with gold braid. His face was powdered, and there was a black dot next to his mouth. His hand rested on the head of a tall silverheaded walking stick. Juele felt dowdy beside him in her plain pink smock. He stamped the stick on the ground.

"State your business, young woman!"

"The queen sent for me," Juele said, nervously. She remembered her white card and presented it. "I'm her . . . I'm an artist." The man eyed her severely, and his mouth closed down to a minute oval.

"You will refer to her as 'Her Majesty, the Queen,'" he said.

"I'm very sorry."

"I am the chef de protocol. I am to be addressed as 'sir,'" he said, rolling right over her apology like the carpet had over the floor. "You will follow behind me. You will not touch anything. You will bow to royalty when you are addressed by them. You will not speak first. Do you understand?"

"Oh, yes," Juele said. "Sir."

"Good," the man said, beginning to walk toward the open doors. "You will not open any doors that are closed. You will not close any that are open. If you receive anything to eat, you will wait until the senior person in the room has begun before picking up your fork—and you will use the outermost fork, or spoon, at your place setting. You will not mention asparagus. If the ceiling falls in on you, pick yourself up, curtsey, and sit down again. Bodily functions are *never* to be referred to at any time. . . ."

Juele trailed after him, tripping over folds in the rug and the admonitions that fell from the chef de protocol's lips.

". . . And this is the first royal reception room," the official said, leading her through a pair of doors into a large room. Juele didn't think much of it. Surely the king could afford better decoration than steel lamps and pewter ornaments. The walls were paneled in a plain, gray wood. Opposite the doors there was a low dais on which was placed three chairs. There was nothing special about the appearance of the chairs themselves, but they *felt* significant. Juele stopped when the official did. His silk costume had changed to plain gray serge. Juele's dress had started as simple blue cotton, and it remained that way.

"Bow," he said. Obediently, Juele bowed to the empty chairs. Her art case hit her in the knees.

"Good. This way." He beckoned her toward a door at the rear of the chamber, and turned left.

The second reception chamber was much nicer. Large, airy and painted white, it was furnished with carved wooden tables. The chairs on the dais bore simple tapestry cushions. Juele repeated her obeisance, then trotted after her guide to the next chamber.

The official led Juele through chambers whose adornments increased successively in value until she lost count of the number of rooms she had seen. She saw rooms furnished with pierced and embossed tin, enamels and bronze, glittering silver and semiprecious gems, gold and precious stones. The chambers were ornamented, plumed, filled with paintings and statuary, gems, mosaics, fountains, wall hangings, gauzy or velvet curtains, but always the three thrones sat on the dais in precisely the same position as in the first chamber. Juele wondered if they weren't merely going around in a circle, spiraling upwards through higher and higher chords of the same room. The chef's attire changed to fit the setting, growing more glamorous as they went along. Very proper, she thought, for a trusted servant of the king. Her own costume remained modest, growing only a little more stylish or expensive-looking as they progressed.

Occasionally, tour groups passed them, and a tiny girl with golden skin and black hair took their picture with a flash camera. In one corridor, Juele walked under the scaffolding where dozens of men in dusty T-shirts and blue jeans were setting up enormous floodlights. A man in a beret seated below them in a canvas chair shouted at them through a megaphone.

At last they arrived in a room so large and grand that Juele was intimidated by the very ostentatiousness of it all. The floor was a mosaic of solid gold tiles inlaid with lapis lazuli and cut gems. The ceiling resembled the night sky and glittered with stars. At the center of the ceiling was a circle of seven faces with closed eyes, representing the seven Sleepers. In between fantastic patterns of inset jewels, each wall had a silk tapestry borne on a rod between golden bosses shaped like the heads of dragons, unicorns, bears, and lions. The dais stood higher than her head, and on it, the three ornate golden thrones had canopies of red and blue silk velvet suspended from the ceiling by chains of gold with angels clambering up and down them. This was the royal throne room, the center of the castle. She stood on a silk carpet three inches thick in the middle of the room and trembled.

"Wait here," the chef de protocol ordered, and left her.

To calm her nerves, Juele studied the tapestries hanging on the walls. The ones on the side walls were famous throughout the Dreamland, depicting the pursuit of the pegasus and the fighting of the dragon. She'd seen echoes of these images nearer to home, but of course these images were the originals. Things changed in the Dreamland, but there were enough minds that had dreamed of pegasi and dragons that their legend, if not frequent existence, was assured. The tapestries behind the thrones depicted other fantastic sights from the Waking World. Juele picked out televisions, automobiles, space ships, and countless other devices she did not know. All these were superimposed over two huge circles of blue and green. She'd learned in school that the Waking World was spherical, so this must be a map. Juele stared in fascination, wondering how the people at the bottom kept the blood from rushing to their heads. Much better to live in a flat world, where everything was right side up all the time. Well, most of the time.

The edge of the tapestry was twisted, rucking up the picture of a big car with swept-back sides that made it look like a mechanical fish. Juele went over to turn down the corner of the hanging and found that it was hooked over the top of a door hidden behind it. The door was ajar, and a warm glow shone out from the room beyond. Juele peeked through.

The walls of the hidden chamber were painted a warm red, in contrast to the white pillars and ceiling and the rich mahogany of the woodwork around the windows and the fireplace. In the center of the cosy little room was a man seated at a wooden table. A tall bronze lamp over his shoulder projected a round beam onto his hands, which were busy with bits of brightly colored fluff and twists of wire. He had a pipe clenched in his teeth and half-glasses on his nose. His hair was dark, but going white at the temples. Juele thought he was handsome and noble looking. He glanced up, and a pair of direct gray eyes stared into hers.

The glasses, pipe, and feathers vanished, and a tall, pointed crown appeared on his head. His countenance, already regal, became fiercely imperial, and he became twice as large as he had been. Juele clutched her art box. She was in the presence of the king, who, if she was not mistaken, had been tying trout flies until she had invaded his privacy. She trembled and tried to stammer out an apology. Seeing her properly at last, the handsome face changed at once to one more gentle and approachable. His hawk-sharp eyes tilted slightly down in the outer corners, giving them a friendlier shape.

"Why, my dear, who are you?" he asked.

"I . . . Your Majesty, I'm so sorry to intrude."

"Not at all," he said, with a smile. "I was only enjoying myself. What is your name, child?"

"My name's Juele, sire," she stuttered. "I'm an artist—I mean, I'm studying to be—at the School of Light. It's just down the street. I'm trying to find the queen. I thought she would be in here, but she's not. He told me to wait, but the tapestry was twisted." She looked desperately over her shoulder for the courtier who had escorted her, but he had vanished. In fact, so had the door. She had no escape.

"Oh, of course you are an artist!" the king said, taking in her smock with a shrewd eye. "You're here to create my wife's portrait. I know she is very much looking forward to it. First year at the School, eh?"

"First week, actually, sire," Juele stammered.

"Really? Congratulations on the commission, then. I am impressed. You must have considerable talent for one of your years, or for any age. Her Majesty is very fond of your organization. It is very dear to her heart. I am sure she will like you very much."

"I am most honored, Your Majesty," Juele said, warming to him. Her heart was still racing, but she felt much less nervous. The king, for all his imperial majesty, was easy to speak to. "She . . . Her Majesty is expecting me." His Majesty nodded.

"Of course. I look forward to hearing great things about you in the future, Juele," the king said kindly. He waved a hand, and Juele almost jumped out of her shoes at the silent arrival beside her of a royal page. He was dressed in an embroidered cap and the cloud-white livery of the palace. She had no idea how the king had summoned him, or where he'd come from. "Please help this young lady find Her Majesty."

"At once, my liege," the young man said, bowing deeply.

"Girl? Where are ... oh." The chef de protocol glided up alongside them holding his walking stick aloft. He made a grand bow. "Your Majesty, I am so sorry that this inconvenient child interrupted you." Juele watched as the king's face sharpened, and his brow rose higher.

"You are interrupting *us*," the king said sternly, waving a hand. "You let her become lost. She was your responsibility, and you failed. You are excused." The white-wigged courtier jogged backward out of sight. Juele glanced back. The door had not reappeared, but the chef de protocol had taken his king's order literally, and disappeared. Byron turned to Juele. "Farewell, my dear. I look forward to seeing your work."

Juele curtseyed. The page waited a moment, then touched her arm. The king assumed his glasses and pipe once again, pushed the crown to the back of his head, and bent to tie a red feather to an amber bead. Starry-eyed, Juele followed the page toward a blank wall. As the page reached it, a door appeared in the wood paneling and swung open. The king was perfect, her heart sang. He was noble, handsome, and kind, with a keen eye for every kind of detail. She couldn't wait to write to her parents!

Queen Harmonia glided up and back, the long skirts of her amber and gold quilted dressing gown sweeping the floor. Rugs and carpets swirled and eddied in her wake like the surface of a pond behind a swan. A woolly shawl lay draped over her shoulders. Juele found it an odd addition to Her Majesty's wardrobe, but even that homely garment looked magnificent on the elegant person of the queen. Her hair, a deep red-gold, fell unbound down her back. Her creamy skin was just barely touched with peach, and her eyes were aquamarines given life. Juele, looking more-than-usually average that day with light brown hair and tan skin, was overwhelmed by being so close to such beauty and grace. Having asked permission, she had her sketchbook open on her lap and was taking down curves and arcs as quickly as she could bend lines. The dark green, velvet chair in which she sat had been intended for a much larger person than herself. Her feet swung high off the floor, and her back didn't touch the cushions.

The room was as good a setting as a ring for the jewellike beauty of the queen. The long room had been paneled in cherrywood. The floor, of glass-smooth cream marble, was scattered with handloomed rugs in warm, autumn colors. There was a good deal of objets d'art that only enhanced the most lovely presence in the room, that of the queen herself. A narrow porcelain vase showed the same lift and arch of its neck as she did. The gilded tables flanking the window had slim, sleek legs joined at rounded curves to their tops.

"Naturally, the image will be full length," Queen Harmonia said, drawing her lovely, tapering fingers down through the air from the top of her head and off toward some undetermined point near the ground. "It must fit into its place in the gallery. I have ordered a marble alcove, suitably placed for the best light, and out of any drafts. Won't that be nice?"

"Yes, Your Majesty," Juele said. Capturing the queen's grace was difficult. The sketches she'd made so far only showed her movements, not her person, and Juele was barely satisfied with those. She kept the book carefully turned toward her so the queen would not see the clumsiness of her efforts. She was so nervous everything was coming out wrong. "Have you a setting in mind for the image? This room? A garden? A library? A . . . natural setting?"

"Oh, I don't know, dear Juele," the queen said, pausing a moment to consider. "The castle, surely, but whether in or out I don't know."

"You *do* want an illusion, don't you? I'm not very experienced with nebulosity."

"Oh, no, illusion, please. Of course," the queen said, with a smile. She pushed back her hair with her hands. Juele admired a huge topaz ring on her forefinger, and a carved gold band on the third finger of her left hand. "I am familiar with the various art forms practiced by the School, and the innovations they have made. They—you—have enjoyed my patronage for many years now. I chose *you* because of your facility with *illusion*, not woodworking. It's all symbolic, as well. I want my image to be as ethereal as the Dreamland itself. Nebulosity is distressingly down to earth, isn't it?"

"Very often, Your Majesty," Juele said, trying to sound as if she knew what she was talking about. It wouldn't do for a picture of the queen to transmogrify into a set of bowling pins or a box of insurance forms. Nebulosity was one of the few things in the Dreamland where form hardly ever followed function. "Er, even a portrait will change over time, influence and all."

"True. As for initial form . . ." Harmonia turned and paced to the grand window, where she posed with her back to it. "I have not made up my mind. A traditional framed portrait might be nice. But a sculpture has its attractions as well. Or perhaps something really abstract. What do you think?"

"A representative illusion is always the best," Juele said promptly, hearing an echo in the back of her mind from the Idealists. "As close to nature as possible." She saw a grand image of the queen with the noon sun lighting her shoulders and her hair from behind. It'd be so easy. All she'd have to do was copy what she saw. She was so glad the queen wanted symbolism. What a chance to make Rutaro proud of her.

"Really?" the queen asked, surprised. "But what about all the other forms that are possible? Don't you think that impressionistic illusions evoke a greater emotional response."

"I . . . no . . . I don't know, ma'am," Juele said, in a very small voice, feeling herself shrink just a bit more. "I'm new at this." The queen smiled warmly.

"Of course you are, my dear, but you have talent," Harmonia said, in a reassuring, motherly voice. She put her thumb and forefinger to her chin. "Now, let's see. I think a traditional portrait, following all the forms, would be just the thing."

Juele felt as if she had been helped back into her depth. She relaxed a little. "Would you like to be pictured standing or sitting, Your Majesty?"

"I believe that I would like to be seated. More restful to the eye, don't you think?"

Juele nodded. She was ready to agree with anything. With the queen's approval, Juele placed a chair with the fireplace visible behind it. Harmonia sailed over and sank into it with the grace of a leaf falling from a tree. Juele abandoned the abstract lines and started a sketch on a new page. Let's see, she thought, what symbols does one use for a queen? The king had put the world at her feet, so Juele made the hearth rug a rough image of the Dreamland, both homespun and idealized at the same time. Having recently done an image of the Dreamland for class, it was easy to recall the map and replace the lines of topography with embroidery. Art was a particular interest of Her Majesty's, so over the mantelpiece, Juele placed a painting of the School of Light. The Idealists would be pleased when they saw that. Through the hearth, she made visible an image of open, green meadows at noonday. The strong yellow light outlined the edges of the thronelike chair very nicely.

The queen was also a mother. Juele thought for a moment, then put a wreath heavy with ripe pears and apples around the figure's head. It looked a little old-fashioned, but very pretty. At the center of the wreath, Juele limned an image of the full moon, denoting a woman at the fullness of her life. The benevolent silver face was not unlike the queen's below it. The moon was also associated with illusion, most appropriate for the queen, as the School's patroness. She put a cat nursing her kittens at the queen's feet. Juele bit her lip.

Would all these symbols in combination translate well to other media when the portrait changed form?

A man appeared at the door of the study. He wore a spotlessly clean white tunic that buttoned at the neck, over equally pristine white trousers and shoes. Around his neck hung a device consisting of rubber tubes and metal pipes, and he held the traditional black bag of a physician. "Your Majesty," he said, bowing.

Harmonia gestured to him from her seat. "Ah, Doctor Eyebright! I have been expecting you. You won't mind, will you, Juele? The doctor has come to give me a medical consultation."

"No, not at all, Your Majesty," Juele said, erasing part of the wreath. The adoring cherubs she had placed on either side of the queen's chair looked unhealthy. But the queen did not. She wondered what could be wrong.

"And what appears to be the problem?" the doctor asked, solicitously, sitting down in the chair opposite his patient. He had a strong, sympathetic face with large brown eyes and large ears, most suitable for his profession.

"Oh, Doctor," the queen said. She leaned toward him with her hands clasped, in great distress. "I have a stabbing pain in my left leg. There are blisters on my tongue, and I run a slight fever in the evenings. And there are other symptoms. The small of my back feels as though it is twisted out of shape. And my feet!" She went on to enumerate her aches and pains, until it sounded to Juele as if Harmonia never spent a moment out of agony. Her heart went out in sympathy to the queen.

"Um-hm, um-hm, um-hm, I see," Doctor Eyebright said, ponderously. He looked at Juele, who tried to make herself smaller in the big chair. She didn't think she ought to be here during a private examination, even though the queen had asked her to stay. The doctor didn't appear to mind an onlooker. His eyes lit on the sketchpad. He gave Juele a kindly smile and turned back to his patient. "And is this something you might have had before?"

"No, not yet. I think it is Hopkirk's fandango," Queen

Harmonia said, definitely. "I have consulted several medical texts, and they were all agreed."

"I see," the doctor said, and produced a small, shining glass rod from his bag. "Open your mouth, please? Yes, I see." He put the rod under the queen's tongue. Juele watched with interest. Under the doctor's care, the queen began to look less tense, even appearing to enjoy herself. Juele had to stop herself from putting all sorts of medical paraphernalia into her sketch. Hopkirk's fandango sounded serious, but the doctor seemed to be a competent and sympathetic man. One consultation ought to clear it right up.

Doctor Eyebright waited a moment, looking at his wrist, then retrieved the glass stick. The queen waited, her large eyes anxious, as he put it away in his bag.

"I don't think you have anything you need to worry about, Your Majesty," the doctor said, taking her hand and giving it a paternal pat.

"But the ache in my leg? It's terrible."

"Tell me about it again, Your Majesty," Doctor Eyebright said, leaning back in his chair with a thoughtful expression. *Perhaps a second consultation*, Juele thought, *to clear up severe pain*. The queen began once more to describe the very quality of the stabbing feeling she felt, how often, and where it was. The doctor tented his fingers together and nodded gravely as she spoke. His brown eyes were always on his patient. This was quite a long consultation, Juele thought, noting down bunches of grapes and gentle cows at the margin of her drawings. Her uncle hadn't had such a comprehensive examination when he'd broken his leg. The queen must be chronically ill, to judge by how long it was taking to heal her. Such an examination ought to cure anything, but queen didn't seem to be feeling any relief. Juele began to think that the others might have been right when they told her Harmonia was a hypochondriac. Juele's respect for the queen dimmed ever so slightly, although she still felt devoted to Her Majesty for her understanding and acceptance. No matter what her

personal quirks, she had given Juele this job, and Juele
was grateful.

"Mother, you must see the design for my gown!" A
pretty young woman with black hair came into the room
holding an armload of moonlight and diamonds, or at
least that was how it looked to Juele from where she sat.
The tall girl shook out one of the swatches of pearl silk,
and it became the front panel of a glorious wedding
dress. She held it up to herself and turned this way and
that so the queen could look at it. So this was Princess
Leonora, Juele thought. The princess stopped twirling
as she became aware of her mother's visitors. "Oh, I am
sorry. I didn't realize you had company."

"Doctor Eyebright was just leaving, dear," the queen
said. The doctor rose and bowed.

"I will come back later, Your Majesty," Doctor Eyebright said. "Four o'clock, our regular afternoon appointment." He opened his black bag, stepped into it, and
pulled it in after himself.

"Thank you, dear Doctor," the queen said, absently.
"And this is Juele, dear, who has come to capture my
image."

"How nice to meet you," Princess Leonora said, pleasantly. "Mother has been looking forward to having her
portrait done."

Juele smiled back and tried not to stare. The queen's
daughter was a beautiful woman. She was not that much
older than Juele, although her graceful carriage made her
seem timeless. She was slim and dainty, with long tresses
of shining dark hair that streamed down her back and
ended in a little curl. Her eyes were a bright green. Too
blue a green for the golden room. Juele saw her realize it, and the eyes changed to a more hazel color that
went better with the decor. The change was real, Juele
recognized with a small shock. Leonora had a superb
control of influence. Such command was only fitting for
the daughter of the queen and heir to the throne, but
it was amazing to see it in person. No one in all of Wandering had strength of mind like that.

"The dress is quite exquisite, dear," Harmonia said, smiling. She stretched out a hand, and Leonora came to bend down for a kiss.

"It's only a sketch, of course," Leonora said, fluttering one side of the silk. Taking a closer look, Juele saw that the piece was a kind of illusion. Underneath the semblance of cloth and jewels, it was only tissue paper covered with colored pencil marks showing darts and stitching lines. "This is as far as Berthe got. She'll continue to work on it later, when I come back from Bolster."

"Are you sure you should go?" Harmonia asked, full of concern. Leonora knelt beside her.

"Mother, I know the exhibit is important to you, but I will be bored to *pieces* if I wait here while it's all being set up. If Berthe had been able to work on my dress, I'd stay." Leonora rose and swirled around the room, holding out the paper skirt. The designer had covered the expanse of silk with rosebuds and orange blossoms picked out in diamonds, and ivy in sprays of long, oval pearls. The dress was going to be absolutely beautiful, and just laden with *symbolism*. Juele sighed with satisfaction. "We'll be back in time to attend the opening."

"Ah, here you are," said a deep male voice. "Your Majesty, good morning."

"Dear Roan, come in!" the queen said, holding out her hand to the tall man at the door. He had dark hair and wide gray eyes, and a strong, angled jaw that made Juele want to draw it. His dark brows angled upward, too, from a straight nose in the middle of his thin face. So this was Roan. Juele studied him. He was rather handsome, with his gray eyes and broad shoulders. She had heard a lot about him from other students. He was the one who had some kind of special connection to the Sleepers. Word around the School had it that he never changed at all, under any kind of influence. That would make him a good artist's model, since it would be so easy to pick up the next day if one didn't finish. She wondered if the image itself would shift, and what it would look like when it did.

"Roan, you must see the design for my dress!" Leonora said, starting to turn toward him with the sparkling fabric against her chest.

"Oh, no, dear," Harmonia said, twitching a forefinger at her daughter. A peach-colored haze sprang up around the princess, obscuring the gown panel from view. "That's bad luck. He can see it on your wedding day. Not before." Leonora frowned, and her brow took on a mulish look, complete with gray donkey's ears. Juele giggled, then ducked her head, abashed. She was witnessing a private moment between mother and daughter, something that would never be repeated in public. Leonora's expression changed almost at once to one of elfin mischief, and she was restored to her beauty. She gave Juele a sly grin, daughter to daughter. Juele felt honored.

"All right," the princess said, folding up the length of silk until it was no more than a small handful of tissue paper. She stowed it away in the air. "I'll *describe* it to him."

"That's fine, dear," the queen said, imperturbably. "The tradition says nothing at all about that."

Roan bowed to the queen, then addressed his fiancée. "I have made all our travel arrangements. We'll be on the same train as the party from the Ministry of History, but in your private car. It will be hitched just in front of the caboose before you arrive."

"That's splendid," Leonora said. "I'll be traveling very light. Only two or three trunks, plus six servants."

"Practically by yourself," Roan said, with a droll expression, and a small fish on a string appeared above Leonora's head.

"Very nearly," Leonora said, refusing to jump for the bait. The fish swam away in the air, pursued by a winged cat. "It means you hardly have to share me with anyone. Mother, I wish you were coming with us."

"Oh, no, thank you, darling," the queen said. "I do hate traveling out of town. There's too much *outside* out there."

"We would see to your personal comfort, Your Majesty," Roan said.

"You are very good, Roan, but I plan to enjoy myself here," the queen said. "I hope you have a lovely time."

"I must get back to my packing," Leonora said. With a kiss for her mother and another for her fiancé, the princess swept out. She *was* lovely, and by the expression on Roan's face, Juele wasn't the only one who thought so. He caught her watching him and gave her a kindly look.

"So you are one of the artists from the School," he said. "May I peer over your shoulder and see what you're doing?"

"Only if she doesn't feel shy about it," the queen said. "You can tell him no if you would like, my dear. His inquisitiveness is purely professional."

Juele kept her eye on him as he walked around behind her and looked at her sketchbook. She half expected his nose to grow ratlike whiskers as he indulged his curiosity, but he didn't change in any way she could observe. She'd have to wait for a wave of influence to see if the rumors about him were true or not.

"It's very interesting," Roan said, pointing at the ornamentation Juele was crafting with such care, "but what's all this?"

"May I see, too, my dear?" the queen asked. Juele laid her sketchbook flat and made the drawing stand up so it was visible to both of them. The queen's image was present in the center, glowing from within with a golden light as befitted a mother-goddess figure. The arbor of vines, heavy with grapes, apples, and pears, hung above the queen's head. The moon blessed her with its silver light. Angels flew to either side, supporting baskets of fruit and grain, baby animals, and small images of various kinds of artwork. The colors were rich and summery, with plenty of gold ticking the arms of the thronelike chair, the pillars, and the angels' wings, to reflect the gleam of the queen's hair.

"I can *almost* see myself in there," the queen said, her mouth pursed with amusement that brought out her cheeks in dimples. "What is all the rest of it?"

"Symbols," Juele said, wishing she had Rutaro's

eloquence to express herself. "Representing your attributes and offices." The queen's brows drew upward.

"Oh, my dear, there's too much in the frame. It
detracts from the image."

"No, ma'am," Juele said boldly. "They're meant to
enhance Your Majesty. Symbols found in nature and legend that are appropriate for royalty and . . . and moth-
erhood . . . and art." Roan's face was very still, but Juele
saw laughter in his eyes. She felt hurt. The queen shook
her head gently.

"All right," Juele said, feeling her cheeks burning with
shame. She peeled away the wreath, scrubbing it out of
existence, and sent the angels away. But, the image
looked so bare like that!

A wave of influence came rolling through the castle.
Juele felt it coming and wished she could enjoy it. The
room's decor altered to blond wood and cerulean blue
hangings. The queen became tall and willowy with long,
pale gold hair. In contrast, the figure in the little sketch,
now reclining on a velvet couch, bloomed with rolls of
voluptuous flesh and hanks of thick, dark hair. Her classic
stola slipped off the lush breasts and became a white
drape hiding only the figure's lower body. Juele was
embarrassed. She smashed the image flat on the sketchbook, crumpled the strands of light together and stuffed
them back into her workbox. It wasn't a true image after
all. She'd have to try again.

"I think that's enough for today," Harmonia said, rising
and offering a hand to Juele. "You have done so much.
You must be tired."

Juele started to protest. She wanted badly to make
another attempt, to prove to the queen that she was up
to doing the job properly, but the kind words were a
dismissal. She didn't dare protest.

"I'm sorry to rush you, but I haven't a moment more
time today," Harmonia said, trying to soften her words.
"I have a dress fitting of my own—for the opening at
the School, my dear. And another consultation with the
doctor. He is so sympathetic, don't you think?"

"Oh, yes," Juele said, hastily gathering up her paraphernalia. Disgrace and dismissal. She'd have to go back to the School and say she had failed.

"Good," Harmonia said. "Will you come back Monday at the same time? Will that be all right?"

"Oh, yes, ma'am," Juele said, relieved. She hadn't lost her commission after all! "I'll be here, ma'am. On the dot."

Chapter 16

Rutaro sat on a hard, orange, plastic chair in the linoleum-floored corridor, kicking his feet and drumming his fingertips on his thigh. Juele sat in a gray chair next to him, wondering why he was so nervous. He was one of the founders of the School. Surely the review board would approve his idea. She still didn't know what that idea was, but he had brought along an armload of rolled blueprints and a portfolio stuffed full of papers, suggesting many late nights preparing for the interview. For once he looked like any other student at the school, a fresh-faced young man with high cheekbones and a wing of glossy, straight brown hair over straight brows and serious gray eyes, wearing a pale blue, button-down shirt, khaki trousers, and tan lace-up boots underneath his white smock. No, Juele amended her thought, he looked like the *ideal* of any other student. He was too polished, too bandbox-fresh. Juele smiled and shook her head. None of Them could *ever* look like ordinary people.

Waiting gave her too much time to worry about her problems with the queen's portrait. Rutaro had been too nervous that morning to talk technique, and no one else wanted to talk about her commission. She hated to make an unadorned portrait, when the queen deserved to have the best. Maybe Mayrona had some ideas, although symbolism was not her strong suit, either. Juele tilted the back of her chair up against the lockers and rested her head on the cool enamel paint. Maybe she could look in the library, or wander the School's galleries for some inspiration.

Besides Juele, Rutaro had brought along a few more

supporters to help him in his presentation. Manolo and Sangweiler, frequent visitors to the inner circle discussions in the Ivory Tower sat in the uncomfortable chairs on Rutaro's other side. Helena's apprentice Borus had come along, too, keeping quietly to himself in a seat across the hall. To Juele's pleased surprise, Gretred had also been asked. That'd put a spoke in the wheels of the clique, who never could see that the big Wocabahtian was alive, or that she had considerable talent, especially in symbolism and color. She had her nose in a book, only looking up now and again when people came out of the door beside Rutaro. Tynne, the artist who had created the upside-down fountain, made seven. That was a lucky number with its own monumental symbolism. Juele didn't know what difference the size of an entourage could possibly make, but she was willing to back Rutaro up as much as she could.

In the room behind them, Juele could hear the voices of other students as they offered their ideas for graduate projects to the board. She was unimpressed by most of it, dismissing the ideas as substance without style. A pair of young men in snappy suits and carrying linen suitcases bound with leather bands had brought in an entire dog-and-pony show to promote their presentation of an empty tent.

"This is intended to show the emptiness of life," one of the men had announced. He got no further in his dissertation. The board, accompanied by a thousand voices from a studio audience who appeared momentarily in the chamber, booed them loudly. The men had reemerged at the end of a long hook that dragged them out into the hall. The dogs and ponies were never seen again, at least not in that form. Juele suspected they had changed into the winged moneybags that flew out of the room a little later.

One woman wanted to make money appear to grow on trees as a protest against profligacy in government. A serious young man had the notion of putting cell bars on every window in the School. *Small minds*, Juele

thought, listening to the teachers and administrators
drone on about theory and relevance. Some of their
projects were approved, and some of them weren't. The
constant hum of voices was hypnotic, lulling Juele into
a trance.

The door opened again, catching Juele in the middle
of a yawn, and a woman leaned out to beckon Rutaro
inside. He gestured at his papers, which sprang neatly
to his hands, and cocked his head to Juele. She and the
others followed, eager and nervous.

The chamber was dark around them. Seven administrators and teachers in smocks and berets sat with their
hands folded at a long table at the head of the room.
The only light came from dull spotlights illuminating the
faces of the board from below, throwing their eyes and
the hollows beneath their cheekbones into shadow.
Rutaro and the others went to stand beneath another
beam that shone directly down onto a low, raised platform, some twenty feet away from the panel. Juele
tripped stepping up onto it in the dark, and the sound
of her footfall echoed throughout the silent room until
she thought the echo would kill her with mortification.
As the sound died away, she huddled with the other
students in a knot at the rear of the platform. Rutaro
stood forward and put his bundle down on a podium
before him.

The members of the board had muttered among
themselves when Rutaro entered, then fell silent for a
long time, studying him. Rutaro rocked back and forth
with his hands clasped behind his back.

"Well, Rutaro," said the chancellor. He still looked
elderly, although instead of being short and stout, today
he was a big, hearty man with wildly curling eyebrows,
and large, flat hands that he folded together on the
tabletop. The other dons seemed surprised by Rutaro's
presence, but the chancellor regarded him with the same
impassivity he offered to any other student. "Good
morning to ye."

"Good morning, chancellor," Rutaro said, respectfully.

"I am pleased to see you here today. What have you got to show us?"

"I wish to offer my proposal for a graduate project," Rutaro said, projecting his voice to carry to the very edges of the chamber. A susurrus of excited whispers told Juele that they and the board were not alone in the room. There were others hidden in the shadows.

"So I have gathered," said the chancellor, drily, leaning forward over his clasped hands. "And may we hear your idea?"

"Yes, sir," Rutaro said respectfully. He opened his portfolio and propped it on an easel that came into being near his right hand. He threw the cover up and over, revealing the first page that showed a handsome pencil sketch of the Castle of Dreams. Juele admired the detail. Even the tiny flags on the turrets were waving. "Premise: the running of the government is a necessary function in the Dreamland, but I believe that little care is taken with aesthetics, which I believe to be a necessary facet. In other words, the appearance of dreams is left wholly to chance, form following function, without planning or correction except by the minds of the Sleepers themselves. Hence, many of the dreams that we solve on behalf of the Sleepers, nay, all dreaming minds, are unnecessarily ugly. Dreams should be beautiful—all dreams!"

"And what would be the purpose of this exercise?" the chancellor asked, cutting through Rutaro's dissertation. He didn't seem as impressed as the others. Rutaro turned to him earnestly.

"The function of art is to draw importance to worthy concepts and important subjects. Government function tends to be . . . utilitarian. The Sleepers have entrusted us with their most pressing concerns. Is it not appropriate to offer them their solutions in the most beautiful possible representation?

"You might argue," Rutaro continued, "that the castle already looks perfect, but it's not so. Even though it is the heart of the Dreamland, there are many prosaic elements to it. I feel that it should be an ideal that surpasses human nature, an ideal beyond the ordinary imaginings of all the minds of the Waking World!" Juele felt the latent energy in his voice filling her with excitement, like charging a battery. Manolo, Borus, Sangweiler, Tynne, and Cretred nodded, their eyes brimful with enthusiasm.

"My project will be to surround, nay, *replace* the Castle of Dreams with a grand illusion showing the ideal of the castle as it ought to be, as a symbol of all the Dreamland, and the ideal toward which we should strive."

Gasps came from all over the dark room. Juele clasped her hands together in excitement in the sleeves of her smock. This was big thinking, just the kind of thing she would have expected from an Idealist.

"And how do you mean to accomplish this goal?" the chancellor asked. Rutaro's eyes were lit from within as he flung over sheet after sheet on his drawing pad.

"I intend to wrap the capital around with a single, enormous illusion. The size of the canvas will allow everyone who views it to share in the appreciation of beauty." The images protruded out from the surface of the paper. The first showed a faint black-and-white tracery overlaying the castle, which was shown in color. The tracery started with a few frames set at various points around the castle grounds, until the keep was surrounded by a ring of tapestries. Each subsequent image had more detail filled in: first color, then texture, and, finally, life. Light shone upward from the ring, growing until it encompassed the castle. Where it touched, stones acquired sharper angles, trees stood straighter, and flowerbeds filled in. The very colors were as pure as slices of rainbow. Rutaro turned the easel so it lay flat, and the image stood up in three dimensions, a perfect little model. "I will show the Dreamland how nature can be improved in beauty and form, correcting what is wrong, and enhancing the light. It is my hope that seeing the ideal will inspire the common Dreamlander to reach higher for the goals that will best serve the Sleepers and every mind in the Waking World." On the last page, the castle itself was invisible within the walls of Rutaro's illusion. Rutaro pointed at the final image with a stick. "Once again, the School will lead the way—art leading reality to enlightenment."

The unseen crowd along the walls broke into spontaneous applause. Rutaro smiled, flexing the stick between his hands. Juele stood in the shadows, absorbing the beauty of the revised image.

"I see," the chancellor said, nodding. "It sounds most interesting, Rutaro."

"This is a big project, worthy of both the School of Light and the capital of the Dreamland," said a woman with a warm, musical voice. "I say he should go ahead."

"I think it sounds too ambitious," said a narrow-faced academic at the far left of the board. Juele thought it was a woman, but wasn't positive. "We would like you to report on the project in stages."

"Oh, no," growled a deep-voiced trustee, raising his eyebrows. "Hear about a half-crafted illusion? How tedious. We want to see it when it's done!"

"Should we make him stand or fail on a single viewing?" the chancellor asked, lowering his eyebrows almost to his nose. "He is not a beginner. He will ask for review if he requires guidance. I say, proceed."

Rutaro laid a hand on Juele's shoulder and leaned over to her. "Let's go." He beckoned to the others.

"But they're still debating whether or not your project is approved," Juele whispered back. "Shouldn't we stay?"

"No, they'll let us know what they decide when they're ready," Rutaro said, gathering up his blueprints and folding them down into a small book filled with cramped handwriting. He put it into the pocket of his smock. "They want it. You can tell at once when they *don't* like something." He drew a forefinger across his throat with a *snick!* sound. "No, they're intrigued. They're just as likely to demand a time-limit, too, and I don't want them to surprise us and say it must be done before it is. We can start at once. Come on, this will

be fun." They left the room quietly while the board went
on with its argument.

"Why are we going this way?" Sangweiler asked, as
Rutaro led them through the gate of the quadrangle, out
into the grounds, and down the path leading out of the
school. "We could have just cut through the exhibit hall
and gone into the castle directly."

"Because my project has nothing to do with the *inside*
of the castle," Rutaro shouted, striding on ahead. "It is
to show the ideal of how the castle should appear. My
project will have nothing to do with its inner functioning."

Rutaro led his party out onto the road. The shining
turrets of the Castle of Dreams were visible over the
trees ahead, different yet again, though equally majestic and beautiful. Today they were made of a rosy granite
that sparkled in the sun. The pennants snapped smartly
in a stiff breeze that scattered the clouds into narrow
rooster-tails of white. Juele buttoned up her smock,
expecting to have to walk several blocks—past the entire
shopping precinct—to reach the castle, but to her surprise, the red stone walls were only half a block up the
street.

"Is the castle moving?" Juele asked.

"No, the School is," Rutaro called over his shoulder.
"As we grow in importance to the crown, we approach.
At present, thanks to the upcoming exhibition and Her
Majesty's interest, we are more important to the crown
than most other concerns. When my project is complete,
I hope we will be closer yet!"

As they crossed a side street, Juele glanced down in
the direction of the stores. She could see rows of arcades
and shops crowded together, as if the merchants had
been shouldered aside, perhaps blocks out of the way,
by the school grounds. Juele was proud to be part of
such an important organization that could change the very
face of the city of Mnemosyne.

Rutaro entered the tall, black gates of the Castle of
Dreams as if he was coming in to take possession. As

they had before, the guards on duty saluted him. Juele followed as though in a trance. They saluted her, too.

The students stood on the lane looking up at the great stone keep as courtiers, carters, traveling salesmen, and tour groups angled around to avoid them. Rutaro looked supremely confident. Juele felt very small and meek. The castle was enormous and majestic. For the first time Juele experienced a moment of doubt. How did she or anyone else dare to improve upon the heart of their homeland? What could they possibly do to make it more beautiful than it was? But, no, it was as Rutaro had said: there were subtle imperfections in it. The complex sprawled in all directions. It lacked ideal symmetry. It could be done.

"How are we going to surround the whole thing?" she asked.

"Like this," Rutaro said, gathering them around him with a gesture. He flicked a finger, and a perfect miniature of the keep hovered among them in air. He put his two forefingers down just inside the castle gates and drew them out and around until they met again at the back. Bright lines of light followed his fingers, until the whole building was surrounded by a ring of white light. The glow grew until the castle seemed to be a beautiful toy encased in a glass globe. The glass globe itself acquired an image of the castle, but it was castle plus one, castle to the nth degree. Gradually, the glass skin melded with the real thing, covering the flaws and enhancing the best features until it all shone like a big rosy jewel.

"It looks beautiful," Juele breathed.

"That," her mentor said with satisfaction, "is the whole idea."

"Simple, when you think about it," Manolo said, peering at the floating castle. "I wonder why no one else has done it."

"Because," Rutaro said, "no one else has thought of it."

❖   ❖   ❖

Rutaro took them on a walk all the way around the building at a distance of a couple hundred feet to survey the terrain. He was possessed of boundless energy, and Juele was fed by his enthusiasm. They walked and walked and walked, surveying and making notes, but she didn't feel the least tired or footsore. The others were as excited as she was.

"It will be a lot of work," Tynne said, her cheerful face aglow, "but what a showpiece it will be."

"My intention is to have this ready for the opening of the exhibition," Rutaro said, as they returned to the front entrance. "I know that does not seem like very much time, but it will be enough. All of your names will be added to the acknowledgments," he added, graciously. "For now, let us begin. We will set the framework for the whole piece. I am counting upon you. You will all follow my lead, but we are working on this as a coherent group, with a single vision." Juele thought that sounded rather as if he was trying to start a new Seven of his own, with himself as its head.

"What about people?" she asked.

"We will enlist more assistants as soon as the initial sketch is in place," Rutaro said. "At first, there will not be a whole ring of canvases around the palace, but focal points in specific places, to catch and lead the eye to the next one."

"No, I mean, people," Juele said, gesturing at the crowds that bustled around them. "Will we be including moving images?"

"As needed, as needed," Rutaro said, thoughtfully. "Yes, of course. A building without inhabitants might as well be a mountain or a mushroom. Excellent observation, Juele. Excellent."

Juele felt a flush of pride and amazement. He had accepted one of her suggestions. Gretred brought a friendly fist around and chucked her on the shoulder.

"Let me begin upon the initial sketches. I am dividing the area into six, one for each of you to oversee," Rutaro said, taking a pencil out of his smock pocket, "as

I will oversee all of you." The little model of the castle divided into six roughly equal, pie-shaped sections. "We must begin at the reception point for most visitors to the castle." Rutaro spun it so the entrance was facing him and started to sketch on the air.

The pencil left thick black lines hovering in space. Juele watched as the few spare lines became high-peaked Gothic doors, deep relief carvings on the panels deftly drawn, without a curlicue out of place. The ones the castle had at present were of plain, heavy, hewn wood. They looked as though they were meant to be Gothic in design, but the Sleeper or Sleepers dreaming the palace hadn't quite finished the thought. Juele thought they looked nice, but not majestic enough for the Castle of Dreams. Rutaro's vision was much better. He was assisting the Sleepers to make their dream come true.

"Manolo," he said. The intense young man came forward and lifted the delicate sketch by one side. The lines wavered a little, too thin to stand up well against the sunlight.

"Get that propped up, secure it with a few lines and scribbles," Rutaro said, sketching furiously on the next panel. "We'll begin to fill in the sketches as soon as the preliminaries are done." He dashed down irregular lines peppered with squiggles and spots that became the east gardens and the Royal Maze. Juele was astonished that he could do so much from memory. Strokes of the pencil suggested exotic flowers and trellises, statues, fountains and ponds with birds sitting on the surface and on the limbs of the sculptures. Inspiration lit his eyes as he kept drawing until the image was more than twenty feet wide. It was as lovely a landscape as she had ever seen.

"Gretred!" The tall girl started at one side and began to roll the image into a tall cylinder to move it.

A heavy-featured man in a humble, blue suit who had been hovering on the grass at the perimeter of their little group finally made up his mind and came over to speak to them. He homed in on Rutaro, whether for his official-looking white smock or his air of authority. He took off his hat.

"I beg your pardon," he said. "I am looking for Royal Geographer Romney."

"You must enquire in the castle," Rutaro said, pointing to the doors with the point of his pencil. He went on drawing. The man walked a few paces into the court-yard, looked at the castle, looked at the sketch Manolo was securing in place with scribbles from his own stick of charcoal, and came back again.

"But, isn't this the castle?"

"No, this is not the castle," Rutaro said, with an eye-brow raised into his hair. "It is Art."

"Don't know nothing about Art," the man said dubi-ously, comparing the two portals again. But he obviously knew what he liked, because he asked, "Could I please be announced? I've got an appointment. I've come a really long way."

Juele giggled behind her hand. Rutaro's illusion was already having the effect he'd wanted. People were mistaking the ideal image for the castle, dismissing the real thing as not being perfect enough.

"I regret that I cannot help you," Rutaro said, haughtily.

"Dang it, another Displacement Dream," the man said, spitting on the grass. "Look, let me in. I'll find my own way."

With a heavy sigh, Rutaro erased the lines that held the illusory doors latched, and redrew the right one to appear open. The whole image trembled for a moment. Juele was afraid it might collapse. Manolo jumped to secure it with a few strokes of his own, then went on drawing guy lines to stake it into the ground. Rutaro continued on with his large sketch. Juele and the other three students watched in fascination as a huge stable took shape. Using complicated perspective, Rutaro man-aged to suggest individual stalls with horses leaning out, grooms walking up and back, and the double-door of a smithy with the smoke from the forge puffing out from the open top half. Rutaro drew in the raised arm and sweating face of the smith with a few quick lines.

"Sangweiler," he said.

The bearded youth gathered up the stables and made off to the left. Tynne got the lawns and the huge glass wall of the ball room; Borus, the solar tower and fountain gardens. Juele held her breath, waiting for her turn. Rutaro swept down a number of vertical lines, crossed them at the top with horizontal lines, and described a small half-oval in a large blank space. Juele was dismayed as she recognized the kitchens, workshops, and postern gate, the most utilitarian and least pretty section of the castle. Of course, she was the youngest and most inexperienced of the group, she told herself. Her disappointment was not lost on Rutaro. He took her arm and leaned close, his intense blue eyes boring into hers.

"I'm trusting you," he said, solemnly. "This is the greatest challenge of the project. You can make something of this. Anyone can make something pretty prettier. Look for the compelling soul, and bring it out. For me. I know you can do it."

Juele nodded fervently, and Rutaro smiled at her. How could she refuse after that? She set to work folding up her share of the tapestry. She couldn't wait to get started. She'd make the kitchens beautiful if she had to take lessons from interior designers and turn them inside out!

"Excuse me," the man said, leaning out of the line drawing of the door. "I can't seem to find the rest of the castle."

"It's over there, man," Rutaro said, impatiently, pointing at the castle keep. "Please go over there. It's only a hundred feet!"

"Oh, no, I know it's one of those detachment things," the man said, dubiously. Juele was beginning to think the man was a nuisance, meant to interfere with them getting anything done. But he seemed like a real person who was genuinely in distress. "I'll go over there, but the whole thing will actually be over here. I know how it works. Why does it always happen to me? My

wife never has Displacement Dreams." Rutaro closed his
eyes and shook his head. His left hand gathered up light
behind his back.

"Look there," Rutaro said, pointing behind the man.
"What a lucky coincidence! Here comes the Royal Geographer now!" The stranger turned around, squinting. A
figure began to take shape out of the light behind Rutaro.
With a flick of his wrist, he tossed the mass through the
image of the door. It formed into a short, slim man with
curly hair, walking toward them, carrying a large rolled
canvas meant to be the Great Map of the Dreamland.
Juele had never met Minister Romney, but knew that
he, or she, was reputed to be good natured. Rutaro must
have known all the rumors about the Royal Geographer's
character. The figure came toward them smiling. The
stranger turned back, with a confused look on his face,
and breathed with relief when he saw the simulacrum.
Juele thought it looked like an older version of Rutaro,
but realized the stranger wouldn't know the difference
between it and the real minister.

"Master Romney, I am Folbert from Middle Doze in
Somnus," said the visitor. "I came to ask for official
intervention from your office."

"What seems to be the problem, my friend?" asked
the simulacrum in Rutaro's voice.

"Both Upper Doze and Lower Doze are trying to level
out until they're at the same height above sea level as
we are. We like things the way they are, Minister. We'll
all be one big Doze if this keeps on. What can we do?
Will you help us?"

"He already sounds like a big doze, if you ask me,"
Manolo whispered to Juele with a mischievous light in
his eyes. They grinned, listening to the false Minister
carry on, sounding just like one of Them.

"My friend, try to accept the changeable nature of the
Dreamland," said the pseudo-Romney, unscrolling his
map so the stranger could see the section that referred
to Somnus. Rutaro's capacious visual memory had not
failed him; there in a corner near the border of Swenyo

were three dots marked "The Dozes." "There will be times when the Sleepers themselves decree that your three villages will rise or fall or combine. The beauty of change is that there is no right altitude and no wrong altitude for Doze to take. Indeed, there's only the right *attitude*."

"Attitude?" the man asked, puzzled.

"Go on, my dear," Rutaro said, flicking a hand at Juele. She picked up her sketch and started walking around the perimeter of the keep. Juele was disappointed not to be able to see what happened to the stranger from Somnus. She found the spot where Rutaro had taken his reference to the rear of the castle and planted her tapestry there. The sun was not quite as strong behind the postern gate at that hour of the afternoon, so the sketch held its shape quite nicely as she painted lines along the bottom and perimeter to hold it in place. She hurried back to the entrance. Manolo had begun to fill in details on the door frame. She hoped he wasn't going to tear himself open again.

"Ah, Juele," Rutaro said, beckoning her over. "I have a most important job for you. Would you please take this around the castle grounds. It will tie together all the main canvases. A lifeline, if you will. Once connected, it will carry the flow of energy to every part of the tapestry."

Juele took it and started walking, letting the thin line of white play out behind her. As she joined the various canvases together, they took on a greater coherence, looking more as if they were part of the same structure. Juele had wondered how Rutaro was going to give such a sprawling illusion continuity.

The reel of light played out just as she reached her starting point beside the gates. The simulacrum was still talking. The man was listening, rapt with enlightenment. Manolo stood hidden behind his work, listening with a huge grin on his face. The other students had returned, too, and were enjoying the show. Rutaro stood a few paces away from it. He'd given the simulacrum a sufficient reality to continue on on its own and promptly lost interest in the subject. He was concentrating on another portion of the project.

". . . To comprehend your place is to make your portion of Doze the superior one. You will no longer be acting out of ignorance, but in supreme reverence for love and beauty, in service to the Sleepers. Will that help you?" the figure of Romney said, winding its speech to a conclusion. The man beamed at him. He looked as though he wanted to shake hands, but Romney didn't extend his in return. Instead, Folbert clutched his hat in both hands, and backed away, bowing.

"Yes, Minister. Thank you, Minister!" With one nervous, happy look over his shoulder, the Somnusian set off down the path. The students waited until he was out of earshot, then broke out laughing.

"Should you have done that?" Juele asked Rutaro.

"He was pestering me," he said, offhandedly, winding light between his fingers like a knitter with a skein of yarn. "Now he is happy, and the most important thing, he has gone away."

Chapter 17

It had become a nightly ritual for Juele and Mayrona to talk over the events of the day as they got ready to go to sleep. The roommates had little time to spend together. Besides a full schedule of classes, Juele was working on the queen's portrait and Rutaro's project, playing afternoon sports in the broad field near the School gate, attending occasional lectures on art history at the gallery, and participating in earnest discussions nightly in either the Ivory Tower or the coffeehouse. Still, she missed having friends in whom she could confide. Mayrona was the closest to that kind of friend Juele had, but she, too, was constantly busy with her classes and her offering for the exhibition. In between those, she was rarely to be found around campus.

Their little room was becoming filled with half-finished images and sketches from homework or ideas they were working out for the exhibition or, in Juele's case, that were assigned to her by Rutaro. Surrounded by reminders of all the things she did during the day, Juele no longer saw the dowdy dormitory walls, although the inadequate bathing facilities continued to be a challenge.

"What did you say?" Juele called, over the groaning of the pipes as she washed her face in the sink. No matter what her new status was as Rutaro's favorite, the School's tyrannical presence held sway in the Garrets. However Juele concentrated, the dull and awful fixtures remained. The necessary was always terrible, whether it was a thundermug, a hole in a board, or a flush toilet with a gurgling floor underneath it. Juele used what measure of influence she was capable of to keep the hem of her nightclothes and her feet from touching the always damp floor. The shower, when it was a shower, was also unspeakable, smelling of mildew or worse. She was grateful when the facilities actually had a door or a curtain. When they didn't, she or Mayrona would turn her back to give the other one privacy. The sink was the least appalling item, even when it was no more than a bucket. "Why are all the vital fixtures so *ugly*?"

"So we'll look for the beauty of the natural world and appreciate it when we see it!" Mayrona shouted back, with a giggle in her voice. "So we will concentrate on externals instead of internal comforts! So we won't spend all our time in here!"

Juele pulled open the wooden door, which screeched a protest, and leaned out. "As if I'd spend one second more in here than I have to," she said, wiping her face with a towel. "I cannot wait to get past the formalities, when I've achieved enough education to live in nice surroundings instead of squalor."

"Oh, me, too," Mayrona exclaimed, sitting on her bed, brushing her curly chestnut hair with a round-backed brush. "I said, if you can squeeze in any more activities, Festy would like to speak to you tomorrow. He was very happy to hear that you'd be willing to take outside jobs. Since you were chosen for the queen's commission, you can get higher rates than an ordinary beginner. He could fill all your spare time with paying work."

"I am running out of spare time," Juele said with a laugh. She hung the rough towel on the iron hook next to the cracked mirror. "Not that I'm unhappy about being busy, but my professors are pressing me to put something in the exhibition. I don't know if with all I'm doing I'll have time to do anything."

Mayrona shook her head. She put away the brush and curled up with her teddy bear in her arms. "Oh, you don't have to put in anything of your own this time. I think they'll understand. You'll be showing the queen's portrait, after all."

"But I want to," Juele said, kicking her slippers off

under her bed. "The portrait's less my ideas and innovations than hers. I won't be able to show anyone what I think, how I work."

"Don't underestimate yourself," Mayrona said with a smile. "I am sure your personality will shine through. What are you doing on Rutaro's great project?"

"For the last two days I've just been preparing canvases," Juele said, plumping down on her thin mattress. She felt awkward going into too much detail, since Mayrona wasn't being included on the initial stages. As she had promised, Juele had asked Rutaro to allow her roommate to participate, but Rutaro had said bluntly, "not good enough." Juele had made excuses to Mayrona, but continued to press him to let Mayrona come in later when the time came to fill in predesigned sections of the tapestries. No matter what Rutaro thought, May was more than good enough. She could bring a genuine vitality to the images. Juele swung her legs up and threw her dowdy coverlet over them. "I hope it will liven up soon. How is your Life and Sound project going for the exhibition?"

"Not too badly," Mayrona said abruptly. "Good night." She reached for the light. Juele jumped up out of bed and caught her hand.

"No, please, May, don't go to sleep," Juele begged. "Talk to me, please. You've done this every night. Have I done something to offend you? Is it because you wanted a room of your own?"

"No, you haven't done a thing," Mayrona said, troubled. She looked as if she couldn't make up her mind whether to say anything.

"Then, what? Just when I think we're having a friendly conversation, you put out the light!"

"But I *have* to go to sleep first. If *you* do, then you'll find out. Then you won't want to room with me any longer."

Juele sat down on the edge of the narrow bed beside her, still gently holding her hand. "Find out what? Tell me."

"You'll think I'm crazy," Mayrona said, turning her face

to the wall. "All right. I have problems with monsters at night. If I'm alone, the furniture chases me around the room."

"The *furniture*? But that's impossible," Juele said, frowning. "Form follows function. Furniture can't act like monsters. It's . . . inert stuff to put other inert stuff in."

"No, you're wrong," Mayrona said, her eyes wide and haunted. "One night, my footlocker nearly bit my leg off."

Juele suddenly had a mental picture of a dresser pursuing Mayrona, the drawers snapping at her heels, the spindle legs galloping, as closets lining the corridor yawned and snarled. She giggled. "I'm sorry. It just sounds so funny."

Mayrona jerked her hand out of Juele's and shoved it under her pillow. The room widened suddenly. Juele was thrown back onto her own bed, as a seventy-foot chasm appeared in the floor between them. May, on the other side, looked like a copper-haired doll with red cheeks and pouting lips, in a toy bed with a minute china teddy beside her on the pillow. "It's not funny when it happens to you," Mayrona's voice said, faint in the distance. "Good night." The tiny figure turned over.

"I'm sorry. I shouldn't have laughed. That was really insensitive. May?" Juele climbed down off her bed and clambered into the divide, trying to get back to her roommate's side of the room. The walls of the ravine were sharp and steep under her bare feet, and the going was dangerous, lit only dimly by the ceiling lamp. A sharp wind whistled through the canyon, blowing her nightdress against her legs. Juele stopped near a rocky outcropping and looked down. Her stomach lurched as she saw the sheer fall below her disappear into darkness. There was no way down or across. "May?" she called, but her roommate wouldn't say another word. She seemed turned to stone under her blanket. "May, I'm sorry!" Someone in the floor below thumped on the ceiling.

"Hey, hold your noise up there!"

With a rueful look at the silent form of her room-mate, Juele crawled back up and into her bed as quietly as she could.

The next morning, Mayrona was up and out of the room before Juele was awake. Juele looked around. The room was back to its normal proportions. All of the furniture was in place. Not a stick of it was disturbed from its position of the night before.

Overnight, the mood of the Sleeper dreaming Mnemosyne had changed from modern to extremely primitive. Juele set foot out of the school grounds and looked around in shock for the houses. The terrain around her had altered to rough, grassy, rolling green hills, and shaggy-haired mothers in skins and pelts played with their naked, dirty children at the mouths of caves. The predatory traffic was gone, but in its place she feared the threat of animal attack. In a cluster of huge, old trees that lined the hill running alongside her path, she distinctly saw the long, ringed tail of a saber-toothed tiger disappearing among the branches. Small animals, mostly scrawny dogs and colorful lizards, still threw themselves in her path, hoping to pose for her. Juele dodged around firepits and refuse piles containing huge bones as she walked in the direction of the castle.

Not that it resembled a castle as she would normally define one. In approximately the correct direction, at the right distance from the school gates, lay a mountain of the right size riddled with cave entrances. The parts of Rutaro's project already erected were suggested by landscapes daubed on rocks with moss paint and mud. Even thus the canvases looked prettier than the cave complex.

Bearded guards dressed in bearskin kilts and holding spears eyed Juele suspiciously as she approached them at ground level, but let her pass. In the high anteroom, now a stalactite-filled cavern, a page with a deerskin tied around his waist and wearing a bone necklace met her and bowed as gracefully as if he had still been wearing silk. The gallery through which he led her was filled with roughly hewn rocks and paintings in ochre and manganese depicting a hunt.

On leaving the school, Juele's clothes had shifted at once to a loose tunic of small skins stitched together. She didn't like the smell of the cured hides, nor the itch of invisible bugs crawling through the fur of the pelts, but she accepted them as part of the Sleepers' will. This appearance was a new experience for her; caveman stuff had never touched Wandering as far back as she could remember. Her artist's smock was represented by a cluster of pink feathers tied at her shoulder, and her box was a skin bag full of chunks of pigment. Juele wondered how, when the whole of Mnemosyne was in the thrall of an influence that changed it so drastically, the School had managed to stay fixed in a fairly modern, genteel appearance. Its grasp of itself must really be well maintained. However the Idealists had done it, they'd given the School a coherent reality independent of the vagaries of Sleeper's whim. The School was saner than the rest of the city. But then, it was made up by the focus of seven specific minds, much in the same way as the Dreamland itself, instead of millions plus the additional input of the Collective Unconscious.

The queen looked fetching in bone and amber earrings and a leopard sarong. Her body was as rounded as the Grecian vision Juele's first attempt at portraiture had accidentally become, and her shining raven hair was pulled back with a deerskin tie braided with coral beads. To her surprise Juele found it easier to make sketches of Queen Harmonia in the pure, primitive essence of prehistory than it had been in elegant surroundings. Her hands, driving crumbling chunks of charcoal and ochre over a scraped skin, automatically picked up on the symbol of the queen as the personification of the Earth Mother. Juele had to rub out most of what she created, but kept the essence, which was good. In the absence of the usual palatial opulence, Juele was inspired to keep her symbolism to a minimum, and she got a truer resemblance as a result. She was pleased, because she had actually made progress on the basic sketch for the portrait. The queen was pleased with the results, too.

Doctor Eyebright was there again for a consultation. A fire in a firepit at the center of the chamber gave off thick smoke heady with incense, and a complicated sand painting had been laid out on the floor at the south side of the cave. Harmonia sat at her ease on a heap of tiger and wolf pelts on the floor in the light of the small cavern mouth, while Juele sketched and the doctor danced around her, whooping and whirling. A tall bony individual with brown skin, almost naked in a leather loincloth decorated with beads and feathers, the doctor wore plumed bracelets and headband, and a necklet of long fangs separated by beads. He still had his customary calm voice and bedside manner, even when performing the healing ritual. His gyrations came to a halt, and he shook ringed bone rattles at the queen until the plumes on his wrists danced. Harmonia put a delicate hand to her breast and smiled.

"I feel very much better," she said. "I think we'll stop now, dear Juele. I'd like to go out and walk in the garden for a while."

"Do not overdo," the doctor warned her. "Perhaps a short walk, and then a cup of tea. Not too much sun."

"All right," the queen said, with a smile. "Thank you, doctor. I always appreciate your advice."

Juele rolled up the skins she had been working on and waited until the queen had left. The doctor parted the sandpainting on the floor with a finger, preparing to depart. The floor opened up, showing steps down into a mysterious underworld. Juele called out to him.

"Doctor, please, may I ask you a question?"

"Certainly," Doctor Eyebright said. He returned from the edge of the abyss, pulled a large rock around and sat down across from Juele, his eyes meeting hers sincerely. "What seems to be the matter?"

"Is it possible for two people to perceive something really differently?"

"My dear girl, that's the very nature of the Dreamland," Doctor Eyebright said. "Do you have a specific 'something' in mind?"

Juele recounted Mayrona's story and explained the way she had behaved since she and Juele had become roommates. "I'm very worried about her. She really believes what she said."

"Well," the doctor said, flicking out his wristlets with professional briskness. "There are only three possibilities. She's telling the truth, she's lying, or she is mad. It *may* be true."

"But I've never seen anything like that happen. Snapping and, er, pursuing is not a function of furniture."

"Ah, but to her it might be an object of terror, and then it could do all the things that she claims. It could be serious. People have been killed by their fears. Perhaps she was frightened by a chiffonier when she was small. An impressionable age. A single incident can form one's whole life path."

"Oh," Juele said, light dawning on her. "My mother is like that about spiders. I like them, but they're big hairy monsters to her."

"That's exactly what I mean," Doctor Eyebright said. He produced a chunk of ivory bearing a black glyph from his medicine pouch. "Give her this. She can come and consult me. I will help her if I can."

"Thank you," Juele said, clutching the card. "In the meanwhile, I'd better make sure I'm the last one to go to sleep, and the last to leave the room every day, so she doesn't get hurt."

"That's the ticket," the doctor said, rising and patting her hand. "You have a kind heart. Just keep listening to her. That may be all the medical attention she needs."

Juele laughed. "But I'm not a doctor."

Eyebright nodded wisely. "There are many kinds of doctors in the world."

Juele gathered up her things. She had to find her way on her own, for the castle was undergoing yet another metamorphosis. The page was no doubt busy elsewhere, helping show confused visitors around or out of the changing castle. Whatever had caught the attention of the Sleeper slipped away again, bringing Mnemosyne back to a familiar modernity. Juele was able to enjoy the feeling of the passage of energy, and most blessedly, being rid of bugs. She allowed herself a good scratch around the ribs under her smock and went out through the maze of corridors looking for the exit.

It was now quite a busy day. Keeping her art box flat against her, Juele wove through crowds of people carrying suitcases, porters in bow ties and red caps, an infinite line of women in silk saris carrying bundles on their heads, and frantic couriers in short orange tabards, some on bicycles.

In the midst of all the hubbub, she spotted the tall figure of the princess's fiancé, Roan. He wore a dark blue suit and a long, fawn-colored coat, and he played with the hat he carried in two fingers while looking around him for someone. Juele found him fascinating. Except for his clothes he looked *exactly* as he had when she saw him last in the queen's apartments. How completely strange. But being locked in a single form didn't seem to affect him adversely. He wasn't insane; really, he had a delightful personality. If she'd been the princess she might have fallen in love with him, too. Juele regretted enormously not getting to see Roan in the prehistoric metaphor and wondered if he had been wearing skins like everyone else. Her waggish imagination stripped him of his respectable suit and clad him in feathers and a loincloth, like Doctor Eyebright. Juele giggled. Just thinking about it left a grin on her face she couldn't erase as she passed him. Unaware of her private fancies, Roan met her eyes with a polite smile and a bow.

"Ah, there you are, my dear," Roan said, waving to Leonora, as she appeared at the top of a staircase leading down to the Great Hall. "Down here!"

Leonora descended the steps to meet him, followed by a train of a dozen uniformed bellhops each carrying at least two bags. When she was close, Roan created an opaque wall of privacy around them behind which he could sweep her up in a passionate kiss in the midst of the crowd. Leonora smiled up at him.

"Why, thank you," she said. "Everything is ready to go. How do you like my travel ensemble?" She took a step away and pirouetted in a circle. She wore a slim trench coat that covered her from shoulders to calves and was belted tightly about her middle. Her silken and shining golden hair, lying unbound on her shoulders, and her dainty ankles below the hem of the coat made what lay in between mysterious and yet inviting. Roan wished heartily that the long-delayed wedding was over and past already.

"You look as though you belong in a Movie Extravaganza, instead of merely attending one," Roan said, kissing her again. Leonora returned it warmly, then tapped the wall with a finger, dissolving it.

"We can't leave this here," she said. "Bergold will never be able to find us in this crowd."

Indeed, when the privacy curtain fell Roan saw Bergold at once, not a dozen feet away from them, looking frantically about. He was short as usual and thin for a change, wearing a tweed suit that looked too hot for the day. Bergold's eyebrows went up when he spotted Roan. He began to elbow his way through the crowd of bellboys toward them. His cheerful face was pink.

"I've had word from Bolster that sneak previews have begun," Bergold said, in great excitement. "We must hurry and catch the train. We could be missing half the event! Reports have already come back about sightings of curious things in the area, particularly in the surrounding forests."

"Oh, the sticks," Leonora said, dismissively. "Mnemosyne is only a short train ride from Bolster. There is a lot of preliminary hype leading up to the event. We shall get there before the opening is fully under way. We surely haven't missed anything of importance."

"That is true," Bergold said, bowing to her. "My

eagerness springs from my profession. As a Historian,
I like to witness events in full."

"Of course," Leonora said, with a charming grin. "That
way you can screen the whole thing and sift out all the
boring parts so we don't have to bear with them later.
Mother will appreciate your ministry's editing." She
turned to Roan. "Wait until you see the marvelous gown
I have for the premiere."

"I hope I can measure up to your glory," Roan said.
Evening dress was something he wore very well, but what
if the premiere happened to occur in the daytime? "Shall
we go? I have the tickets here in my pocket, and a lim-
ousine waiting in the courtyard."

Leonora gestured to her train of servants, and they
fell in behind her, with Bergold bringing up the rear.
Roan offered her his arm and maneuvered his way carefully through the crowd toward the reception chamber.

"You sound remarkably well-informed about Cult
Movie Evocations," Roan said.

"I have been reading a little in the Akashic Records,"
Leonora said, peeking up at him under the brim of her
fedora. "The more I found out, the more I wanted to
see one for myself."

"I think you will find it fascinating," Roan said. "I have
always enjoyed them. I don't think they reflect much
about the Waking World—at least, I hope not—but they
are good entertainment."

As they reached the great portal, a figure in a gray
uniform with white gloves, white plumed cap, crossed
leather shoulder belts, and boots stepped smartly out
before them and held up a hand.

"Your Highness, Master Roan, Master Bergold," Captain Spar said. The head of the palace guard was a most
trustworthy and brave soldier who had a knack for
appearing where he was needed in the castle, but he had
a tendency toward humorlessness. He was a man of
approximately King Byron's age, and he had served the
royal family for as long as he had existed. Of average
height for a soldier, he had grizzled hair cut short, and

sharp features in a timeworn, bony face. Recently, he had married a charming woman from the Ministry of History.

"Captain," Roan said, pleasantly. "Will you let us pass? We are escorting Her Highness to Bolster this afternoon."

"If Your Highness wishes to go, that's all right," Spar said, "but I have orders from His Majesty. He wants Master Roan to stay about."

"Oh, no!" Leonora cried. "Why?"

"Her Majesty's artists, ma'am," Spar said, grimly. "Some of them is building a wall of art right around the castle. You can see it if you go out there."

"I did go out today," Roan said. "It looked harmless to me."

"Well, His Majesty didn't think so," said Spar. "I don't like it, neither. I don't care for what I can't touch. It's all made out of light, see. They're out there playing with the stuff like taffy, and my hand goes right through it. Suspicious, I call it. If any funny stuff goes on, His Majesty wants a good eye on it, and instructed me to say that you are the man for the job."

"But can't *you* look after it?" Leonora asked, bending the whole of her charm on Spar. "I've always thought you and your guards were equal to every situation. I want Roan to accompany me."

"I wish me and all my guards could go with you *and* Master Roan, my lady," Spar said sincerely. "Between everyone preparing to go off and the artists everywhere, there's been more than enough to keep us all busy watching. All we need is a little more construction and confusion. If there'd be a crisis, I'd be grateful for an experienced man who could keep his head." He nodded knowingly at Roan.

"I can hardly refuse the king's order," Roan said, apologetically. He took Leonora's hand and squeezed it. "You'll have a good time without me."

"But, I don't want to go alone," Leonora said, looking very upset. "It won't be as much fun. Please, my love? I'm all ready to go. I've pared everything down to only four servants. It really isn't worth unpacking. I will go and talk to father. How much more trouble can one more work of art be?"

Roan shook his head with regret. "I had better stay, my dear."

Bergold stepped forward gallantly. "Your Highness, if you would accept a very poor substitute, I would be pleased to escort you to Bolster."

"Would you?" Leonora turned to him with a smile that lit the room with a rosy glow. "Oh, how kind of you, Bergold. It wouldn't be too much trouble?"

"Not at all! It would be a great pleasure."

Roan turned to Captain Spar. "I will accompany Princess Leonora to the train station, then I will be at the king's service. Will that suit?"

Spar saluted crisply. "Admirably, sir. I will report back to His Majesty."

"Booo-ooard!" shouted the conductor, walking up and down the platform and holding open in his big palm the gold pocket watch attached to his vest by a thick gold chain. Porters hurried back and forth with two-wheeled carts filled with hefty suitcases decorated with travel stickers. The squeak of the wheels added a soprano shriek to the baritone hissing of the steam from the brake valves of the train. Women in feathered hats, fur stoles, and high-heeled shoes climbed the iron stairs into the coaches, assisted by men in smart blue and red uniforms. Roan and Leonora stood beside the steps to the royal car staring into one another's eyes.

"I wish you were coming with me," Leonora said. Her hair was very yellow under the tan slouch hat, and her eyes were wide pools of blue. Roan felt as if he could happily drown in them.

"So do I. Enjoy the event for me," he said.

"I'll bring you some images," she promised. "Something you can enjoy . . . personally." The coy tilt of her eyelashes made Roan's heart skip a beat. He swept her into his arms for a deep, loving kiss, as a host of tuxedo-clad violinists seated at the opposite side of the platform broke into heartrending farewell music. The music, and the kiss, were interrupted by impatient tapping on the window of the train car. Bergold, pacing up and down inside, tapped his wristwatch and pointed meaningfully toward the engine. The musicians turned into doves, whirling up around the two lovers in a cloud. Leonora sighed.

"I'd better get aboard before Bergold bursts something worrying," she said. Roan picked up her traveling case and handed her up the narrow stairs. He waited until she was seated in her compartment, then took out his handkerchief to wave good-bye.

With a loud hoot, the train lurched and started to move forward. Leonora began to blow kisses to him through the window, which flew out to touch his cheeks and lips. Their fervor was not in the least disrupted by the glass in-between them. Roan threw a kiss back to her and waved until the train had steamed out of sight.

Ignoring the cries of cabbies, hansom men, and rickshaw drivers offering him transport, Roan walked back to the castle to survey the new project. The School itself had shifted closer to the castle since the morning. As the King's Investigator the phenomenon interested him. So far the School had not come close enough to do any damage to the palace grounds. It certainly made the transit easier for the artists involved with the work of art in progress.

The project was indeed on a massive scale. Frameworks had been put up already much of the way around two sides of the keep, just outside the moat. He could see a half dozen or so smocked illusionists engaged in filling in the panels, and he marveled that they were throwing so much effort into what would be a temporary exhibit. Was he really needed here to help maintain security? How much of a nuisance would it be to have the artists underfoot until the exhibition opened? As Roan skirted an enormous representation of a set of magnificently beautiful double doors on the path leading to the castle entrance, he wondered what the project would be when it was finished. So far it looked remarkably representational.

Chapter 18

Juele sat with Mayrona in the dining hall. The buzz of conversation around her centered on nothing but the great illusion taking shape around the castle. Senior students and habitués of the coffeehouse who had never had much to say to Juele before kept popping around to their table.

"You'd put in a good word for me, wouldn't you, dear?" asked the greasy-haired man with the beret, patting Juele on the hand. Mayrona shot her a veiled look of amusement.

"Honestly, I have no influence as to who Rutaro will want when he wants them," Juele said, apologetically, as she had said over and over again. The greasy-haired man wasted no more time on her, but disappeared, leaving another hopeful student in his place. Juele spotted him next at Tynne's table. The serene older woman paid no attention, but went on eating her lunch in peace. All Rutaro's assistants were being subjected to the same pleas.

At the end of the meal, the chancellor rose from his place and banged the table for attention. Rutaro stood up beside him.

"My friends, many of you have heard rumors of my graduate project," Rutaro began. Instantly, the horde of students seemed to surge toward him. "I am working on an illusion—dare I call it a single piece?—that will surpass anything that I have done before. I wish to offer you *all* the opportunity to join in. It will be a lot of work, but I believe the concept to be unique, and it is all being done for the greater glory of the School of Light. If anyone wishes to participate, follow me now to the Castle of Dreams!" He gestured with one raised hand and marched down the center aisle of the hall toward the door.

The rush of artists following Rutaro was like a river freed from a dam. Juele and Mayrona had to jump to one side to avoid being trampled. Sharing a smile, the roommates joined the end of the queue.

"I have assigned you all to a particular section of the tapestry," Rutaro called, when his new workforce was assembled at the section near the castle gates. "The outlines are set and will be given to you by one of my assistants. I want you to make an image of the part of the castle you see before you. But remember, you are trying to capture the pure essence of the *heart* of the Dreamland, not just a building. It is vital to comprehend the spirit, not just the appearance. You must believe absolutely nothing of what you see. It is what you *feel* that is important. Am I going too fast for anyone?"

Mayrona stood beside Juele with a delighted smile on her face. To Juele's relief, May had been assigned to her crew. Her roommate didn't mind that she hadn't been involved earlier. To be allowed to play now filled her with joy. Not so the clique. All of them had made their appeals in the dining hall, and all had been placed by Rutaro under Juele's aegis. Without any guesswork, Juele knew they were all unhappy about it. She could feel little digs in the soil underneath her feet, threatening to undermine her where she stood, and knew it came from the group clad in loose-fitting blouses and baggy trousers standing together at the edge of the crowd. Shifting a little bit onto solid soil, she tried to ignore them and concentrate on what Rutaro was saying. He left the front gate and led them to an empty spot beside Tynne's section on the west side of the castle, near the ballroom and formal gardens, talking all the time. Juele had elbowed her way through the crowd to be with the rest of his assistants, taking Mayrona with

her. The clique had come right behind them, pushing
forward and hogging the best view.

"On your canvases, you are to fill in the foreground
and background as well as giving life to the illusion itself,"
Rutaro explained, concentrating on the blank area before
him. Images began to pour from his brow. The blank
tapestry took on color as scenes of knights on horseback
fighting dragons and ogres appeared. Rippling cylinders
unrolled across that scene and became the banners
hanging from heralds' trumpets. Vines stretched toward
the sky, concealing the heralds. These clung to the walls
of gardens as gorgeous ladies in flowing gowns wandering
through. Elegant processions of men and women attired
in scarlet and cloth of gold swept across the field of view.
Acrobats, jesters, and artisans leaped about. Musicians
plied their instruments at the knees of lovely ladies and
regal kings. As each layer of color blended in, it enriched
the beauty of the successive image.

He dipped into the images that came close to the
section of tapestry with a long brush, and used lighting
strokes to create sections of wall and window, surmounted
by banners snapping in the breeze, all informed and given
life by the history of the capital that Rutaro wove into
them. Bravery from the knights made the walls strong,
the ladies and musicians lent them grace. A wash of army
over all made the castle defensible against all enemies.

The colors whirled together, melding into white light
that was shaped into blocks and window embrasures. It
was very beautiful, and very deep. Juele admired the
way that the finished illusion seemed to flow outward
from the baseline, swirling back around their feet for
yards, and forward to the very wall of the castle itself
as if his illusion could throw a shadow both ways. Juele
could no longer see the real wall. Her whole field of
view in that section was filled with Rutaro's idealized
dream of what it should be. The sighs of admiration
throughout the crowd told her she wasn't the only one
who was impressed. He began upon another one, throwing his considerable talent into it. How strange that when

a part was finished, it looked like ordinary stone, but one could feel its history subtly taking hold of one. This was Art.

Rutaro stood back from the canvas, brush at rest.

"Are there any questions?" he asked the crowd.

Gretred shyly raised a hand. "You can see in-between the pieces. What should we do about that?"

Rutaro pointed a finger at her, and a gold star appeared over her head. "A very good question. You have all had basic color class. We will use a technique similar to Mr. Cachet's character-building exercise." Laughter erupted throughout the crowd. Juele and Sangweiler exchanged grins and raised eyebrows. "At the edge of your canvases, leave out at least one shade to be filled in by the piece beside yours."

As Rutaro held up his hand behind the last few inches of the section nearest Tynne's, Juele could see he had created it without any black. He pulled the two sections together and ran the brush down them in a zigzagging pattern, blurring the edges. They married together like jigsaw puzzle pieces. The line between them was visible for a moment, then faded. The two parts might have been of very different styles, but within a few moments she forgot that they had been separate. It was a far more seamless method than Mr. Cachet had taught them. Rutaro moved on to the third piece, which appeared to be a sickly green at the rim. He joined it to the first two, and red spread into the third piece, warming the hues to normal. The colors blended together smoothly.

Juele put out a hand to touch the join before it faded. The light felt faintly sticky, and where it joined with another part, it adhered and went back to its normal dry, airy texture.

"But what if it doesn't fit right?" asked someone in the back of the crowd. Rutaro looked blank until Gretred, nearest to the querent, repeated the question.

"Oh, well," Rutaro said. He took hold of the image in both hands and tore it apart. It made a horrendous ripping noise, and the real castle became visible in the gap. "Start over. But get it right in the end. The idea is to make all here beautiful." He patted the two halves together again.

"How do you know it's a true image?" asked Daline, shoving herself forward into the row nearest him. She was still enough in awe of Rutaro to ask politely, but Juele recognized the faint expression of scorn on her face. Rutaro held a hand to his ear. Juele repeated the question, somewhat louder. She'd thought Daline was perfectly audible.

"You'll know in your heart," Rutaro said passionately, pounding a fist against his chest. "But if you don't believe me . . . wait and see."

Like Juele, he must have sensed the oncoming headiness of a wind of change. So had they all. The students braced themselves in their own way to experience the alteration. Juele closed her eyes and let influence pour over her like warm water. When she opened her eyes, she was six inches taller than before, with teak-brown skin and filbert-shaped fingernails at the end of long fingers. Mayrona was a dainty redhead a foot shorter than she. Rutaro had gone from being a model student to a more old-fashioned young gentleman, the way Juele was accustomed to seeing him, with tightly curled, slightly long black hair, an olive complexion, and intense, round brown eyes. Under the white smock, his blue oxford-cloth shirt had softened and faded to a flowing white blouse with big sleeves, and a black ribbon tie.

The castle behind him had turned to golden granite, its sides higher and more forbidding. Black wrought iron guarded the deep window embrasures where hints of jewel colors caught the sun. Juele had to remind herself to look at the real castle. It looked the same as Rutaro's illusion. Not as perfect—of course not! But, he had captured the underlying essence, so that when it changed, so did his art.

"Hmmph," Daline grumbled, and was swept back into the tide of people surging forward to ask Rutaro questions. He answered anything they cared to ask, but all queries had to be filtered through his six assistants. He couldn't seem to hear anyone else directly. In the absence of the Ivory Tower's teleological salon, he'd established a mobile chain of command that served the same exclusive purpose of limiting direct access to him. That must have been very embarrassing for the people at the bottom of the social scale. When Juele hung back, refusing to push herself forward, others grabbed her arms and shoved her ahead of them toward Rutaro, shouting their questions at her so she could relay them. She tried to take turns with the other five, but there were too many people pleading with her, loading her with queries. In the end, she was shouting, too, just to relieve the pressure of being too full of other people's curiosity. Rutaro answered them all. Then, he held up his hands for silence.

"Now, let us begin!" Rutaro called out. From his pocket he produced a small, linen-bound sketchbook. He opened it and took from the open page a wicker basket of seeds, which he handed to Juele. He turned the page and offered the basket that appeared there to Gretred. He continued to thumb through the little book until each of the six had been given one. "My dutiful assistants have my assignments for you. Choose a view of the castle. Make it your own—within my parameters, of course. My assistants and I will be available to answer questions or to offer help as needed."

May smiled up at Juele and gave her arm a little squeeze. She was so happy to be there. Juele was proud, too. She looked at the crowd surrounding them, and could see no end to it. She never knew there were so many students at the School. It was as if hundreds of people had come from everywhere to participate in Rutaro's project. She'd have traveled far, too, to be here. Almost every face was aglow like Mayrona's. They wanted to be part of this experiment, in service not only to Art, but to the Sleepers. Probably, like everything else in the Dreamland, the enrollment changed depending upon influence, circumstances, and the number of sleepers in the Waking World whose attention turned to the pursuit of the creative. The great Seven made all things possible. Perhaps they themselves had an interest in Rutaro making things beautiful for them. She felt a little shocked at herself for thinking that Dreamlanders did anything but serve the Sleepers and accept anything that came to them from the creative source, but she was sure the Sleepers would like it if things looked nicer.

Rutaro shooed them away. Juele gathered up her assigned group and led the way around the castle toward the postern gate. The master sketch, set just beyond the moat, looked lonely standing there by itself, stark black lines rising up like wrought iron. The clique couldn't contain their scorn.

"What's the matter?" Erbatu asked, nastily. "You couldn't get a place closer to the front of the castle?"

"We don't want to be back here," Soma protested. "No one can see our work!"

"Maybe she's not the big favorite she thinks she is," Tanner said, with a twist of his lip. "He put the baby out of the way where she couldn't do any damage. After all, his grade is riding on this project."

"I want to be assigned to the front," said Daline, tossing her hair. "I'm telling Rutaro the next time I see him."

"We have standards to maintain," Bella said, studying her fingernails and not looking at Juele.

Juele didn't know what to say to them. She thought the same things, and felt just a little sorry for herself. It was a challenge, she reminded herself. Rutaro was trusting her, not punishing her. If anything needed beautifying, it was the kitchens.

"There's lots more scope here for creativity here at the back than there is in front," she protested, lamely. "Someone has to take the rear of the castle. I don't mind, really." The clique looked dubious, and ready to abandon her. Hurriedly, she scanned her section and pointed to the left. "Look, we have part of the gardens. You could have that."

Her offer was tried in a brass balance that appeared
before them, weighed, and found to be just acceptable.
The clique sauntered as far as they could along the ribbon of light until an invisible barrier forced them to stop
at a spot overlooking part of the Royal Maze at the border
of Gretred's section. With many sly glances at Juele, they
spread out to claim as much as they could of the pretty
area. The rest of Juele's crew, all strangers except for
Mayrona, divided up the rest without protest. Gallantly,
her roommate chose the spot beside hers, which offered
the prospect of a blank wall and the compost heap.

Juele took her basket to each person in turn to hand
out assignments. She felt vulnerable and silly crouching
down at their feet, but it was the only way to plant the
little seeds of inspiration. She dibbled a small hole in
the ground at the center of each canvas and watched the
seeds sprout into a framework like the main sketch. They
were only rough suggestions, leaving room for each artist
to express his or her imagination. Rutaro had managed
to capture something interesting about even the dullest
part of the castle. Juele felt her hands itching to fill in
each outline as it grew up before her, but her enthusiasm was not shared by all. The clique accepted their
sketches without grace and ignored her pointedly from
that moment on. Juele tried to think of something to say
that would appease them, but there was nothing. She'd
done the best for them she could.

The ground changed frequently under her feet, making
the going unsteady. Rocks grew up out of depressions,
catching her toe and making her stumble. She recognized
that it was because she had never been in charge of a
large group before. All she could do was watch her step,
and be the kind of guide that Rutaro trusted her to be.

The clique intended to make that role as difficult for
her as possible. Juele set to work on the master sketch,
using a broad brush to fill in blocks of color, with an
eye toward putting in detail later. How could she capture the soul of a kitchen? Would it have more to do
with the enjoyment of the meals prepared there or with

the work itself? She tried to do what Rutaro had done, emitting images from her brow that she could use to fill in the picture: baskets of eggs, sides of beef and braces of fowl, milk in huge painted cans, vegetables by the cartload—each with its own tasty colors. How interesting the way the hues blended, almost like soup. She became engrossed in what she was doing, forgetting to check on anyone else's work until something tapped on her shoulder. Juele spun around, but saw no one. The tapping came again, and she looked down. A little yellow bird sat on her sleeve looking up at her. It turned a beady black eye to the left. Juele followed its glance. Mayrona, twenty feet away, was staring intently at her. She cleared her throat meaningfully, then nodded with her head tilted. Each nod produced a small orange arrow that flew in the direction of the garden end of the arc.

Juele put down her brush and followed the warning arrows into the clique's territory. Colm let out a whistle as she approached, and the clique glanced up disinterestedly from where they were seated in a circle on the lawn. The In Crowd had abandoned their sections and were designing fashion garments. Illusionary models of skeletal thinness paraded in their midst with their hips stuck forward at unreal angles, displaying loose-fitting dresses, coats, and trousers in excruciating color combinations.

Juele stared at the tapestry with horror. She was grateful to Mayrona for paying attention. Instead of following the instructions they had been given, the clique had created wild murals colored with discontentment. Why, they hadn't even stayed within the lines! Brightly hued scribbles hung in the air over the suggestions of bush, gate, and tree. Tanner hadn't bothered to draw at all. His space was full of insulting graffiti. Juele caught a few uncomplimentary references to herself and turned crimson. The mess went right up to Gretred's section, where it stopped as if it had hit a glass wall. Gret was keeping her workers in order. The clique stared at Juele as she came over with her hands clenched in frustration, daring her to defy them. If it hadn't been for Rutaro, Juele might have slunk away and let them do what they liked, but he was trusting her.

"This isn't what Rutaro wants," Juele said, summoning up all her courage. "You are supposed to draw the part of the castle you see in the sketch."

"That's what we saw, darling," Bella said, with an amused glance at the others. She fluttered a delicate hand. "That garden is an absolute riot of color. So I drew the riot. Don't you like it? Don't you think it's a riot?"

"I . . . I don't think this is what he had in mind," Juele said.

"Well, it's too late," Cal said. He lay down on the grass and crossed one bent knee over the other. "It's all filled in. We can't change it."

Embarrassed, Juele went back to the center panel to study it. There must be something she could do to start over. Rutaro seemed to think of everything. If she couldn't fix the problem, she would let him down. She scanned the black lines that seemed to encompass one sixth of the arc of the castle. But what was that spark of red down at the bottom, underlying the base of the postern gate? Juele knelt to examine it. The spark was a small round button marked RESET. Juele pressed it.

Suddenly, all the color and depth in the drawing was wiped away as if it had never been there. Juele stood back. To her alarm, all the other pieces in her section had been erased as well, leaving only the outlines. All the artists on the right turned to glare at her.

"Sorry," she said.

"I don't mind," Mayrona said, at once. She never did, Juele thought, sending a mental blessing toward her roommate. "I wanted to change the color of the grass anyway. Thanks!" She grasped a hank of sunlight and began to wind it into a skein.

The inoffensive strangers at the other end of the line gamely started to repaint their sections. Juele went back to the clique, promising herself to keep an eye on them and make sure they did it right this time.

They all groaned when they saw her coming, but Bella and Erbatu got up to work on their segments, shaming the rest of the clique into action. Audaciously, Tanner resumed scrawling words onto his canvas, but they blurred and shifted, filling in the outlines Rutaro had set. It wasn't exactly the way Juele herself would have done it, but they were getting the job done.

Resolved to be more vigilant, she walked up and down the line to see what everyone was doing. The strangers at the west end of her arc were quiet and hardworking. The outbuildings beyond the kitchens were starting to take shape and color. Juele was very pleased. The artists themselves didn't have a lot of personality, but they had plenty of talent. Mayrona's was the best of all. She had picked up on the people coming and going out of the rear door of the castle, and had reproduced a few of them, giving them life as if she knew everything about them.

On Juele's other side, though, the tapestry dissolved into wild sketches, wide blank places, thumbnail sketches, and Impressionism. Once Juele had taken her eye off them, the clique had again started to do what they pleased. Colm sat on the ground daubing in enormously complex detail a cluster of tiny purple blossoms that lay in the foreground, paying no attention to the bushes the flowers were growing from. Most of his friends had disappeared.

"Colm, where did they go?" Juele asked. He shrugged without turning. Juele looked around for the flyaway garments the group had been wearing. Near the curtain wall Cal and Erbatu were talking with an artist still engaged upon one of the works of public sculpture. She went down to retrieve them.

"Please come back," she said. "I'm sure you can get a little more done today. There's only a week until the exhibition opens. Please." Cal ignored her and went on talking. She reached out to take his upper arm. He turned into a large white cat, who wriggled out of her arms and jumped to the ground. Erbatu, standing a little closer, became a sleek calico cat. Juele reached for her, and she hissed, raising a paw with claws bared. Surprised, Juele backed away, then made a pass to catch them both. They scooted out of reach and ran away in opposite directions. Juele thought for a split second, then started running after Cal, trying to herd him back up the slope to his canvas. The cat vanished among the legs of a delegation of men wearing somber black suits and carrying briefcases. The men, in an endless double file that led out the castle gates, moved so slowly Juele became frantic waiting for them to pass. In the end, she wriggled between two rows, apologizing all the time.

Cal-the-cat scrambled over the drawbridge. Juele ran after him and almost got him cornered near a guard station beside the castle walls. He dashed between her legs and shot over the drawbridge again, making for the Maze where Bella, Daline, and Sondra were talking with Davney Farfetch, who was in Gretred's group. Juele spun around, cursing Frustration Dreams and Impossible Task scenarios. Why couldn't she just have to drain the ocean with a leaky bucket, instead of dealing with egotistical artists? As she neared the four of them, Bella, Daline, and Sondra turned into cats, too. Cal leaped into their midst, rolling over and over with them in a cloud of screaming fur. Juele dashed up, trying to gather them in her arms. A flailing paw scratched her face, and more lacerated her hands. She managed to catch hold of one paw and one tail, but the cats kicked loose and scampered off with Juele in pursuit. Davney watched them go, laughing.

Juele chased the clique of cats all over the grounds, unable to get any two to go in the same direction. She wished she could manipulate dreamstuff the way the policeman in town had, and gather them all up in one long arm. To her dismay, she spotted Rutaro coming around the corner of the castle from Tynne's side. In a moment, he would see that half of her section had been abandoned. It was her fault for being an inexperienced manager. She would confess her problem and ask for his help in managing the senior students. Maybe it would be better if they worked with someone else. At least she would have proof that they were refusing to cooperate with her.

But the cats had spotted him, too. Faster than she could run, they raced back to their canvases and became human beings again in a twinkling. In contrast, Juele felt as if she was trying to swim through molasses. The air was thick and hot, draining her of energy. By the time she trudged back, Rutaro had arrived, and the clique was hard at work flinging colors. Juele, red-faced with exertion and embarrassment, tagged along behind Rutaro, who was cool and collected as he surveyed the progress her group was making. He examined Mayrona's dustmen.

"Very nice," he said to Juele. "Really very good." He nodded approval. Juele gave her roommate a thumbs-up. Mayrona beamed with pleasure. She grabbed Juele's hand and gave it a delighted squeeze as Rutaro passed on to the next part of the tapestry.

This was Colm's station. The senior student was innocently filling in clumps of greenery, acting as though he was concentrating too deeply to notice he was being observed. He smiled up at Rutaro, but refused to meet Juele's gaze. She fumed, wondering if he could feel the laser beams shooting out of her eyes at him. Where the red dots touched his clothing, it smoked, but he didn't even flinch.

"Darling Rutaro," Daline said, throwing her hair fetchingly as they reached her. She had filled in some of the flowers and bushes on her canvas. Even Juele, as annoyed as she was, had to admit how pretty they looked. Daline enhanced her own image with a quick powder puff of illusion, bringing up the rosiness of her cheeks to match her creations. "I'm so happy to be part of your experiment."

Rutaro looked at her with a bemused smile. "What did you say?" he asked.

Daline held up a mask of a smiling face on a stick toward him. Behind it, the real one glared at Juele. "What did he say?" she asked.

"He said, what did *you* say?"

"Do you mean he will not speak to me directly?" Daline shrieked. The shell-like pink ears under her waves of hair sharpened, taking on just a bit of the aspect of the fury she had been in town. The rest of the clique was listening, and Juele knew she didn't enjoy being embarrassed in front of her peer group.

"He just did speak to you," Juele said. "I guess you couldn't hear him."

"Well, tell him!"

Feeling uncomfortable, Juele repeated her greeting, word for word. Rutaro bowed to Daline politely.

"I am delighted that everyone has agreed to participate. You are very welcome." Juele passed his statement along, including the little bow.

"I'm a little confused about the way you've got all this set up," Daline purred, sidling up closer to him. "I'd appreciate it if you could give me just a little personal guidance as to what it is you want." A little embarrassed, Juele repeated the other girl's words.

"I am afraid you are attaching too much importance to direct contact with me," Rutaro said, looking her up and down with pleasurable speculation. He did like women, and she was very attractive. "Part of my experiment is to introduce the diverse feelings that all of the artists have concerning the ideal nature of being. I've given you all the base material you need," he added, pointing to the outline. "I regret that time is short and supervising the project as a whole is taking up all of it that I have been allotted. I am so sorry."

"But I find your personal view so inspiring," Daline insisted. He beamed at her.

"You appear already to have a fundamental understanding of the nature of beauty," Rutaro said, still relaying through Juele. "What I wish you to consider while you are working is evoking love for your subject. Enhance the ideal, bring out the character underlying the imperfect. If you need any more help, my assistant here will give you all that you need."

"Oh, but she isn't much help," Daline said, walking her fingers up the lapel of his smock. "Why, everything got so disordered because we were here on our own with her that we had to start all over."

Outraged at the lie, Juele hyperventilated with anger and puffed herself up to say something. Daline deflated her with the end of her brush, then held up a warning hand as she tried to reinflate.

"Tell him what I said. No additions! Remember I can still hear *you*. You can tattletale later. This is a private conversation between me and him. Now, say it!"

Juele repeated Daline's libelous speech. She tried to add her own comments afterwards, but no sound came out of her mouth. Her own voice didn't belong to her. She was no more than the conduit between two strong personalities. How frustrating!

One of the strong personalities, however, was on her side.

"Well, if you won't be guided by me, and my chosen representative, you must not want to be part of this project," Rutaro said, in a very calm voice. Her mentor gave Daline a sweet smile, almost as blithe as one of Peppardine's. Daline was flustered.

"But we do! It's just that this view doesn't offer much opportunity for creativity," she said, stooping to gather up her wits that had dropped about her feet like marbles. Juele bent to help her, but the girl pushed her away, putting the marbles back into her head as quickly as she could. Daline straightened up, tossing her hair back sensuously. "In fact, it just bores us to *death*. My friends and I would *really* appreciate it if we could move to a more interesting part. It would give us more natural subjects to *love*." Rutaro raised his eyebrows into his curly hair.

"I observed you dashing about on the lawn earlier, my dear. Most undignified, in the presence of our sovereign, don't you think? Such a perspective didn't give you much opportunity to study the part of the castle to which you *have* been assigned. I wouldn't *dream* of moving you, under the circumstances. I look forward to seeing what you make of this part. Think of it as Sleeper's whim. The symbolism should be most interesting." He smiled, swept her a gallant bow, and walked on to the next section of tapestry. Daline stood stiff with shock. The others, who had been listening, started painting furiously, pretending they couldn't see him behind them. Rutaro vanished around the corner of the castle, tossing a wink to Juele.

Juele was relieved and grateful. The clique were momentarily chastened. They didn't believe they could be thrown out for noncooperation, but that was exactly what Rutaro was suggesting. She didn't like having to be in the middle, but by the end of Rutaro's tirade they had clearly forgotten she was relaying his words. That was a good thing, because in a week this project would be done, and she didn't want to make enemies of them all for life.

Chapter 19

She worked for a while, filling in broad blocks of color and wondering if they were true enough to reality. It would be hard to tell until she added shading and detail. Knowing she had only a week to complete her mission, her insides wound up tight as a watch spring with tension. The anxious feeling relaxed gradually, tick by tick, as she counted off the finished parts. But she still had to keep an eye on the others working under her. That wasn't going to be as much fun as working alone. With a sigh, Juele left her brush hanging in the air and went to patrol her territory again. She felt like a sentry. If she had to behave like a policeman much longer, she was going to sprout a uniform and a truncheon.

The clique had abandoned their stations again, but they hadn't gone far. The whole group was clustered at the edge of Juele's arc, shouting over the invisible barrier to Davney, whose tapestry was the second one in on Gretred's arc. The student in the middle was listening to the gossip with a grin on his face and his ears as big as funnels, but not saying anything.

". . . So, Manolo said the poor fool couldn't tell Rutaro's minister from the real thing!" Davney called, painting an exclamation point in black on the air. "The idiot townie walked off thinking he'd had an audience, when it was all a joke."

Cal laughed heartily. "What a great idea," he said. "We ought to do that."

"If we made them, they'd make far more sense than real bureaucrats," Bella said, brushing her hair out of

her face with her wrist. Her hands were glowing with
blobs of colored light. "Think how we could improve
things."

"The Royal Geographer must have been easy to duplicate," Sondra said, looking up at her friends slyly through
her eyelashes. "Go for a real challenge—the Historian
Prime! You'd have to age the light until it was almost
rotten." The others laughed.

"No, use old light!" Colm said, waving his hands. His
tilted eyes in his narrow face gleamed with mischief.
"Look: my impression of Micah." Gathering up handfuls
of the color lying about his feet, he made the image of
a little old man with white hair, clad in a parchment-
colored robe, and wearing a sour expression. The figure hobbled jerkily. It walked over to Sondra and eyed
her up and down.

"You're not historically accurate, young woman!" the
image said. The clique burst into laughter. Sondra looked
offended for a moment, but allowed herself to relax and
get the joke. She sent it back to Davney.

"You, young man! The records show you did not sing
'Happy Birthday' at your sister's party four years ago. Do
it right now to set the archives straight."

"Darling, stop that," Bella laughed. "What if the real
thing comes out and sees it?"

"He left for Bolster," Davney said. "I saw the whole
Ministry go a couple of days ago, bag, baggage, and
boring old books."

Juele hurried up to them, and started to erase the fake
Micah. "You can't do this!" she said, in alarm. "Please.
We'll get in trouble!"

"I'll do one," Cal shouted, spinning light into a column that undulated into the form of a beautiful woman
in a diaphanous blue dress.

"And who's that?" Daline asked, with a sneer.

"I dunno," Cal said. "The Minister of Gorgeousness."
The figure started to walk, swiveling its hips from side
to side, but it quickly deformed and lost proportion. Juele
ran after it. It split in two before her eyes. The limbs

walked off in two different directions. In a moment, the whole thing vanished.

"Life never was your best illusion," Bella said, shaking her head sadly. Cal shrugged.

"Please!" Juele begged them. "You shouldn't be making people."

"Why not?" Davney asked, reasonably. "Rutaro did it."

"Well, that was just to stop someone from pestering him," Juele said. "It's not part of the project."

"We're supposed to put people into the tapestries. The castle isn't supposed to be unpopulated, is it?"

"Well, no, but you're supposed to enhance the ones who are . . ."

"Did he erase his?"

"Well, no . . ." Juele said, "but . . ."

"So it's still out there somewhere, isn't it? Within the range of an overwhelmingly powerful illusion like Rutaro's castle, a sufficiently perfect pseudominister would survive." As Davney said that, the Micah figure suddenly sank into a pool of color on the ground that was quickly lost in the ambient light. He glanced down and shrugged. "Oh, well, I guess he wasn't perfect. I'll keep trying."

"Don't!" Juele pleaded. She appealed to all of them. "There's only a week left to finish the project, and you're wasting time."

"All right," Davney said, kindly. "You're right. We'll go back to work."

"Right after this one!" Erbatu said, cackling with glee. Juele spun around. Beside the young woman was a pudgy, middle-aged man in a blue and white robe that had a pocket protector over the left breast. "What do you think, my dears?"

"You can't make the Minister of Science," Bella protested. "*I'm* making the Minister of Science." She indicated a column of light she was molding into a tall woman.

"Yours can be the assistant minister," Erbatu said, tossing her head defiantly.

Cal had modeled another woman, this one more well

defined but more scantily clad than the first. "This is the new Minister of Gorgeousness."

One after another, fake people popped into being. Some of them were deformed creatures that wandered away and stopped existing in a few moments, but others held their shapes for a distressingly long time. At first Juele ran from one to another, scrubbing them out of existence, but as the crowd grew, she backed away. There was only one thing she could do. She would have to push the reset button again and blank them all. Mayrona and the others would be upset with her for making them start all over again, but she needed to get the clique back on track. Another monster lurched forward, to the loud amusement of her classmates. She turned to run toward her tapestry.

A hand grabbed hers and pulled her onto an ample lap. She found she was sitting on a stout redheaded woman in a calico dress, who was seated in a flowered, overstuffed armchair.

"Oh, child, aren't you the cutest thing?" the woman said, gathering her up for a squeeze. "Aren't you going to say hello to your Aunt Daisy? Isn't she the cutest thing, Howard?"

"You bet she is," said a rangy man, leaning over them both with a camera in his hand. He patted Juele on the head. "Why, I haven't seen you since you were pin-sized! Smile pretty!"

The flash exploded in her face. Juele's eyes were dazzled, and little blue dots danced before them. She tried to extricate herself and get up. The woman held on to her tightly and planted a highly perfumed, smooching kiss on her cheek. Juele's heart sank. She'd been captured by an Overbearing Relatives nuisance.

"I have to go . . . over here," she said, wriggling off the woman's lap.

"Well, then, I'll come with you, darling." Aunt Daisy kept hold of her hand, patting it all the time as she walked with her, and babbling about hundreds of relatives so it was impossible for Juele to think. The nuisance moved at a slow pace that made Juele frantic, but she couldn't get loose from its grasp. ". . . And Gordon, him that married Ethel Barnsworth, they've got five children now, one as big as you, and they live right next to the Reverend Timmel. You remember him. . . ." The only thought Juele could keep in her head was to get to the reset button.

She bent down and shoved foreground images out of the way, searching for the red dot. Where was it? It was so small, and the picture it was hidden in was so large. It seemed an impossible task. It was almost as if she had to find a reset button to clear the image out so she could find the reset button. At last, underneath a stone from the path, she saw it. She stuck out a finger to push it.

Uncle Howard was quicker, though. His bony hand shot in ahead of hers.

"Well, what's this pretty little thing?" he asked, picking up the small dot between thumb and forefinger. "Isn't this nice? Look, Daisy!"

"Oh, no! I need that. Please, give that back to me," Juele begged. She glanced over her shoulder. The crowd of pseudopeople was growing larger. The individuals looked more real than ever, some of them holding their shapes quite well. Now they were walking away, intermingling with the crowd of servants and courtiers in the palace grounds.

"Well, thank you, little darling," Uncle Howard said, holding the reset button high up over Juele's head. "This'll be a right nice souvenir of our visit. I'll put it up in our sitting room, over the mantelpiece, right next to little Kevin's diploma, and we'll always think of you when we look at it."

"You come and visit us, you hear?" Aunt Daisy said, beaming. She pinched Juele's cheek painfully. "Oh, you are just so cute!"

"Smile pretty!" Uncle Howard said, aiming his camera down at Juele with his free hand as she jumped for the reset button. In a burst of flashbulb glare, they vanished. Gone! Juele threw up her hands in frustration.

Now she'd have to erase the clique's messes by hand, if she could locate them all. She ran back to the clique's area, and looked around in dismay. The crowd of simulacra were not in sight. The group stood by itself, looking puzzled.

"Where did they go?" Juele demanded.

"All gone," Bella complained. "Every one of them popped."

"We're doing something wrong," Cal said, frowning. He eyed Juele. "You saw Rutaro make his puppet. How did he do it?"

"I'm not going to tell you," Juele said, aghast.

"We'll figure it out on our own," Daline said, with a dismissive wave of her hand. "All right, this time you make it, Tanner, and we'll all critique you as you go so it really lasts." They gathered in a circle around Tanner, who started molding a shape out of thin air.

Juele tried to get into the middle of the circle to erase the image that was forming. She ducked under Bella's elbow and got knocked backwards off her feet by an invisible bumper. Juele clambered to her feet. Circling around, she looked for an opening. Cal and Colm were waving and pointing, yelling suggestions at Tanner, and not paying attention to their backs. Juele slipped between them. As one, their arms came down and formed an impenetrable barrier. Putting her head down, she pawed the ground to the tune of a trumpet somewhere in the air, then charged toward the space between Daline and Sondra just as the girls stood aside. Juele thundered through the circle and out the other side, just in time to see a coherent image that looked like the Historian Prime walking down the garden path toward the front of the castle past a group of courtiers in somber velvet robes and skullcaps. The clique was laughing. Juele caught herself and spun on her heel to run and erase it. Tanner caught her as she passed and held her in the air by the upper arms.

"No, leave it! We want to see what happens. Look, they're talking to him! They think he's real!"

The rest of the group gathered around Tanner and pounded him on the back.

"Congratulations," Colm said. "That's perfect. Now we can do it again."

"No!" Juele protested, struggling. "You can't let that exist."

"Sure we can," said Cal. "Uh-oh. Cheese it! The King's Investigator!" Juele looked up. The tall form of Roan Faireven appeared on the path leading from the postern gate. He hadn't seen the simulacrum yet, but he would in a moment. "Call it back! We'll have to hide it."

"No time," Tanner said. He made erasing motions in the air, and the image of Micah vanished with an audible pop. Juele kicked Tanner in the shins and dusted herself off as he dropped her. Roan looked up and waved to her. In a moment, he came up the hill to join them.

"Good afternoon! I've been looking at your work in progress," the tall man said, pleasantly. He nodded to the rest of the group. "Going very well, isn't it?"

At a glare from Juele, the clique sprang to work on their sections. "It's coming along," she said.

"What is the purpose of the image?" Roan asked. Juele explained Rutaro's aim.

"What an undertaking," the King's Investigator said, impressed. "I look forward to seeing it. Good day." He nodded to the others and continued along the path toward the Maze.

"He's very nice," Juele said almost to herself, as he walked out of sight.

"So that's the freak, huh?" Cal asked, coming up behind her to watch him go. Juele gave him a fierce look and exploded a flashbulb's worth of white light in his face. She knew whom she thought was the freak around there. Cal jumped back in surprise, but regarded Juele with a measure of respect.

"Let's get on with it," she said.

Roan was impressed with the prospect. A work of art that would enhance the appearance of the castle, drawing upon its history and its emotional impact on the people of the Dreamland, was indeed a fascinating and ambitious concept. It would seem that the designer understood the symbolic importance of the castle as the heart of the land. He was enjoying seeing the formative phases. The attention to detail was amazing. If the queen's little artist was correct, when this was finished the real castle wouldn't be visible. His professional side was concerned about having the castle surrounded by a curtain of unreality. He didn't feel completely comfortable having the actual face of government obscured, making it look as if the castle had been changed by any minds but those of the Sleepers, yet he liked the notion of displaying the ideal. He hoped people wouldn't get too fond of the improvement, since the work would only be in place during the queen's exhibition. Roan liked the concept, though. It was worthy of the Sleepers. Somehow he was surprised. He never expected that depth of reverence in a group so egotistical as the School of Light.

The chief artist, a grand type in a floppy cravat and white smock, stalked around the castle precinct giving orders to his volunteer staff. The queen's artist seemed to admire him very much. From the short time Roan had observed him, he understood her respect. He carefully kept back from standing over the man's shoulder, not wanting to interfere with the creative process. How did the artists think up what they wanted to do? Roan considered himself practical rather than imaginative, a necessary function for his job, but he envied those who could conceive grand designs. He was interested in the illusionists' skill at manipulating light. Such a measure of influence was more powerful than it would at first seem, since they were not working with a physical substance. Illusion-crafting was a delicate process. He didn't possess the control to do it. It was like dancing ballet in work boots. He'd played with nebulosity as a child. Anyone could mold that, but light was different. He had more respect for their talents than before.

Roan was sorry Leonora wasn't there to explore the

huge illusion with him. He missed her with all his heart. It was so strange being there while Leonora was not. Normally, he was the one who departed on missions. The castle felt so much lonelier without her and Bergold. Their absence, and that of his father, had left him almost without allies at court in the midst of so many others who saw him as a freak. It was an uncomfortable existence, and he avoided his enemies whenever he could.

Illusion attracted him. It couldn't hurt him or change him any more than influence could, but it could make him believe in what he saw. Now, as he explored the gardens as recreated by artists, he came upon the reflecting pool in the center of the queen's rectangular lilac garden, and looked into its depths. His image shone up at him, unchanged as always. He reached down to touch the water. It wasn't there, of course. His hand passed right through the mirror-bright surface. He wondered where the real pool was and if he would walk into a knee-deep surprise if he kept going. He smiled, and his face smiled back up at him.

A wave of influence rolled through the castle environs, shifting the golden sandstone keep to yellow brick with peaked, enameled tile roofs. The courtiers wandering along the paths were no longer in business suits or jerkins and hose, but silk robes or cotton smocks and pointed straw hats. The illusion altered to suit. The plants in the garden had taken on more exotic forms, becoming lilies and orchids. Even the shape of the clearing had changed from rectangular to round. Roan caught a glimpse of color. He glanced down and frowned, puzzled. His clothes seemed to have changed from a suit to a long, rainbow-hued caftan. He knew it wasn't a true alteration because he could still feel his trouser legs and the chafe of his collar. He wanted desperately to see a mirror, to know what it was like to look out of his eyes and see a different face.

The pool in the midst of the illusion was farther away now and surrounded with succulents like a desert oasis. Roan went to part the plants, and his hands passed through them. This was an illusion, he reminded himself. Not real. He leaned through them and looked into the pond, almost feeling his heart stop. His eyes met the black, slightly bloodshot ones of a stranger. He had a broad nose and thick, frizzy hair under a colorful hood. His skin was dark and glistened with oil. A thrill ran through him. Oh, he liked this illusionary landscape. It gave him the dream that he could be different like everyone else. He wondered if perhaps he had any hidden talent for illusion that could be trained. Roan's head jerked sideways, to see if anyone was looking down over his shoulder, to make certain this was supposed to be him. As he turned back, he saw the image's head moving, too. Their eyes met. He smiled, and the image lifted its upper lip to show strong, white teeth that gleamed against his dark skin. They were very square, not at all like Roan's more rectangular, everyday teeth. The illusion was treating him as if he was an ordinary Dreamlander.

He felt a pang of longing, wishing it could be so. His resistance to the strength of others' minds was useful, but sometimes he felt that he would trade it all to be able to wake up in the morning and have no idea what he'd look like in the mirror. He sighed with disappointment. He had hoped that now that he had seen the Sleeper dreaming him he might begin to change, but it seemed that the Sleeper liked having an echo of his personal self walking the landscape of his creation, no matter what distress it caused the echo. Roan had to remind himself he was there for the Sleeper's comfort and pleasure, not his own. But he could enjoy this masquerade while it lasted.

Roan had been going through a lot of personal issues since he saw his dreamer. He wondered what it really meant to be created in the image of a Sleeper. Bergold and Roan's father, Thomasen, had searched the Akashic Records thoroughly. His situation was unique. No Dreamlander had ever met his avatar before. When he was a child Roan had heard a legend that anyone who met the dreamer who dreamed him, would be forever altered, or die. Roan had seen his. Now he knew the legend wasn't true. He had not died. He did feel himself forever changed, mentally and psychologically, though not physically. Everything around him had changed, too. It was everchanging. That was the nature of the Dreamland, but was it altered *because* of his new knowledge?

Not that he could tell. The government was still running exactly as it had before his journey. The Historians and Continuitors still mostly hated him. The princess was still lovely and in love with him. Roan found her thoughtful now and again, unable or unwilling to share her ponderings with him. She said she couldn't put her feelings into words. Roan blamed himself. His likeness to one of the great Sleepers must have made her doubt her own reasons for existing, her own validity, even her royalty. Why couldn't he be normal and not have this tremendous onus hanging over his head? If she'd asked, he would have released her from their engagement, but that would have broken his heart. The Continuitors and Historians would get their wish, then, because he wouldn't want to continue to exist without her.

Roan walked out of the clearing. The path ahead of him seemed to be marked in three big blocks of slightly different colors. The center one showed a white line of light running parallel to the castle wall. He realized that center space represented the gap between two sections of illusion. As soon as he stepped over the delineation that marked the end of the illusion he was in, the colorful caftan he wore blinked out of existence. Quickly, Roan looked at his arm, checked the color of the skin on the back of his hand. It was light again, and the shape of his arm was as it had been every day for years. He hadn't changed even a little. For a moment, he'd been able to enjoy the illusion of being different. The reality remained unaltered.

A grand gentleman clad in bright red silk from his neck to the tops of his round black shoes and a lacquered black cap with a feather on top came toward him from the other side of the illusion. He, too, stepped over the line into the gap, and his face changed enough that Roan could recognize him. He bowed.

"Good afternoon, Synton," he said. The Minister of Continuity eyed him up and down.

"Did I see you alter a moment ago?" Synton asked, suspiciously. "You are back to your base shape."

"A temporary illusion," Roan said. "I was within the images on the other side of this hiatus."

"You *should* vary," Synton said, peevishly. It was an old argument, and Roan hated it. Quickly he changed the subject.

"What do you think about this massive undertaking?" he asked, gesturing about him. Synton's face contorted with anger. His mandarin headdress was no longer surmounted by a feather, but by a lightning bolt.

"It should not be allowed!" Synton shouted. "We must be able to see things as the Sleepers have made them, not as someone wants them to appear. Some mere *constructs* of Sleepers' will deigning to dictate to them!"

"It's intended to be in praise to the Sleepers," Roan said, mildly, wondering if it would rain on the chief Continuitor's head. "I've just been talking to one of the artists. I am rather enjoying the illusions."

"You would like them," Synton thundered. "They are a perversion of the normal stream of consciousness, like you."

Roan refused to allow the Continuitor to drag him into defending himself. "It is only temporary," he pointed out. "In a week it will be finished, and it will remain in place only a short time after that."

"It should come down at once. I shall speak to the king. He must do something about it—as he should have done something about you many years ago."

Roan sighed. He wished more than before that he had been permitted to go with Leonora. He bowed as the minister stalked off, silk robes changing into a burnoose and djellabah as Synton passed into the illusion that Roan had just left. The lightning display over his head showing his fit of temper became a sandstorm. The artists needed to fix that section of their masterwork. It wasn't quite in sync with the main image of the castle.

A pity that the alteration of appearance couldn't change people's personalities, too, but even influence couldn't do that. A kinder, gentler Synton would be a greater attraction than even an ideal castle.

Chapter 20

"Pardon me," said a woman in a sensible dress and shoes. "Can you tell me how to find the Royal Geographer?"

Juele stood up and pointed toward the castle entrance. "You can find Minister Romney in there, ma'am," she said.

"Oh, thank you! I hope he's not too busy today," the woman gushed, confidingly. "I'm from Doze. Master Folbert came back with such wonderful advice from the minister. We've all come to ask questions that have been bothering us, too." She gestured to a hopeful crowd standing behind her. "We're so looking forward to meeting him. Or is he her today?"

"I don't know, ma'am." *Uh-oh*, Juele thought. She escorted the woman and her friends to the castle door, then went looking for Rutaro.

He was inspecting the stables, standing over the unlucky student drawing the stalls with Sangweiler to translate for him. "No, this is not satisfactory! More empty horses," he ordered. "Do you think the king has only one steed to bless himself with? Look at the real thing, for pity's sake!"

"I apologize, Rutaro," the line artist said. "I thought I could *suggest* more . . ." Sangweiler had his hand in front of his mouth, hiding a grin of rueful amusement that he shared with Juele when she appeared. Rutaro cut off the relayed excuse when it was only half delivered.

"One horse with seventeen heads will not suggest anything other than the rider has no idea where he is going! Bad symbolism! For the Seven's sake, take the time to create the proper number of horse's posteriors. If you need a model I suggest you look in a mirror."

Abandoning the volunteer to Sangweiler's care, he came over to where Juele was waiting out of the line of fire. She told him about the visitors from Doze.

Rutaro shook his head. "Please go back and deal with your section," he said. "That is the most important thing right now. They won't bother us."

But Rutaro was wrong. As Juele was leaving him, the woman and her friends rounded the corner of the castle. The woman shrilled a joyful cry as she spotted the white smock.

"There you are!" she said, swooping down like a bird of prey. Her talonlike hand closed around Rutaro's arm. Rutaro backed away, but she held on tight. "Minister Romney didn't know what we were talking about when we stopped to see her, and she couldn't answer our questions. Obviously I made a mistake. I realize I should have followed Master Folbert's instructions to the letter. I should have started with you. I recognized you right away from his description—the grand one wearing white, he said. He said you were the one who directed him rightly in the first place. And, *then* Minister Romney came along and helped him, he said. I did everything out of sequence. No wonder it didn't work. Now, can you please help us?"

The student whom Rutaro had chided for being lazy hung about, openly snickering as Rutaro sputtered. He'd really dug himself into this one. There was a murmur of shock from the others, who had never seen one of the Idealists discomfited. Juele was embarrassed for Rutaro.

"Madam, he was incorrect," Rutaro said, as patiently as he could, although Juele saw signs of temper building.

"Oh, but anyone can see you're the man who gets things done around here," the woman said, looking around at the scaffolding holding up the tapestries and canvases around the castle. "You must be very important." Rutaro ignored her. He tried to go about his business, and the crowd followed him. Juele stayed as close to his side as she could. She felt him vibrate with irritation.

"Is there anything I can do to help?" she asked.

"No! Go back to work," Rutaro said, through his teeth. As they passed artists' work stations along the line, Juele could see images of the woman and her friends popping up in the midst of everyone else's tapestries. Juele wondered how word could spread so fast and so accurately, until she realized that each section was tied to all the others along the silvery land-line. Rutaro would use it to tie the whole thing together into one coherent image when it was finished. In the meantime, anyone could tap into it to send pictures to someone else.

More strangers appeared on the path, letting out cries of joy when they saw Rutaro. Folbert must have told everyone in the world about his wonderful experience. The crowd around the Idealist grew more assertive, pushing in closer and closer to see him. Juele was shoved away from his side. She lost sight of the white smock in the milling mass of bodies. Suddenly, a glowing figure wearing blue and green robes appeared in their midst.

"There she is!" cried the woman from Doze. "Minister, why is the moon only blue once in a while?" The crowd surged away, leaving Rutaro staggering. Juele rushed up to support him. He waved her away.

"I am all right," he assured her.

"Cool!" one of the students behind her exclaimed, watching the pseudominister addressing the mob of people. They were listening with rapt expressions on their faces. "I want to try that!" Automatically Juele and Sangweiler relayed the statement. Rutaro was outraged.

"No," he said. "That was done in the name of expediency. These people don't have real problems. They are only curious. For that they do not need to consult a genuine minister. This will keep them busy so they do not interfere with us."

"It looks like a laugh," said another student. "What fun! We should build a whole set of fakes! Collect them all!"

"Don't do that," Rutaro said, imperiously. "I want you to do what I say, not what I do." But the damage had been done. Juele saw the tiny image of the false Romney appear in the tapestry window. Word spread around the circuit. In no time, everyone was talking about it, and speculating on what they would do if they created their own government officials.

Juele went back to her station and tried to lead by example, as Rutaro wanted her to. She threw herself into her work, trying to ignore the tiny picture frame that appeared at the bottom of her canvas indicating someone was sending her another image of what the false Romney was doing at that moment. She didn't want to look at it, although she was tempted. Her work didn't go anywhere near as fast as Rutaro's had. The distraction, and her lack of experience, slowed her down. His skill and years of practice—hundreds, possibly—made the miracles he performed appear easy.

Rutaro certainly did not need the distraction of tourists coming up to talk to him. His undertaking would have occupied the entire mind of a more ordinary being. As he had told Daline, it did keep him too busy to spend much time with individuals. Though he passed through Juele's section several times to supervise, he didn't stop to talk. What with Mayrona deep in concentration on one side, and the clique ignoring her on the other, Juele began to feel neglected and lonely. Mayrona was working on the shadows that fell deeply along the north side of the complex. This was the hardest part for her, and Juele didn't dare distract her just to chat. The In Crowd was enjoying the network of artists, laughing over relayed pictures and scandals, and paying no attention to her attempts at conversation when she came by to see how they were doing.

They worked faster than she did, too, leaving them more time to make their own images and fuse them into

the huge illusion. Juele thought they would ruin Rutaro's
design, but the little pictures vanished into the ether,
leaving the landscape unscathed. The white strand of
light along the ground flashed as the images sped away.
The method, discovered earlier by someone on Borus's
team, proved to be an efficient way to send messages.
The system had been intended to supply needed information so no one had to run all the way around the
castle to ask Rutaro or one of the group leaders a
question. After that, somebody began using it to circulate
the latest rumors and jokes to his friends. Pretty soon
everybody was sending pictures to one another, making
them pop up in one another's canvases. Everyone on the
circuit got to see and hear gossip and funny pictures
without having to move. The more Juele ignored it, the
more she felt out of the loop, but she wasn't there for
the society of others. The important thing was to get
the project finished. She ignored the little twinges of
woe, and buckled down to work.

The sun had moved from one side of the sky to the
other when she felt a tap on her shoulder. She looked
up to see Rutaro. Instead of his usual pressed perfection, his clothes looked a trifle askew, and there was a
haunted look in his eyes.

"Are you all right?" she asked.

"All those people are gone at last," he said, with
evident relief.

Juele cocked her head. "I thought you liked lots of
people watching you."

"I don't like crowds," he said, with a small frown, as
if she should understand that. "I like an audience." Juele
realized he was telling the truth. No one ever crowded
him in the School. Usually the students and dons alike
cleared a respectful path for the Idealists. Strangers
wouldn't know to keep their distance.

"Come along," he said. "We need a short break, and
I have something to show you. In appreciation of all your
hard work." Refusing to answer any questions, he set out

from the castle gates, leaving her to hurry along in his wake.

The school was only steps outside the walls. Juele was surprised. It seemed to have moved closer since that morning.

Rutaro led her through the archway that led toward the museum. Outside the main gallery in the quadrangle was another attached structure that Juele had never noticed before. With its tall, white pillars and elegantly carved entablature it seemed far too grand for the usual student works. Perhaps the School only allowed it to exist for special occasions.

"Come and see. This is your doing," Rutaro said, holding open the door for her.

"Mine?"

"Yes. No one else ever dares to tell us what we must or should do. It's a nice change."

Juele was abashed at her boldness in possibly having overstepped her bounds. "I would never order you to do anything," she protested. "I don't remember."

"Perhaps you don't," Rutaro said with a little smile, "but we do. I've been keeping it as a surprise until it was finished. If I have been a little distant, forgive me. There is so much involved in the execution of my project that I have had little time to spend with you."

"Oh, that's all right," Juele said, forgiving him from the bottom of her heart. "I'm happy for whatever time you have."

She walked in—and gasped. The sound echoed into the corners of the airy entry hall, thirty times larger than her dormitory room. Including the castle, this was the most elegant place she had ever been in her life. If this place was reserved especially for the Idealists' special works, that would explain it. Only for Them would it be good enough. Blank-eyed statues supporting the ceiling on their heads stood in imposing rows against the walls. They were made of the finest alabaster, and the cornices of the carved, white plaster ceiling were gilded. Doors opened up on small galleries to the right and left that were hung with paintings and adorned with three-dimensional art displayed on pedestals. Scholars and teachers in their smocks browsed slowly around or sat on benches in the middle of the chambers, studying particular illusions at a distance.

"Senior students' projects," said Rutaro. "But We're in here." He led her between two of the statues to a pair of mahogany doors with gold handles. Though a maroon ribbon looped across them at waist-level prevented entry, the doors stood open. Through them Juele could glimpse rich colors and textures. A sign on a post read THE GRAND GALLERY.

"Go ahead," Rutaro said, gesturing her forward and handing her a large golden scissors. "You will be the first. Tell me what you think." He folded his arms and leaned against the carved rosewood lintel.

Honored beyond words, Juele took the scissors and cut the ribbon. The satin whispered as it touched the floor, emphasizing the ominous silence beyond. Juele crept through the doorway, keenly aware of the hollow sound of her footsteps on the hard floor, and stopped just over the threshold to gawk.

The main room of the gallery was so huge that she could just barely discern the opposite wall. It had been opulently decorated as if time and detail were of no moment. Over her head, the ceiling had been fully ornamented with handsome classical figures, encrusted in gold and gorgeous colors, depicting the hours, the signs of the zodiac, the seasons, the muses, and the absolutes. Blank-eyed gods and goddesses held up ivy vines and gilded laurels. The art overhead seemed to flow toward the corners of the room where tails of color and texture streamed down the walls to the floor, outlining sumptuous velvet panels on the upper walls in vines and festoons of flowers. Ancient paintings of landscapes and people in odd clothes were framed in warmly glowing gold against the velvet. Where no ornament was present, the walls and floor were white marble, like most of the galleries she had seen on campus, but no marble she had seen yet was as translucent and shiny as this. It was a grand, glorious setting. She felt as if she was in the presence of something of great artistic importance. And yet, there seemed to be nothing displayed here at all. In the center of this vast chamber, a gray kitten was playing with a ball of string. Juele walked closer to watch it. She noticed a white line on the floor. She thought that must mark where she was meant to stop, so she did.

She watched the kitten for a while. She thought it might be eight or nine weeks old. Its delicate ears were too big in proportion to its little face and round, green eyes. The ball of string escaped its minute paws, and it bounded after it, needle claws spread, with the ferocity of a miniature tiger. It rolled over and over on its prey, which appeared to try and get away, only to be captured by its persistent hunter. Once or twice the kitten's antics made Juele laugh, but she didn't see anything in its presence of overwhelming importance. She left the kitten to its game.

When she came out, Rutaro left off leaning against the wall and came to meet her.

"What do you think?" he asked.

"Well, it's very realistic," she said. She didn't want to say she didn't understand it, or insult him in any way.

"Nice gray kitten, eh?" Rutaro asked, in a noncommittal voice.

"Well, yes," Juele said, and stopped, trying to think of something complimentary to add. To her dismay, the disappointment in her voice was plain to both of them. Rutaro didn't seem at all upset. He nodded.

"You didn't go far enough in," he said. He tilted his head toward the door. "Come on."

Juele followed him back into the grand chamber. A blue glass bowl had appeared by the kitten. It noticed the food in the bowl and abandoned the string at once. Squeaking happily, it fell to, enjoying its meal with tiny comments to itself. Juele looked questioningly at Rutaro.

"The trouble is that you didn't step over the line,

either physically or figuratively," Rutaro said. "Few do. Go on. Slowly."

Juele returned to the line. Feeling a bit silly, she glanced back at him for permission. He nodded encouragingly, and she stepped forward. The scene around her changed violently to that of another chamber, full of hot steam, every surface covered with teetering, dirty crockery stacked to the ceiling. The whole thing smelled unpleasantly of floor wax and spoiled food. "Oh!"

"Do you see?" Rutaro asked. He was still in the corner behind her, propping up the wall, although he was almost hidden by the piles of dishes. "It's all in the symbolism. The kitten is the symbol of simple joy, frolic, innocent play. It's the string that denotes the intricacies of mass illusion. You must see that, and then you must look for more." There was another white line on the floor. She stepped over it.

The room changed. Now it was full of flowers in vases, and the air was full of the heady, waxy scent of lilies. She took another pace.

The room changed. Jewel-colored songbirds flitted freely around her. One made to land on her finger. Its wirelike claws almost felt real. She let it take off and stepped over the line on the floor.

The room changed. She was almost knocked to the dirt floor by the bull that charged past her. It was aiming its terrifyingly sharp horns at the man in the tight, brocaded suit who waved a red flag. Another pace took her into a deep jungle. The air was hot and steamy with the smell of spice. Unseen birds hooted and called, and more than once she heard the rush of wings over her head. The white line on the ground was a fat, pale snake. It lay quiescent now, but Juele feared that if she stepped over it, she'd wake it.

"Go on!" Rutaro commanded.

Hastily, Juele obeyed. She stepped over the line. She was on a pointed cliff of yellow stone and clay, looking down on slate blue waters. White clouds floated lazily through the sky. She squinted to see the birds that were flying in an arrowhead formation in the distance, then realized with a shock that they were jet airplanes, a rare vision in the Dreamland.

"Go on," said the voice behind her.

She looked down for the white line. It was at the very edge of the cliff. Going forward meant certain death. It's only an illusion, she told herself. She could not fall. Beyond it was only floor. Her mind knew that, but her stomach doubted. Gathering all her courage and her trust in Rutaro, she stepped over the line. To her relief, the sole of her shoe touched something solid in the air. She put her weight on it.

Suddenly, she was back in the gallery, but howling winds surrounded her, carrying furniture and debris around and around, obscuring the walls. Juele's hair whipped violently against her cheek. The only place of safety was in the center where she stood. She glanced back. Through the haze of windstorm, she could see the fuzzy figure of Rutaro in his bright clothes still standing in the corner.

"This is amazing," she said. Her voice was snatched away by the wind, but the figure nodded its understanding. "How is it possible to fill this huge room with successive illusions? How can you overlap them like this?"

"Illusions take up no space," Rutaro said, over the roaring. "You ought to understand that. They are just around *you*. As you move, the room can change, because illusions are not made of the usual solid dreamstuff. You can overlap them infinitely. Even in life, two people standing side by side and observing the same sight can see two very different things, and neither may see the truth."

"What do you mean?"

"Put out your hand." Juele hesitated, fearing being whisked into the maelstrom. Even if it was illusory, if she believed in it, it could hurt her. Rutaro's voice barked over the screaming gale. "Put your hand out!"

She did. The wind buffeted it, but she forced herself to think *it's only an illusion!* Within a foot, her questing fingers bumped into something solid. Juele put out her other hand and looked up, but she saw only the swirling wind. "Why, what is it?"

"The wall," said Rutaro. Puzzled, she looked up and around. She tried to break through the layers of illusion and couldn't. She didn't see anything but the tornado and had to trust her hands. She felt over to her right. Her fingertips touched an angle and another wall. "It's the outside of the museum," Rutaro said.

"The whole room is an illusion?"

"What a dear innocent child you are," Rutaro said, fondly. "Of course. Illusions are everywhere. Never believe anything you see or hear."

Speechless with admiration, Juele touched the wall over and over. She closed her eyes and realized her eyes and ears were telling her something quite different than what her hands knew. The Idealists *were* the masters of her craft. She wished she had been smart enough to step over the line and spot the subsequent illusions without Rutaro telling her, or better yet, had been the first to realize that one could put a whole imagination's worth of visions into a thimble-sized reality.

Rutaro reached through the hurricane and touched her hand. "Come along. Lesson's over for today. You have classes to go to."

"That's the most wonderful thing I've ever seen," Juele said, as she followed Rutaro out of the Grand Gallery into the foyer, her voice hushed with awe.

"Not bad," he said, although she could tell he was basking in the glory of her admiration. "Come, let's take a short cut." He took her hand and led her toward the door of the foyer. Instead of opening it, he stepped through it, taking her with him. She had believed wholeheartedly in that door until that moment.

"Why is that an illusion?"

"The whole gallery is an illusion," Rutaro said, swinging his arm through a solid-looking wall. "There's nothing here but a glade, but you see that everybody else believes in it, too. Where layer upon layer of illusion exists, it becomes harder to believe in reality."

Juele shook her head. She was determined to try and learn the skill herself. If anything, she admired Rutaro more than ever. He had been her first friend here. In only two weeks, she had seen more wonders than in all of her life put together. He smiled at her.

"I must go back, and you must go to class," he said. "I will see you later."

Juele looked up at him devotedly. "I'll be there."

Chapter 21

In the late afternoon, Juele returned to the castle. She had an idea how to manifest in physical terms her concept of the aromas and smells that emanated from the kitchens and outbuildings, and she wanted to work it out in living color. How did one express the melange of garbage mixed with compost and cooking, all in visual terms? With deep concentration, she was sure she could imbue the image with a sense that all these elements were present and serving an important function. In one way the clique was correct. There was little of the heroic or historical at this end of the castle. Still, without the guts, the arms and legs and especially the head wouldn't function at all.

Most of the clique was still present, if not accomplishing much. They shut her out when they felt like it and admitted her to their little circle when they wanted an audience. To her relief they had stayed in their places and gotten more work done that day than ever before. She attributed their attentiveness to the little pictures-in-pictures that had begun to appear on the tapestry at everyone's station. Still images were the easiest to send along the glowing land-line, but soon the more advanced students were sending live images.

"Did you hear?" Daline asked, her face repeated in every tapestry tuned in to the network of gossip. "The Minister of Science wants to have everyone examined once a year and ask how many times they've changed with influence or by free will. Why do you suppose they want to know something like that?"

"Oh, who knows?" Soma asked, popping up in the

pictures in her turn. "It's voyeuristic, if you ask me. Totally IYF."

Juele couldn't resist asking. "What's that mean?" Out of the corner of her eye she saw her own face appear on Tanner's tapestry.

"In your face, darling," Bella explained, shaking her head sadly. "How pathetic that you didn't know. Everybody knows that."

"I think they want to IYM," said a male student with a moustache. "That's 'invade your mind,' for those of you out of the loop."

"IYD, dear," Daline said. Even Juele could figure out "in your dreams." "They'd be stumped for lack of material." How odd that the group scorned her because she wasn't up on the most current gossip, slang, and images. They claimed to pride themselves on their individuality, but none of them dared to be different from the other. In her experience over the last few weeks, she had found it was too much work to try to be someone else. She decided to ignore the trends and be herself, fashionable or not. Sooner or later they'd get used to her the way she was.

Numerous others joined in the fun, offering their suggestions for the Ministry of Science's survey, each more outrageous than the one before.

"What do you think of the reappearance of the apparition?" asked a student from Manolo's side of the castle. "His Leadershipness whips off a quick image to get out of a jam and doesn't want anyone to try it themselves."

"Hypocrisy, my dear," said Sondra. "Why should he have all the fun?" Juele firmly put the picture-in-picture to one side, determined to not to get involved in the gossip. She could have spent all day looking and listening, and getting nothing else done.

Toward dinnertime, Juele looked up from her visualization of the smell of compost. It was much too quiet at the clique's end of the line. Juele abandoned her efforts and went to see what they were doing. The tapestries showed a lot of progress, but they'd been abandoned. None of the group was on the line. Where had they gone?

Juele heard giggling and looked about, scanning the edge of the gardens. She didn't see anybody. A huge rosebush sat right out in the middle of a clearing, not far from the path. A critical look told her it was too perfect to be real. It had to have been put there by one of them, and recently. From Juele's recollection of the outline, it was not part of Rutaro's original design. She circled around to the other side of it and found Bella and Daline making cushions out of nebulosity to pad a wooden park bench. The rosebush was invisible from their side, like the wall Davney had built to protect him from onlookers.

"What's this for?" Juele asked. "Rutaro didn't say anything about one-way illusions."

"It's for us, darling," Bella said. "Freelance. Our idea. When the patrons come, we'll come up here and hide out and listen. Townies do say the funniest things about art. You should come, too, my dear."

"I . . . I don't know if I should," Juele said. "Is this the only one like this?"

"Does it look big enough to hold us all?" Daline asked, shaking her head with pity. "Of course not, dear. They're *all* over the place." She put two fingers on Juele's lips, forestalling her comment. "It'll be our little secret, dear, won't it? We'll have everything else finished in time. Let us have our fun?"

Juele didn't like to refuse them something that seemed so harmless. "All right," she said.

At the end of the day, it was soothing for Juele to go up into the Ivory Tower. The salon room was now full of pedestals of works in progress, including her own. Their brief sally into public works had urged the Idealists to start creating more dynamically. Even Von came close to finishing most of his pieces before they vanished. With their advice and encouragement, Juele had made progress on her askance reality project for the exhibition. She was pleased at the way it was coming along. With her time limited by all she was doing, she had decided to model something very simple, just a still life of flowers in a basket. Keeping from looking directly at the creation growing on her stand, she drew a few stems of bluebells and tucked them in among little purple irises and bright red dianthus.

"Juele! Think fast," Soteran called. Juele had just time to turn around and catch the glass egg he pitched to her. Instead of resting in her palms, the egg spun in mid-air. It was a wonderful little ovoid of brilliant greens and blues arranged in coiled patterns, embedded in pure crystal. A teardrop of pure gold lay at the heart of the egg.

"Add to it," Mara urged her from across the room where she sat at her easel. "Nicely. Then you have to remember what you've added and keep it real even if you can't see it. Can you do that?"

"I'll try," Juele said. What an exciting idea for an exercise! She was very pleased to be included. To think that her work, in however small a piece, would be melded with Theirs made her hands tremble so much that she nearly lost her grip on the egg.

"Quicker!" Soteran shouted. Nervously, Juele spun an image. She had detailed structures of flowers in her mind, so she drew a dancing frieze of marigolds over the blue and green, and tossed the egg to Peppardine. His fine, long hands spangled her flowers with dew. The silver droplets formed their own complicated pattern which clashed neither with the marigolds nor the spiral ground. Juele watched him with fascination. He grinned companionably at her as he threw the egg underhand to Von. Juele sighed. They could make such beautiful illusions together.

"Try not to lose the mood," Rutaro scolded her. Because his main project was outside, Rutaro worked on small pieces for his own amusement in the tower. As an exercise he had chosen to model her again, this time in light. She wondered how he ever found time to do all the things he did. "You were in a state of pensive concentration."

"I'm sorry," Juele said, trying to school her face back into solemn contemplation, but she couldn't help sneaking a glance through her eyelashes at Peppardine. He wasn't looking at her, but she knew he was aware of her attention. She wondered if she and the Idealists would ever develop the kind of mental rapport Rutaro and Peppardine enjoyed. Although she'd die right there if Peppardine could read her mind now.

"No apology needed," Rutaro said, spinning shades of green between his fingers as he chose the right hue to go with her eyes. "You're a good subject. And," as he watched the egg fly through the air to Helena, "a good artist. You've got potential," he said, molding an eye between his hands. "You could be one of us one day. If you work hard."

"And learn," Mara added severely.

Juele was speechless with joy. One day she could change her pink smock for a white one! She didn't know if They could have said anything that would have delighted her more. Instantly she went back to her project, vowing to make it a paragon of beauty and design worthy of Them.

She studied her piece with a critical eye. It wasn't a bad bouquet, but the arrangement looked incomplete. What it really needed was a special accent at the top, something to symbolize the advice she had received from Them, which had helped guide her skill to a level that her teachers at home could never dream of. A rose, she thought. A white rose, that was it. Juele picked the brightest white she could find and molded the petals with the greatest of care. A rose that showed seven petals, one for each Idealist. She kept wanting to look directly at the flower, to make sure of its perfection of form, but knew it would disappear if she did. She was grateful for her good peripheral vision.

Remembering the gallery exhibit she had enjoyed, she

stopped molding for a moment to wonder if she should work in a smell factor, too. The rose scent would waft a sweet note over the more ordinary aromas of garden and wild flowers. No, she shouldn't. She'd gone to so much trouble to create an original technique, she didn't want to be criticized for including anyone else's ideas. She wanted to do her own thing. Symbolism, though, she could add, since that was everywhere. She was sure Rutaro and Peppardine would enjoy the attention to detail. Green and growing things were healthy. Along the sides of the basket she put the icon used by physicians. People in love gave flowers to one another. She drew in a valentine card with big pink hearts on it.

"Why an egg?" Von asked thoughtfully, capturing the now-bejeweled ovoid as it sailed through the air between Helena and Callia. "Why an egg, and not a sphere or a cube?"

"Eggs are a comfortable shape, but not a completed one, like a sphere," Peppardine said, dropping into lecturing mode. A white egg took form between his long fingers. He tossed it into the air, spinning, and caught it. "They're a perfect example of form following function—they contain possibilities. Eggs are the beginning of all ideas, not where they stop. They are the ultimate in prefigurative symbology. That is so important. An egg is promise. It foreshadows a chicken or a snake or a lizard at some time in the future." He dropped it. The egg broke on the floor into a perfectly oval white splash with a yellow-gold hemisphere in the center, and the two empty halves of the shell rocked. "Like this, it denotes failure. Disguise is impossible—you cannot stuff the egg back into its shell."

"Seems like too much for one poor little shape to encompass," Von said, tapping the decorated egg on the edge of his glass. The multicolored contents slid out of the shell into his drink, and he downed them in a gulp. "Now, does that mean I contain all possibilities?"

"You always did, you fool," Mara said, "but you don't always use them."

"How are you coming along?" Callia asked, coming over and putting an arm around Juele's shoulders. Juele suddenly felt shy about showing Them her piece, but she couldn't very well hide it.

"You have to turn sideways," she said. Callia glanced away, then broke into peals of laughter.

"My dear, it's like a traffic jam," she said. "Save something for your next picture." Von and Soteran came over to see. Juele felt like running down the stairs into the night.

Soteran regarded the piece gravely. "You do know that these are things that the flowers symbolize, not symbols of the flowers themselves."

"I . . . but they mean these things to me," Juele said, trying to defend herself.

"Felicity of composition, my dear!" Rutaro said, expertly flicking her superfluous symbols out of the picture with a fingertip.

"You know, the simplest things are often best," Peppardine said, with amusement in his beautiful eyes. "Sometimes a basket of flowers is just a basket of flowers."

Juele felt like crying. It was her own fault. She had jumped straight into the depths, and she felt the floor under her tossing like a sea again. Helena came over and tipped her chin up with a finger. The touch steadied her.

"You're doing well, dear," she said. "But the execution is up to you, and in the end your piece must stand on its own merits. Perhaps you are trying to do too much at once."

Juele nodded. "Will you help me?"

"We'll guide you," Peppardine promised. "That's what we are here for."

Juele felt better. With their help, she could do anything.

Chapter 22

"My goodness, it's getting thick out there," the queen said, looking out of the window at the growing illusion. "Very soon one won't be able to see the city any more. It's quite marvelous, though, isn't it? Almost *perfect*."

"That's Rutaro's purpose, ma'am," Juele said.

"I am just delighted," the queen said, sitting down in her thronelike chair. Juele erased a tassel on the pillow at the queen's elbow, then dabbed it in again as it reappeared. "It's so splendid and huge, like nothing that's ever been done before. I should feel almost humble, shouldn't I, to know that this is being done in my honor? All these people working so hard, for my gala exhibition?"

"Oh, not at all, ma'am!" Juele protested. "The honor is ours!"

Harmonia smiled, lifting her chin high. "You are very sweet, my dear. My, the illusions are getting most intense and interesting. I went for a little walk in the garden yesterday, and would you believe it, I got lost! Instead of the reflecting pool, there was a glade full of mirrors, almost like a funhouse. I looked different in every one. It took me a while to find the least true reflection, so I could come out again. There are quite a lot of people about already. So many people came up to tell me they are enjoying it. It looks as though the exhibition will be a popular success."

"I hope so, ma'am," Juele said, keeping her eyes on her portrait, and not meeting the queen's. Hundreds of those people weren't there for the art; they were there for Rutaro's pretend Romney. The word seemed to have spread all over the Dreamland about the minister who gave good, high-minded advice, because even more people had appeared that day looking for her. Rutaro hadn't wanted to set up an advice bureau. He had tried to send them to the real court officials, but the palace was curiously empty. Hardly any of the other ministers seemed to be around. They must all have gone out of town to the Cult Movie Evocation. The curious and the hopeful had returned to Rutaro in demanding, relentless hordes.

Worse yet, some of the students working on the project wanted to try making their own ministers, and they were increasingly resistant to being told they couldn't do what they saw the Idealist doing. She knew Rutaro hoped the crowds would go away so he could finish before the exhibition was due to open. In the meantime he was making himself deliberately hard to find so he couldn't be pestered. Unfortunately, that meant he was often out of reach for legitimate problems, leaving the students to do what they liked. Juele didn't dare mention the situation to the queen. She might order Rutaro to stop. That would be the end of his graduate project, when it had taken such an effort for him to propose it.

The queen was full of plans for her exhibition. "I have written a short speech, should I be asked to deliver a few comments before or after the official opening. My ladies-in-waiting have instructions to bring large handbags, should I be given floral tributes or little gifts. I am of several minds on what to wear," she told Juele. "The event is in the afternoon. Of course, it will all depend upon the weather."

"I'm sure the chancellor will make sure the weather is good," Juele said, adding to the translucency of the queen's complexion. If he didn't, she was certain that They would. The talk in the Ivory Tower in the evenings referred often to the queen's visit. For all their seeming aloofness, the Seven were looking forward to the day with great enthusiasm.

"Ah, the chancellor," the queen said fondly. "He's

quite a courtier, your chancellor." Harmonia rose from
the chair and opened a drawer in a handsome walnut
cabinet. From it she drew a ribbon four inches wide
and a couple of yards long. It appeared to be made of
silver and gold light woven in a complex and beautiful pattern, studded with cascades of jewels. Juele recognized that it was made of true dreamstuff laden with
illusion. "Glorious isn't it? He has given me this to wear
for the presentation, to reflect my beauty, he said, 'however inadequately a mirror may reflect the sun.' Isn't
that nice? I was most flattered."

Juele smiled shyly and nodded. Roan, who had come
by to watch her work, examined it with interest.

"It's remarkable," he said, turning it so the bright lights
twinkled. "A very nice tribute." It made a good contrast
to the queen's beauty. She reminded him more of a pearl,
with her light coming from the inside. Leonora, young,
intense, and in love, was more like a diamond: sharp,
clear, and focused. The comparison was deceptive,
because the queen only appeared to be vague. It suited
her to let people underestimate her. He handed it back,
and she shut the ribbon in the cabinet, stifling its cor-
uscating light.

"Will you be staying for the exhibition?" the queen
asked Roan.

"Yes, Your Majesty," Roan said. "The Movie Extravaganza does not require my attention. It's not common-
place, but it is predictable, controllable, and therefore
safe." He didn't want to mention the king's reasons for
having him stay to watch over the goings-on at the castle
in front of Juele.

Queen Harmonia turned to her little artist, who was
working hard on the portrait. "Well, I wish His Majesty
would go, too. He should, but he isn't. With no courtiers to pester him, he's having a little holiday in his
chambers. He said he wants to concentrate on hobbies.
Building a bottle around a ship, that sort of thing. Painting pictures. Cutting gems. Planting a garden. He is full
of plans."

Roan knew that what the king did, even on a casual basis, put the Dreamland in order. He never knew if the king had to do it, knew *what* he had to do, or if it was an impulse from the Sleepers, but Byron always did what was right, and it always came out right. Works of the good kings were enduring, changing with influences as everything—well, almost everything—in the Dreamland did, and yet were still recognizable as the work of the reigning monarch. The king kept all his realm well, secure, and prosperous, and that was what counted. Leonora, possessed of her father's good organizing mind and mother's love of beauty, would be an excellent queen one day, and he would be titled the Consort Royal. Contemplating the title made him feel a trifle uncomfortable. He only wanted to be the King's Investigator, or when the time came, the Queen's. He would be honored to serve Leonora, as well as being a devoted husband. He let out a small sigh. He was always thinking of her, more so now since she was away.

A trio of doctors appeared at the chamber door. "Ah! Time for my consultation," Queen Harmonia said.

"Then, I should leave you, Your Majesty," Roan said, bowing. "Thank you for allowing me to watch you, Mistress Juele. I envy you your skill."

The girl beamed with pleasure. "I'm just a beginner, Master Roan. You should see what the others can do."

"I am still impressed," Roan said sincerely. "It's a thousand times more than I can achieve." With a smile, he slipped out the door.

"May I go, too?" Juele asked the queen, flexing the small brush she was using between her hands. "I should get back. There's so much more to do."

"Of course, my dear," Harmonia said, affectionately, sweeping over to kiss the girl on the forehead. "I look forward to our next meeting."

Juele picked up all her tools and folded the portrait carefully into the portfolio she now carried in her art box. One, maybe two more sittings, and it would be finished. On the threshold she smiled and curtseyed to the queen, but Harmonia was already engaged in explaining symptoms to her attentive physicians.

To her surprise, Master Roan had only gone a few yards down the corridor. He was engaged in an argument with some men. By the dark green robes, Juele guessed them to be the Minister of Continuity and some of his staff. Roan wasn't so much arguing with them as listening to the minister, who was in a terrible mood.

". . . Trust you for security! And look at the place! Can't see a true thing to save your life!" Minister Synton shouted. His whirling arms glinted like knives. He was in a dangerous mood. With faces like brass, the other Continuitors kept Roan from moving away. Juele glanced up and down the hall. To her dismay, she realized that they were standing in the way she needed to go. She didn't dare walk through and interrupt them, and she couldn't go back into the queen's apartments. The minister paced up and back. In a moment he would see her. Juele ducked into the nearest niche and hunkered down behind the statue of a past queen of the Dreamland, which kindly spread out its marble skirts to shield her. She peeked out over the exaggerated hipline of a centuries-bygone gown.

"Master Synton, it's all harmless appearance," Roan said. "I've said that be—"

"You *would* consider this harmless. Anything nonstandard must be all right with a man with only one face. The issues go very deep. You say they are conforming to the shapes below their images. I have seen places where this is not true. I can't ask you to understand it. I am not certain a mutant like you would have the capacity to comprehend."

"Synton, there is nothing wrong with my intelligence," Roan said, very patiently. "You are overwrought. If you would see this as a temporary situation, not a permanent affront to the Sleepers . . ."

"Change can come quickly! Any affront is as good as if it was permanent!"

"Minister, if it will help I will speak to the artist in

charge and ask him to take greater care with the continuity of the images. From my understanding, that is his intention in any case."

Synton grunted and stalked away, followed by his entourage. Roan sighed and leaned back against the wall. The awful things the minister had said must have hurt. Juele was ashamed that she had heard him abused. She wished he would go away so she could sneak out without him seeing her.

But, he was the King's Investigator. In a moment, he came and leaned over the arm of the stone queen.

"You may come out now," he said, kindly. Juele blushed. He'd known all along she was there. She scrambled out from her hiding place, taking care not to bash her inanimate protectoress with her art box.

"I'm sorry," she said. Roan shook his head.

"Never mind," Roan said. "It's an old argument. How is the work going outside?"

"Very well," Juele said, grateful to change the topic. "We'll be done very soon. I think."

"I think your portrait is going well, too, though I am not an expert. Are you satisfied with the progress?"

"Oh, yes," Juele said.

"I had better let you get back to your tasks," Roan said, "as I must return to mine. I look forward to seeing you again." He swept her a deep bow, just as if she was a member of the court. Blushing, Juele hurried away, clasping her art box. He was so nice. She couldn't understand why anyone would treat him so badly, even if he didn't change.

Juele bounded down the wide steps that led from the upper floor into the rear section of the castle. Her hand passed through the banister before coming to rest on something solid. She was alarmed for a moment, then realized that the stairwell was touched with illusion. Rutaro's image had spread in places all the way inside the castle, flowing like oil from the original canvases. Perhaps that was his intention, to have all the sections covering the castle eventually meet at the hub. She hoped the queen wouldn't mind. It did make things look more perfect than before.

Voices floated up from below. Juele slowed as she saw a man in a red velvet tunic and tam bowing to a woman in blue and white ministerial robes who held a tall staff with a globe at the tip. She didn't want to intrude on another ministerial meeting.

"I would be grateful for the favor, Mistress Carodil," the courtier said. "If you sent an analyst to examine the river waters to explain why they are solid enough to walk on, it would be a great relief to those of us in Ephemer."

"Such a task does fall within my ministry," the woman said. She turned to pace, her thumb and forefinger thoughtfully cupping her chin. She came to a jerky halt. "But not this month." The woman turned into a parrot. She fluttered up to stand on top of the orb on her cane. "Many councils are of one head."

"I beg your pardon?" the man in velvet asked.

"Awk!" exclaimed the parrot, turning into a blue and white pig. Juele was puzzled, wondering if the Minister of Science had taken one too many of her own potions. Then she noticed the boy in the smock sitting on the floor against the wall, almost hidden by a potted plant. On his lap he held a device with several knobs and buttons. Over his head hovered an illumined box displaying red numbers that surged ever higher. When he pushed one control, the figure of Carodil spoke. When he moved a ball set into the surface of his device, Carodil moved around. When he slid a lever, the minister changed appearance. But he seemed to be having trouble with the module. The look of panic on his face told Juele that it wasn't behaving the way he expected.

"Conviction framis belknap proof dorbimbit," Carodil said, changing from pig to jointed marionette to a phonograph, as the hapless courtier tried to understand her. "Hop zamboni." At last, the Minister of Science turned into a fig tree and stopped babbling. Over the young artist's head were the words GAME OVER. He slammed a fist down on the module.

"You are indisposed," the courtier said, bowing deeply and retreating on velvet-shod feet toward the door. "If it would be convenient for you, I would like to broach this matter again later."

Naturally, the fig tree didn't say anything, but the courtier didn't appear to require an answer. He backed out of the room. The student gave Juele a guilty look.

"I'm not very good at this yet," he said, "but no one seems to have noticed." He squirmed uncomfortably. "Don't tell anyone I said that. I know it should be perfect. Please, promise you won't!"

"I won't tell," Juele said. "But you shouldn't be doing it at all."

The boy gave her a shamefaced grin. "But it's fun."

"Well, don't," Juele said, lamely. "We could all get in trouble." The student shrugged. As one of Rutaro's assistants she felt a certain amount of responsibility to keep the project in line, but Juele had no real authority and he knew it. She would have to refer the matter to Rutaro and suggest that he pull the reins on people a little tighter.

The crowds were even greater within the castle walls than when she'd left. There were several ministers in their robes of office holding court around the grounds. She hoped they were all real, but very soon she figured out that none of them were. The clique and other advanced students had definitely gotten the hang of creating realistic administrators. Instead of working on the project, they were running their creations, vying for the attention of visitors to the castle grounds, and enjoying themselves thoroughly behind their one-way screens at the expense of the hapless Dreamlanders who came to ask for help. The land-line buzzed with excitement. Where the assistants had been sharing gossip, jokes, and pictures before, now they were swapping techniques.

"We should replace *all* the ministers with ones of our own design!" one student suggested. "How much worse a job would they do than the ones already in office?"

"No," Rutaro said, his face and voice appearing a hundred times larger than life on every canvas around the castle. Juele backed up. His face was red, and he looked mad enough to explode. "It is *not* part of my vision to take over the work of government. This is Art! All these beings are to cease to exist at once!"

There was a lot of complaining from disappointed students, but almost all the copies dropped out of sight. The tourists looked around in dismay and began to leave the grounds. Yet, as soon as Rutaro turned his back or disappeared, the false ministers popped up, only to be surrounded by querents again. So far no one in the court seemed to have noticed. The royal guards hadn't tried to arrest either the images or the students for usurpation. Juele did what she could to prevent visitors from getting caught up in groups around the illusionary ministers. If she could get to them first, she sent them into the castle to see what real officials were still in Mnemosyne. It was a disadvantage being at the rear of the grounds where most of them wouldn't come until it was too late.

Rutaro saw that this new hobby was diverting attention away from the work at hand. He spurred his volunteers to paint quicker, but he insisted they still maintain the quality he sought. Many of the canvases had been neglected. Their artists couldn't concentrate properly on more than one thing. Rutaro was becoming fraught as the hours ticked away. As the opening of the exhibition drew ever closer, his temper shortened in proportion. While exhorting students to do their best, he often went off on fits of rage that had his six assistants struggling for euphemisms. Juele tried to work with the students assigned to her and bothered him as seldom as possible. Visitors still threatened to overwhelm him with cares more properly the province of the administration. Wherever he went he was pursued by men and women shouting about taxes, noise ordinances, leash laws, and property rights. He ran away from them.

During the very next wave of influence, he turned into

a large, white butterfly, skipping from place to place, whisking away before anyone could stop him and ask him questions. His assistants were left to fend for themselves. Juele couldn't catch his attention at all. She had an outside job to do in Mnemosyne that afternoon, and she wanted to ask his permission to go. As her part of the tapestry was well along, she had felt confident enough to accept a small commission from Mayrona's friend Festy to decorate and entertain at a child's party. After watching the frantic butterfly flit past her for the seventh time, Juele realized she couldn't wait any longer or she would be late. She created a message of her face and her voice and integrated it into her tapestry, set to go off when he came by, then headed off to her job.

Chapter 23

Juele walked along the street heading toward the castle, tossing coins up into the air and catching them. As far as she was concerned, Festy could send her on all the jobs he could give her.

It was so nice to be earning some money. She'd become so used to living on a little that she didn't know what to do with the windfall. Maybe she'd spend it on clothes, she thought, or, passing purveyors of food who wafted tempting aromas out of their shop doors, upgrade her level of food service in the dining hall. Juele knew there were nicer things to eat in the kitchens than she normally got, although she certainly was not as badly off as some. One could tell how impoverished some students were by their diet. The ones who never had any lettuce, cabbage, or kale on their plates, for whom the black-clad ladies rarely brought out the bacon, hardly had a bean, or at any rate, not too much bread. Poor aristocracy, of which there were a few in the studen body, had the upper crust, but not a very big piece of the pie. The students at Juele's level had a more varied diet, featuring peanuts, small potatoes, and a *little* sugar. Juele held onto her pride, balancing her meals in between as much as she could. If she stretched out her luxury items to look like more, well, all's fair in illusion, wasn't it? With a steady income from side jobs, she could look forward to just desserts, if she chose.

Down a small street that led between the shopping precinct and the castle grounds, Juele spotted Sangweiler hard at work with a trowel and a bucket. She waved to him. The bearded student put aside his tools and stood up to stretch.

"So you *can* come outside," he said. "I've hardly seen you past the gates except to go between the castle and class!"

"What are you doing?" she asked curiously, examining the wall he was building. "It's different on both sides!"

"Oh, it's a camouflage wall," he said. "Meant to screen the houses back there from the busy part of the city. I've even put in a noise damper to cut traffic noise—" he looked around "—when there is any traffic. It gives the homeowners a nice view to look at."

The side facing the street showed a row of neat little homes with pretty gardens. Figures moved around in the yards, and children and pets played, although they bore little resemblance to what was really going on behind the wall. That meant passersby couldn't peer into the front windows of the homes. But Sangweiler's best work had been reserved for the inside. Instead of shops and streets, the homeowners now overlooked miles of green meadow full of black and white cows, and a river at the bottom. The cows were a little stiff, but Juele didn't feel comfortable pointing that out.

"Very impressive," Juele said. She examined the edge of the illusion. It was not as thin as the illusions that Rutaro and his friends could produce, but a very workmanlike job to put all that depth of focus into a small package. "And so compact."

"Yeah, pretty good, if I do say so myself. I didn't want to be a civil engineer," the senior student said, "but here I am. This wall won't keep a carriage from bashing into these people's gardens, but it gives them the appearance of privacy."

"What's it pay?"

"Not much for the initial construction," Sangweiler admitted, "but there's an extra charge for maintenance, plus I change the view of the seasons every three months."

"Job security!" Juele exclaimed. "I like that."

A woman in a flowered dress walking a small, spotted dog approached. Juele and Sangweiler moved aside so she had room to pass. She gave the two artists in smocks a suspicious look. The woman noticed the meadow, frowned, and attempted to walk into it. As soon as she found it was only a few inches deep, she stalked back, dragging the dog, with her face red and steam pouring out of her ears. The dog barked at the students.

"That's a fake landscape!" the woman exclaimed, pointing at it, and transferred the accusing finger to them. "How *dare* you! You're making a mockery out of the Sleeper's will!" Sangweiler ignored her and pretended to yawn.

"It's a commission, ma'am," Juele started to say, politely, but she railed on.

"Pay no mind," Sangweiler said, holding up a hand. "She's just a nuisance. How did your job go?"

"Very well," Juele said. She held up her fee. The big coins clinked together with a satisfying sound she could never duplicate in an illusion. "Three chickens!"

"Good going!" Sangweiler exclaimed.

"*Who* are you calling a nuisance, young man?" the woman fumed. "Why, I have a good mind to call the police and have you both thrown in jail for disturbing the landscape!"

"Did you say you were entertaining at a birthday party? Did it go well?"

"Wonderfully, after a while," Juele said. "In the beginning I thought it would be one long Embarrassment Dream. For the longest time I couldn't coax a single smile out of the birthday child or his friends. It's just the same kind of things I did at home. I was afraid my small town illusions weren't sophisticated enough for city children, but they warmed up when I increased the color saturation and speed. I guess they get more stimulation here. And they loved it when I made them jewelry and party hats out of light."

"You sound like quite an expert," Sangweiler said, with a smile.

"Oh, yes. I did lots of spare jobs to pay for train fare to Mnemosyne: birthday parties, coming of age celebrations, wedding decorations. You know, helping the bride look beautiful no matter what else happened." She grinned. "I used to make my friends' rooms look clean so they could come out to play."

"That must have made you popular."

"Did you hear me?" the woman shrieked, pushing up closer to them. "You have no right to paste fake scenes all over this city! Post no bills!"

Without thinking, Juele threw up a wall between them and the woman and splashed a sound-deadening wash over it to cut out the shrill noise. At once, she was horrified at what she had done. She took the wall down, revealing the astonished woman's face.

"I am so sorry," Juele said. "But these people hired my friend to paint this landscape. . . ."

The woman wasn't interested in explanations. She turned into a pigeon, fluttered above Sangweiler's illusion, and voided on it. The dropping fell right through the insubstantial landscape. Sangweiler laughed. The pigeon made an indignant noise and flew away. The dog ran after its mistress, trailing its leash. Juele watched her go. A small part of her was ashamed for behaving so badly to another person, but she was surprised that the rest of her did not care. The woman was a townie. She didn't understand art.

"Forget about her," Sangweiler said.

But Juele couldn't. She had started to behave like an elitist. Sangweiler was staring at her. He wouldn't understand the remorse she was feeling. She changed the subject.

"I . . . I certainly hope I can get more jobs like this," she said, forcing herself to smile while her conscience rifled through her memory looking for more evidence to berate her.

"I know exactly what you mean," Sangweiler said. "Rutaro's project is great experience, but we're all volunteering our time. Still need to pay the bills! That's why I'm doing this for suburbanites and mundanes. Look here." He opened a package of lightproof paper and held it up in the sun. A brilliant array of colors lay revealed over his palms. Juele caught her breath.

"How beautiful. I bet they were expensive."

"And how," Sangweiler said, letting out a whistle that sounded like a moth escaping from an empty wallet. "They're imported to Celestia by a fellow I know who's just come back from chasing rainbows in Rem. He likes to go to far-off places where there are different and exotic kinds of light. He pays for his travels by selling the pigments he finds. He gets tropical sunsets, arctic whiteouts, darkest jungle. . . . I overspent a little. You wouldn't care to buy a share, would you?" Juele gasped at the depth and purity of color, and thrift lost its argument with beauty.

"Well, I don't know . . ." Juele said, knowing intellectually how thin her finances were, but the remains of the latest payment on the royal commission was heating up in her pocket, threatening to burn a hole through. She got paid a little whenever she went in to model the queen. And there were the chickens she'd been paid for the party.

"They're amazingly durable," Sangweiler said. "I've found that most of them keep their color for ages, even in the most boring surroundings. Helena and Rutaro bought some, too." He turned his hand, and a brilliant, deep red caught her eye, almost driving into her brain. It must have come from the very farthest edge of the rainbow, even more rich than the light she'd saved from that rainy day. And if Rutaro had bought some, that was endorsement enough for her. Sangweiler dangled the strands again, and Juele nearly gasped with delight.

"That's *glorious*. All right." The two of them struck a bargain, and Juele found herself a chicken and two loaves of bread poorer, but the proud possessor of a pool of red light the size of her palm. It felt warm and smooth, as if it was alive. What a treat! She knew that Mr. Cachet would tell her to learn how to tell that color without looking at it. A red of such intensity would be no trouble at all. Juele tucked the strands away in her work box, picturing how well it would go in her askance reality project. Such vivid color ought to go a very long way, spun out in minute quantities in the blossoms and the ceramic heart on the basket. It would create marvelous eye-catching glints. Mayrona would love it, too. Touches would add life to their miserable dormitory. As an accent it should last a long time. Perhaps with its help, they might be able at last to tack up some neutral colors over the dreary walls. As she walked away she was already deep in planning. She had to laugh at herself. After all the sensible notions she had made for the money, she ended up spending it on art supplies. As always.

"See you back around the castle," Sangweiler called after her.

Juele enjoyed her walk back, gawking at the old buildings and the gardens on her way as avidly as any tourist. She loved Mnemosyne. Never had she seen colors that were so bright, nor people who were so different and interesting. It made her feel as if her hometown was drawn in plain black and white. If there was a kind of gravity in the Dreamland that attracted color, it pulled toward Mnemosyne and the School in particular.

Life here was such a change from her normal, ordinary existence at home. She looked different, carried herself differently, and enjoyed new things. In spite of her earlier resolution not to be changed, the pervasive atmosphere of the School itself was altering her to suit itself. In only a few weeks, she had stopped seeing both sides of the Town and Gown disagreements. When once she had had more sympathy for the townsfolk, she now placed herself fully on the side of the School. It was a natural adjustment. She knew almost no one outside, and from the way the people of Mnemosyne talked when she was out, hardly anyone outside knew anything or anyone inside. They called the scholars "they" with a small "t." At first when Juele heard "they" whispered behind her back, she thought the townsfolk were referring to the Idealists, but how would they know of them?

Peppardine said he and his friends hardly ever went out of the school grounds. But she discovered the townies meant any of the students. The smock set them apart, made them objects of curiosity, misinformation, and occasionally, fear.

In their turn, the students all but ignored the towns-folk and abhorred the tourists, laughing at them behind their backs. Anyone who looked awkward or lost was a target, even if she or he had managed to blend in physi-cally as the Dreamland was wont to make people do. More often, the prevailing influence in an area pointed up a stranger's lack of belonging, making them stand out. Juele had caught herself laughing at people who seemed out of place, forgetting how she had felt her first day. Consciously she tried not to be offensive, but her per-spective had changed. Whether or not she felt as if she belonged at the School, she was acting as if she did. She fought it now and again, seeking to regain the Juele who had left home with her heart wide open, but the influ-ence of the School was as powerful on a willing heart as any Sleeper. So long as she was there, she remained changed. She wondered if it would affect the fundamental Juele inside. What would she be like when she went home?

But would she just go home? She wondered about it as she walked through the castle doors, heading for her dormitory room. Many of the older students on the line talked about the posts around the Dreamland they were going to take after graduation. While she was sitting for Juele, the queen had spoken of possible jobs that might be offered to her later on. Juele thought it might be nice to work in the castle. Could she earn that? She knew she was improving in her skill and gaining a more critical eye. Every time she went to model the queen she saw the fundamental mistakes she had made in the portrait the time before. It was a temptation to tear it all up and start again, but she was also learning what to erase and what to keep. She was gaining perspective, as the queen said. Juele was pleased with herself and

her progress. Her future didn't have to be decided right
that moment, she told herself, putting away her party
supplies and her new red pigment. She left the dormitory and cut through the royal gallery toward the postern
door and the kitchens.

When Juele returned to her station, things were in
more of an uproar than when she had left. None of the
clique were in their places, and color was leaking out
of their tapestries like sand from an hourglass. Hastily
she built a dam of shadow to catch it and went looking
for them.

Seeking eight people in the vast castle grounds was
not an easy task. The terrain had become hilly, and thousands of people milled up and down the slopes, getting
in the way of the artists at work. Juele spotted Rutaro's
white smock moving hastily through the orchards. To her
relief he was human again. Behind him were Bella and
Daline and, a dozen paces behind them, a hundred sheep
in flowered shirts and baseball hats clicking away with
cameras.

"There she is," Daline said, putting a hand on Rutaro's
arm. He turned as Juele came up to them. His face was
red with anger.

"Where were you?" he demanded, growing a yard
taller so he could loom over her menacingly. "I have had
to speak to *your staff* directly. That is not what I want
to have happen!" He looked strained.

"I had a side job, Rutaro," Juele said apologetically.
"I left you a message."

"A message is not enough!" Rutaro said, and the
whites of his eyes showed. He tossed his head like a
frightened horse. "I need you *here*. You should have been
here!"

"But, but, Sangweiler was working in town, too," she
stammered. "I thought it would do no harm."

"What does it matter what someone else is doing?"
Rutaro demanded. "I count on *you*, and you let me
down!"

A few yards away to her left, Tanner snickered and muttered a comment in a low voice. Juele heard him and quietly fumed to herself. Rutaro's head snapped around. He could hear him, too. Sondra and Erbatu made an excuse to come over and hang over Tanner's shoulder as he pretended to work, but they were watching Juele. They were pleased with themselves. They'd managed to break down the chain of command and pierce the sound barrier Rutaro had set in place. It was all Juele's fault, which pleased them even more. She was sorry. Her section must be causing Rutaro more trouble than any other. Probably Sangweiler didn't have such aggressive people working for him who tried so hard to get around the rules.

"It won't happen again, Rutaro," Juele promised. He wasn't listening.

"It is not as if I don't have other concerns. I have been pursued all day by fools wishing to be advised on everything from colors for interior decoration to defense agreements between warring villages," Rutaro said. "I've given them plenty of alternative people to speak to. I have sent them to the appropriate authorities in the castle, but those seas of people all still want *me*." He smacked himself in the chest. The sound reverberated through the air. In the distance, Juele heard a cry.

"There he is!" shrieked a female voice. A woman clambered to the top of the nearest ridge at the rear of the castle and pointed straight at Rutaro. "He'll tell us where to go!" Glad shouts filled the air. From behind her came dozens of people, eagerly reaching out. Rutaro blanched.

"Oh, no, here they come again." He backed away from them, seeking an exit.

But his escape was cut off. Pouring into the castle gates came hundreds, thousands of eager people. They came up the hill in waves, surrounding him from all sides, clamoring for Rutaro's attention. His eyes rolled until all Juele could see were the whites. Spreading out her arms, she threw herself against the rising tide of humanity, trying to hold them back, to protect him. He stumbled backwards. The crowds of people came together with their hands out, seeking to touch him. Juele found herself lifted up off the ground by the sheer press of human bodies and bobbed along helplessly in their wake. Rutaro was driven to the castle wall. The crest of the wave gathered and rolled inexorably toward him, threatening to drown him. Just before it washed over him, he threw up his arms.

"Enough is enough!" he cried, and disappeared. The wave receded, and the crowd stopped in its tracks.

"Where did he go?" a man bellowed, casting about for a sign of the white smock.

"Spread out!" another man called, raising his hand high. "We'll find him!"

"Stop!" a quavering voice ordered. "He's not the one you are here to see." From the heart of the mob emerged an old man in maroon and dusty-beige robes. Juele recognized Micah, the Historian Prime. She groaned. It was one of the clique's constructs. But, to her surprise, the crowd began to gather about him. They couldn't tell the difference between him and the real thing. She began to make her way forward, ready to erase the image on the spot. Arms grabbed her and held her back.

"No, darling," Bella said, in her ear. Most of the In Crowd was standing behind her, watching "Micah" avidly. "Watch and learn."

"Minister!" a man shouted. "One of my neighbors is shifting most of my yard over our mutual property line. What can I do?"

"It's shifting that way by itself," protested the man standing next to him, obviously the neighbor.

"There's historical perspective for land grabs," Micah said, lifting a trembling finger. "You ought to be fairly compensated. If he acknowledges that he is taking your property, then he should give you money for it."

"How much?"

"A fair price," Micah decreed. "Not more than the current value of property in your area." The two neighbors eyed each other for a moment, then nodded and shook hands.

"Master Micah, my boss has stolen my good name!" a woman cried. "They call him Chloe, and that's my name. I worked hard to attain it! I want it back."

"That is uncalled for," Micah said, severely. "He must give it back, or you are entitled to attach his reputation."

"Thank you, Minister!" The crowd murmured approval. Juele was impressed. The illusion was making reasonably wise judgments. More distinguished-looking persons in robes appeared, attracting their own circle of querents and curiosity-seekers. Few of the visitors broke away in search of Rutaro. The flow of tourists receded, pulling away from the line of canvases. The artists returned to their places in peace. Bella shot Juele a smug look.

"There, you see, my dear?" she said. "We can do it as well as he does."

"But, don't you think that what you're doing is derivative and representational?" By suggesting they were copying another's designs Juele hoped to goad them into stopping, but it didn't work.

"Oh, no, my dear," Bella said, with satisfaction, "it's *interpretive*. This is how we think things should work." She flicked her fingers. "Run along now, like a good little drone, and do your dabs."

Stung, Juele went back to her canvas. She didn't know whether to be annoyed that they were disobeying Rutaro's instructions or grateful that they had distracted the crowd away from pursuing him. She had to admit that the pesty things were doing a good job. As Rutaro had said, most of the problems people had were trivial things they could have worked out themselves, but it should have been up to the real ministers to tell them so. If it kept the tourists away from them while they were finishing the illusion, what harm was there? Tossing between the horns of the dilemma, Juele went back to work. She wondered where Rutaro had gone. She was worried about him. He'd seemed more than a little frayed around the edges when he disappeared. She hoped he'd be more himself when she saw him later.

But he had no intention of being found. When Juele

went looking for the Ivory Tower that night, she couldn't find her way. Fruitlessly she wandered through the turnings of the ancient stone passageways, seeking access to the square garden. A passage just off the old quadrangle that usually led to the garden had become a dead end. There, she found a dozen men and women she knew well from the inner circle, all questing about in vain. Tynne shook her head as Juele appeared.

"You, too, eh? I've been searching for hours." Juele stared at the mute gray walls of the corridor, feeling bereft. "Don't take it personally," Tynne said kindly.

"Locked the door and pulled it in after Them," said Borus, forlornly.

"Oh, well," said Tynne. "Let's go to the coffeehouse."

"I'll wait here," Borus said. "Helena might decide she needs me." He turned into a large dog, found a cosy spot near the end of the corridor, and settled down with his muzzle on his front paws.

Exciting conversation might do Juele a world of good, and she could see how her fortunes fared with the clique. She hated supervising them; it made it hard to socialize, and she did want them to like her. She enjoyed being In. Her continuing goal was to gain acceptance into the In Crowd for Gretred and Mayrona. She also realized, with a guilty twinge, that she had been spending fewer evenings with Bella and her friends as her time had been taken up by the Idealists. The clique probably would like to hear the latest news from the Ivory Tower. If they hadn't wheedled it out of Rutaro that afternoon, when they'd made him talk to them.

The more Juele thought about the smoke-filled room with the occluded atmosphere and veiled barbs, the more she thought a night off from all of it wouldn't do her a bit of harm, either. "No, thank you," she said to Tynne. "I think I'll just go to bed."

The second senior under-attaché for Provincial Affairs folded his office into his briefcase and prepared to go home for the day.

"Cudo!" called a familiar voice as he turned into the corridor. The under-attaché smiled at his friend, Jarold, the assistant minister of science. "Nice day."

"Very nice," Cudo said, pleasantly. "Fewer problems than yesterday. Everybody's been in such a splendid mood. Every diplomatic and trade mission from other provinces that came to this office today all worked out almost immediately, even the most difficult. And, I ran into Master Micah tonight. He seemed more than usually amenable. I didn't have any trouble getting him to assign one of his staffers to do some research for our department."

"It *has* been very peaceful around here lately," said his friend. "Maybe it's even affected the old page-turner." Cudo laughed. "I was expecting a shipment of imaginary numbers from Swenyo today. It didn't arrive, and they guarantee delivery."

"Sleeper's whim," said the under-attaché with a sigh. "Though there was a lot of traffic today through the castle. Still is. Quite a lot going on, even though nearly everyone's away. Did you see the new laws posted today? Nearly fifteen, I should say."

"What do you think of the great civic engineering project?" asked Jarold.

"I thought the artists would be a pest, but things look very pretty."

"All our apprentices are having fun with the optical illusions," said the assistant minister. "I've got to keep on them every minute to make sure they're doing their assigned experiments. But for once, I'm not having any trouble getting them on the measuring committee. All of them want to be outside, and seeing what's going on."

"Right and proper for your department," Cudo said approvingly.

"Mmm. But too much leisure time is having a strange effect on Minister Carodil. She keeps changing her mind. Every other time I go to ask her a question, she says something different. I'm not getting bad advice, you understand, but sometimes she contradicts herself."

"How odd," said Cudo, as they came to the main corridor near the side entrance used by junior civil servants. "I say, what's that dog doing posing in that window? He's been there every time I've passed for the last few days."

"Nice window," Jarold said. "Always seems to be sunny there. Well, this is where I go. Good night, old man."

Cudo walked through the door that opened onto the shortcut that led directly from the palace to his small home. His wife greeted him at the door with a smile. "Good evening, dear! Your dinner is ready!"

"Very good, my love," he said, putting his briefcase down. To his way of thinking, life was good. His wife was perfectly beautiful, his house was perfectly clean, his children perfectly behaved, and his job had been perfectly easy that day. He sat at the head of the gleaming table and tucked a napkin into his collar. His wife whirled about, placing dish after sumptuous dish before him. She arranged generous servings on his plate, brought him a cold drink, and danced off to let him enjoy it in peace.

To his way of thinking, the meal seemed a little insubstantial to him, but it looked so pretty and smelled so good that he didn't like to mention it.

Jarold started down the long hill toward the castle gates. Just before he reached it, the path turned, diverting him back into the grounds. Jarold frowned. He had checked out for the day and was entitled by covenant to eight hours rest in a domicile of his own choosing. He backed up and began sprinting toward the gates again, putting on a burst of speed at the curve of the path, hoping to outrun the diversion, but he found himself halfway around the castle precinct, in the midst of the royal stables. No matter how hard he tried, he couldn't leave. The castle meant to keep him overnight.

"Oh, well," he said. "Sleeper's will." Briefcase in hand, he went back to his office. His secretary raised her eyebrows from her typewriter as he appeared. Jarold folded back his desk chair, fluffing it up until it was a comfortable sofa, and prepared to go to sleep.

"Get me up at six, will you, Mabel?"

"Of course, minister," the secretary said brightly. She turned into a rooster and flew up to a perch near the window to wait for dawn.

Chapter 24

The assistant to the undersecretary in charge of cataloguing the Akashic Records had gone home early from work with a severe case of dislocated features. With his eyes on the back of his head it was easy to keep track of the people coming and going from the royal archives, but impossible to do any of the work on his desk. Thanks to a restorative wave of influence during the night the condition had straightened itself out.

In the morning, he left his humble abode in Mnemosyne and trudged up the hill toward the castle. He was not looking forward to plowing through the backlog. It was just something that had to be done. He reached the gates and gawked through them at the desolate, ruined landscape beyond. Not a brick or stone stood on top of another anywhere in the blackened grounds. Shardlike embers glowed angrily everywhere. An unhealthy smoke rose from a huge crater in the center of what yesterday was not an empty field. His eyes, newly restored to the front of his head, followed the plume of smoke upward. His mouth, which had always been in the same place, dropped open. Miles above his head, the Castle of Dreams floated on a lofty bed of cloud.

"Oh, my," said the assistant to the undersecretary in a quavering voice. "I think I'm going to be late for work today."

He never glanced at the tiny gray kitten playing with a ball of yarn just inside a white line at the edge of the destruction.

❖   ❖   ❖

Juele left the queen's apartments after another successful session. She hugged her art box against her side with pleasure. Unless something went completely wrong, she could be through with the portrait after one more sitting. The queen had said she liked the way it was coming. Juele could almost *feel* the pink fading out of her smock. When half a dozen doctors had appeared at the door for Her Majesty's morning consultation, Juele had withdrawn, feeling content.

She wanted to share her joy with Rutaro. He still worried her, disappearing like that the night before. He probably just wanted to rest undisturbed. The cares of the project weighed heavily enough on him to flatten any lesser artist. When it was all over, she bet he would sleep for a month. Now that the excitement of the modeling session was fading, Juele realized she was tired, too. She hadn't been sleeping as well as she could, and there was so much to do.

It was going to take her some time to reach her section of the tapestry. As Rutaro had said might happen, the School of Light was now entirely contained within the castle itself. The way the school buildings intersected the castle, there was no way to avoid passing through parts of it. She was fascinated by the way that the two buildings seemed to overlie one another. Rooms rarely intersected, though corridors and streets did, and all of them were surrounded by Rutaro's illusion. Servants and students mingled in the open spaces, all looking equally confused.

What with the constant movement of the School toward the center of the castle, it was difficult to follow a single route directly to anywhere. Just now she had turned left at the Prism Building and found herself in the Vermeil Room, one of the higher-up reception chambers, all decorated in silver-gilt. Dutifully, she bowed to the chairs on the dais, one of which was draped with a bundle of silk cloth, and kept walking. A man in gorgeous satin livery bustled toward her with a staff in his hand and a frown on his face. Juele jumped guiltily. It was the chef de protocol. He was going to chide her for being there without permission and without going through the lesser rooms first. She hadn't meant to. It was just where that part of the School had ended up at that moment.

He seemed to walk in place for a distance, then he stopped and bowed deeply, no doubt to the chair behind her.

"Your Majesty," he said, bowing again. Juele stared at him.

"I'm not the queen. Or the princess," she said, backing away. "I'm sorry. I'll go."

He did not seem to hear her. The truth dawned on Juele. There was an illusion in force here, but it only went one way. She could see and hear him from her side, but he could not see and hear her from his. The courtier bowed again, as if hearing an invisible presence on the throne speak.

"Yes, Your Majesty," he said, bobbing up and down like a glass bird, almost banging his head on the ground. "Your most humble servant, Your Majesty. It shall be done, Your Majesty."

Juele rather enjoyed seeing the man prostrate himself. The uppermost courtiers were so snobby, particularly this one. She sat down on the edge of the dais to watch. The chef de protocol agreed humbly with everything the invisible presence said, even chiding himself.

"But, of course, Your Majesty. I haven't been sufficiently vigilant. I will do better."

After a while the spectacle became boring. Juele remembered that she had better get to work.

On the way out of the chamber, she spotted the place she had missed her turning before. The main quadrangle intersected the corridor at an acute angle, leaving a steadily widening sliver of room for her to wiggle into the School's environs. If she could just find the museum, she could pass easily through into the royal gallery and take the back stairs down to the kitchens. In the corridor, she passed a grandly dressed man in dark green robes whom she recognized as the Minister of Continuity. With him again was Roan, the King's Investigator. Roan seemed to be suppressing his temper, but he bowed to Juele and gave her a pleasant look. Juele smiled shyly at him and shot away into the quad.

"There is too much interference being caused by this . . . this oil painting!" Synton insisted. "Things are not as they should be. The castle ought to be inviolate. Reserved for government business only!"

"Mm-hm," King Byron said. He was building a house of cards, concentrating on placing the seven of diamonds on top of a pyramid made by the fours of clubs, hearts, and spades. "Certainly it should. If the Sleepers will it."

"The artists do not appear to be abusing their trust," Roan said. "Their gallery has been open to the castle's for weeks, now, and they have caused no real trouble."

"But the building itself is now encroaching! They are frightening people away from here," Synton said. "I would normally see a dozen to two dozen people per day with questions relating to my department, and practically no one has come to me in days."

"That could be a perfectly normal hiatus," Roan said. "The Sleepers may not be needing the clarification that you and your staff offer them."

"Do you presume to speak for the Sleepers, you abomination? Your Majesty!" Synton said, appealing to the king.

"Yes, yes," the king said absently. The house of cards melted down into a single sheet of paper, a crossword puzzle. Byron clicked the top of the pen in his hand and filled in a six-letter word.

"Moreover, Your Majesty," Synton continued, narrowing his eyes at Roan, "the cooks are complaining that food isn't arriving as it should be. They are having to make do with other sources of nutrition for the court."

"All of us have seen Thin Times and Feast Times Dreams," Roan argued. The king was obviously in the throes of creation, one of the means he had of setting the Dreamland in order, and they were interrupting him. His Majesty was trying to be cordial, but he was too preoccupied to pay them more than cursory attention. Synton saw none of the signs, though. He was determined to make his point.

"You are wrong, Master Roan. Such a dearth of activity in the castle is unprecedented, Your Majesty."

"It may be," the king said absently, frowning at his crossword. "And then again, it might not."

"But most importantly, Your Majesty," Synton said. He had become a bulldog, and Roan knew that there was no reasoning with him now. He would hang onto his topic until he got the answer he wanted. "I must protest at all the uproar of what is going on about the castle."

"Your Majesty," Roan said, with a trace of irritation, but he tried to keep his voice level. "It's just an illusion. Her Majesty's favored artists are preparing a spectacle for her exhibition. It will be quite amazing when it is finished. I have been speaking . . ." Synton interrupted him, shouldering forward toward the king.

"Yes, but they are preventing the normal operation of the court. It is difficult to tell what is proper, and what is illusion, any more. I have been walking into doors that are actually walls, and tripping over chairs I cannot see. This is all wrong."

"Your Majesty," Roan said, reasonably, "it will all be over soon. I have asked his excellency," with a bow for the minister, "to hold off his wrath for the brief period for everyone to enjoy the finished illusions. When it's over, all will be removed. For the meantime, it's harmless entertainment."

"Now! I want it done now! Now-wow-wow!" the minister snapped, grabbing the king's trouser leg and pulling at it. "You are on the side of all this interference, Your Majesty!" he growled, with a mouth full of cloth. "You must see my point!"

"I agree with Synton," the king said, a little absentmindedly, Roan thought. "You must let him do his job, Master Roan."

Roan bowed. "I would be delighted to do so, but I hope he will balance his assiduous wish for order in the court with the queen's pleasure at her patronage of the art school in our midst. I might mention, in the interests of security, that the guards keep watch upon the proximity of the school itself. It does seem to be closer than ever. I saw an annex of it encroaching upon the royal kitchens yesterday morning. It did give the cooks quite a start. Now it seems to be intruding upon part of the dining chambers without actually opening into them. The halls are completely accessible if one approaches them from a door not covered by the School. I am surprised that Master Synton is not upset about the movement of the building."

"This is a normal Dreamish function," Synton said, with a disapproving look at Roan. "It is not at all uncommon for things of importance to achieve greater propinquity. What I object to is the illusion."

"Very well," Roan said. "It would help if I could enlist Captain Spar and the guards to assist me in watching the perimeter, to direct people safely around it. If they keep watch upon the School, they can also oversee what is real and what is not, then warn the unwary of hazards that are concealed by the illusion. That should satisfy Master Synton's concerns and mine at one time."

"Ah," said the king. "I agree with you. It shall be done."

"Thank you, Your Majesty," Roan said. "I will take care of the matter at once." He bowed and excused himself.

Minister Synton watched him go, then turned back to the king, who was filling in more clues. He glanced at the king speculatively. The king had favored most of his propositions that day. Synton resumed human state, but kept the bulldog's jaw for emphasis.

"It is strange how, Your Majesty, how Roan never changes in any way," he said.

"Hmm? Yes, it certainly is."

"That is an offense against the continuity and the view of the Sleepers, wouldn't you agree?"

"Why, yes, I agree with you," Byron said, amiably. He exclaimed to himself and jotted down a long word that ran down the length of the puzzle.

The minister was surprised by the king's concurrence. In all the years Roan had existed, Byron had been tolerant of the affront the Historian's son represented to the face of the Dreamland. But, today, for whatever reason the Sleepers had sent, he had changed his mind. While the opportunity presented itself, Synton was determined to make his case.

"In fact, my liege, I have long been of the opinion that Roan upsets the delicate balance of the Dreamland's reality, if I may call our state of being reality," he said, cautiously, watching the king with care. Byron was capable of righteous rages that could burn down forests, and Roan had always been a favorite of his. "Not only that, and I realize that I may be far overstepping myself, but if he is indeed an avatar of a Sleeper, not that I believe that wild tale for a moment, such a being as he pierces the veil between this and the Waking World. How can we continue to be the agents of the Sleepers' solution to their concerns if such an irritant remains? He is an abomination of nature. Although he does his job."

"Yes, I agree with you," the king said. "He is an abomination of nature. Although he does his job."

"Such a situation could not be a healthy one. I feel it would cause more harm the longer it goes on."

"Do you?"

"Yes," Synton said, with all the conviction that was in him. He set his bulldog's jaw. "In fact, I think that the only solution is discontinuation, my king. With apologies. I realize that your daughter is attached to him. But you are the king."

"That is true," Byron said, mildly. He finished his puzzle and clicked the pen closed. "I am the king. I agree with you. It shall be done."

Synton was flatly astonished, but realized that after all, things in the Dreamland did change. Except the monster Roan. He pressed his advantage.

"Then may I see to his apprehension at once, Your Majesty? The sooner he is removed from society, the sooner the rift between this world and the next will begin to heal."

"If you wish," the king said, his attention wandering off to a brightly colored vase on the dresser behind the minister. "If you wish."

"May I have a signed order to that effect?" Synton asked. It was best to create a paper trail in case his instructions were questioned later. Byron shrugged and turned over his crossword puzzle. He clicked his pen open again and scribbled a few sentences on the blank paper. At the bottom, he wrote his name in big letters and swirled a flourish underneath. He handed the sheet to the Minister of Continuity.

Gleefully, Synton accepted the order and read it through. It was everything he had hoped for. Arrest, incarceration, and discontinuation. True, this action might hurt the princess's feelings, but it could not happen at a more opportune time, while she was out of town. She would have prevented Roan's removal in spite of Synton's reasonable concerns. The sooner the freak was out of the way, the sooner Princess Leonora would forget him. One day she would find a normal husband, who changed according to the Sleepers' will. The thought that the Dreamland narrowly escaped having an anathema as a royal consort sent chills through him. Bowing to the king, Synton excused himself and went looking for Captain Spar.

The figure of the king sat motionless upon his throne. As soon as the room was empty of expectations, it resumed its base shape as a man's shirt stuffed with cloth.

Roan shook the manacles on his wrists, not believing they were real. One moment he had been in Captain Spar's office, giving the commander instructions regarding the observation of the castle perimeter. The next thing he knew, he was being led to the dungeons under armed guard. Spar had looked as if he regretted his action, but he never called back his men.

"Why are you doing this?" he asked Corporal Lum, who led the squad of red-clad soldiers escorting him.

"Orders, sir," Lum said, miserably.

"What have I done?" The guards had to help him down the narrow stone steps because of the short iron chain hobbling his ankles.

"Being different, sir. I mean, the same. By order of the king. Only it was Minister Synton who done it. He had the arrest order right there in front of us. Signed by the king, it was. We all saw it, but the minister held onto the order, wouldn't let Captain Spar handle it. I'm sorry, sir. I don't think it ought to be allowed, but orders is orders."

Roan knew Synton thought of him as a freak and felt he posed a threat to the continuity of the Dreamland, but he had never suspected Synton would stoop to such tactics. "I must appeal this outrage to the king!"

"Don't know if you'll have a chance, sir," Lum said. He tripped on an invisible bump underfoot, then helped Roan over it so he wouldn't stumble. "The punishment's already been decided."

"Punishment? What punishment?"

Lum gulped. "Discontinuation, sir. I'm sorry, sir. I wish it was different."

"I don't blame you, Corporal," Roan said, his calm voice belying the confusion and outrage he felt inside. "You've got to do your job."

The dungeons in the great granite pile were small cells hewn into solid rock, with only a horizontal slit of a window at the top of the outer wall that let in limited light and air. Lum stood by as Roan stooped to go into the cell. The ceiling was low, and Roan was tall. He peered around the gloomy enclosure and found there was a wide stone shelf that served as bed, seat, and table. A covered bucket huddled in the corner. The door began to close upon him. Roan held it back with desperate palms. "Wait, I am entitled to one telephone call."

"That's true, sir," Lum said, opening the door again. Roan released a breath he didn't realize he was holding.

"I'll get the phone," Lum said. He closed the heavy door on Roan, who saw it as a solid wall of black iron. The guard's footsteps receded into a faint echo.

Roan sat down on the shelf and thought hard about his last conversation with the king. It had seemed perfectly normal. The king was perhaps a little distant, but the queen had said he was taking a vacation, enjoying his hobbies. He had not appeared to harbor any ill will against Roan. Surely after so many years of loyal service as King's Investigator he had earned the consideration of being informed of any displeasure he had incurred?

A short time later, the measured pace returned. Lum opened the door and handed him the receiver of a tremendous, old-fashioned black telephone so heavy that it could be used as a weapon in other hands. So long as Lum held onto it, it remained a communication device.

Roan clicked the cradle and held the receiver to his ear. He heard a mournful hum, a click, and finally a human being. "To whom do you wish to speak, please?" asked a nasal female voice.

"Her Highness, the Princess Leonora," Roan said. "She's in Bolster."

"One mo-ment, puleeze," the voice said. But it was more than one moment. Roan paced up and back impatiently, tethered by the curly cord to the device. "I am sorry. The party to whom you wish to speak is outside the calling radius."

"Try again, please," Roan said, desperately. "This is important." Shaking his head, Lum clicked the cradle, and the receiver fell silent. The curly cord retracted, yanking the receiver out of Roan's hands. The guard hung it up.

"I'm sorry, sir. One call is all you're allowed."

"Lum, I have to let someone know that I am down here," Roan pleaded. "Won't you inform the king?" On second thought, Roan recalled that it was the king who had condemned him at Synton's request. He couldn't look for any help there. His family and all of his friends were at the Cult Movie Evocation in northwest Celestia with the princess. "What about Her Majesty? Could you speak to her?"

"I'm only supposed to let you communicate with one person, and one only," Lum said unhappily. "That's the rule."

"But I didn't get through! Please, Lum, you must get a message to Leonora. Send a page. It'll find her no matter where she is. I must tell someone where I am. I can't . . ." His voice faded. Die alone in the dark, he nearly said. "Please help me."

"It's highly irregular, sir," Lum said, looking guilty and sad. "But, seeing as it's you, sir, I'll do anything I can."

"I appreciate that, Corporal."

"I'll send the message at once," Lum said. He started to swing the heavy door around. A thought occurred to him, and he opened the door to say, "And if it means anything, sir, I don't mind that you're never different."

"Thank you, Lum," Roan said, touched. "It does mean a lot to me." The iron door slammed shut with a boom that echoed up and down the gloomy corridor, leaving him alone in the dark. He shook the bars, then went to sit down on the bench to think. Discontinuation! Could this be a sign his Sleeper was abandoning him because Celestia was about to undergo Changeover? Oh, surely not so soon! None of the other many indications of catastrophe had been noted. On the other hand, all the Historians who would have observed them were in Bolster, and the mass of illusion around the castle might have prevented them from seeing any. He had to wait until Leonora or Bergold returned to Mnemosyne. Then, the mistake would be straightened out, and he would be reprieved. It must be. In the meantime, he had to try and think his way out, before it was too late.

Shaking his head with regret, Corporal Lum went in search of a page. Captain Spar would consider him being derelict of duty if he didn't go right back to his patrol, but Master Roan was special, related to the Sleepers and all. It'd be worth demerits and punishment duty to help him. To his relief he didn't have to go far to find pages. In a big empty hall not far from the postern gate dozens of them in yellow, white, and orange livery were skipping back and forth up and down stairs, laughing and calling to one another. Empty-headed little wretches, Lum thought.

"Here, lad!" he called. One of the boys left their game and came to a bounding halt before Lum.

"I've got a job for you."

"Yes, sir!"

"Take this message to the Princess Leonora. She's gone to Bolster. Tell her that Master Roan is in the cells, and he's in real trouble. He needs her to come and help him. They're going to discontinue him in a couple of days if she doesn't do something right smart. Do you have all that?"

"Yes, sir!" the boy said, wide-eyed.

"Well, go on!" Lum said. The page scampered away. His heart lighter, Lum turned and marched back to his post. If Captain Spar chose to put him on report, well, it was for a good cause. The princess would fix everything. *She'd* raise holy murder. The Minister of Continuity would be lucky if he didn't find himself in the cells.

The page ran across the hall, up three steps, and out onto an upper passage, where he turned into a duck-shaped target in a row of identical ducks swimming through bobbing waves of cardboard cut out to resemble water.

Colm, seated on a buttress twenty feet away from the target, took aim with a slingshot, pulled back the elastic, and let fly. A blob of light went sailing through the air, missing the duck. It struck an alabaster bust in a niche above the row of ducks, making the statue's nose glow blue.

"Missed him that time," Colm said to Tanner, who sat beside him in a window frame. The duck swam to the end of the passage, where it went nose down, disappearing into the lower level. "I'll get him the next time he goes around."

Chapter 25

The brutality of the schedule Juele was keeping began to tell upon her. When she woke in the mornings, she felt as if she had never gone to sleep at all. Her dreams were full of running from place to place with her heavy art box full of pieces of a jigsaw puzzle and a loud timer strapped to her chest. Each piece had to be put into its place before the buzzer went off, or Juele would lose her spot in the School and be banished forever to the nether reaches, where no one ever talked about art, and everything was pedestrian and ordinary. Everything depended upon her being in the right place at the right time. She had no choice, no one she could appeal to. People swam up out of the gloom through which she ran, their faces distorted. Their mouths were stretched open in hysterical laughter that was strangely muted. Juele could never understand what they were saying. They were all strangers.

Juele jerked awake, and found herself sitting all alone in a classroom, surrounded by empty desks. Horrified, she realized she had fallen asleep during class and was no longer following the teacher.

"Listen carefully to the nuances," a woman's voice was saying in the distance. Guiltily, Juele recognized the crisp tones of Mrs. Dowsabell, the sound instructor. "And this one indicates extreme crisis." Another buzzer sounded, with a little more edge to it. Juele attempted to follow her, to catch up with the others without having heard the first part of the instruction. She rose, taking her box with her, and found herself in a narrow, linoleum-floored corridor with three doors to choose from. Juele opened one at random onto a new passageway and could hear the teacher's voice a little closer. She dashed through, throwing open doors and following the voice through twists and turns until she all but ran into the back of the class, which was wending its way through a difficult and tortuous passage.

"So you have caught up with us at last, Mistress Juele," the teacher said, disapprovingly. Juele bent her head with shame. The other students snickered.

"I'm sorry, Mrs. Dowsabell," she said.

"Sorry? Sorry doesn't ring the decibel. How can you learn about sound if you aren't awake to listen?" Juele didn't know what to say. The laughter that she feared rose around her, and Mrs. Dowsabell spun on her heel and scolded the other students. "Stop that at once!" she ordered, and turned back to Juele. "I thought there might be trouble because you were so young. Are you a baby at other times? Do you need an afternoon nap?"

"Oh, no, ma'am!" Juele said in alarm. "I'm pretty generally a teenager."

"I see," Mrs. Dowsabell said, in strident tones. "A teenager. Not a nuisance, set to disrupt my classroom?"

Juele was horrified at the thought. "No, ma'am!"

"Hmph! Well, then, take your naps when you are not in this classroom. Otherwise, we will begin to wonder whether there was an error in your acceptance to this School." Juele quailed, hearing an echo of her nightmare in the teacher's words. "These are years unlike anything you will ever have in your life. Don't waste them."

"No, ma'am," Juele said, contritely.

"Oh, she's just going to live forever, like Them," Tanner sneered, and she could feel the full scorn of the clique in his words. He yanked a string, and Juele's right arm jumped. "She can catch up on everything later."

It was all very well for him to jibe. He wasn't putting his whole heart and soul into Rutaro's project. Nor was any of his group working so hard to keep up with all her acquaintances as she was, in the Ivory Tower and elsewhere. Juele was furious. Why had she given them

so much power over her? She found it hard to pull back
control. Tanner flicked another string, and she felt her
leg dance a step.

The bell rang, saving Juele from further humiliation.
She left the classroom, feeling her bottom pierced by
the multiple horns of a dilemma. It was true, she had
been saying yes to everyone. She was afraid if she said
no to anything that she was offered that she would be
left out, and never get another opportunity. She was
spending so much time on her outside projects and
socializing in the coffeehouse and the Ivory Tower in the
evenings that she was beginning to neglect her school-
work, the very reason she had come to the School of
Light in the first place. Honesty compelled her to admit
that in attempting to do everything at once she might
not be giving her best efforts to anything. Desperately,
she went over her schedule, not knowing what to sac-
rifice. Something was going to have to give way. If she
didn't make the choice herself, someone else would
undoubtedly make it for her.

One thing she did not want to give up were her vis-
its to the Ivory Tower. It was still a privilege to be
admitted, to sit in the exalted inner circle and listen to
the Idealists. To her enormous relief the passage opened
that evening on the square garden. The tower stood there
under the cloud-heavy sky like a finger of moonlight:
inviting, tantalizing, infinitely desirable, and accessible.

When she entered the salon room, everything seemed
normal. Rutaro and the other Idealists greeted her with
pleasure. Her easel was waiting for her. She sat down
at it, determined to finish her askance reality piece with
the minimum of extraneous detail. It was nearly through,
anyhow. She waved to Bella and Soma in the crowd. For
the first time in a long while, their group stood in the
closest ring to the inner circle.

The Idealists were engaged in a discussion of another
of their lofty topics. This one was so elevated that their
voices sounded to Juele as though they were very far away

and high up. If she listened upwards, she could hear them faintly. After a time the talk became more comprehensible, and their voices sank within reach of her ears.

"Putting a purpose into words makes certain the purpose will never be fulfilled," Soteran said, concluding a point he was making. "Only presenting the illusion without preamble assures that it will be accepted without question."

"And does that mean that doing something without saying so assures success?" asked Von.

"Certainly," Soteran said, his young-old face alight with mischief. "It goes without saying."

"So if you draw attention to something it jinxes the endeavor?" Juele asked, turning around from her design.

"Ideas can certainly be destroyed by perception, yes," Peppardine said.

"Then," Juele blurted, making up her mind all at once, "I have to say we're getting too close to the center of the Castle of Dreams because certain people are sort of taking over the government."

"What?" Helena asked, vaguely troubled. "Who would want to do that?"

"I don't think anyone wanted to," Juele said hastily. "It's just been happening bit by bit. I mean, you've talked about how things could be better run, on a more natural and artistic line. People," she was aware of Bella and the others boring holes in her back with their eyes, "listen when you talk."

"Of course they listen," Rutaro said, his eyes flashing dangerously. "Are you saying that is an ill thing?"

"Oh, no! I mean, you do encourage people to strive, but there's some things people shouldn't be doing. I mean, you set a terrific example, but sometimes you're not there. You have to get in control of your project again. They're making laws. They're trying cases," Juele said urgently, raising her voice above the grumbling from the outer circles. The clique was pushing forward, almost penetrating into the inner sanctum. "I mean, they're not too bad at it, but it's not their job!"

"You're not trying to destroy my project, are you?" Rutaro asked.

"Never!" Juele protested, springing to her feet. Her self-doubt swam up, but she knew what was right. She was determined to spout it out until her nerve deserted her. "Peppardine said to keep the impression in my mind. I have. The project isn't what it was to start with. It's not just pretty any more. It's not proper reality, or an ideal of one. We should have a king and everything, not artists running our own version of dreams. It might upset the Dreamland itself. Absolute power is corrupting the images absolutely. I . . . I *like* the people who are doing it, but they are doing wrong, and will keep *on* doing it, unless you're more . . . active."

"Don't you trust my judgment?" Rutaro asked, his voice low and silky. He looked relaxed, with his legs over the arm of his chair, but she heard a rattle of warning, like the shake of a snake's tail.

"Oh, of course I do," Juele hurried to assure him. "But you're not controlling everything the way you could."

"Don't say I'm losing control, don't *say* it!"

"But if you're not there, people can do what they like," Juele pressed. "They're ignoring your vision, making it, well, perverse."

"No!" Rutaro thundered. "You'll cause my project to fail now!"

"I want it to succeed," Juele insisted. "It *will* succeed, I know it!"

"Aaah!" Rutaro cried in anguish, tearing at his hair. Helena and Callia rushed to his side, murmuring soothing phrases in soft voices. Mara glared angrily at Juele, who realized her mistake. She had stated something as fact, and by their rules, now it couldn't come true. Peppardine looked at her with disappointment in his eyes.

"I'm sorry," Juele began, with her hands out in supplication. "Please, I didn't mean that. I mean, I *did*. . . ."

"I don't want you here any longer," Rutaro said, raising a sorrowful face to her. "Go away."

"Please, don't!" Juele begged.

An unseen force pressed against her, pushing her backward out of the inner circle. Juele protested, walking against the invisible wind, but she was pulled ever deeper into the jeering crowd. Suddenly, she found herself on the landing at the top of the stairs. The door slammed shut in her face. Juele shouted and banged on the door with her fists, trying to make herself be heard over the loud party noises that issued through it. Her eyes filled with frustrated tears. When she blinked them clear she found she was pounding on a different door, the one that led into the tower from the courtyard. She'd been repelled outside.

Juele turned the knob. Thank the Sleepers, the door still opened. She started to step inside, and her body began to swell. In a moment, she was four or five times her normal size. She wedged one leg in the antechamber, squeezing the rest of herself to fit. Her leg popped loose, and she found herself floating in the air like a balloon, unable to bring herself close enough to make another attempt. Great Sleepers, no! She no longer fit in.

"Oh, *look*," said Daline, sailing down the spiral stairs with the rest of the gang behind her. She smiled, cat-like, at Juele. "Here is the door. I can step out—" and she suited the action to the word with one dainty foot "—but then, I can step in again! Out. In. Out. In. Out. In. *You're* Out."

She stuck out a sharp finger that Juele felt pierce her side. Air jetted out from Juele's belly with a whoosh, propelling her away, sending her whizzing into the night sky. Derisive laughter followed her and faded away in the distance.

When Juele finally fell to earth, deflated and exhausted, she couldn't find her way back to the Ivory Tower. None of the ways she tried led to the square garden. When other intimates passed her, they looked down on her with pity.

Chapter 26

Juele owed Rutaro an apology, but found it almost impossible to deliver it. Now, when and if she saw him in the castle grounds, he was accompanied by no fewer than three members of the clique, acting as a combination bodyguard and buffer. Juele was horrified to see that as a sign of their assumed status they were wearing white smocks. These robes were decorated with colorful embroidery, ribbons, badges, even jewels, completely overbearing the pure symbol of Idealism. Not only the smocks were overbearing. If anyone else but the In Crowd tried to speak with Rutaro they ran interference, preventing words or people from interrupting his concentration with layers of sound insulation. Juele heard her opening remark to him rebound out into the ether before the whole sentence was out of her mouth.

Rutaro, walking along deep in worried thought, didn't seem to notice this or anything else around him. He was surrounded by his own personal fog, which issued from his brow, thickening the air around him. When he did speak, Juele couldn't hear his voice, and his manner was testy and discontented. The In Crowd relayed his statements, adding their own interpretations. Juele waited for an unguarded moment when they were standing apart from him and tried to scoot close. A spongy, invisible barrier bounced her right back into her tapestry. She landed on the ground, surrounded by picturesque mounds of imaginary compost wound with ivy, while her interpretations of kitchen staff passed her with barrows of perfect vegetables and sides of beef. Underneath her illusion was the messy and smelly reality. She had to hide the stains on the back of her smock when she rose to her feet. Tanner, Cal, and Soma, Rutaro's current escorts, grinned at her with insufferable satisfaction.

"You'd better get back to work, my sweet," Soma said, tossing her an airy wave. "We might have to start erasing your trash. It isn't perfect enough."

"Wait a moment," Juele said, planting her hands on her hips. "I am in charge of this section, not you."

"Not any more, little girl," Tanner said. "You're not a natural leader. You couldn't handle command. Now, it's ours."

"That's right," Cal said, leering. "If you make waves, we can force you right out. Fft! Gone."

Juele opened her mouth and shut it again, realizing they were right. She couldn't let them push her away. She must stay on the project so she could keep an eye on things. Rutaro was not himself. When he woke up to what was really going on, he needed loyal followers standing by. She just hoped it was soon. The opening was only days away.

Rutaro, staring at the ground deep in thought, continued to walk on, leaving a trail of haze behind him. His escort caught up with him in a few quick strides. Juele looked after him longingly. She took her place at her canvas, thinking how she could get his attention. It wasn't going to be easy. He seemed to be carrying his own isolation chamber around with him.

Fake ministers were everywhere. The advanced students were changing things openly now, creating whatever and whomever they wished. As soon as a robed apparition was formed, it was immediately surrounded by curiosity-seekers. The clique was enjoying being in charge. Because there seemed to be no one else around to assume authority, they were the de facto government.

Directing the day-to-day operations of the kingdom was a fascinating new game. Dilettantes of all sorts of skills, the clique picked up just enough diplomacy, justice, and tact to sound wise. People came to them and, for the most part, went away satisfied. Juele watched, half in alarm and half in admiration as Sondra, in the person of the prime minister, mediated a dispute between two factions from Wocabaht who were warring over water rights. They'd brought their missiles and armaments with them, which each side turned on the other whenever the argument wasn't going their way. Juele hit the dirt as a badly aimed missile went winging over her head. Guns blazed, and men in uniform fell everywhere. Sondra was enjoying herself very much as her creation held forth in the middle of the battleground. Gradually, hostilities ceased, and a little island of calm emerged around the prime minister. A beam of light from the heavens shone down on him, lighting up his very wise-looking eyebrows and white beard.

"This agreement shall be formalized in a treaty which will be artistically correct," the PM announced. "Neither party shall break it, on pains of . . . whatever pains you would find most painful. Water is a silly thing to be arguing about. You should find more important things to argue about." The warring parties nodded gratefully and shook hands.

This is *wrong*, Juele wanted to cry out to the crowd. Don't listen to him! He's a fake! But she was afraid to say anything. The disputants were happy. If she broke the spell, they might turn on her, as they had turned on Rutaro.

Bella noticed the artists on the line watching Sondra in action, and she came over to exhort them to work.

"All must be beauty and symmetry, darlings," Bella said, waving her gauzy sleeves at them like an apparition in the fog. "Awkward, unfinished dreams are *ugly*. They must never happen. We want the Sleepers to feel comfortable with what we're doing and show us favor."

Juele growled to herself. How dare they suggest *guiding* the attentions of the very Sleepers in the Waking World by ordering the world of their dreams? That was as ridiculous as trying to make function follow form! This wasn't just art any more. It was sedition. How could Rutaro put up with it?

"Bella?" she asked, as the senior student turned away. "Where's Rutaro? He hasn't been through here in some time."

Bella looked vaguely troubled. She frowned at Juele. "He's . . . safe."

"I want to see him," Juele said.

"You don't *need* to see him," Bella said, impatiently. "And what you want hardly matters, does it? If it ever did."

Juele worked at polishing up her section, thinking now and again of how she could help pull the project back on track. She was making her tapestry the best she could possibly draw. The buildings had been created from her heart. Even in their incomplete state, they looked a thousand times better than the real thing concealed under the glamour. Her hands were moving almost automatically, giving her plenty of time to consider the situation. She had a carton of eggs beside her. Every so often, she broke one onto her palette and used the goo to touch up her images, making them fresh and new, like the egg itself. Rutaro ought to approve of the symbolism.

She hadn't seen Rutaro in a few days. His absence worried her, not just because his oversight of the project was now lacking, but because the others had co-opted his vision for their own purposes. He had given them access to the castle, and they were abusing the privilege. They were having a good time playing government. The worst thing was that no one seemed to notice the difference. She kept hoping somebody would call attention to the fact that nearly all the people in the castle giving advice and instructions were make-believe. But no one did. Even the guards took their orders from the illusions. Sooner or later, something was going to go very wrong, and Rutaro would be blamed for it. She couldn't let that happen.

Someone had to be told about it. Someone in charge. The Historians had all gone out of town to the event in Bolster. She didn't know if the Scientists would believe her. The Continuitors, Juele had seen for herself, were hostile with regard to the School. They wouldn't be of any help, even if she explained that the continuity of the Dreamland was in danger. At the very pit of her belly, Juele had a nervous feeling that she knew perfectly well who ought to be informed. She must tell the king.

She stood up, wiping her hands together as Bella and Daline came around on one of their patrols.

"I'm going back to my room for a while," she said, giving them her most innocent smile.

"Sorry," Daline said, tossing her head. "You can't have a break yet. You work."

"But, I need to," Juele said, concerned. "I need to mail a letter to my parents. I'd like to tell them all is well."

Bella and Daline looked at one another. "Not right now," Bella said. The fashion for the day was black again, but this time the dark circles around their eyes looked real instead of cosmetic. "Sorry, dear. Once this is finished, you can stop. As you kept on saying, we haven't got a lot of time."

They already felt the weight of ruling the Dreamland, Juele thought. She was certain they hadn't stopped to consider what would happen when the exhibition opened and the castle was full of more discerning critics. They would be found out. Probably they were already out of their depth and heading toward a crisis point, but they'd rather die than tell her of their worries. And the issues were getting more complicated.

"Darlings, help!" Erbatu's face appeared in the picture-in-picture. "I've got a handful of punters who want to know about Export Trade Regulations, and I don't know a thing about that."

"My dear, just tell them to come back later," Bella said.

"That's the trouble!" Erbatu wailed. "They have."

"Where are you, darling?"

"In the Brass Chamber."

Bella and Daline exchanged glances. "We're coming, darling."

What nerve! They were in the royal chambers. Under pretense of improving the border that ran along the path, Juele made her way to the right where her tapestry connected with Mayrona's. She didn't dare use the picture-in-picture communication. May saw her coming toward her through the fog, and she sidled close.

"I must get out of here," Juele muttered. "I have a plan."

"How can I help?" Mayrona asked at once. Juele blurted out the details in a whisper, hoping to get it all said before one of the others came near. Cal walked by, grinning at the two girls on their knees, and deliberately smudged the brickwork that Mayrona had taken so many pains over.

"Too bad!" he snickered. "You'll have to do it all over again."

"If anything you're doing is going to give them their comeuppance," Mayrona whispered when he'd moved away, "I'm behind you all the way."

As soon as Cal was out of sight, Juele created a one-way illusion to cover her actions. She needed at least an hour's grace. With Mayrona's help, she constructed an illusory replica of herself. It would act as a decoy while she was gone, working away quietly at her assigned tasks. To give the impression that something was really getting done, she filled in layer after layer of shading and detail and covered them over with thin veils of illusion. She'd been saving up plenty of easy, quickly finished tasks for such a moment as this. The veils would be timed to disappear, revealing the finished work in stages. Mayrona would make sure the double's actions coincided with the shifting veils. When the replica deteriorated, there'd be no way to conceal her absence, but they would have to guess how long she had been away, and where she had gone. She didn't want to make them so mad at her they would never speak to her again, but she was doing this for their own good. They should be made to stop what they were doing and redirect their abilities to something really worthwhile, like Art and Beauty.

Her hands flew almost as swiftly as her thoughts, shaking out sheets of color and tacking them in place with lines and shadows. She made a long fuse out of rainbow-hued light. It would disappear in sequence from red to violet. By then, she'd better be back.

Juele took a last look at the figure. She had made it look as much like her as she could. But how could she keep the clique from interfering with it and discovering the subterfuge too soon? Ah, she knew. Humility. Juele concentrated on bowing the head and shoulders. If she appeared to be meekly going about her business, the others would believe she was cowed into cooperation. She hoped no Sleeper-sent influence would come through and change the whole thing into some other representation of a trick. The figure started spinning a blob of light between its long, capable hands. As a symbol to Rutaro, should he come by, she made the blob a series of spheres within spheres, so he would know to look beneath the surface. It was all she could do in such limited time. She just hoped that the clique hadn't converted him to their ideas in the last few days.

May watched her work with the first sign of envy Juele had ever seen in her. "You learn fast," she said. "You know, you really are as good as the Idealists think you are."

"I owe Rutaro for that," Juele said. "That's why I have to help him." She struck a match on the bottom of her shoe, touched it to the fuse, and ran.

Juele crept through the castle corridors, not knowing where to look first. Servants and courtiers in proper black suits passed to and fro. She wished she dared to ask one of them to guide her to the king, but who knew if any of them was really an illusion in the control of the clique? She scanned the hallway. Some of it was definitely illusionary, but she couldn't tell how much. She couldn't trust anything but her own eyes.

The logical place to start was the reception rooms. The basest chamber was easiest to find, just beyond the grand staircase to the upper floors. It led to all the others. She scurried into the plain, wood-paneled room, realized it was empty, bowed to the chairs on the dais, and hurried through the exit door into the next. He had to be in one of these. Where else would he be?

Juele took great care to watch where she was going. Illusion had seeped in from the outside, imbuing almost all of the interior of the castle as well as the exterior, putting up walls or statues to give rooms more artistic appearance, and hiding the structural features that were less than AC. After the first time she walked into an obstacle she couldn't see, she started eyeing everything for perfect configuration, a sure sign of illusion, and walking with her hands out before her like a sleepwalker. Perhaps that would be a good excuse to give the clique if they found her missing. But she must hurry.

She sneaked through the Brass Chamber, sliding unseen behind a crowd of wealthy-looking men and women in long velvet skirts and houppelandes clamoring for attention from Kaulb, the Royal Treasurer. Erbatu was sitting in the center throne on the dais, looking flustered and unhappy, occasionally directing her creation and putting words in his mouth. Things were clearly not going well. Bella and Daline flanked her in the outer thrones. Daline, looking too much at home, was listening carefully to the proceedings, and offering occasional suggestions. Bella had the grace to seem embarrassed to be where she was. None of them was happy. They were in over their heads, Juele thought. She felt the urge to erase Minister Kaulb and let them take the consequences. Turning her back, she tiptoed into the Bronze Chamber.

She had almost given up hope of finding the king by the time she trotted from the Vermeil Room into the gold reception chamber. Time was running out for her doppelganger. If she didn't find His Majesty soon, she must go back. To her relief, she saw a regal figure sitting erect on the center throne. Thank the Sleepers, here was the king!

Byron's handsome face was frowning as he stared down at a point a yard or so beyond his feet. No servants were present. He had probably sent them away so he could think. Juele regretted invading his privacy again, but this was an audience chamber, the proper venue for asking royal favors. As she scurried in the door, he glanced up at her and his brows drew down. Juele felt like fleeing, but fought her shyness. Too much was at stake.

"Your Majesty," Juele said, bowing. "Do you remember me? I'm Juele. I'm painting Her Majesty's portrait."

"Ah, yes," the king said, a warm smile lighting his face. "How nice to see you."

"Your Majesty, there's a problem going on outside."

"Outside?"

"With the queen's illusion. I mean, Rutaro's illusion. I mean," Juele said, swallowing hard, "the illusion that Rutaro is doing for Her Majesty's exhibition. The one around the castle."

"Yes?" the king asked, wrinkling his forehead. "What is the problem?"

"Well—" Juele hesitated, then the words poured out of her. "It's not going exactly as it was planned. And there are so many people interfering, and now I can't find Rutaro at all. Your Majesty, there are people taking over who don't have the best interests of the Dreamland in mind. This was meant to be something beautiful, and they're making a joke out of it. All the fake ministers are theirs. It's not responsible. Rutaro only did it because they were bothering him. Art *must* be separate. It should be the symbol of reality, not the thing itself." She stopped for breath. "I'm sorry, Your Majesty. Words aren't my best medium. I should put it in pictures for you."

"And what do you think we should do about it, Juele?" the king asked.

"Why, stop them, Your Majesty!" Juele exclaimed. "They don't know what they're doing."

"They don't?" Byron asked. Juele couldn't believe how calm he seemed. He wasn't at all upset to hear that art students had taken over the functions of his government. Perhaps he wasn't the ideal ruler that she had originally thought he was. She was disappointed. But her intuition told her something else was wrong. It wasn't the way he looked, but the way he felt. He wasn't really noble clean through. She looked deeper, as the treacherous clique had taught her to do. In his eyes, instead of the intelligence and warmth of man and king that she had seen before, she saw cloth. With buttons. And cuffs! This King Byron was nothing but a stuffed shirt, left to fool those who got through the barriers of illusion. Juele worried where the real one had gone. Had the others locked him up somewhere, so they could continue to rule the Dreamland when the exhibition was over? The king was the symbol of the land—if they imprisoned the king, they imprisoned the country. This was not only sedition, but treason. The clique's damage must be undone immediately.

It was too late to keep looking for the real man. She had to get back to her tapestry. The illusions would be almost used up, and everyone would figure out that she was gone. They'd lock her up, or do to her whatever they must have done with Rutaro, and then no one would be left to help while things went to pieces. The scattered energies of Rutaro's illusion was a descriptive symbol of the chaos which would overwhelm the Dreamland. This was too much for one very young, very new art student to bear alone, but she didn't know whom she could trust.

She bowed automatically to the fake king, who nodded politely, and went back to staring at his feet. Juele peered out into the hall. She heard footsteps approaching and hoped none of the ad hoc ruling class was wandering through the corridors in search of dissenters. Where could she hide? The room across the hall was lined with mirrors, but otherwise empty. The next nearest was full of antique furniture, all with spindly legs, useless for concealment. The wall hangings in the corridor were too short. They wouldn't cover her legs. Juele put out her arms, in hopes of using her sleepwalking defense.

Worse luck, the footsteps belonged to Queen Harmonia. The queen, all in emerald green with silken brown hair wound in braids around her head, was making purposefully for the golden throne room, and the false Byron. Juele couldn't let her see him!

"Your Majesty!" Juele called, waving a hand.

"Oh, hello, my dear Juele," the queen said, with a warm smile. "I need to see my husband. Is he in there?"

"Yes, I mean, no! No, he's somewhere else," Juele said hastily. "I was looking for him, too. I had to ask him something." She racked her brain, trying to think of what that would be, and hoping the queen wouldn't ask.

"Well, he must be here," Harmonia said, throwing up her hands. "I've been in all the higher chambers—and, if you'll forgive me, my dear, your School makes it just a tiny bit difficult to get about close to the center of the castle—but I didn't find him there. He might have arrived just ahead of us. I'll just have a peep inside."

Juele scooted between the queen and the door, hoping she didn't look as panicky as she felt.

"Oh, I wouldn't do that, Your Majesty. He's been preoccupied lately, hasn't he?"

"He seemed quite contented the last time I spoke to him," said the queen, stepping to one side.

"Maybe he is dining!" Juele stepped along with her, hoping her inventiveness would hold out. The queen put kindly hands on her shoulders and looked her straight in the eye.

"My dear, please let me by. I don't want to think you're hiding something."

Lowering her head, Juele let her pass. Harmonia might be satisfied with this king and not realize he was a fake. But one look was enough.

"My dear Juele, that's not Byron," the queen said. "I know him. I can't be fooled so easily. Where is my husband? What is going on here?"

Juele desperately wanted to spill out the whole story to her, but she was afraid that someone would overhear her. There were one-way illusions throughout the castle, connected to the ever-present land-line that now seemed to lead everywhere, including the royal chambers. If she was overheard, it would be all over the tapestry in no time.

"The illusions have spread inside the castle, ma'am," Juele said, in a low voice. "Some of the students who were helping are trying to make the project, um, more than decorative."

"It has gone farther than that!" Harmonia said, in high dudgeon. "I have all manner of attendants and eight doctors at my beck and call, but only one of them is a real person. The others are who knows what? Do you think I don't know the difference between a real doctor and an imaginary doctor? This is my hobby! I may be a hypochondriac, but I'm not a hysteric. Do you know what those foolish doctors have been saying to me? They think because I support the arts I should become reigning queen! Undoubtedly with *themselves* as the *eminences grises* behind the throne. As if I did not have a full program of activities already. And my health! Oh, I couldn't permit it. We must find the king. No doubt these students have him wound up in a vision of a perfect world, and he has no idea anything is wrong."

"Can you help, Your Majesty?" Juele asked.

"I can't do much," Harmonia admitted. "I am hemmed around by seeming servants and seeming doctors who are all keeping a close eye on me. If you are so cautious about discovery that you don't feel you can speak freely to me when we appear to be in private, then we need a little assistance. We need someone with a good head on his shoulders, who is steady, stalwart, and unchanged by appearances. Or unchanging." Harmonia nodded decidedly. "Yes, the ideal person would be Roan Faireven. He is the King's Investigator. You have met him." Juele nodded.

"Yes, ma'am. Where is he? I haven't seen him lately."

"Nor have I," said the queen. "My daughter went to Bolster. I am certain that Roan has gone to join her. Do you know where that is? I can't leave here myself, but

if you go I will keep our would-be controllers occupied."
She took the emerald ring off her finger and pressed it
into Juele's hands. Juele looked up and down the hallway, hoping no one was observing them. "Take this and
buy train fare to Bolster. Find Roan. He's the one with
sense. He will help straighten this all out. Oh, here come
my suffocating servants. I must go."

A flock of ladies-in-waiting in pale green fluttered
toward the queen and surrounded her.

"Your Majesty, we didn't know where you'd gone!"
"Oh, Your Majesty, aren't you lovely today. Doesn't she
look lovely, ladies?" "Oh, yes!" The queen sent Juele a
long-suffering look over their heads and allowed herself
to be swept away in their midst. It was almost a pity that
the queen didn't want to reign. She was so clear-headed.
She would have made a wonderful national leader.

Juele's time was up. She must get back.

"Where is she?" howled a voice, growing louder as
it came nearer. It sounded like Daline in the extremes
of rage. *"Where is she?"*

Juele clutched her art box. They were coming toward
her. She'd better find a place to hide, and quickly. She
whipped together a one-way illusion and hid behind it,
hoping it wasn't so crude it would stick out in the elegant hallway. She didn't have time to do it over.

"I don't know where she is!" Juele's ears perked up.
That was Mayrona's voice. The clique had discovered her
absence. But it was too soon! Or, was it? Cal and Tanner stormed into view, hauling a shrinking Mayrona
between them. Soma and Daline looked like furies again.

"We saw the puppet you were playing with, pretending
she was still there," Soma said, holding a talon-clawed
fingertip under May's chin. Oh, nightmares, a wave of
change must have come through while Juele was hunt-
ing for the king. She checked. Sure enough, her skin and
clothes had sustained an alteration. "Now, where did Juele
go?"

"I don't know," Mayrona protested, trying to pull away
from the sharp nail. "She's gone, that's all, and I don't

know if she's ever coming back." Daline looked worried and chewed on her own talons nervously.

"You'd better tell us," she said. "How'd you like to see the dungeons here, darling?" She pointed to the Gold Chamber. "We can arrange it."

"No," Cal said, with an evil leer. "I know her weakness. Over here!" He and Tanner hauled Mayrona toward the room full of antique furniture. May looked in the door and went pale. Her hands froze onto the doorposts like vises.

"Oh, please don't put me in there," she pleaded with her captors. "Please, no!"

Grinning, Cal pried her loose, shoved her in, and slammed the door. Immediately Mayrona began pounding on the other side. More sounds erupted, that of wood sliding on tile, and a weird keening like the creak of old cabinets that had been closed for centuries. Juele was horrified. Mayrona's ailment was real. The pounding became more frenzied. "Let me out!"

Colm's ruddy face popped up in the nearest tapestry. "Good news, my dears! She said she'll go along with us."

Daline breathed a sigh of relief. "Good, darling. Give her some more doctors."

Silently, Juele blessed the queen. She was keeping her word. Daline shot a quick glance at the door, from behind which was issuing squeaks, thumps, and cries for help.

"Leave her there," Daline said, turning on her heel. "We've got things to do." She stalked away, her bat-wings quivering. The others followed.

As soon as they were gone, Juele threw herself at the door. It was locked. For once Juele cursed being unable to manipulate dreamstuff well. If she was an ordinary Dreamlander, she could open the stupid thing. Oh, she could make a perfect image of an open door, but that would do her roommate no good at all!

"May, it's me," she whispered. "I'll get you out of there." The pounding stopped.

"Juele?" Mayrona shouted. "Did you find the king?"

"Not yet. There's been a change of plans!" Juele threw a cautionary glance over her shoulder at the tapestry on the wall. The pastoral image showed no signs of life, but she didn't dare say too much. She shook the door handle. "May, I can't get this open. I'll have to get help."

"Never mind me," Mayrona insisted. "Go do what you have to do."

"But it'll be night soon!" Juele cried. Mayrona must not be alone in the room with all that furniture after dark.

"No! I can handle it," Mayrona shouted. "Stop *them* first. I'll be all right. I promise." More squeaking and grinding noises broke out, sounding even closer to the door. Juele rattled the handle and threw herself against the panels, begging the Sleepers to alter it to an open door, to take away all her talent with illusion and replace it with locksmithing ability. Mayrona's voice rose to a high crescendo. "Don't worry about me! *Go!* Now!"

The very force of her voice threw Juele away from the door. With a backward look of regret and admiration for her roommate's courage, Juele ran.

Chapter 27

The dungeon changed from an iron-walled prison with solid steel doors to featureless tan rooms that appeared to have no doors at all. Roan tried to walk out of his cell at once. He was thrown violently backward against the opposite wall. The force field keeping him in was invisible to the naked eye.

Roan sat down on the tan bench against the inside wall and mused on the nature of invisible barriers. He couldn't be affected by influence, though he could be injured by physical objects. But the highest power he knew, the one that kept him from overpowering his guards and attempting an escape, was his respect for the law. He was a prisoner of rules and regulations, and his own sense of honor.

There still was no word from Leonora. Time was running out. If nothing stopped the course of events, Roan faced discontinuation the next day. He could not believe that in less than twenty-four hours he would cease to exist.

He still could not understand why the king had turned against him. Over the many years that Roan had served the court, he had thought they enjoyed a deep mutual respect. What had he done to offend the king? For one panicky moment he wondered if this was an extreme measure that Byron, an overprotective father, was taking to prevent Roan from marrying his daughter. No, that was absurd, Roan told himself, pacing back and forth. The shape of the cell shifted from square to rectangular, making it more convenient in which to pace. All His Majesty would have to do to put an end to the engagement was to decree that it was over. Neither of them would defy his wishes.

No, Roan was bothered by more than that. There had been something unreal about his last meeting with the king. He couldn't put his finger on exactly what. In fact, there had been something unreal about the king himself. Minister Synton was right about strange forces invading the castle over the last weeks. What if one of them had taken the king's place? What if he had been an *illusion*? If the order for imprisonment had been imposed by a being who was masquerading as the king, well, then, the arrest and the sentence were null and void.

Roan stopped pacing, hope rising in his heart. He could not wait until Leonora or Bergold or his father returned to Mnemosyne. He had to find the truth for himself. To do that, he must be free. But freedom was not so easily obtained.

He faced the transparent barrier. The moment he set foot into the corridor, he would be breaking his word to obey the law. But he was certain he was being denied due process. He'd been given no chance to defend himself. It was vital that he get back to that audience chamber and determine to his own satisfaction whether the king who sat there was the real thing. Not only he, but the whole Dreamland could be in danger.

Roan pushed his hands into the force field, concentrating all his strength of will on finding a weak point. The barrier was strong, as strong as the steel wall would have been. Lancing fire raced up his arms into his body, making his back teeth rattle. Ignoring the pain, he tore a hole in the energy wall. Sweat poured into his eyes. He blinked it away, half-blinded by the blue-and-white lightning. He feared he wasn't strong enough, that it would defeat him in the end, but he persevered. Slowly, the opening enlarged until it was big enough for him to squeeze through.

Sirens blared deafeningly the moment he pierced the wall. A shadow fell on his face. Roan looked up in alarm.

Captain Spar was standing in front of him at parade rest, with his hands behind his back. He was unarmed.

"You don't want to do that, sir," Spar said, in a calm, even voice. "Don't try to come out, Master Roan."

"Captain, I *must*," Roan said. "I have to find out . . ."

"*No*, sir, you must stay there. Or else . . ."

"Or else, Captain?" Roan gave a bitter laugh. "I am facing oblivion. What more could you possibly do to me?" Spar stiffened.

"Sir, I regret highly having to keep you locked up, but I am bound by the laws of the Dreamland. You are, too. I know you could overpower me in an instant. You've got the strength. But you won't do it," Spar said, looking at him steadily. "You're too law-abiding. I know it in my bones. I've got to do my job, sir. This has to be handled in the correct way. Master Roan, if this is really your last day of existence, wouldn't you want to go out knowing you lived it in the same way you lived all the others?"

Roan's heart sank. Spar was right. His conscience kept telling him so. He sighed. "Yes, Captain, I would."

"I'll keep asking the king for a reprieve," the guard captain said. "I will keep sending appeals upstairs, and I'll allow you to do the same. You can't say fairer than that."

"It may not really be the king," Roan said, urgently. "Haven't you noticed anything strange about the castle while you've been patrolling?"

"Aye, sir, but I've reported it all to His Majesty. He's certain there's nothing to worry about, and he ought to know."

"But what if that's not really the king?" Roan pressed.

"He's in the position of authority, sir," Spar said, slowly raising Roan's hands off the force field wall, so as not to alarm him. "Chain of command, sir."

Roan could see freedom over the guard captain's shoulder. All he would have to do was paralyze Spar with a blast of influence, and he would be out. But never free, not in his own mind. The captain had hit him in his weak spot. It was a point of honor. Where honor was at stake, everything else must be sacrificed. He was wrong to have attempted to escape. Very reluctantly, he backed away from the barrier.

"That's good, sir," Spar said, in the same calm voice. "I'll keep on asking, sir. They'll pay attention to me. You have my word on that. I keep my promises, same as you."

"I'm depending upon you, Captain," Roan said, as the invisible door sealed itself off. The alarms and flashing lights stopped, and the dungeon fell quiet as a tomb. His tomb. He sat down on the bench to think.

Juele ran through the gallery. She must get out of the castle at once, but how? She mustn't go by way of her station; they'd be watching that, now. She would have to risk the front entrance. Could Manolo be trusted? Had he fallen in with the clique?

Terrified of being observed, Juele stayed alert for signs of the land-line snaking through. Even though there were no tapestries in the hall, she still felt eyes on her. All the portraits on the walls turned their eyes to follow her as she ran. It seemed as though the whole castle was against her. A suit of armor stationed against the wall near the door stepped forward as she dashed toward the exit. It swung its halberd up in an arc, then chopped it down. Fortunately, Juele was quicker than a hollow man. She ducked the sharp blade and kept running into the next chamber.

The entry hall was full of people in elegant clothes, mingling and discussing weighty-sounding matters. Audiences were usually over for the day by this time. These officials were no doubt preparing to leave. Perhaps she could sneak out with them. She spotted Tanner at the entrance, near the sentries. He must be looking for her. Juele crouched behind a cluster of statuary. She noticed it looking down at her. To her surprise, it was the griffin and cow from the sculpture garden. The museum must have melded with this part of the castle.

"Is this hide and seek?" the griffin asked.

"Shh!" she hissed. "It's not a game!" Tanner had a dozen guards with sunglasses and whips with him. She was terrified. What would they do to her if they caught her?

"What's that?" the griffin asked, his voice getting louder.

"Please be quiet," Juele begged. The griffin opened its beak to the widest.

"She's over here!" it bellowed.

Tanner's head went up. He started through the crowd toward them. His guards followed, elbowing dignitaries aside. Juele ducked into the crowd, between women in bell skirts and men in gorgeous cloaks. An endless line of men in solemn black robes was winding slowly out of the castle toward the gate. Inspiration struck her. Hastily, she put on the semblance of the man nearest her and butted into line behind him. She heard a murmur of protest from the next man in line, but he made way for her. Slowly they progressed, a measured pace at a time. She passed Tanner. He and his enforcers cast about, looking for her. She forced herself to keep her eyes fixed forward. Her heart was pounding so hard she didn't believe he could not hear it. At one point he was only a step away. He'd see through her disguise! Then, the line moved, and she was a pace closer to the door. Tanner disappeared past the griffin, which was muttering to itself. As the queue curved along the path from the drawbridge, Juele risked a glance back. Tanner was nowhere in sight.

The illusion hung over the castle in stripes and tatters, not the elegant picture that Rutaro had envisioned. He would be devastated if he could see the way his marvelous project looked. Juele worried about what the clique had done with him. What had Bella meant when she said he was "safe"?

The line of men seemed to stretch out of the gate and all the way into the town of Mnemosyne, but Juele realized as she neared the exit that, as they reached the walls, the men were popping like soap bubbles. They weren't real. Only flat pictures of them were marching into a two-dimensional picture of town. Just before she got to the gate, Juele detached herself, resumed her own appearance, and trotted out into the street. The streets were remarkably deserted. There were usually crowds of curiosity-seekers hanging around the castle. The few that were there had looks of horror on their faces. Well, really, the unfinished illusion didn't look that bad. She turned to glance back. Her heart stopped for a moment.

So *that* was why there were so few new visitors coming through the last few days, Juele thought. No one in their right mind would set foot in there.

Beyond the gate was a steaming, radioactive bomb crater, as hot as the caldera of a volcano, with shards of stone and metal studding the bleak landscape like the spines of a long-dead beast. If she hadn't come from inside that disaster area only a moment before, she would never go near it. Everyone thought the castle had been blown to bits.

No, not destroyed, she realized, as she looked up into the evening sky. The Castle of Dreams had become a Castle in the Air. Juele had to hand it to Bella and her friends. The clique had figured out a way to keep their mayhem from being discovered. If the castle wasn't accessible, nobody could question who was making the laws and decisions that came down. It was remarkably good work, better than she thought they were capable of. Then, she noticed the kitten. It was a little gray cat, playing with a ball of string, not far from a white line drawn on the ground.

Suddenly, she realized that *they* hadn't drawn the picture of devastation, Rutaro had. He had done it so he could get his work done in peace. He had fallen into a trap of his own design, only it hadn't been meant as a trap in the first place. Juele had to get to Bolster and Master Roan right away.

Trains were one of the few things that had a presence in the Dreamland regardless of what face the rest of the country wore. The railways were comforting in their solidity. The trains themselves remained reliable under most circumstances. However, the Mnemosyne railway station at night lacked all the friendliness and charm that it had had when she had arrived there in the daytime weeks before. The ceilings, once adorned with wooden bric-a-brac, were soaring sheets of dark glass held up by soulless metal struts. Porters, jolly and kind during the day, had blank eyes and neckties that reflected her frightened face back at her. Juele held tightly to the queen's ring in the pocket of her smock as a kind of talisman against fear.

Were there any more trains to Bolster that night? She found the timetable chalked on a blackboard nailed high on the brick wall over the tracks. Yes, several were listed. The next departure was about forty minutes away. A huge clock hung from the ceiling, ticking ponderously. Here, every minute was of importance. As the red second hand swept past the twelve, a train screamed, emitted clouds of steam, and chugged away.

Juele got in one of the lines at the ticket office. All of them were long, and moved with frustrating sloth. When she reached the window, the clerk in the eyeshade on the other side of the glass slammed down a rack of wooden bars and put up a sign that said, "Out to lunch." Juele tapped politely on the window, but the man glared at her and pointed to the sign. With a groan, Juele moved to the next shortest queue.

The minutes ticked away. Thirty. Twenty. She reached the next window and presented the queen's ring.

"One ticket to Bolster please."

The clerk, an older man, glared down at the ring. "What is this? I can't accept jewelry as legal tender."

"But form follows function," Juele said, frantically. "Isn't it enough to pay for my fare?"

"Sister, you could buy the whole train for this, but I can only take legal tender. Is this all you have?"

Juele searched her pockets. "Yes. But someone must accept this. It's an item of value."

"Over there," said the clerk. He pointed out of his

window at another desk. The long line in front of it was full of people leading chickens, goats, horses, or pigs, or carrying bundles of wood, baskets of fruit or eggs, or bundles of writing paper secured with rubber bands, all noncash means of paying for their tickets.

Reluctantly, Juele went to stand behind a woman and a baby leading a pair of goats. She fidgeted uncomfortably as the minutes ticked away. Another locomotive screamed its farewell, and the first train to Bolster left without her. The next was going soon, but the line didn't move. Juele worried that the clique would figure out where she had gone and catch up with her here. They mustn't find her. If Rutaro's project failed now, it would be all her fault. And now, poor Mayrona was trapped in a room with her own personal nightmare. Hurry, she begged the ticket agent. Hurry.

The baby looked up at her from its mother's shoulder and took its chubby fist out of its mouth.

"Betrayer," it said.

Juele recoiled. Oh, this was a nightmare. Master Roan must help her!

With ticket in hand at last, she looked up at the timetable. The next train for Bolster was about to depart on track 2. Juele hefted her art box and began running. Men in top hats and frock coats were assisting ladies in tiny hats and huge dresses up the brass-bound step-boxes into the cars. Juele's assigned ticket put her in car A, immediately behind the locomotive. The train seemed to stretch for miles as she ran past porters with carts, newspaper vendors, and families with dozens of pieces of luggage. Keeping one eye on the great clock, she banged into men with briefcases. She threw apologies back over her shoulder. Just as the conductor was preparing to pick up the step-box, she thrust her ticket at him and clambered on board the train. There was one seat left. She flung herself into it. At last!

The sweeping red hand on the clock moved up past the ten, the eleven, and swept over the twelve. Juele watched it, bracing herself for the scream of the whistle and the great surge as the train began to pull out. She jerked her body forward, encouraging the train to move. It wasn't moving! She stared at her ticket. The time was right. What was wrong with this train?

She looked around her. Her surroundings had changed. She wasn't in a real train. This was a waiting area. The real train was pulling out beside her. Juele leaped up and ran out of the car, waving her ticket. She was too late. The locomotive chugged away down the tracks. Juele whirled to look at the timetable for the next train. It was going from track 8, halfway across the station, in only five minutes. Juele ran, dodging passengers and carts. Her heart pounded. She was trapped in a Missed Connections Dream. She must keep trying. Too much depended on her.

The train on track 8 shrieked as it jerked into motion. Juele ran alongside it, reaching for the brass rails to pull herself up into a car. It was going too fast for her. She managed to catch hold of the caboose and hopped onto the rear platform. Her footing was none too steady. The conductor, swinging a red lantern, held out a hand to her. Juele reached for him, but the train jerked again. She fell off the rear of the train onto the tracks. Her art box sprawled beside her. Juele jumped to her feet, grabbed the strap of the box, and ran to catch up. It was no use. The train pulled steadily ahead, increasing the distance frustratingly between them a foot at a time. Juele stopped running. Try again, go, try again, go, try again, chugged the litany in her brain. Track 3 was the next train to Bolster. She *had* to try again. She must get to the Movie Extravaganza and find Master Roan.

Chapter 28

For the tenth time that day, bright white letters rolled up into the sky over a backdrop of roseate clouds. Bergold let out a sigh of deep pleasure.

"Most satisfying, isn't it, Princess?" he asked, removing his flat straw hat with a bow to the girl seated at his left.

"Oh, yes," Leonora said, her round blue eyes red at the corners. She dabbed at her upturned nose with a handkerchief. Her own flat straw hat with a swathed veil under her chin was slightly askew. She removed the hat pins and resecured it on her thick, golden hair. "Look at me. I'm a mess! No matter how many times I see it, I can't help but be touched to my very heart. What wonderful minds they have in the Waking World!"

"So they have revealed to us," Bergold said, hooking his cane over his arm and pulling his notebook from the pocket of his striped flannel jacket. He opened the book to a page upon which were ticked such entries as "tidal wave," "exploding car" and "space craft," and put a checkmark beside "happy ending." "As Cult Movie Evocations go, this is a very fine example. There must be millions of sleepers who have experienced the extravaganza itself, so we are getting very clear concentrations of images. Although it has taken several days for the entire story line to be revealed, I believe it was worth it. I am so pleased you decided to come and see it for yourself."

"I didn't want to stay in the castle," Leonora said, glancing around the sunlit streets. "I couldn't properly concentrate on planning my wedding with all the hubbub going on, even though Mother was so happy about her event. I had few other duties—everyone else was coming here. There were no state occasions for which I had to play hostess—not a tea, a dinner, a reception, or an opening of any kind. I'm glad, really. Two weeks ago, there was nothing but! I was stuck in the midst of an Endless Repetition Dream that didn't end until Roan noticed and helped me get out of it."

"His powers of observation are most admirable," Bergold said, gallantly, "although most especially where you are concerned." Leonora smiled at him warmly as she took his arm. They promenaded down the cobblestone street past glinting puddles and the piles of flat film cans that were everywhere. Bergold had explained that Cans were an integral part of a really detailed Cult Movie Evocation.

"Poor Roan, having to stay there in the midst of it all and look after Daddy. Bless him for being so responsible, although I do miss him. Thank you for volunteering to be my companion, Bergold. It's nice to have a friend along who is such an excellent guide! You've explained the phenomenon so precisely. I am enjoying it so much more for understanding it well."

"It is my pleasure," the Historian said, bowing to hide his blush. Leonora smiled. How like Bergold to be modest about his expertise. He might not be the most senior Historian in the Ministry, but he had a good mind unspoiled by the pigheadedness many of his colleagues possessed. It was a constant source of pain to her that her father's ministers considered her beloved Roan to be a freak. If Bergold hadn't been a good friend in his own right, she would have loved him for the devotion and understanding he showed Roan.

Now that the spell of the movie ending had broken, other people were beginning to move about again. Leonora tapped Bergold on the arm with the handle of her parasol.

"Oh, look, there are the lovers again!" She nodded toward the handsome young man and beautiful girl who walked hand in hand, their shoulders pressed together, whispering soft endearments to one another. They gazed deeply into one another's eyes. They were in their own precious world, one that would, Leonora knew from seeing the events repeated many times, be shattered by a disaster not of their own making.

How tragic their story appeared to be, Leonora thought, with a shiver of delight. To see the entire event from beginning to end in order she would have to wait for the Historians to piece it together. Most of what she had seen at first in Bolster was a series of brief scenes showing their affair that could not be in proper chronological order. That was simply how they were fixed in the millions of dreaming minds who had experienced the Movie Extravaganza itself in the Waking World. Bergold called the phenomenon Trailer Memory. The star-crossed pair kissed; they sobbed on one another's shoulder; they rolled together in the grass with husky whispers and a hiss of skirts. More had been revealed over the course of several days, and she felt it was well worth the wait. Leonora fumbled in her bag for her handkerchief, wondering if this was one of the sad scenes. Oh, how lovely, it was the proposal.

"I miss Roan," Leonora said, looking wistfully at the young man, on one knee beside his lady who sat on a park bench at a bus stop along the main street. The other passengers had had enough of the event already, and were ignoring them.

Bergold smiled at the couple, as the girl accepted the nail bent in a circle, which was all the young man could afford as an engagement ring. The pair kissed shyly, but with veiled hints of passion to come. "I am certain he would rather be here than there," he said. Leonora sighed.

"I'm sorry Mother didn't come," she said. "She would have enjoyed this. Parts of the love story are tragic enough to keep her miserable for weeks. She'd be so happy!"

"She has her doctors to amuse her," Bergold pointed out. "And her exhibition. I hope that's going well."

"I'm sure it is," the princess said. "Well, I'm all cried out. I would enjoy something to drink. Shall we go in here?" She dodged a pillar of cans, one of two that flanked the entrance to the sweet shop. Bergold gallantly handed her around it, and into the midst of the paparazzi near the door. Flashbulbs exploded in their faces, and people filling the stands cheered. Leonora waved gaily to them, smiling in all directions.

The event had attracted all sorts of fascinating freaks of Dreamish nature to Bolster. Bergold had seen a number of these before. The characters got more extreme and more numerous each time. The stands full of people near the entrance to every building had become very tiresome. The princess was gracious as ever, waving to the cheering mobs.

"If you ignore them, they'll continue to do exactly the same thing," Bergold said. "They're only nuisances."

"Oh, I know," Leonora said, keeping the bright smile on her face, "but if even one of them is a true Dreamland subject, I owe them the consideration befitting their reality. Besides, it's fun to be this popular."

Bergold grinned and concentrated on guiding her inside. At least most of the fans stayed in the stands. They still had to contend with lots of mobile nuisances who jumped in and out of their path with cameras. Paparazzi seemed to be everywhere. Flashbulbs as big as his head exploded in front of their eyes, dazzling them. Only the ever-present uniformed doormen kept him from banging into doors. Leonora seemed to have a protective shell around her, preventing her from being bumped. She turned to allow one more barrage of picture-taking.

"Princess Leonora!" one of the paparazzi demanded, coming up to snap off another huge flashbulb in their faces. "What do you think of the rumor that the Castle of Dreams has been blown up? Can we have a quote? Hey, man, how about you?"

Leonora's face went pale with shock. Without a word, she picked up her skirts and headed for the train station. Bergold followed in worried pursuit. When they got to the platform, Leonora's maid and servants were waiting there beside the royal coach with all her bags packed.

"Blown up, indeed!" Bergold exclaimed, staring up at the sky as he trotted behind the princess down the Mnemosyne station platform. "Will you look at that?"

"Good heavens!" Leonora said, staring. "Blown up is right!" The Castle of Dreams, all white marble turrets and rosy tiled roofs, floated high in the air on a pillow of clouds, as if blissfully unaware of the consternation its flight had caused on the ground below. It seemed to be intact, for which Leonora was grateful.

"That must have been the explosion to end all explosions," Bergold said, measuring the distance with an eye. He calculated the building had to be at least ten miles in the air. "It's as if we never left the Motion Picture." He signaled for a cab, and a shiny, black motorcycle with a double-sized sidecar striped in red pulled up beside them with a screech. Handing Leonora in, Bergold clambered over the side. The servants piled in the suitcases and crowded in behind them. "To the castle! Or, what's left of it." The driver tipped a hand to his visored helmet and leaned over the handlebars.

"Poor Father!" said Leonora, still gazing upward as they shot through the streets of the city. "Poor Mother! I hope they're all right. Mother never has had much of a head for heights."

The motorcycle passed through the crowds of bystanders, which parted respectfully when they saw its royal passenger. At the curtain wall, the guards on duty in the sentry box saluted Leonora. Everything looked normal, until she looked between the gates. Nothing within the walls was left standing. At the heart of the destruction was a deep pit from which smoke was still rising. All around it were the charred remains of the outbuildings. Leonora stared at the blackened remains of the stables and pleasure gardens and felt like weeping.

"Your Highness!" exclaimed Carodil, Minister of

Science. The tall woman bustled forward with her orb-headed staff in hand. "Thank all verifiable existence! We thought you had been caught in the explosion! I had gone out into the city to investigate a claim that I instructed people to measure their noses twice a day to detect propensity for untruthfulness! Naturally, I had done nothing of the sort! When I attempted to return, I saw this!" She swung the cane in the direction of the gates.

"What happened?" Leonora asked.

"We don't know yet. It occurred three days ago. No one heard an explosion, or witnessed the castle lifting off." Carodil pointed to a dozen of her apprentices, all examining and measuring the edge of the glowing ruin with meters, dowsing rods, sextants, and graph paper. "We are trying to see if there is any clue in the debris left behind. Don't get too close, Your Highness. The radiation that the site is giving off may result in destruction of us all. The temperature is so high it doesn't measure on our graphs."

Juele pushed determinedly through the crowd toward the princess. She had a stitch in her ribs from having run all the way from the railway station. She wished fervently that she had been possessed of sufficient influence to transform herself into a muscular, long-distance athlete.

After running after phantom trains until the small hours, she had sat down for just a moment on a bench to await the 3:00 A.M. express to Bolster. Instead, lulled by engine noise and sheer exhaustion, she had fallen asleep. She had missed the princess disembarking her train, but woken up just in time to see the cabbie drive the party away on his motorcycle. She knew where they were going. The whole of Mnemosyne was converging on the castle grounds and Rutaro's scene of disaster. At last, she ducked under the arms of the guards surrounding the princess and dropped, panting, at Leonora's feet.

"Your Highness, your mother sent me to look for you."

"You're her artist," Leonora said. The plump man beside her helped her up. Juele brushed off her smock, in an effort to look more presentable. "What do you know about this?"

"It was going all right," Juele said, "but it's gotten out of hand. Where is Master Roan?" She scanned the cluster of court officials, but she didn't see the familiar, handsome face.

"He's not with me," Leonora said. "He remained here in Mnemosyne while I went to Bolster."

Juele frowned. "He can't be here, Your Highness. The queen said he was with you! She told me to find him."

"No, my father the king asked him to stay behind. If you'd ask him, he'd tell you that."

"We can't find the king, either," Juele said, wringing her hands together. Even they felt less capable than usual. "I found a stuffed shirt that they left to take his place, but not him."

"Who?" Leonora demanded. "Who did it? Has something terrible happened to him?"

"I'm sure they wouldn't have *done* anything," Juele said, in alarm. "They might just . . . keep him from finding out anything has happened. Like the explosion."

"But, the castle?" Leonora looked upward at the building floating above her. It was almost large enough to block the sun. She squinted, hoping she could see her mother looking out of her sitting room window.

"That's not really the castle," Juele said. "It's an illusion. A big one. The castle is in there." She pointed at the disaster area.

"No," said Leonora, shaking her head in disbelief. "It can't be. Form would follow function. It's not the first time the Castle of Dreams has become a Castle in the Air. She's right," she said, turning to Bergold. "Very probably Daddy has no idea that the place has taken off. Otherwise, he'd have made arrangements for transportation from here to there. We'll have to tell him."

"How can we get up there?" Bergold asked.

"We need to find a messenger," Leonora said. "Send a page . . . oh, I can't. They're all up there!" She turned to her servant. "Eurika, will you go into town and find an express messenger? Someone who specializes in air mail?"

The lady-in-waiting picked up her skirts and shot away downhill. Within minutes, she had returned, riding behind the saddle of a young woman in black on a broom.

"Find the king," Leonora ordered. "You must succeed, no matter what form you have to take."

"As you wish, Your Highness," the witch said. She spurred her wooden steed and whisked into the air. From the mouth of the castle issued an enormous shape. Gasps from the onlookers broke out as they realized it was a red dragon. Its slitted yellow eyes glittered. It flew at the tiny figure on the broom, its jaws open. The witch veered away, avoiding the toothy maw, which snapped down on nothing.

"It's only illusion," Juele shouted. "It's just to discourage you from getting near. Don't believe in it. Ignore it!" Such an order was easier to say than to obey, but the woman on the broom squared her shoulders and bravely flew right down the gullet of big dragon. The crowd waited, holding its collective breath. In a moment, the witch flew out the back of the huge beast's head. The onlookers cheered. The witch joined both hands over her head in a victory salute. Leaving the beast behind, she vanished into the castle. Soon, she emerged again. Juele squinted. The woman was alone on her broom. She flew down and landed before the princess.

"I'm sorry, Your Highness," she said, spreading her black skirts in a curtsy. "Everything looks normal, but it's all insubstantial. I found His Majesty, but he paid no attention to me. He was putting together a jigsaw puzzle."

"Take me," Leonora said. She pulled in her skirts, which became wide trousers, and prepared to mount the broom. "I'll make Daddy listen."

"Don't go. He's an illusion," Juele insisted, taking her arm. The princess stiffened, and Juele let her hand drop. "I'll *prove* it, Your Highness. Pace the keep. It's supposed to be a thousand by a thousand no matter what, isn't it?"

"Yes, of course," Leonora said, impatiently.

"It is always one thousand paces on a side," Carodil said, with a disapproving frown.

"I'll bet you anything it isn't. I'll bet my life. I'll bet my career!"

The princess gave her a curious look.

"Very well." She signed to the Minister of Science, who barked an order at her apprentices. Instantly, the dozen or so young men and women sprang into action. In no time, they had assembled a device consisting of a huge lens marked with cross-hatching mounted on a swiveling tripod with a sighting mechanism. One of them gazed through it, while three of them shifted the framework from side to side. More stood by with notebooks to record the results. They ran back to Carodil.

"Initial measurement was one thousand by one thousand," the sky-gazing apprentice announced.

"There," said Carodil, authoritatively. "What did I tell you?"

"Second sampling recorded nine hundred paces by twelve hundred," the apprentice continued. "Third reading was five hundred by eight hundred."

"It *is* varying in size!" Carodil exclaimed. "But this never happens! Where is the Minister of Continuity? He must explain this." She gazed around her, as if expecting Synton to spring into being beside her.

Leonora looked at Juele with new respect. "Very well," she said, "where is the castle?"

"Still in the same place you left it," Juele said, relieved that they believed her at last. "It's in there. Follow me."

"No!" Carodil said, alarmed, stepping in Leonora's way. "The heat, Your Highness! The radiation! It could result in damage or discontinuation."

"No, Your Excellency," Juele said, patiently. "It's only an illusion. A fully formed, coherent illusion made of light with sound, heat, and even smells. It was constructed by a master illusionist."

"This master must be superlative, if he can fool my instruments," Carodil said, skeptically.

"Your instruments can only believe what they see," Juele said. "It's affecting them, too."

"And you know who this master of illusion is?" Leonora asked.

"Yes, I do," Juele said, reluctant to name Rutaro. "And I think he's in trouble."

"Is my mother all right?"

"She's fine," Juele said, hastily. "They've given her a lot of doctors to keep her happy." She felt like a traitor saying it out loud, but the princess had to know the facts. There was no time for further illusion here. She had seen too much of that already.

"We have to find Roan," Leonora said. "Please take me inside."

"Your Highness, I can't allow this," Carodil said.

"There's no time!" Juele said. "Watch me."

Rutaro's skill was superb. Juele felt heat drifting over the line, smelled the sulphur and scorched earth. Intellectually, she knew none of it was real. Her senses truly believed the castle was not there, and had departed the site violently. It took a moment to steel herself to step over the line. She took a deep breath. One pace was all it took to leave the crowd behind. She heard a faint cry from the princess, cut off by the insulating quality of the illusion.

Inside the thin shell, everything looked normal, or as normal as it had been when she left. During the hours she was gone, someone had joined together all the pieces surrounding the castle. The resulting whole wasn't at all perfect or ideal. If Rutaro had done it, he must have been out of his mind. The grounds were surprisingly empty of life, except for all the constructs wandering around. There wasn't a single person in a smock to be seen, nor was the School anywhere in sight. The main quadrangle should have been sticking out through the wall of the solar tower.

She put one foot back over the line, which was etched on the ground in white ash and stood straddling the line. When she looked down, she saw herself bisected by the thin film of illusion, standing half in and half out of the castle environs.

The others still looked unwilling to follow her. She tried to think of how Rutaro would convince them to trust her. She held out her hand, palm up, confidently, and waited. The Historian and the Minister of Science held back. Only the princess was brave enough to come forward. She gripped Juele's hand with a strength born of fear. Juele pressed her fingers confidently, then pulled her over the line. Leonora took a deep breath and plunged forward with her eyes closed.

"There, Your Highness, do you see?" Juele said, as the princess opened her eyes.

"Oh! The castle *is* here," Leonora said, in wonder. "Look, the Lullay still leads through the moat. It's still flowing. Oh, no, what if the Night Lily Lake was contaminated by the explosion?"

"There was no explosion, Your Highness," Juele insisted. "It's just an illusion. Step out again, and you'll see. I swear it."

Together they crossed back over the white line on the ground. Leonora looked up at the castle hovering above them. "That's astonishing. Inside, you can't even see that."

"I didn't know all this was there myself until today," Juele said. "That would explain . . ."

"Would explain what?" Leonora asked, looking closely at her.

"Nothing, Your Highness," Juele said hastily. "Come on. We've got to find Master Roan."

Leonora followed her. The girl was hiding something, but she could wait to find it out until they discovered why Roan hadn't been there to meet them. Mistress Carodil appeared at her elbow. She immediately directed her apprentices to begin measuring the keep. The young people ran over the drawbridge and set to work. Bergold popped through what appeared to be open air and stared about him with his eyes wide open.

"My hat," he said. He looked at the endless stream of men in black coming from the castle doors and all the colorfully dressed courtiers circulating about the grounds who seemed to be coming and going freely from Mnemosyne. "The view looks normal from in here. Who are these people?"

"Most of them aren't real," Juele explained. "They were made to keep everybody in the castle happy. I'm not sure how many real people there are here. Most of the tourists, the queen, and a couple of her doctors. Oh, and him." The artist pointed at Master Synton, who came bustling down the path toward them, followed by the green-clad members of his staff.

"Your Highness!" he exclaimed. He seemed surprised to see her, and not a little nervous. "Is it . . . is it all over?"

"No," said Leonora. "Don't you know what's happening out there?"

Chapter 29

The clunk of the key turning in the lock made Roan look up with a jerk. He hadn't slept at all. From the weary look on the faces of the guards who now chained his wrists and ankles, neither had they.

"You must come now, sir," Spar said.

"No word from the king?" Roan asked, hopefully, and was dismayed at the cracking of his voice.

"No, sir," Spar said, stiff with regret. Followed by a dreary-voiced parson reading from a book in a voice that went up and down like a church bell, an honor guard marched Roan down the dark corridor. Shouting and banging erupted from barred cells all along the way, and arms reached out at him, nearly touching him. From his prison, they led Roan to a dim room with soldiers standing in a line facing a pockmarked wall, against which Roan was now placed. At a signal, the ceiling would be rolled back, and as the blaze of noon sunlight touched him, he was expected to discontinue. Snare drums began an incessant roll that picked at his nerves.

"What about Her Highness?" Roan asked, as they undid his shackles and tied his hands behind his back.

"No reply, sir," Corporal Lum said. He earned a sharp look from Captain Spar, although the chief guard not entirely unsympathetic. The guard captain was a stalwart, honest individual. Roan would be glad to leave the safety of the palace in his hands, as he had whenever he had gone on missions for the king.

The worst of it, the crowning insult of all, Roan thought, was that because no one else's influence affected him, he was going to have to make himself disappear.

He just wished he could have seen Leonora once more before the end.

"What do you mean, the castle is full of illusory impostors?" Synton asked, furiously. "I have said all along that permitting artists to range about the palace unsupervised was a grave mistake, and now see what has happened!"

Leonora interrupted him. "Minister, it would have taken a more persuasive man than you to keep my mother from having her art show. Have you seen Master Roan? We need to find him to get to the bottom of all this unreality. He will help us clear all the illusion away."

Synton looked away from her. "I have not seen him today, Your Highness. Nor yesterday." His evasive tone struck Leonora as false.

"Where is he?" she demanded. "You do know! As the daughter of your sovereign I order you to tell me."

"Your royal father himself gave the order for the removal of the freak—I mean, Master Roan, Your Highness," Synton said. He glanced up at the sky. The sun was almost at its height. "It was ordered for noon. It must be all over by now."

"What must?" Leonora asked. Her pedestal, never entirely absent from under her feet, grew until she stood a foot taller than the minister. "Tell me!"

"Your father signed an order for his discontinuation, my lady," Synton said, with a nervous bow.

"*What?* Why?"

"Because of his failure to fit into the patterns set down by the Sleepers millennia ago," Synton began, taking a deep breath. Leonora was shocked. She glared down at him, fire in her eyes.

"You! You asked him to. And he said yes this time. Why?"

"I don't know, my lady," the minister said, wringing his hands together guiltily. "For once he appears to have seen what harm an unchanging being does to the Dreamland. Sleepers know I have *tried* to persuade . . ."

"I have no time to deal with such perfidy now," Leonora said. The pedestal under her feet shrunk to the ground. She turned to Juele and seized her hand. "My fiancé's life is in danger. The sentence will be passed at noon. There may still be time to save him. Quick! You must get me through to him at once."

"I will, Your Highness," Juele promised.

"Wait a moment," Carodil said, alarmed. "Your Highness, I can't allow you to follow this . . . person alone."

"She won't be alone," Bergold said. "Roan is my friend."

"Who knows what monstrosities lie hidden within the false appearances with which her fellows have festooned the castle?" Synton said, regaining his dignity.

"You can *all* come along," Juele said, impatiently, thinking of the quickest route to the dungeons. "But we have to hurry." She eyed the front entrance, so beautifully crafted by Rutaro, and fully realized by Manolo. The intense young student was nowhere to be seen. She still had no idea if he had allied himself to the clique, or whether he had been caught blindly up in the project as all the others had. She didn't think the clique would attempt to harm her or the others in order to keep the secret of their perfidy—such a good word—but who knew how much the strain of the last days was telling on them? They wouldn't dare to make a physical attack upon the princess. The doors stood open, invitingly. Juele beckoned the group to follow her through and walked smack into a solid object. Dazed, she backed away and wiped away part of Manolo's lovely illusion. Behind the image was a blank wall. The castle door must have moved. The laughter Juele feared rose around her. Her invisible tormentors were joined by Minister Synton.

"And this is your great expert?" he asked the princess, guffawing. Stung, Juele felt her face redden. She hadn't time to feel every inch of the front wall to find where the door had shifted, but the illusion at the back door was all hers.

"Come on," she said. "We'll have to go in through the kitchens."

"A fine thing for the princess and heir to the throne," Synton muttered, trailing along behind.

"Shush," Juele said. "Please let me concentrate. Um, I'm sorry, Minister."

The princess smiled. "No apologies needed. Let her do her job, Master Synton."

"Wild discontinuities everywhere," the minister grumbled to himself as he followed Princess Leonora around the side of the castle.

Master Synton was right. So much that was here didn't fit in, and yet the illusion clearly was not finished. Plenty of gaps showed in the outlines, letting the original castle peep through. She could see where some of the artists had departed radically from the guidelines Rutaro had set. When she found him, she would have to make him see, no matter how angry at her he got. It troubled Juele that no one from the School was around, finishing it. Only a few days remained before the opening—if there would now be an opening.

She led the others around the edge quickly but cautiously. Farther away from the castle walls the illusion was relatively shallow, at most rising to cover their ankles. Crowds of people passed by, bowing to the princess and the two ministers. The hilarious laughter followed them as they went, distracting Juele from being able to tell where illusion left off and reality began. The clique must be watching them. She kept an eye out for the telltale signs of one-way illusions and erased them, hoping to surprise the spies in their hiding place. In the fifth blind she found a small box that was the source of the roars of derisive laughter. Juele threw it to the ground and jumped on it, smashing it into bits. Once it was silent, her head cleared. She must not waste precious time. Juele liked Master Roan, and she worried that they might be too late. The sun crept ominously higher as they rounded the corner of the castle.

The terrain was blessedly flat that day, giving Juele

a view of almost the whole rear section. The area around the postern gate was empty of people in smocks. Mayrona wasn't at her accustomed place, sketching the compost heaps and repairing illusory bricks. Juele guessed she was still a prisoner in the lumber room. The first thing she intended to do when they freed Master Roan would be to get Mayrona out. The very next thing would be to kick Cal in the pants.

"The castle seems to be lively today," said Master Bergold, watching the kitchen workers come and go.

"There are illusions everywhere," Juele cautioned him. "Be careful."

"How do we tell what's real and what isn't?" Leonora asked.

"Illusions are insubstantial," Juele said. "And they look more perfect than reality. If it looks too good, it's probably not real. Ah!" The carton of eggs was sitting exactly where she had left it when she went looking for the queen. Juele picked it up and took out an egg. "Watch this."

A clean but humbly-dressed man hauling a basket of perfect, rosy apples on his shoulder trudged between them. He was one of Juele's better constructs. Juele took careful aim and threw the egg so that it struck him in the middle of his back. The yolk hung like a yellow sun directly between his shoulder blades, and the white spread out in an irregular alabaster oval. Leonora let out a little gasp. The man kept walking.

"And what are we to learn from this?" Synton asked. "That you artists are vandals? That we already knew!"

"No, sir, look at the pattern," Juele said, pointing as she followed the illusory man in the kitchen door. He never looked up at them. "Real eggs don't look like that. Uncooked egg whites are clear. Nothing real ever makes a perfect splash like that. But all the illusions will."

"Ah!" said Bergold, with an enlightened smile for her. "Good night, I hope *we* can tell!"

Juele loaded the rest of the eggs into her art box and set the empty carton on top of a trash barrel near the door that she could only smell, not see. The Minister of Science stared at the carton sitting there in midair. Juele felt like grinning.

She was pleased to see that part of her illusion had spread inside the castle here. It appeared to have enhanced the real kitchens. The hustle and bustle and actual workings was unchanged, but everything had an air of beauty. The kitchen help were given a semblance of cleanliness and rosy cheeks that didn't interfere with their efficiency at all. Roasts were symmetrical in shape and turned neatly on their spits over vast wood fires by dogs or well-scrubbed boys in tunics. There were no stray bits of rotting meat or heaps of spoiled vegetables visible. It wasn't that she didn't think those things should be true, but they were ugly. She had worked hard on making her part of the castle more idealistic, as Rutaro had wanted her to. A *ping!* made her turn her head just in time to see a plump cook remove a beige casserole dish from a box with a shiny black glass front. Another cook was taking beautifully prepared meals out of a magazine, lifting them straight off the pages.

Juele glanced back at the dignitaries following her, wanting to see what they thought of what she'd done with the kitchens. She hoped Rutaro would think that she had captured the spirit of ideal kitchens. She thought it looked pretty good. Everybody was too busy to notice. She couldn't really blame them. She was concerned about Master Roan, too.

Soft-footed waiters in immaculate suits carried trays in and out of the swinging door that led to the series of dining rooms, but Juele was bound for the wine cellars. The stairs leading underground were near them, in the coolest part of the complex. She led the princess out of the cooking rooms. A chorus of barking erupted, and a dog lunged at them to the end of its chain. The black, deep-chested hound had three heads, and each of its sharp-toothed jaws slavered. Princess Leonora jumped back, and the ministers recoiled.

"It's vicious," Carodil said. "Can we get by?"

Princess Leonora put out a hand and flicked her fingers at it. "That should have made it a poodle," she said. "How can it resist influence? Is it a creature of the Sleepers themselves?"

"It's a nuisance," Bergold said.

"It's a classical reference, ma'am," Juele said, hefting another egg. "The Underworld Dog. Somebody's idea of a joke." By the heavy-handed construction, she guessed it had been made by Cal in between attempts at making a Minister of Gorgeousness. She tossed the egg at the dog. The middle head leaped up and swallowed the missile in midair. Suddenly, the dog hiccuped and broke out in egg-shaped spots like single-petaled daisies. "See? Fake."

The dog snarled fearsomely when they hurried by, but when it lunged to bite, its three sets of jaws passed harmlessly through their targets.

"Whew!" Bergold said, recoiling. "Very convincing."

Only two turnings remained until they reached the cool haven of the cellars. A rushing noise like a loud waterfall echoed through the vaulted brick hallways near the vegetable stores. Juele was puzzled by the sound. When she turned into the next corridor she was astonished to see a veritable cascade of brown objects like stones pouring out of the ceiling and disappearing into a gap in the floor. One bounced to her feet. It was a turnip.

"Not only impassable, but inedible," commented Mistress Carodil.

"Fifty percent right," said the princess, as Juele's ovoid missile scored a hit in the center of the tumbling vegetables. "I *thought* the root cellars were elsewhere."

They hurried through the vaulted brick hallways toward the last junction. The corridors ahead and to the right were clear, shadows in the brick walls picked out by flickering torches at intervals, but the turning to the left was blocked by a sheet of flame. Hot, yellow tongues licked upward with a roar like wind in the trees. Heat drove the party backward.

"One of those disrespectful daubers has set fire to the

castle," Synton exclaimed furiously. He put out his hands, and Juele felt the waves of influence under his control. "I can't put it out! It must be Sleeper-caused."

"It could be a natural conflagration," Carodil said, regarding it with a professional eye. "Function: impassability. A locked door? The egress of a one-way corridor?"

"That *is* the way we need to go!" Bergold said, casting about in alarm. "We can divert—we can take the stairs near the historical archives."

"Which way?" Leonora asked. Bergold took her hand and started running down the empty corridor ahead.

"Your Highness!" Juele cried. The princess glanced back. Juele flung an egg at the flames. The white-and-yellow bull's-eye splattered on the sheet of flame and held its shape. The princess's mouth opened, but she wasted no time. She flung her arm up to protect her eyes and followed Juele through the fire. Bergold was right behind them. They heard an outcry of protest from Mistress Carodil and the Continuitors, who followed. The princess's lovely face in the torchlight was concentrated and troubled.

As Juele had remembered, the spiral of gray stone steps began only a short distance beyond. Thankfully, the stairs were wide and flat in this incarnation of the castle. Bergold led the way down flight after flight until Juele felt almost dizzy. They emerged in a lower chamber smelling of damp stone and moss. Several corridors radiated off into the darkness.

"We should have brought torches with us," Bergold said, lengthening his legs. "I can run up and get some."

"Don't, Master Bergold," Juele said, fumbling around in her box. She took out her neatly-sorted hanks of light and offered them around. Mistress Carodil reached for one, but her hand passed straight through it.

"Manipulation of a nonphysical substance," she said, with interest. "We must speak later."

"I can't touch it," Leonora said, trying again and again to take hold of a skein of bright white. "How can we use it?"

Juele took the princess's arm and wound a festoon of light around her sleeve so it clung as close as lace. The others immediately held their arms out. Juele's hands flew as she issued everybody with gaily colored personal illumination systems. Synton accepted his reluctantly, although his staff watched themselves being lighted with open curiosity and admiration like the children at a birthday party. Juele was so used to being among fellow artists that she'd forgotten the effect of even the simplest forms of light-bending on the general public. She wrapped the hank of costly red around Master Bergold's hand without a single thought of regret. She was sacrificing it to save a life. The princess pointed them all down different corridors.

"We must try every way until we find Roan. Hurry! There's no time to lose."

Box flopping on her hip, Juele ran down her assigned passage. Everything down here seemed distressingly real. Few of the comforting illusions had seeped down into this level. Huge webs draped from the corners of the ceiling, and their hairy, many-legged occupants turned glittering eyes toward her as she passed. Dim, dreary cells along the passage were lit with a single torch burning in a sconce or a lightbulb hanging from a strand of wire in the ceiling, all reminding her how close the sun was to midheaven. The princess's exhortation rang in her ears. "Hurry!"

Captain Spar looked at his watch, then at the red telephone hanging on the wall for the thousandth time since they had entered the chamber of execution, and shook his head. Roan's heart sank into his shoes.

"It's time, sir," he said. His back straight as a tree, Spar drew a sword from his belt and held it high in the air. Corporal Lum shot Roan a look of misery and remorse, but he stood properly at attention with his head high and heels together beside the rope that worked the ceiling. A page stood forth and began to read from a scroll.

"We, Byron, by power of their Creative Eminences the Sleepers King of the Dreamland, do hereby order and decree . . ." Roan steeled himself. What a fool he'd been to think that because he resembled one of the Seven Sleepers that they had a special purpose for him. He had been so sure he would be preserved from harm, as he had been so often in the past. There was a saying from the Waking World that you should never believe your own press releases. Roan straightened his spine and looked his executioners right in the eye. He wanted the last notice to read that he died bravely.

He wondered if discontinuation would hurt.

Juele could smell fresh air ahead of her. She wondered if the scent was another illusion, meant to tantalize the prisoners in the cells, or if there truly was an opening to the surface nearby. Through an open door ahead she caught a glimpse of light. It was dim yellow in color, but in comparison to the darkness of the dungeons, almost blindingly bright. Juele heard voices ahead, talking in the unnatural intonation used for official business, and started running. She burst into the room and hung in the doorway, taking in the scene. In a high-ceilinged, rectangular room painted white she saw a page, a pastor, and a line of black-clad soldiers raising rifles to point at a man standing proud and defiant against the pockmarked wall opposite. It was Master Roan! He still existed!

But he wouldn't for long. Juele saw another guard, a square-jawed, older man in a more ornate uniform, spic and span and spit-polished from head to toe. The gold epaulets on his shoulders shone like embers. He even had knife-sharp creases down the front of his trousers. He held a sword point high in the air, ready to drop it to signal the execution. That man was clearly too perfect to be real. He must be one of Tanner's illusionary enforcers. She had to mark him. When the soldiers saw that he was a fake, they'd stop. The princess would explain everything. Oh, she couldn't believe the clique were prepared to discontinue people, no matter what they thought of townies!

"Ready . . ." intoned the enforcer.

Juele took an egg from her art box.

"Aim . . ."

With all her strength, Juele flung the ovoid end-over-end at the simulacrum.

"Blub!" shouted the commander, as the egg hit him square in the face. He pawed at the clear goo that dripped down onto his immaculate tunic. Juele stared at him in dismay. He was no illusion. The commander was real. And she had made him angry.

"Young lady, what in Nightmare's name do you think you're doing?" the commander bellowed, wiping egg off his face. Juele cowered, her eyes wide. "You've interrupted a process of lawful justice!"

"Not justice," Princess Leonora stated, pushing past Juele into the chamber. "Murder! Halt this travesty at once!"

Spar looked surprised for an instant, then saluted crisply. "As you say, Your Highness!"

"But, Your Highness, this proceeding is by your father's own will," Synton protested, following at her heels like a dog.

"That is *impossible*," Leonora said. She turned to Corporal Lum. "Untie him right now!" The guard sprang forward to undo the bonds around Master Roan's wrists. Roan and the princess fell into one another's arms and kissed passionately.

"My darling, I thought I would never see you again," Roan said, all his heart in his eyes.

"This is all perfectly legal," the Minister of Continuity said imperiously, brandishing a document at the pair. "I have the order of execution right here. This must go forward. Captain, do your duty!" Spar glared at him.

Leonora put out a hand glowing with white light to Synton. "Let me see the order!" She stamped her foot as the minister hesitated. "At once, do you hear me?"

Synton looked upset, but he handed the document to her. Leonora read it over, and her cheeks turned pink.

" 'We, Byron, blah blah, do hereby blah decree, blah blah, that *you shall use no starch upon our collars*'? This is my father's laundry list! You used *this* to put my fiancé in mortal danger?" She loomed higher and higher with every step she took toward the cowering minister until she was standing on a pedestal almost eight feet high. In contrast, Bella's and Daline's furies were no more terrifying than rubber spiders. The minister fell to his knees.

"But that's not what it said before," Synton babbled. "The king himself gave it to me."

"You weren't talking to my father at all," Leonora said. "Just one of his shirts. The list was probably in the cuff. That's where he always puts it."

"Nonsense, er, Your Highness. Do you think I can't tell the king from a shirt?"

"But, it *was* a shirt," Juele said. "I saw you. Do you remember? I was coming out of the Vermeil Chamber when you were going in."

"I remember," said Roan, raising his eyebrows. "That king *was* an illusion?" He looked relieved.

"But he looked like the king," Synton said, his voice rising in bewilderment. "How do I know the document isn't an illusion now?"

The princess turned to Juele. Juele took a fingerful of egg off the captain's otherwise immaculate tunic. "I'm sorry about the mess," she said.

"Perfectly all right, miss," the captain said, stiffly, staring straight ahead. His eyes dropped to hers for a moment, and he winked. Juele hid her smile as she smeared the egg down the length of the parchment. Instead of turning perfect yellow and white, it remained clear.

"There, do you see?" Leonora said.

"It has changed!" Synton insisted, desperately. "The list showed one of the things His Majesty wanted cleaned up . . . oh, very well." Everyone in the room stared at

him stonily. He bowed his head in resignation. In spite
of the trouble he had caused, including very nearly his
own discontinuation, Roan felt sorry for Synton. The
minister had a noisy bee in his bonnet about his, Roan's,
existence, but he was an honest man. Synton took his
hat off his pale, thinning hair, and let the bee fly out.
"Very well, it was a mistake. But I blame the illusionists for misleading me! Their interference is not in the
Sleepers' plan."

"What we must do now," Roan said, "is put an end
to the confusion and bring the illusion back outside
where it belongs. It's only the surface, not the substance
of things that has gone wrong, after all. Can you turn
it all off, Juele?"

"Not me," Juele said. "Rutaro would have to do it.
It's his project."

"And where is he?"

"Some of the others have got him somewhere," Juele
said, unhappily. "They said he was safe, but I don't
believe them. We have to get him away from them.
They've done something to his mind."

"Ah. Where are *they*?"

"At the center," Juele said, promptly. "Rutaro said the
School moves close or far from the Castle of Dreams
depending upon how important it is at the moment. Right
now, the School is running things, so it's one hundred
percent important to the kingdom, so I think that's where
they went."

"The throne room," Leonora said, her eyes wide with
alarm. "Daddy."

Chapter 30

Only the night before, the School buildings had over-lapped the castle, with classrooms skewed through dining rooms. Quadrangles had run alongside galleries and corridors. The castle was now almost entirely unencumbered except for the layers of illusion radiating inward from the tapestries outside. The people with Juele changed appearance frequently as they went through the work of artist after artist. If Rutaro had maintained control, each person would retain a single image, a true, enhanced image of the person, all the way through the castle, until influence changed both the reality and the shell. He'd be so upset if he could see the mess made of his lovely vision. Juele had to reassure herself that Rutaro was almost certainly safe, not like Master Roan, who was sharing his harrowing experiences with his friend and the princess as they went toward the center of the castle. She was only listening with half an ear, concentrating instead on leading her growing party through the maze of passages. Usually, it was very easy to find the throne room. Several routes led there, including the way through the chain of audience chambers. Juele didn't want to take all the time to stop and bow before all the chairs, so she took the corridor used by most visitors of state that led from the front entrance hall.

Some effort had been made by the clique to obscure the way with false leads that dumped them into alcoves, closets, and fish ponds, no doubt to put off discovery as long as possible. Juele had to use all her wits to keep from falling into the simple traps that had confounded

others. Ahead of them, in a gallery beyond the main
reception chamber, she saw several men in court costume, who rushed toward the princess as soon as she
crossed the threshold.

"Your Highness!" exclaimed one, in alarm. "How did
you get in here?"

"Oh, dear! Now she is as trapped as ourselves,"
another said. Juele glanced around. The room had no
visible doors, and the walls looked as though they were
made of crystal shards. Incongruously, handsome oil
paintings in carved gold frames hung on the walls in
between the gleamingly sharp crystal.

"How long have you been in here, gentlemen?" Princess Leonora asked.

"Three days, madame." The princess shot Juele a
meaningful glance, who tore down the one-way illusion
covering the portal. Without another word, all of the men
hurried out to freedom. Juele opened the corridor on
the opposite wall.

"This is ridiculous," snarled the Continuitor, as he
dodged fake spider webs and plunging ravines that Juele
walked over casually. "I do not like having things appear
differently from the way they are."

In some places it was harder to tell what was real and
what was not. Illusion hid physical obstacles and placed
imaginary ones where there were none. Master Bergold
stumbled against an invisible wall that half-filled a doorway. Juele smashed an egg on it to warn anyone who
might come behind them.

Corporal Lum politely held aside a curtain for the
others to pass into the hallway beyond. The princess
smiled at him as she walked by. Juele caught the flash
of something silver. Captain Spar had seen it, too. He
threw himself in front of the princess in time to save
her from being chopped in half by a razor-sharp pen-
dulum that swung down from the ceiling.

"What is that?" Leonora asked. "That was never there
before." Juele studied it and the rows of swaying blades
that filled the hallway beyond. The light struck miniature

rainbows off the edges. No edge of real dreamstuff could be honed so perfectly.

"It's not there now, Your Highness," Juele said. She recognized the style of illusion-crafting. It bore all the hallmarks of Erbatu's elegant but dangerous lines. Juele marked the first axe with a carefully thrown egg to prove its unreality. "You see? We can go through."

"It's too dangerous," Master Bergold said, with a frown on his round face. "I don't trust it. What if one of them is real? Your Highness, perhaps if you would wait here?"

"Certainly not," Leonora said. "It's insubstantial. Juele said that it is. We'll all close our eyes. She will lead us." She took Juele's hand and reached out to Roan. Mistress Carodil tied on an antiseptic-looking blindfold and took hold of Master Roan's arm. Master Bergold screwed his eyes shut and formed a link between her and the disapproving Continuitors and guards behind.

Juele led the train of blindfolded court officials through the shifting shadows. She used her free hand to feel for obstructions. She flinched now and again when one of the silver blades swished down, looking as though it would cut off her fingers. At the far end, she felt her way through a seemingly solid wall. The hall of razors disappeared behind the more comfortable illusion of solid, brown wood panels, probably Corey's work. It had the mark of his serenity on it. She stopped, and let everyone get their bearings.

"This is absurd," Minister Synton declared, opening his eyes. "If all things are illusory, then there is nothing to fear. Let us get this charade over with."

He flung open the next door onto the roar of cars passing by. Juele gasped in recognition.

"Hmph!" Synton snorted at the rows of rushing automobiles and started through.

"No, Minister, don't!" she shouted. Roan saw her alarm. His long strides carried him to the Minister of Continuity, pushing him to the side of the doorway before he could go in. A huge articulated truck rumbled past, ejecting black smoke into everyone's faces.

"Wha-ha-hat was that?" Synton gasped, picking himself up.

" 'Traffic,' by Wimster," Juele said. "They must have brought it over from the museum. It's real dreamstuff, sir. You could have been flattened."

"You have an excellent visual memory," Roan said. "It looked like any of a dozen automobile nuisances I've seen in my life, not all of them substantial."

"It's an artist's gift," Master Bergold said, with a kind smile. Juele straightened her back proudly and led on. She edged into the room around the free-standing sculpture, making sure where the traffic vanished before signaling the others to follow.

Juele saw movement as she came into the antechamber that preceded the throne room. She knew it was the antechamber by the ornamental ceiling with the constellations made of inlaid gemstones, but the walls looked like nothing, disappearing into infinity, except for the crowds of people who seemed to be coming toward them. She jumped, and the girl at the head of each group jumped. Juele crept closer to examine the phenomenon and found the walls were completely covered by mirrors.

"Where's the way out?" asked the princess.

"Out . . . out . . . out . . . ?" said the multiple reflections.

"I don't know," Juele said. She felt in her art box. "I've only got one more egg."

"Egg . . . egg . . . egg . . ."

She walked into the middle of the room, facing all the life-sized images of herself that regarded all the others with doubt. She was nervous. All these people were trusting her. So was Rutaro, whether he knew it or not. Juele weighed the egg in her hand.

The illusion had to be the most perfect image. She looked at all the possible Jueles and chose the reflection in which she looked the most beautiful, tall and mature. Yes, it had to be the one opposite her right hand.

"That one," said Master Roan, pointing over her shoulder,

as she aimed the egg. *Sklutch!* The white blob with the yellow heart hung in the air like a bull's-eye.

"One . . . one . . . one . . ." said his echo.

"That was right," Juele said, looking at the King's Investigator in surprise. "How did you know?"

"Look," he said, pointing to the mirror. She and the princess looked. The illusionary egg hung on the insubstantial glass, but it still reflected the contents of the room. Nothing seemed very much out of the ordinary, until she noticed Roan's reflection. It didn't look like him. He let out a sigh. "A beautiful dream."

The princess squeezed his arm. "I like you the way you are."

"Mmmph!" grumbled Minister Synton. Bergold chuckled.

"Through here," Juele said.

Behind the false mirror stood the grand doors of the throne room. Roan and Bergold swung them wide, and they saw a solid wall of white stone.

"It's the School," Juele said. The royal chamber had expanded to contain it. Juele could see light coming out of the windows over her head. Were all the other students trapped inside? "I think we can just squeeze around it."

There was barely room to move around the edge. The School would have touched the walls if not for the protruding gargoyles, flying buttresses, and bay windows on the upper floors. Juele flattened herself and edged sideways to the corner, with the tapestries and pedestals brushing past her back. Master Roan followed beside her, and Princess Leonora beside him.

Beyond the second corner the room opened up where the royal dais prevented the School from expanding in that direction. All the furniture and works of art that had been standing in the way were piled in heaps to the left and right of the high platform. The room was dark, except for a column of blinding white light that reached to the ceiling. Surrounding the finger of white was a broad, shallow caldera of spiky black. Juele popped out

from between the stone of the School wall and a gold-
fringed tapestry for a better look and had to throw up
her arm against the brightness of a beam of red light
that lanced toward her. Master Roan pulled her down
behind the nearest mound of expensive debris. The red
beam struck the wall above their head, etching a black
line into the gold-inlaid panel. The familiar fume of ideas
floated thickly in the air. It adhered to the illusions,
changing and altering them. Everyone else started to
cough, then realized the smoke didn't tickle. They
stopped and looked at Juele. She shrugged.

Lightning cracked from the ceiling, picking out a circle
of dark shapes in the column of light. Juele thought she
could count eight heads. At least she knew where the
clique was. She hoped Rutaro was in there, too.

"Is my father in the middle of all that?" Leonora
asked.

"I don't know, Your Highness," Juele said, peering over
the high mountain of darkness which lay between them
and the center. "There are too many illusions."

"If it's all illusion," Captain Spar said, "we can charge
right through it!"

"Er, no," Juele said. "You won't be able to figure out
what's real and what's not. I can paint a solid wall with
an image of what's behind it. Even a moving image,
constantly updated. It'd look like clear air, but you'd
smash yourself if you tried to run through it. Child's play,
really." Despite the seriousness of the situation, she was
enjoying being the authority in the midst of all these
adults.

"A very sophisticated and subtle form of child's play,"
Roan said, with a wry smile. Juele blushed. "I'll see if
I can get in there. Captain, guard the others."

"Yes, sir," Spar said. "Do you want my men with you,
sir?" Corporal Lum perked up. Roan shook his head.

"Better just one of us, captain. I have certain . . .
immunities."

Spar gave him his flinty smile. "As you say, sir."

Juele watched Roan with admiration. He was truly

courageous. As soon as the red beams deflected away from their hiding place, he leaped over the nearest obstruction and started running toward the center. A white-hot beacon swung around and slapped him across the middle. He fell backward. Juele feared the light had wounded him, but he rose quickly and dodged to the right, avoiding the spot where he had fallen. Master Roan couldn't be hurt by influence, the rumors said, but he could still hurt himself on physical things hidden in the illusions. There must be an obstacle concealed by the darkness. Juele reached out and erased as much of the illusion as she could. She uncovered a fallen chair just before Roan stumbled over it. He dodged and continued running. As quickly as Juele undid the menaces, more and deadlier ones appeared in his path. He bounded over cresting waves that shone in the actinic glare.

A monster with eight heads and an infinity of legs hurtled out of the darkness toward him. Roan reached into his pocket and pulled out a small red device, which he unfolded into a fighting staff. He swung the staff at the beast's heads. It opened mouths full of needle-pointed teeth, trying to bite his head and arms off. Juele clenched her hands in fear. Roan threw himself backward as the beast shot out a dozen claws to grasp him. He brought the staff down on the nearest head—and connected with nothing. The stick struck the floor and rebounded, almost shaking it out of Roan's hands. The beast wasn't real. At once, Roan turned his back on the eight-headed monster and kept running toward the center. The beast flew away, replaced by a lizard-bird with a gaping, saw-toothed beak that dive-bombed him as he ran. Flashes of light exploded around his feet. Roan tripped on something, but kept limping forward. The shadows kept shifting as he neared the center, creating a maze of whirling blades through which he had to thread his way or be sliced to ribbons. Not only was illusion in force here, but influence and plenty of real obstacles, too. Juele felt that was cheating. The clique must have been desperate.

As he got closer to the high barricade, the lasers swung in toward him, burning lines into the floor. Roan dodged them all to scale partway up the dark mound of spikes. He staggered backward, tried again, and came leaping back over the floor. He vaulted the fallen table to land beside Juele.

"I struck a blockade when I tried to get in," he panted. "What's real here?"

"None of it should be, if it was good illusion," Juele said, looking desperately at the complex combination. "It's too mixed up. I can't even see Rutaro in there. They're hogging all the view of him to themselves until there's nothing left."

"Can't we break through?" asked Bergold.

"They've piled up things behind genuine illusion, and they keep changing the images to make it hard to find your bearings. I don't have enough experience to help unpuzzle this whole thing by myself."

"Who does have enough experience?" Princess Leonora asked.

"Peppardine," Juele said at once. "He's Rutaro's friend. He'll help us." *I hope*, Juele thought.

There was no way to enter the School with the doors jammed up against the walls of the throne room. Juele led them back through the corridors of the castle, upstairs and out through the royal gallery into the museum, and across the old quadrangle to the garden where the Ivory Tower stood.

"Who lives here?" the princess asked, curiously, looking at the handsome tower with approval.

"The Idealists," Juele said. "They're the heart of the School of Light. It's their design. Rutaro is one of them."

She ran up the three steps to the door and found herself rebounding across the garden. Master Roan caught her almost in midair and set her on her feet.

"They have a way of showing they don't want visitors, do they?" he asked, as he set her on her feet. Juele hung her head.

"I was expelled the other day," she said. "They probably won't let me in."

"They will admit *us*," Minister Synton said. He pounded on the door. "Open in the name of the king!"

"That won't work," Juele said, frankly. She faced the door and shouted, "Open in the name of the *queen*!"

Instead of swinging on its hinges, the door opened a cutout in the shape of a stately woman wearing a crown. Juele tried to fit through it, but it refused to pass so much as a finger. Synton pushed by her and slammed his shoulder against the panels, to no avail.

"Master Synton, let Her Highness try," Master Roan said. The Minister of Continuity stepped aside. The princess put a dainty toe through the opening. The woman-shape admitted exactly half of her.

"It's very precise in its requirements," Roan said, with a smile. "You are both your mother's and father's child."

"Never mind," Leonora said. Her modest traveling clothes shimmered into silk, and a sapphire-encrusted tiara formed in her hair. "I will get in. Announce me."

Master Bergold's plump shape shifted until he was larger and fatter, and his clothes turned a brilliant sea green. He lifted a trumpet to his lips and blew a deafening blast that echoed around the square garden. "Her Most Admirable Highness, Princess Leonora!"

"You do that very well, Bergold," Leonora said, beaming. The door swung wide, and she started through. Juele and the others came right behind, but as soon as the princess was inside, the portal slammed shut in their faces. Leonora opened it and beckoned to them.

"You are my entourage," she said. "Let them dare to say I can't have you with me." Roan took the three steps in a single bound. Juele followed more tentatively and was relieved to find she could pass over the threshold. She did not feel welcome, but she was in.

The round room at the top was filled with the usual eclectic crowd. When the princess appeared they murmured among themselves and opened a path for her. She marched regally between them to the center. Juele saw the six remaining Idealists chatting quietly in their Victorian finery and their overstuffed easy chairs. There were no pedestals, no bubble pipes, no vending machines. The seventh chair, forlorn and empty, stood by the hearth. As the crowd parted, the six sprang respectfully to their feet.

"Your Highness," Peppardine said, bowing very low. All the others followed suit. As he straightened, he kept his beautiful, compelling eyes on the princess. They were a deep gray today, a fascinating contrast with his caramel-brown hair and fresh complexion. Juele could see Leonora immediately taken by his charm, but just as quickly defending herself against it. This man's colleague had her parents in thrall and was responsible for imprisoning her fiancé. "To what do we owe this very great honor of a visit?"

"This mass illusion around the castle will cease," Leonora said, crisply. "It's not art any more. It's a nuisance."

Chapter 31

"It is not our illusion, Your Highness," Peppardine said, gesturing her to a seat. "Our colleague created it as an exercise of his talents."

"It started out that way," Juele said, piping up from behind Master Roan in the second tier. Only the princess had been admitted to the inner circle. "The others have made a mess of it. He needs your help."

"*She* isn't to be here," Von said, staring hard at Juele. "She was expelled from this society days ago."

"But this is important," Juele protested. She looked around at the six Idealists, who regarded her blankly. "I thought you liked me, even if Rutaro was upset."

"But, we never question one another's selection of protégé," Helena said, turning up a hand in an elegant gesture of helplessness. "Or deselection. I'm afraid you and we have no say in the matter."

"She is here under my protection," Princess Leonora said, drawing herself up.

"Oh, well, that's different, Your Highness," Von said, with great respect. "How may we be of service?"

"Juele, please explain," the princess said.

Everyone looked at Juele. The girl seemed flustered and embarrassed, but she outlined the situation, beginning with Rutaro's "Romney," and ending with her race to the railway station.

"I'm sure this isn't what they intended in the beginning. It just kind of happened," she finished, lamely. "But now they're occupying the throne room, and the king is nowhere in sight. The queen said they want her to take over as sovereign. She doesn't want to," she added hastily, for Leonora's benefit.

"I see," Synton thundered. "It was all a plot! The School will be closed at once as soon as everything is back in order. As soon as we find him, I want this Rutaro thrown into the darkest dungeon with no light he can use to attempt overthrowing the crown ever again!"

"No!" Juele cried. "You can't do that."

"Why not? He has essentially engineered the takeover of the kingdom. This must have been his plan from the very beginning."

"No, he didn't do that," Juele said, wringing her hands together. She looked at the Idealists for support, but They were watching her. Wouldn't They defend their friend? "You have to believe me. There was no prefiguration at all for that in his plans. He would never do such a thing without symbols showing that was the direction things were meant to go."

"No prefiguration?" Peppardine asked, meeting her eyes directly at her for the first time. Juele shook her head. "Then, it is settled. He did not intend to conquer."

"Are you that sure of his artistic integrity?" Roan asked, gently.

"Of course," Peppardine said, simply. "He's an Idealist."

"He did put the disaster around the castle," Juele said, "but that was just to stop people bothering him. He put indications there for anyone to see. I saw them."

"What disaster?" Synton demanded, then flung out his hands dismissively. "Never mind! All illusions will be stopped at once."

"Nonsense," Roan told him. "Illusion is a part of dreams. The Sleepers themselves make illusion possible, so it must continue to exist. Your own mandate is to protect that which They create. That includes errant artists and opportunistic politicians."

Synton deflated slightly with a huffing noise. "True. Then it should be placed under stricter control."

"With respect, sir," Juele said, "that's a really bad idea.

The best thing you can do, if you want to control illusionists, is to hire us. That way we have a good reason for doing what you want."

"A vested interest," Roan agreed.

"Otherwise, we'll just keep trying to break out every which way. And you can't stop us, sir," Juele said, feeling very bold. "You couldn't stop this."

The Continuitor was silent, but Juele could see she'd made her point. The princess drew the Idealists back to hers.

"Juele tells me your assistance is required to remove the obstructions to the throne room so that government can resume its normal operation."

"We do not like to interfere with the oeuvre of another," Soteran said, gravely. "The resulting vision would not be pure Rutaro. It would spoil his reputation."

"It wouldn't be all Rutaro's work if it had gone the way he wanted it to anyhow," Juele pointed out. "He's had hundreds of people working on the project under his guidance for weeks. You've worked together before. I've seen what you did. It was *beautiful*. As for his reputation, the way Daline and the others have got the media mixed, they're going to think *he* stooped to using solids because he couldn't accomplish his design with illusion alone. The chancellor will ask what he's doing dealing with substance instead of form. He could *fail*." She appealed to them. "What's the matter with you? Aren't you worried about him? Don't you miss him?" Some of the Idealists looked at one another, but Peppardine kept his eyes on hers. Juele spoke directly to him.

"He's doing it because of *you*," Juele said. "He's jealous of the adulation people show you. I mean, he admires you himself, but he'd like to be admired, too. Not that all of you aren't admired," she added, blushing. "I think he reached for too large a subject."

"He has a restless spirit," Peppardine said, fondly. "Emotion merely urges him to greater heights of invention."

"He's responsible for having taken over the government!" sputtered Synton.

"But, government, like civilization, is just a shared illusion of authority," Peppardine said, waving a dismissive hand. The simple gesture made the Continuitor turn red. Steam rose out of his ears, and he stamped a foot. The gesture was rendered impotent by the thick carpet on the floor. "Illusions may cause reaction—indeed, that is their purpose, but they are not in themselves solid."

"But they are spurring direct action. The fake king ordered Roan to be put to death," Juele said. Peppardine turned startled eyes to her.

"What? It's getting out of hand."

"Got out of hand," Roan said. "If Juele hadn't come along when she did . . ." He made a sharp gesture across his throat with his hand.

"Point taken," Peppardine said, seriously. "But if we help you, what will become of us? The School must continue. I don't care to be arrested as a perpetrator, especially when I am trying to put things right that were not going right. Nor do I want Rutaro to suffer. He isn't breaking any laws, is he?" He turned to the princess. "Everything is continuing to function, isn't it?"

"That's the trouble. It is behaving exactly like a real government," Princess Leonora said. "Including capturing rule- and lawbreakers."

"It's a work of art," Helena said, with an expression of sincere admiration.

"But he must allow the Dreamland to come back to its normal self," Roan insisted.

"Oh, that's simple," Peppardine said. "Break the cycle. He'll come back to normal."

"It isn't as easy as that. To dismantle the mechanism requires expertise none of us have. It could put us all in danger, including Rutaro."

Mara looked at Peppardine, fire in her dark eyes. "You are not leaving him in there alone to suffer." He patted her hand reassuringly.

"Of course I'm not, but it will take time and

deliberation to thread our way into the toils of the web he wove."

"I'll get us in there," Juele promised.

At the bottom of the tower steps the Idealists stopped to gaze up at the Castle in the Air. It had changed to reflect the warming glow of sunset. Juele couldn't believe that the day had passed so quickly. The pennants fluttering from tower tops bore crossed paintbrushes over a palette. Juele hoped the princess wouldn't notice that detail.

"Look at that!" Peppardine said, craning his head back to take in the whole picture. He put his hands in the pockets of his white smock and swayed back and forth, shaking his head approvingly. "My, my, my!"

"*Look* at it?" Synton exclaimed. "Great Night, you act as if you've never seen it before. How could you miss something that massive? It must have been hanging over our heads like doom for weeks!"

"I haven't been outside in weeks," Peppardine said, as if everyone should know that.

"It hasn't been there very long," Juele said in a small voice. "Rutaro only put it up there when the people coming in from outside overwhelmed us asking us for advice and favors. They were interfering with the project. I wondered why the crowds thinned out so much."

"Asking *you*?" Synton asked, horrified. "Asking *what*?"

"Advice. Favors. They just really wanted someone to listen to them," Juele said, apologetically.

"They were using our names?" Carodil asked, angrily.

"And your faces," Juele admitted. Roan, Bergold, and even the princess were amused, although the ministers were not.

"They *were* running the government," Roan pointed out. "It sounds like they made a good try, but it's not really their field, after all."

"Very good," Peppardine said, nodding critically at the cloudborne castle. "*Very* good. Almost like something I would do. He's really stretched himself. Really very impressive. I can't tell you how proud I am of him."

"Proud?" the Continuitor shrieked.

"Yes," the tall artist said, shaking his head in admiration. "Wonderful work. I thought he'd never learned anything from my example. I've learned a good deal from him. I was wondering if it would ever go the other way." The officials looked puzzled, but Juele knew exactly what Peppardine meant, and she gave him an insider's smile. He returned it. And his eyes spoke to her, just as they to Rutaro had in the gallery: *They don't understand*. Juele felt happiness explode inside her.

"I don't believe it," Von said, with a sneer up at the floating castle as they walked into the museum, heading for the royal gallery. "He actually finished something."

"Bickering's useless," Mara snarled, and the others could see she meant business. Juele quailed. "We'll take care of this out here. Look at this rubbish!" Mara seized a handful of gaudy hallway in both hands and tore it apart with a rending growl. The color faded from the rip outward, revealing a dingy-colored wall underneath. "We'll fix this. You are correct, Your Highness. At this moment, this is *not* art, but it will be again. You get him out," she said, glaring at Peppardine and Juele. Peppardine patted her on the shoulder and gestured to Juele to lead the way.

The beams of red and white light sliced through the darkness at the edge of the throne room, lighting the wings of grotesque monsters flitting through the air. With an effortless gesture Peppardine captured one of the passing beacons of white and reeled it in like a hawser. He rolled the light into balls and sent them flying through the air like small suns. They picked out the shadows of objects strewn throughout the room that had been hidden by veils of illusion. The nightmare monsters fled, chased away by light bright as day. Now that she had a good look at it Juele realized the tossing sea that Roan had jumped across was only a pool of spilled

oil. Shadowy figures flitted in and out, passing right
through the walls of the throne room and the School.
The mountain surrounding the central column of white
light was real enough.

"An untidy composition," Peppardine said, eyeing it
critically. "It looks like . . . chairs?"

Juele followed his gaze and realized he was right. The
heaped ring around the inner ring of light was a spiky
mass of legs and backs. Where had all those chairs come
from? She started toward them, but was pushed back
by a feeling of awe.

"The audience chambers," Leonora said. "Those are
royal chairs, with their own power to command respect.
Those miscreants in there are hiding behind the glory."

"Not a symbolic sculpture, then," Peppardine said,
sadly.

"No. Just a defensive barrier," said Roan.

"It will take us an hour to burrow through all that,"
Master Bergold said.

"No, it won't," said a quiet voice behind them. Juele
turned. A tall girl stood there, pale but erect. "I can make
them move."

"Mayrona! I thought you were still trapped," Juele
said, running to hug her. "But aren't you . . . ?" She
glanced back over her shoulder at the others. She didn't
want to talk about her roommate's weakness in public.

"I'm not afraid of furniture any more. Shock therapy,"
Mayrona said, with a slight smile. "Dr. Eyebright said
it might help, but I was afraid to try, even after three
consultations. Cal *forced* me into it. I could almost thank
him. But I won't."

She clapped her hands. The mountain began to quiver.
A small gold chair at the very top of the slope began
rolling downhill. With an increasingly loud rumble, an
avalanche of others followed. Juele and the others took
cover behind an overturned table, holding their ears
against the din. When the noise stopped, Juele stood up.
The mass had flattened out to a single tier. Mayrona
clapped her hands again. Chairs picked themselves

upright, formed with a gallumphing four-legged gait into groups of three, and stood waiting at attention.

"Where do you want them, Your Highness?" she asked the princess.

"Why, back in the audience rooms," Leonora said. "Thank you." Mayrona pointed a finger toward the exit. The triple file of furniture trundled out, led by a trio of diamond-encrusted gold thrones. When the last, plain wooden seat had vanished around the corner of the school buildings, Mayrona swayed. Juele hurried to support her, but May shook her head.

"I'm fine. Just tired. If you'll excuse me, Your Highness," she said. "I have a few things to go say to the wardrobe in my room." With a curtsy, Mayrona marched out.

"Stop this intrusion at once," said a sour voice. The group spun around. Facing them was a wizened figure in dull red. He shook an admonitory finger at them. "Leave these people alone. They are doing you no harm."

"Micah?" Synton asked, bewildered. "I thought you were still in Bolster."

"He is," Bergold said. "I left him there only this morning."

"No, he isn't," said Galman, the Royal Zoologist, coming forward. "He came back a while ago. He took an express." More figures flitted out of the shadows to stand beside him.

"You're simply making trouble here," said Kaulb, the Royal Treasurer. He brushed dust off his drab robes. One by one, all the court officials confronted them. Only Royal Geographer Romney, standing at the edge of the group, didn't speak.

"Go away," said Minister Synton, pushing his way through the crowd of his colleagues. He pointed at Roan. "You have no business here, one-faced freak."

"That's me!" said the Synton standing beside Juele.

"So it is," Roan said. "Perfectly true to life, isn't it?"

"Now, daughter," said the king, coming forward out of the beam of light. He looked regal, benevolent, and masterful. His eyes bored into the princess's compellingly. "There is nothing wrong here. This is a perfectly normal function of dreams. Everything will sort itself out. Do not interfere." Leonora nodded, entranced. The jeweled coronet on her head became a garland of daisies.

"Yes, Daddy," she said, in an obedient voice. "I won't."

"Very clever," said Peppardine, stepping forward and swatting a hand past all their faces. Leonora gasped. Not one of the ministers blinked. As Peppardine's hand touched the person of the king, Spar and Lum leaped forward and grabbed his arms.

"No," Leonora said. The spell was broken, and she was herself again. "Let him go. They are all replicas, aren't they?" The Idealist nodded. The guards stood back, but remained watchful. Leonora studied them in amazement as they continued to scold and threaten. "Now I can see why everyone believed in them."

"They will cause you no more trouble," Peppardine said. He flicked a finger, and every figure collapsed into a small paper doll, except the king, who was a white silk shirt on the floor, and Romney, who stood by quietly. "This one has more coherence than the others, but is still not real."

"Rutaro made her," Juele said. Corporal Lum bent to pick up the shirt and presented it to the princess. A loud rumbling broke out almost over their heads, and the wall of the School of Light began to recede slowly through the wall to the east. A cry of anguish came from the dais. Without the ministers, the clique's source of authority was gone.

Juele turned to look at the column of white light. Peppardine created a huge gum eraser that flew over the scene and wiped away the last of the illusion concealing the people inside.

On the high platform, the eight senior students sat enthroned in a circle, on chairs of gold and velvet. They were clenching the armrests with straining fingers. The cords stood out on their necks as they stared at a narrower pillar of light at the center. Inside it was the single

figure of a man. Juele could just pick out the shadows
of broad shoulders and dark curly hair. Rutaro was standing rigid within the beam, his eyes straining upward,
hands down at his side, clenched, an unnatural pose. The
eight students stared at him, literally pinning him in place
with their eyes. Juele was full of pity. One of the great
creative minds in the Dreamland, who had imagined the
School into being, was helpless before real influence and
strong emotion. For all their pride in the smock, the
clique hadn't remained true to illusion when power
beckoned.

Images flew from Rutaro's forehead, divided eight
ways, and descended into the students on the thrones.
From them other images arose. Juele could see they were
much less perfect in design, but these were what escaped
from the column, filling the room and seeping out into
the rest of the castle. They were draining him for inspiration. With all the ability at their command, they
didn't have a single original concept of their own.

"They have formed their own ivory tower," Peppardine
said, "but instead of Ideas, they have an Idealist."

Juele ran up to the column of light and pounded on
it. "Let him out!"

Daline sat up majestically in her throne, never turning her head.

"No," she shouted. "You had one of Them all to
yourself. Now he's *ours*."

"But he's not mine," Juele said. "He chose me."

"And then he unchose you!" Cal said. "What are you
doing here?"

Juele looked at the haunted face in the glass tube.
"He needs me."

"Why you?" Colm asked. "You're too young. You're
too new!"

"You can't take him away from us," Tanner said, without looking at Juele. He kept his eyes fixed on the prize
in the center. Staring straight ahead, Bella didn't say
anything aloud. Juele remembered that out of the whole
group Bella had been the nicest to her. She looked tired

of the governing game. She'd been there, done that, passed the legislation, and now she wanted to stop, but she couldn't walk away from her companions. They wouldn't let her go, any more than they could let Rutaro go free. Juele read her moving lips.

"Help," Bella whispered. Juele pounded on the wall of light.

"Go away, you baby, you infant, you child! You have no right to be here," Daline hissed. "Take this!"

Juele felt a wave of seasickness take hold of her belly. She started to grow smaller. Her clothes were too big, as if she was playing dress-up in her mother's closet. The reflection in the column's shiny side showed her the face of a baby, wearing booties and diapers, before she fell off the dais. Juele tried to scramble back up again. It was too high for her short, round legs. She jumped, reaching for the edge. At last her hands caught the smooth surface. Her hands would take her wherever she wanted to go. They pulled her up to the platform. Juele tore furiously at the web of light with her fingers. She felt as if she was fighting all eight of them at once.

"Stop," Roan said, catching hold of her wrists. "You'll only hurt yourself."

"They're using influence," Juele said. "It's not fair. They're all working together!"

"No, they're not," Roan said, watching the illusions fly. "I have watched power plays in court for years. Each of them is working for himself or herself, albeit toward a common goal."

"Layers of illusion," Peppardine said. "If you slip past one, the others catch you. Breaking the concentration of one of them isn't enough. You need to distract them all."

"Can you make all of them look the other way?" Roan asked, with a nod of approval for Peppardine. "It works in that fashion with influence—in a trial between equals, distraction is the best weapon."

"I can," Juele said, resolute because Roan, unlike the Minister of Continuity, treated her like a peer. She stood up, a teenager again. But how could she do it? Juele felt Peppardine's long, strong fingers close around hers. He was at her shoulder.

"Make them doubt," he said. Juele looked up at him. He nodded encouragement.

Doubt? she thought. Doubt what? Make them wonder if they really had their prize, Juele realized. There was plenty of light she could use. She took handfuls of it, and began to mold it, looking out of the corner of her eye. Using Rutaro's own techniques, which he had used to make the lifelike image of Romney, Juele crafted images of the Idealists.

"Very nice," Peppardine said, watching her hands fly.

"But she is not doing anything," Minister Synton complained. "Guards, break in and remove these intruders at once!"

"Just a moment, please, Master Synton," Roan's voice said. "Just because you can't see it doesn't mean nothing is happening."

"Oh, I see," Leonora whispered. "It's not there at the front of your eyes."

"Stuff and nonsense, Your Highness," Synton said. "Either it's there or it isn't!"

"Shush!" Peppardine commanded. Synton fell silent.

In short order, beside Juele stood an elegant Helena, a solemn Soteran, a languid Von, a sullen Mara, a nimble Callia. The divine Peppardine didn't need to be created, only copied, which Juele did with her heart in her fingers. And Rutaro, curly haired, energetic, confident, with his ribbon tie crisp over the snowy whiteness of his shirt and smock as she could see him in her memory, not rigid and strained, as he was in the column of light. Juele made her simulacra walk among the clique. Insubstantial, the images weren't turned back by the force field surrounding the thrones.

"Who is that?" Erbatu whispered to her neighbor.

"Are They here?" Colm asked nervously.

The occupants of those uneasy chairs did not turn their heads, but Juele caught them starting, and their gaze shifting as they glimpsed the Idealists out of the corner of their eyes. She heard puzzled mumbling from one to another. Their heads trembled. They *wanted* to look around. The beam of light began to weaken. Juele tried to force her way in again and was thrust back.

"It's not time for direct action yet," Roan said. "Wait."

The disturbance among the senior students grew greatest when they saw the image of Rutaro walking among them. It was the image's confidence that upset them most. Juele had him hold up his wrists and show the chains on them. Broken chains. It was the sole symbol with which Juele had invested her image, and she thought it was the most effective: he was free. Juele saw Tanner's forehead begin to sweat, as his eyes rolled from the figure in the center to the one who seemed to be standing next to him. The maelstrom surrounding the real Rutaro began to break up.

Juele could almost see the thoughts in their mind. The rest of the Idealists had come to take over this place. Any moment now, the In Crowd would be thrust into the second tier. Daline's nerve failed first. The askance image of Rutaro was standing right next to her. She turned her head to look at him. He wasn't there. Her head jerked around to the pillar in the center. He was still standing there, but there was also the ghost at her elbow. She began to tremble. She wasn't concentrating any more. The others blinked, and the real Rutaro swayed.

Roan pushed at the wall of light surrounding the thrones, and his hand went through the surface like dipping into water. He nodded. Peppardine and Juele walked into the circle. The tall artist touched Rutaro on the shoulder.

"It's over, my friend," he said.

Rutaro's head moved jerkily, until his eyes met Peppardine's. They closed for the first time, and Rutaro slowly collapsed in a heap. Juele and Peppardine bent to catch him and eased him slowly to the floor. The beam of light died quickly away. Once the power source was gone, the impressive trappings looked weak and crude. The eight elegant thrones deflated, until the clique was sitting on the floor.

"It's going away!" Sondra wailed. "Quick, bring it back!" The others started weaving light furiously, trying to recreate the column of light, the ministers, the thrones, but their hands shook, and all their images went awry. Spar and his guards came forward and pulled them to their feet.

"Your part of the exhibition is over," Roan told them firmly. Light spilled out of their hands and faded away.

The figure of Minister Romney disappeared. All around the room, tapestries and works of art faded, leaving empty outlines and frameworks everywhere. The reality that remained was not half so bright or handsome, but, Juele thought, it was real. It astonished her how much of the illusion around the castle had been held up by Rutaro's powers of creativity alone. The Idealists were enormously powerful, more than she had ever realized.

Roan watched the images fade with a rueful smile. He must have been thinking much the same thing Juele was.

"It was a good thing that you Idealists didn't really want to take over the world," Roan said. "Together, you'd almost certainly succeed."

"No, thank you," Peppardine said. "We prefer our own version of it." The beams of harsh light faded. Warm, golden light took their place. Three chairs of solid gold fit for royalty reappeared in a line on the dais. New tapestries wove themselves out of the tarnished strands of the old as the winds of change moved slowly but inexorably through the room. Smartly dressed servants tiptoed into the room on velvet-soled shoes and began to tidy it up.

Roan looked at Rutaro, still slumped against his friend's chest. "You'd better take him home."

The senior students stood in a little knot in the middle of the room, surrounded by uniformed guards. For the first time, the enormous authority and awesomeness of the royal chamber overwhelmed them. They looked scared, not at all the commanding presence they possessed at school.

Daline looked at Juele scornfully. "You. You could have been one of Us."

"No, I couldn't," Juele said. "For one thing, you would never let me. For another . . . I wouldn't want to be." She was pleased to realize that it was true. Daline gawked at her in disbelief as she and her companions were led away by Captain Spar and his men. As she passed Juele, Bella sent her a look of gratitude and regret. Peppardine and Juele lifted Rutaro to his feet and carried him toward the door.

"I hope you realize that Rutaro created his great work not just for us, but because of you, too," Peppardine said to Juele at the throne room door. Peppardine wanted to take the shortcut, because, as he said, the School had likely retreated half a mile away already. "You will have a great future in illusion. You can do anything you want to do."

He gave her a smile that warmed her clear through. Juele took it to her heart and treasured it like a love letter. She was tired, hungry, bedraggled, and her art box was empty, but she had never been happier.

"I'm not in a hurry, now," Juele said. "All I want to do now is finish my project and the queen's portrait, and catch up with my classes."

The surface of the floor changed before her, thickening the carpets and bringing out their texture. Color crawled up the walls and gave a rosy flush to the faces in the paintings on the wall. The images were growing more beautiful and more overwhelmingly perfect than ever.

"What's happening?" Juele asked in alarm. "I thought it was over! I thought the illusion was coming down. It's starting again!"

Peppardine raised his face to the ceiling with his eyes closed, as if he was listening.

"That's Mara and the others," Peppardine said, with his gentle smile. "She's remaking the parts of the project that went wrong, so it will look the way Rutaro meant it to. He shall have his dream." He looked at Juele. "His friends will support him."

"Me, too," Juele said.

"I know. We learn from each other," he said, with a warm look. "I would be proud to learn loyalty from you. You gave it, even when we did not deserve it. There is integrity, and there is artistic integrity. You, my dear girl, have both." Juele looked up at him, speechless with happiness. Peppardine pulled Rutaro's arm over his shoulder and picked him up. "I can take him from here. See you tonight in the Tower?"

"Oh, yes!" Juele said. Peppardine smiled at her eagerness and started away. Within two paces the two artists vanished out of sight. Peppardine must have pulled an illusion of invisibility around them to spare Rutaro from being stared at by curious onlookers. The Idealists cherished their privacy.

"Where did they go? Aren't we going to arrest them?" Minister Synton asked, indignantly.

"For committing art?" Roan asked. "No real harm was done."

"And Roan would be the most injured party," Bergold pointed out, "since the illusory king condemned him to discontinuation. Should we arrest you for aiding and abetting a fraud?"

"Certainly not," said Synton, in high dudgeon. "And I would be grateful if you would refrain from mentioning it again. If it is all the same to you, Your Highness," he added, in a much more humble voice.

"If nothing of the sort ever happens again," Leonora said, giving him a withering glance. "In future you will just have to put up with the existence of a glaring discontinuity on the face of the Dreamland."

"I will, Your Highness," Synton said, with a sigh of resignation. "I thank you."

"Don't thank me. I would not be so lenient if your

heinous attempt had succeeded. Thank this determined young woman."

Juele blushed. "I'm just grateful nothing truly awful happened." Synton bowed to them both.

"But what about my parents?" Leonora asked, turning away from the chastened minister to Juele. "None of the servants have seen my father in days."

Juele glanced through the open door of the throne room at the floor-to-ceiling tapestries. The perfection of the wall hangings was marred by the fact one of them was rucked slightly, as if it was hooked over a door. She pointed.

"Daddy!" Leonora cried, as the king emerged from his study. He wore a pair of half-glasses and had a bottle of glue in one hand and a model ship in the other. His daughter met him halfway across the room and flung her arms around him.

Once the clutter of illusions inflicted on the castle by the clique began to clear away, the missing student volunteers began to turn up. Heads wrapped in fog, they were all bound up in little cocoons of concentration, hard at work painting themselves into corners of the castle. All of them seemed surprised when Juele woke them from their reveries and told them they could stop. Manolo, Gretred, Tynne, Borus, and Sangweiler were grateful to put down their paintbrushes and return to the school. Even Davney had had enough of the deception. He went back to his neglected commission with evident relief. Servants woke up, and brushed the spider webs that had been woven over their eyes during the last several days, and went about their business as if nothing had happened.

Juele accompanied Princess Leonora, Master Roan, and the king to Queen Harmonia's chambers. They found her surrounded by a host of doctors, all listening intently as she described her medical woes.

"And occasionally, I have an itch at the bottom of my left foot," she said. "Not usually on weekends, but on weekdays, oh, how it irks me! I am certain that signifies something. Not very serious perhaps, but significant." All of the doctors nodded. Some of them made notes on notepads. A couple whispered into tiny recorders. The air of well-being in the room was so thick it was visible as a bright halo surrounding the queen. Leonora stopped at the doorway, shaking her head with a loving smile.

"She's never looked so happy in her life," the princess said. "I hate to take them away from her."

But the false physicians were already vanishing with the other illusions, leaving behind Doctor Eyebright and a couple of others. Juele looked at them carefully and made sure they were real.

The queen noticed them in the doorway and held out her hands to them.

"Oh, my dears," she said. "Is it all over?" King Byron came in, and Harmonia's eyes glowed with joy. She rose, and he took her hands and kissed them.

"My love, are you all right?" the queen asked. "I was so worried. Were you ever troubled? In danger?"

"Not at all," said King Byron. "I was in my study the entire time. It was the finest vacation I've had since I took the throne. Pity I missed the excitement, my dear."

"It was overwhelming, my love," Queen Harmonia said, throwing her hands in the air. "More of a success than anyone dreamed. I shall undoubtedly have to have several consultations to help me get over it." She, Juele, and Leonora shared a special smile.

Chapter 32

Juele stood in the exhibit hall beside her entry, not far from the entrance to the Grand Gallery containing the Idealists' wonderful illusion. She wore her freshly washed pink smock and her beret, the sign of a working artist. She had done her very best with her still-life, and she was reasonably pleased with the results. The Idealists had given it their seal of approval. Even the brusque Mara had told her, "well done," but whether for her art or her assistance in rescuing Rutaro Juele didn't know. The hall was full of visitors and tourists, all of whom had to pass her stand on their way to the other displays. She enjoyed watching people walk past the empty pedestal, stop, and glance back as they realized they could only see the piece out of the corner of an eye.

"Is that yours?" all of them asked. "What do you call it?"

"Askance reality," Juele said, proudly.

"It's good," some said. "It's rubbish," others insisted. Juele wasn't upset by the latter. She knew they were just being insulting because they were surprised.

The opening of the royal exhibition at the School of Light had been an enormous success. The queen had worn the chancellor's gleaming sash and had made a speech of the utmost charm before cutting the ribbon to the new hall. Juele had waited to see the unveiling of her portrait of the queen in the main salon of the museum. It had been given pride of place in the display. She had finished it in one final sitting, putting in the strong and subtle characteristics she had learned about the queen during the crisis, and making the resemblance just a little stronger. The queen said she loved it. After the exhibition was over, it was to be hung in the royal portrait gallery.

Rutaro's magnum opus was in place around the whole castle, remade and refined in two days flat by the rest of the Idealists and Juele. She knew now that They weren't avatars of the Sleepers, for all that there were seven of them, nor were they demigods or divine beings. The truth didn't stop her respecting and admiring them with all her heart. The door to the Ivory Tower was always open to her now.

The castle had looked utterly perfect, to the delight of the queen and visitors. Juele had no way of knowing whether the Sleepers were pleased with the marvelous outcome, but the weather was brilliantly sunny, setting off the illusion to its best effect. Perhaps that was their way of showing their approval of Rutaro's skill. Everyone else who had seen it was loud in their praise. Unfortunately, the artist himself was not around to accept congratulations. Rutaro had had enough of crowds. Even Juele hadn't seen more than glimpse or two of him for days.

Punishments had been handed down for the members of the clique who had caused so much trouble. They were not imprisoned or expelled, because no matter how Minister Synton searched, he couldn't find anyone who had felt ill-served by the pseudoministers. The erring students were ordered to assist in the cleanup of the castle, and the chancellor had ordered them all sent back to lower classes to start over, putting them back more than a year in their studies. Most of the clique were able to retain their places at the School, but Cal had regressed to a level insufficient to allow him to remain. Juele wouldn't miss him.

Mayrona had truly been cured of her problem. She was grateful to Juele for having sent her to Doctor Eyebright. She now thought that she would go into interior design, beginning with their dormitory room. Her life display was a big success, too.

The two older critics in gray smocks passed by Juele's stand. Their faces were exaggerated masks with long chins and staring eyes, and they looked very much alike except for the long tie on the one man and the bow tie on the other. She was afraid they would heckle her, but they were very complimentary.

"I appreciate the oblique nature of the illusion," said the one with the bow tie.

"Really a clever conceit," said the other. "Well executed." They both gave her a thumbs-up and went on to the next exhibit. Juele hugged herself with delight.

Master Roan came through with Princess Leonora on his arm. Today the princess had long tresses of red-gold hair flowing over a periwinkle blue dress. Rutaro would have itched to model her.

"Here you are," Leonora said, coming over to take Juele's hands and kiss her on the cheek. "We are enjoying the exhibition, but I wanted to thank you again for your help."

"You saved my life," Master Roan said gravely. He bowed to her. "I owe you a great debt."

"Your Highness, it was nothing," Juele said, stammering.

"It was *not* nothing," Princess Leonora said, emphatically. "I understand that my mother has decided you will be named an official court artist. I would like to add that when my father finally consents to set my wedding date, I would like you to be one of the decorators. I hope you would enjoy that." Juele gasped with delight.

"I would be honored, Your Highness. Thank you!" Juele flushed with pride. They smiled at her again, and walked off to tour the rest of the display. Juele gave one little skip for joy, then reasserted a more serene expression to await the public. As a representative of the School of Light, she had a certain dignity to maintain.

She spotted Bella and Daline coming out of the Grand Gallery. Juele waved to them.

"Did you see the kitten?" she asked innocently.

"Yes," said Bella, rolling her eyes. "What a bore."

"You'd think that They could come up with something more exciting," Daline said, tossing her hair. "I think They're becoming passé."

Juele grinned. Then, she heard Rutaro's low chuckle. She looked around, but he wasn't in sight. She spotted him, blended in with the wallpaper not five feet from them, and smiled. They exchanged the nods of colleagues as Bella and Daline, unaware, sashayed away.